D0483049

SUNRISE *on* STRADBURY SQUARE

Also by Doris Elaine Fell
Blue Mist on the Danube
Willows on the Windrush

To
Heather, 22, with all of life
ahead of her
and
in memory of
Julie Lynne, 22, who finished
her journey early

SUNRISE *on* STRADBURY SQUARE

Sagas of a Kindred Heart
Book 3

DORIS ELAINE FELL

Fleming H. Revell
A Division of Baker Book House Co
Grand Rapids, Michigan 49516

© 2002 by Doris Elaine Fell

Published by Fleming H. Revell
a division of Baker Book House Company
P.O. Box 6287, Grand Rapids, MI 49516-6287

Printed in the United States of America

All rights reserved. No part of this publication may be reproduced, stored in a retrieval system, or transmitted in any form or by any means—for example, electronic, photocopy, recording—without the prior written permission of the publisher. The only exception is brief quotations in printed reviews.

Library of Congress Cataloging-in-Publication Data

Fell, Doris Elaine.
    Sunrise on Stradbury Square / Doris Elaine Fell.
       p.   cm. — (Sagas of a kindred heart ; bk. 3)
    ISBN 0-8007-5750-5 (pbk.)
    1. Teacher-student relationships—Fiction. 2. Women college teachers—Fiction. 3. Leukemia—Patients—Fiction. 4. Reunions—Fiction. I. Title.
PS3556.E4716 S86 2002
813'.54—dc21
                                      2002001776

For current information about all releases from Baker Book House, visit our web site:
http://www.bakerbooks.com

A thing of beauty is a joy forever.

"If I should die," he wrote, "I have left no immortal work behind me—but I have lov'd the principle of beauty in all things, and if I had had time I would have made myself remember'd."

John Keats
1795–1821

Prologue

Rachel McCully's stark encounter with her own mortality came at the most unexpected moment. At thirty-seven, she stood without question in the prime of her life, at the peak of her career as a university professor, and had come that morning fresh from the trails of a weekend mountain trip. She had bruises and blisters on her heels to prove it; a burn on her finger from the campfire when the marshmallow prong slipped from her hand; and a nasty snagged fingernail from changing her flat tire on the mountain turnout. But she came down the mountain with wonderful memories, eager to face her students and hand them their final exams.

On this last Monday in May, she walked tall—as she always did—with a brisk, vibrant step and an easy grace while cutting across the campus to McClaren Hall. The flush on her face came from the sun, its warmth invading her body. Contentment stole over her at the thought of another summer holiday abroad.

The heavens above her formed a vault of powdery blue. Wispy white clouds played games with the sunshine. It was not the kind of day for disaster to dog her footsteps. The springtime air smelled fresh and clean, scented sweetly with the crimson and coral roses blooming against the university buildings. Students lazed on the freshly mown lawn between exams, some of them still cramming for their finals. Sprawling pepper trees dotted much of the campus, but a row of magnolias grew just over the footbridge on the walkway to McClaren. Rachel smiled to herself at the young couple huddled beneath the third magnolia—books open, arms around each other, the moment more important to them than their grade point average and graduation on Saturday.

She felt a twinge of envy, a tingle of memory. Her gaze veered from their happiness and stabbed at her own ghosts. The students sat on a white marble bench, its clawed legs stained from inclement weather. On a day much like this glorious, sun-filled morning, a moment on that bench beneath that same magnolia tree lay branded in Rachel's memory forever. The remembered snowy-white magnolia flower, the dark green leaves, the shaded sunlight on the somber face of the man beside her.

Rachel hurried past the young couple, but it was too late. Yesterday was there, the part of her that no one else remembered. No one else knew. She the English professor; he the visiting British don—serious-faced, broad-shouldered, lean.

She had been in her twenties and flattered by the visiting professor's attention. But that morning as she looked into his hooded dark eyes, she blushed under his gaze. They had become such good friends, constant companions. Flustered by his closeness, she said, "Sinclair, you do remember that I want you to speak to the Pen and Quill Club before you leave for London? I thought you could talk to them about C. S. Lewis—"

A scowl nettled his brows, his gaze piercing hers. "Must we talk about literature, Dr. McCully? I want to talk about us."

Her cheeks broiled in spite of the cool shade of the tree. "Us, Sinclair?"

Students walked past them as his fingers entangled hers. Tightened. "I want you to go back to England with me."

"I go abroad every summer," she had stammered.

He remained resolute. "I want you to go back as my wife."

She caught her breath, expecting his face to crease with that wry smile of his. She saw only his familiar studious expression, a handsome face if he would smile more. That morning—as with many mornings—his tie was askew on his otherwise perfect attire. Beneath his brown tweed jacket, he wore a thick V-necked Shetland sweater for what he considered to be the chill of spring. She wanted to reach out and straighten his tie. A playful gesture, a familiar one.

His knee brushed hers as he crossed his long, muscular legs. She drew away. He seemed unaware. He said a second time, "Will you marry me, Rachel?"

"You're joking, of course?"

"That hardly describes me."

True. Other words came to mind: Conservative, professional. Committed, purposeful. She admired his strength of character, but Sinclair was so unlike the carefree, jaunty men who took pleasure in mastering the mountains and skiing with her. What did the two of them have in common? Intellectual pursuits. Art and music. Literature. They talked about tradition—his as a schoolboy in England, as a student at Oxford, as a researcher on the life and works of C. S. Lewis. She boasted about her family tradition—the McCully name a legend at the university. They attended faculty doings as a couple. Walking and dining together. He played soccer and cricket. She favored hiking and skiing. Sinclair viewed mountain heights through a camera lens; she from the top of the mountain. He seemed distant, professional with his students. She entered into their lives. He was reserved. She took risks.

He leaned closer. "Rachel, I am asking you to be my wife. I thought that's what you wanted."

"I do. But—my career means everything to me."

"*You* mean everything to me."

Other images blurred his features. Sinclair catching her eye across the crowded faculty room. The picnic in early spring with the bees buzzing overhead. He detested bees. She swatted at them playfully. He dared her to race across the narrow river, the water as cold as melting ice. They plunged in—his breaststroke powerful and even, his win four strides ahead of hers. But he was the one with a wretched cold and fever three days later. And the Thanksgiving break to his boyhood haunts in England. Meeting his family. Just tiny glimpses of the other Sinclair, the fun-loving man behind the studious expression.

He cupped her chin and forced her to look at him again. "Rachel, are you going to answer me?"

"I don't know what to say."

"Say yes."

A thousand crazy excuses ran through her mind. A thousand uncertainties. His reserve. His brilliance. The less restrained moments with his warm lips on hers. She wanted to ski and climb. To live. To be free. He wanted to marry and settle down and have lots of children. Three at least. And what would they talk about for the next forty years? Shakespeare and Chaucer? Shakespeare's devotion to Anne Hathaway for breakfast. C. S. Lewis or the Lake Poets for supper. And in between poets, they would talk about sending their sons to Eton and the University of St. Andrews in Scotland.

She thought about the sleepless nights she had known since the day they met. The arguments she had with herself. The confusion that paralyzed her about childbearing—the fear of taking defective genes into a marriage, the fear of being a carrier of cystic fibrosis.

"Rachel, I thought you knew that I loved you."

Tears stung her eyes. "I didn't know for certain. How could I? I don't read minds or enjoy guessing games."

His smile was disarming, his quiet reserve unsettling. "But we talked about England and Stradbury Square. And living in Oxford. I told you that I wanted children . . . and marriage. We talked of marriage, Rachel."

"But not to each other."

I hoped. I wondered.

She had sat beside him at faculty meetings for two months, never tumbling to the idea that he had more than an intellectual interest in her. Then at the close of a heated discussion on dropping Victorian literature from the school program, this tall, striking Brit lingered at the back of the room waiting for her. "Would you be so good as to go to dinner with me, Dr. McCully?"

He spoke in the same crisp manner that he used in the classroom. She thought him arrogant then, presumptuous. But at dinner and all the dinners that followed, she found him kind and caring. Utterly captivating. Delightful with his droll sense of humor. Never boring. She expected him to pick a moderately priced restaurant that first evening; he chose the best, lavishing her with unexpected British charm and sending her into spontaneous laughter when he insisted on steaming Victorian tea in Chelsea Rose china. With cup in hand and eyes dancing, he saluted her. "Here's to rescuing you from the chaos of faculty meetings."

Sitting on that stone bench under the magnolia tree, he had said gently, "Rachel, I'm leaving at the end of the semester."

"I know." Whispered. "So am I."

"But you're traveling in Italy."

She ran her fingers over the back of his hand. "Would it help to know that I booked my return flight out of Heathrow?"

"That sounds as if you're willing to leave the door open." He stood and helped her stand. She was tall, but at six-one he was taller. He looked down at her, a twisted smile on his lips. "Perhaps you could reserve your answer until you reach London?"

When she responded, she was half teasing. Wasn't he? "We could meet under Big Ben. I'll give you my final answer then."

He whipped a pocket calendar from his jacket and scanned the pages, his Oxford pen poised. "Would noon on August seventh be good for you?"

Nine years! Had nine years really slipped by? Big Ben still chimed out the hour, but she and Sinclair had gone their separate ways. Back then, with Big Ben booming behind her, she had run away from her chance at happiness—foolish as it might be—with her secret fear of childbearing tucked deep inside her.

Yesterday and today merged. Just for a second, she turned back. Glancing across the footbridge, she gazed at the magnolia tree and the now empty stone bench. Rachel had always prided herself in controlling the calendar and the events of her life, something that her sister, Larea, could not do. Even now, nine years later, Rachel was the sum of many things, her life divided between teaching and sports, and her summers spent abroad. She juggled schedules and negotiated winding curves on mountain roads and the slopes of a ski run, but she could not control her sister's illness, nor this fresh emotional tug at her heartstrings at the awakening thoughts of Sinclair Wakefield.

As she neared McClaren Hall, two students waved. She sent back her winsome smile, anticipating the summer freedom as much as they did. She strolled on with purpose—her life as always disciplined and mapped out. So why, as she sprinted up the last two steps to the language arts building, did she suddenly feel such foreboding, such uncertainty, such pending doom?

One

Shiny glass doors led into McClaren Hall, a mahogany paneled door into her office. She breezed into the room, smiling at her secretary.

"Dr. McCully, you are never late."

"I know. But I picked up a nail negotiating the mountain curves this morning. The trucker behind me almost ran me off the road before I could reach the safety of the turnout."

"Didn't he stop to change your tire?"

She laughed. "I did it myself."

"No wonder you look tired, rushing like that."

"A camping trip is worth it. The weather was perfect. You should go with me sometime, Elsa."

"I'd hate sleeping in a tent."

"You'd get used to it. Anything for me this morning?"

"A faculty meeting at four . . . and an appointment with your doctor at two this afternoon."

"Call him back and tell him I can't make it."

Elsa shrugged. "The nurse said you had to be seen."

"Why all the rush?"

"You're leaving for Europe after school is out."

"Good point."

"I told her this was finals week, but she insisted."

Rachel pocketed the pink memo without reading it. "Two o'clock. Anything else?"

"Jude Alexander wants to see you. She said she'll be back in a few minutes."

Rachel's brows puckered. "Why now? She skipped out on her last two appointments."

"I just posted some of your finals on the bulletin board."

"Oh! Then send her in when she comes back."

Rachel didn't feel chipper as she adjusted the blinds in her inner office, flooding the room with sunlight. In another ten years, she'd retire early, but at thirty-seven, retirement was on the back burner, the prospect rekindled only on bad days, and Jude could easily spoil an already harried schedule.

With a glance in the mirror, Rachel saw her mood mirrored there. Her uneasiness at a confrontation with Jude showed in the scowl ridges tightening around her mouth. She adjusted the silk scarf around her neck, and slipped into her desk chair just as Jude swung the door open.

Jude stomped across the room, every fiber of her body vibrating as she dropped into the wing chair across from Rachel. "You flunked me, Dr. McCully."

Rachel met the girl's sullen gaze. She was a minister's daughter, but anger defined her. Jude was pretty, daring, defiant, a twenty-one-year-old on a crash course with the world.

Rachel saw herself reflected in the angry expression and remembered her own crash course with the world at eighteen. And the jolt that turned her life around.

More harshly than she intended, she said, "Jude, you set yourself up for failure."

"I barely squeaked by last semester in that Victorian lit class, and now, because of some dumb Lake Poets, I won't have enough credits to graduate."

Venting, she was like the hissing tire on Rachel's car, her words falling flat. "You can't do that to me, Prof. My parents are driving from Colorado for my graduation."

Rachel smiled patiently. "You knew the course objectives from the beginning of the semester. Five reports on the poets and *one* research paper of your own choosing. None of them out of reach—especially for an intelligent young woman like you."

What goes around, comes around. Her mother's voice saying, "An intelligent young woman like you, Rachel McCully, wasting your life skiing. Dreaming of Olympic medals. They only last long enough to hang them on your wall—if you win one."

Rachel straightened the plaque on her desk. *When I consider how my life was spent.*

Milton's words drove her to do her best at teaching. Most students respected Rachel; rarely did anyone cross her. She saw students as players on the world's stage and wanted them to find themselves before the curtain came down on their college career and forced them into the cold reality of life off campus. With some she succeeded. With Jude Alexander, she had failed.

"Jude, you turned in only three of the six projects."

Jude switched gears, mellowing her outburst to a plea. "Give me a 'D'—give me anything, but let me graduate." The tears brimming in Jude's eyes quickly lost their remorse. "I don't care what Shakespeare did or what Wordsworth wrote."

"Shakespeare was not one of the Lake Poets."

Jude's lip trembled. "I'm just making a point. It's your fault, Dr. McCully, that I was forced to take these courses. What in the world will I ever do with Wordsworth?"

"Apparently nothing."

She leaned forward in the chair, her fist doubled. "I'm a political science major—I plan on foreign service. What am I supposed to do? Spout poetry to some foreign diplomat?"

The bitter circle kept going around in Rachel's head, kept coming back to confront her. Her own voice defiant like Jude's. "I plan to ski in the Olympics, Mother, and after that I'll be a ski instructor. I don't plan to bury myself in the classroom."

And her mother's controlled voice breaking, "Your sister would give anything to be able to stand up and teach—"

Over the years the stinging memory of coming in from the ski run to the classroom had mellowed Rachel. She understood with hindsight how desperately her mother had needed someone to blame.

"I didn't single you out, Jude. There are certain requirements for graduation. Fortunately, we discovered that you needed additional credits in English before your final semester."

Jude's shoulders sagged. "My parents will be here Friday."

Rachel pushed the box of tissues toward her. How many students had sat in Jude's place over the years? Some ready to quit their university studies. Some troubled over their campus romance. A few wanting to change their majors. She had counseled them, laughed with them, wept with them—especially Amanda Pennyman, the young woman whose fiancé had been killed the night before. For them, there had been sympathy and understanding, and often a prayer. But this morning Rachel made no attempt to blow out Jude's fire with a prayer.

Rachel felt her brows knit together, frowning when she should be showing mercy. "Jude, I'll recommend to the graduation committee that you be allowed to participate in the ceremony—for your parents' sake. But your diploma will be blank."

"What good will that do me?"

"It will get you through the rest of this week. You can make up this class during the summer."

"My folks won't put another dime on my education."

"Then earn the money. It's up to you, Jude."

"Well, I won't take your courses again."

"Under the circumstances, I think that's best. Now, I have another final to oversee. Why don't we talk some more after the graduation ceremony and see how things are going for you then?"

Smoldering eyes glared back. "If you don't pass me—"

"I've turned in your grades—with my recommendations. Now, dry your eyes, Jude. You do have a future and a hope—"

"You sound like my father. Always spouting about God's plan for my life."

"Your father is right. God does have a plan for you, Jude."

"Right now it looks like he has a plan to destroy me. Whatever he has in mind, I hope it's as far from you as I can get."

Rachel glanced at her watch. That sense of pending doom needled her again. Once before she had stood in the faculty room, begging her colleagues to give Jude another chance.

"I guess you think I owe you one, don't you, Doc, just because you kept me from being expelled once. You should have let me go. At least I could have told my parents you threw me out of the university. Now I have to tell them I flunked out."

"You can make up that one course. Life doesn't always toss us a bouquet of roses. Sometimes we get thorns along with them."

Jude's caustic words sliced the air. "I thought you and Wordsworth were into daffodils." She pushed herself to a standing position and gripped the edge of Rachel's desk, her knuckles bone-white. "You're the lucky one, Dr. McCully. You probably wouldn't recognize a thorn if you saw it. Everybody who knows you, raves about you, except me. I think you're one tough lady."

Rachel leaned back in her chair as Jude stalked out, slamming the door behind her. Rachel saw herself as defiant and self-willed as Jude. For long moments, she sat brooding. When her office door flung open again, she expected to see Jude, but Nelson Rodgers, the department head, came in grinning.

"I just passed a tornado coming out of your office. What's wrong with Ms. Alexander this time?"

"It was just a misunderstanding."

"Your fault, of course? I have to admire you, Rachel. You weather every storm. Why don't we have lunch together? We could celebrate the end of another collegiate battle with iced tea."

"I'm sorry, Nelson. I have an appointment at two."

"Then we'll catch lunch in the fall when you get back. You're okay with flying, right?"

"Not a problem for me."

15

He walked over to scrutinize the pictures on her wall. "This is a good one of your dad. And I recognize this one. And this one. But this—" He tapped the photo of Sinclair Wakefield standing beneath Big Ben. "Who's this man, Rachel?"

One of life's painful memories. One of life's special moments. She had taken the picture with a telescopic lens when Sinclair waited for her. She was grateful that the silk scarf around her neck hid the flush. "Don't you remember him? That's Sinclair Wakefield. He spent a sabbatical on staff nine years ago."

"Wakefield! Of course. A year before my time here. For a minute I thought he was my competition. So . . . when do you leave for England?"

"As soon I can tidy up my desk."

"I trust that's after the graduation ceremony."

"Yes, mid-June. I'll be gone two months this time."

He winked. "As long as you come back."

At two, a nurse ushered Rachel into the plush office at the Blue Ridge Medical Center. With a noncommittal smile, she said, "Dr. Risner asked one of his colleagues to see you."

The nurse whipped out of the room, leaving Rachel to stare at the framed records of achievement and soothing seascapes on the wall. They did little to calm her. She was a stickler for time, doctors notoriously late. The minutes ticked away—and with them her patience. 2:10. 2:15. 2:20. She considered stepping back to the nurses' station and rescheduling when the door opened and Eileen Rutledge breezed into the room carrying a chart in her hand. A stethoscope bulged from the pocket of her white lab coat as she settled in the leather chair across from Rachel.

A tiny whipple of uncertainty caught in the pit of her stomach. Eileen had been one of her students in the early years of her teaching—an outstanding student who shared her love of Wordsworth. They were close in age. The last she knew, Eileen had finished medical school and gone on for a specialty in oncology.

Oncology.

Eileen folded her hands on top of the open chart. She offered a vague smile. "Surprised, Dr. McCully?"

"Yes, surprised to be on the opposite side of a desk. I had no idea you had moved back to the area, Eileen."

"A year ago. I moved back with my daughter." She slid a picture across the desk. "That's her school photo."

"She's lovely. Why she looks like—"

"She does, doesn't she? Her name's Rebecca. She's eight."

Rachel stole a glance at the doctor's ringless left hand. Embarrassed, she said, "An eight-year-old? Has it been that long since you took my classes, Eileen?"

"Longer."

"I hoped we'd stay in touch after you graduated."

"After Rebecca came, it seemed best not to burden you with my problems." Her smile warmed. "Even though I didn't stay in touch, I remember the first class I ever took with you. You told us to put our pens and notebooks away, and for the next fifty minutes you made Keats and Byron and Wordsworth come alive for us."

"I loved those lecture periods. They were so much more fun than having my students frantically recording my every word."

"I fell in love with Wordsworth because of you—I still keep a book of his poems by my bed for those nights when sleep eludes me." She met Rachel's gaze. "Were you aware of how your eyes blazed with fire when we were late with our assignments?"

"I've been teased about it many times." The memory of Sinclair Wakefield pierced her, snatching away her joy. "Someone once told me that my eyes and my smile were my best features."

"They still are, Doc McCully. And I remember how you used to snack on celery and cold cuts at our Pen and Quill meetings. And you went wild over homemade fudge and black licorice."

"I thought only my closest friends knew that. But that isn't why I'm here this afternoon. Is it? I expected to see Dr. Risner—I didn't know you were part of his clinic, Dr. Rutledge."

"He calls me in on consult frequently."

"Without consulting the patient?"

She thumbed through the chart. "He didn't call you with the test results?"

"No." The knot in Rachel's stomach tightened as she pulled the pink memo from her purse. "My secretary handed me this memo—*See Dr. Rutledge at two today.*" She met the doctor's gaze again. "I didn't even read this—I thought I'd be seeing Dr. Risner."

Eileen took the picture of her child back. Gently, she said, "Let's back up and start over. . . . Childhood diseases?"

"Measles, mumps. The usual."

"Hospitalizations?"

"None."

"Family history: heart disease? diabetes? cancer?"

"Cystic fibrosis . . . my sister died from it. My parents were killed in a fire."

"Yes, I remember." Eileen made her notations, then with pen poised said quietly, "Were you sick long before you saw Dr. Risner?"

"I'm never sick—except for an upper respiratory infection that sent me to the emergency room two weeks ago. The ER referred me to Dr. Risner for a follow-up."

"When Dr. Risner showed me your white count and chest film, I suggested more labs and a lung scan."

Rachel's lips felt parched. "What's going on, Eileen? Please, be up front with me."

"The way you were with your students? You wanted honesty and had little tolerance for excuses." She made a pretense of shuffling through the labs. "Your white count is much too high."

"There must be some mistake."

Eileen was an attractive young woman with alert eyes and a wholesome expression. An honest woman—the same brilliant student who had sat in Rachel's classroom, with the wisdom and experience of a few years thrown in. "Tell me, what kind of schedule have you been keeping lately? What's your energy level?"

"I just got back from a camping trip early this morning. I hiked without much difficulty." But this time she hadn't been the first one to the mountaintop; she had gone back to the campsite to rest.

"Any unusual bruises or bleeding?"

"You get bruised on the trail sometimes."

"Any fever?"

You should know, she thought, remembering the spiked fever in the emergency room. "It was 101 in the emergency room."

Eileen tapped the chart. "I'm at a disadvantage. I thought Dr. Risner had explained everything to you, Dr. McCully—"

"It's Rachel, please. I'm on this side of the desk now."

"I need to examine you thoroughly. We'll need more tests."

"Dr. Risner knows I'm going on a Rhine River cruise. I go abroad every summer. I can have the tests done when I get back."

"Rachel . . . there's a second concern. The radiologist found a shadow on your right lung."

She felt her heart skip a beat. "A shadow? I've never smoked."

"Your labs are abnormal. Your chest film abnormal. I can't let you go away until I know for certain what's going on."

Rachel focused on Eileen's shiny pierced earrings.

"If you're uncomfortable seeing me, Dr. McCully, we can call in another oncologist. But I offered to see you—you meant so much to me when I was your student."

In a voice that sounded like any but her own, Rachel said, "Be straight with me, Eileen."

"With your white count, we have to rule out leukemia."

The walls caved in on her. She took a deep breath. "Cancer?"

19

"I need to rule it out. If I'm right, God forbid, we'll have to decide on a course of treatment."

A shadow on her lung. Leukemia. These spelled medical tests and hospitalizations and treatments. She would not accept what her sister, Larea, had faced, her life cut short by an illness. No, this could not be happening again. As Eileen pushed back from her desk, her eyes sympathetic, Rachel heard herself rambling, "No. Stay where you are, Dr. Rutledge. Really, I'm fine. I just had flu the night I went to the emergency room. That's how all of this got started."

Eileen's gaze held steady. "Please make an appointment with me before you leave the country. Let's make certain what's going on."

Inside, Rachel felt a wretched emptiness. This couldn't be happening to her. They had made a mistake. But she said, "If your diagnosis is correct, do you have a time frame?"

"Without treatment, possibly months. Traveling abroad first may be unwise."

"They do have doctors in England."

Dr. Rutledge took a book from her lab coat and consulted the back pages. "I have a friend in London. Timothy Whitesaul was a resident when I was in medical school. If you get in trouble—"

"I won't."

Yesterday, even an hour ago, Rachel stood at the edge of tomorrow. On the bend of a river. At the top of a mountain. This was not the time for dreams to be shattered. For hope to be swept away in the current.

She would not cave in to this diagnosis nor fall apart in front of a former student. Her hands shook as she pushed herself from the chair. She wanted to rage against Eileen, against God, against fate. She climbed mountains, didn't she? She had boundless energy, was envied by her friends. She wasn't going to let some error in the emergency room ruin her life.

Recouping her composure, she said, "Mark it down in your chart, Eileen. I intend to beat this thing, whatever it is."

In the car, her courage crumbled. *Cancer! I may have cancer.* She pounded the steering wheel. "No! I have no intention of being cut down before my time like Larea was. I'm still too young to die. God, don't you understand? I promised my sister that I'd do all those things we wanted to do together."

But it took Rachel several days before she stopped crying and set about to defy the odds. As she packed her suitcases, snippets of prose exploded in her mind. They narrowed down to two. She had miles to run and promises to keep—the one to her sister, Larea, the one to Sinclair Wakefield.

Two

Eight months later Eileen Rutledge sat at her desk at the Blue Ridge Medical Center and made a final notation in Rachel McCully's chart.

January 24: Patient has stopped all medication. She is leaving for London to complete the vacation that was interrupted several months ago. Am sending a copy of her medical records to Timothy Whitesaul in London, England.

Eileen closed the chart and took out her own logbook. She thumbed past the weight and dosage charts to the back pages where she reviewed her own private record of Rachel McCully's progress.

May 29: Rachel McCully seen on consultation for Dr. Risner. Elevated labs and abnormal radiology films discussed with patient. Refuses additional tests or appointments at this time.

July 18: Phone call from London, England. Rachel McCully hospitalized after collapsing at Heathrow International. White blood count soaring. Arrangements made to evac her home.

August 8: Rachel had her first chemotherapy treatment today. She has told no one of her illness. How can I send her home to cope alone? That bond between student and professor is strong. I greatly admired Dr. McCully in my student days. Our roles have reversed. She must trust me now. After much soul searching, I took her home with me.

ing me a warning signal that she cannot
gram mapped out for her?

December 12: Rachel and Becki are po
mas catalogues, planning surprises. Rache
will allow herself one shopping spree with
have advised against it. Rachel's immune syste
vive the crowded shopping mall. It's difficult en
ing that she is still at the university part-ti
self to keep her schedule.

They ended the evening
only child a beautiful gift
of beauty is a joy fore
Rachel's cancer, it is t'
three of us give one

December 20: T'
first time, she as'
I remind her
plant. She s
ment pro
to see o
inste
your co

No. Rac
class.

January 1: We we
tion. Just the three ot
daughter looked up into the
me so much about English litera
a New Year's wish?" Becki asked.

"Yes, I asked God for the strength to g
Becki's face clouded. "Will you see Beat
Rachel laughed, that rich melodious laugh o
Potter is gone—and, Becki, I will be gone someday t
understand that, don't you?"

Becki's lip trembled. "You mean heaven?"

Rebecca took an immediate liking
already calling my bright-eyed little im
I done? I know better than to become in
tients. And now I have involved my own

September 5: Seven days post another c
Rachel still violently ill. Will discuss chang

September 26: Rachel refuses to discuss her
views life from a literary landscape; I deal wi
research, cell division and coping. She scorns t
trauma of being dependent on the medical world. Today, for
the first time, she spoke of her sister dying with cystic fibrosis. I tried to reassure her. She shouted back, "I don't like losing control. Or losing my hair. Or the thought of dying. Or
having my students and colleagues know what's happening
to me;"

October 10: I opened the door to the bedroom where
Rachel was resting. Rebecca was pillowed there with her.
Rebecca's long shiny hair spread loosely over the pillow.
Rachel's hair is already coming out in large clumps. They
joked about Rachel going bald, and I heard my daughter say,
"Don't feel sad. My dolls have wigs."
Last night they read *The Secret Garden.* Tonight Rachel is
reading Beatrix Potter's *Peter Rabbit.* They are both much
too old for Peter Rabbit, but they are content together. A
gentle friendship. I remember what joy Dr. McCully gave
me in my university classes, and now she is making literature
live for my daughter.
They adore each other. An eight-year-old and a thirty-seven-
year-old. I think Rebecca reminds her of the child she never had.
I closed the door with a lump in my throat.

October 31: Halloween. This evening when I lost another
patient, I wondered about the masks we humans wear. For
Becki it is an innocent time, a problem no greater than deciding whether she will go about the neighborhood as Squirrel Nutkin or Jemima Puddleduck. She wants Rachel to go
with her as Beatrix Potter. I tell her that Rachel is too ill

... es. But you will remember, won't you? I will always love you. And when I go to England, I will take pictures of Miss Potter's Hill Top Farm and send them to you."

Above my daughter's head, our eyes locked. "It will be a while before you can go," I told her.

"No, Eileen. I have my ticket. I'm stopping treatment."

It was impossible to argue with her in front of Rebecca. "You have a therapy appointment on the third."

"We'll see." And still smiling, she said, "Becki, what is your New Year's wish?"

"Two wishes. I want you to get well." She stole a glance at me. "And I really want to have a daddy. All my friends do."

I am afraid to look at my university professor. I think she knows who Becki's father is. Morrie Chadbourne's name will not pass between us. To even speak his name would make me cry. But Rachel knows. I am certain she knows. Yet it seems an unlikely time to tell her that Morris and I were once married. Divorced.

It was mid-January—the eighteenth—when Rachel arrived at the Blue Ridge Clinic for her final appointment. Eileen had steeled herself for that moment, but she had not expected the tranquility on Rachel's pale, thin face.

"I can't change your mind about England?" she asked, stethoscope in hand.

Thoughtfully, Rachel said, "I'm at peace, Eileen. At peace with God and myself. For me, it's the right decision."

Eileen believed her. But this visit was harder on Eileen and even more painful when Rachel said, "I've been looking into experimental treatments for leukemia."

So had Dr. Rutledge, but she did not volunteer any information. Rachel shared hers. "There's a clinical trial going on in London and Switzerland. The drug they are using is highly specific. It attacks a protein enzyme . . . I have written to ask about it."

---

the
young w...
"I decided ...
said. She turned ...
glistening in her eye...
me the day I turned thirt...
particular age and what mem...

November 19. Dr. McCully ...
Thanksgiving dinner back at her pl...
that we go. But she asked me why Thanks...
year. What should I tell her? Rach...
chemo the day before Thanksgiving. She contin...
erate the treatment poorly and is still in no condit...
biopsy the shadow on her lung. What will I say to Beck...
Rachel loses her battle with cancer?

November 28. Rachel challenges me with the inconsis-
tencies of standard treatment, her desire for experimental
drugs. "Dying does not fit into my schedule," she tells me.
We are fairly close in age, both too young to die. But I
cannot promise Rachel a positive outcome, even if she
changes doctors. She is bartering for time to live in an En-
glish village, far from the madding crowd. She speaks of it often.
I focus on the immediate. I ask myself whether the shadow
on her lung is a primary tumor. She is still too weak for a
surgical biopsy. I wonder whether the cancer has metasta-
sized to her brain. Is she imagining places? Or is she send-

"That's a last ditch effort, Rachel."

"Surely I qualify. My white count stays out of control."

"We don't have enough data on it."

"Enough to satisfy me, Doctor."

The doctor patted Rachel's arm and thought about Wordsworth's words: *The world is too much with us.* She meshed his words with her own. *The medical world is too much with me. It has laid waste my power to separate the patient from the treatment. Rachel McCully knows the difference. But I am not Wordsworth. I cannot gather Rachel a host of golden daffodils. But I must let her choose her own path.*

Still she argued, "We should study the results longer."

Rachel squeezed her hand to reassure Eileen. "As you re-minded me in the beginning, I might not have that long. But a number of those in the study have experienced com-plete remission."

"But for how long, Rachel?"

"Any amount of time is bonus time. You told me that your friend in London worked exclusively with experi-mental drugs."

"I should never have told you."

"If I can get in on his next clinical trial—Eileen, I'm pray-ing that you will contact Dr. Whitesaul for me. He is being very selective."

Eileen couldn't fight prayer, not Dr. McCully's prayer. She tried another delay tactic. "They have the same research in Texas."

With that magnificent smile of hers, Rachel exuded con-fidence. "My dear Eileen, don't you realize that 'my heart still leaps up when I behold a rainbow in the sky'?"

Wordsworth again. She was choosing that part of the world so familiar to her in books. Eileen nodded, letting her go. She sat down on the stool and leaned against the counter. She was being forced to set aside her training as a physi-cian—forced to view the options through Dr. McCully's eyes. McCully was looking for a cure—or for borrowed time. She had never known any patient who loved life more.

"Dr. McCully, what will I tell Becki?"

"That I love her. If I go into remission—and, Eileen, I intend to—then I want you to bring Becki for a visit. I already promised to take her to Beatrix Potter's Hill Top Farm."

Eileen knew that one way or the other they risked losing Rachel, either by progression of her illness or by her moving away. Her child should be outside playing with her friends, but Becki wanted Rachel to come over and read to her that evening. For a moment Eileen felt as though she had done her child a great disservice bringing Rachel into their lives. But no, Rachel had brought more than *The Secret Garden* and the Hill Top Farm into Becki's life. She had brought a special bond of love.

Again, their roles were reversed. Eileen was the student, Rachel her instructor in the course of life. At the office door, Rachel gave Eileen a quick hug. Like a child, Eileen felt sheltered in that embrace. Their two worlds collided. On parting, Rachel spoke of quality of life; Eileen countered with the latest research and the newest drugs being used here at home. Again she mentioned the possibility of a bone marrow transplant. But Rachel smiled the way she always did at the end of a semester.

Resigned, Eileen said, "I'll call Timothy Whitesaul this evening. He knows about you."

"Will he accept me in his program?"

"If I ask him—"

Rachel stood, adjusted her hairpiece, and gathered up her purse and jacket for the last time. "Will it take you long to send my medical records?"

Eileen tucked the chart under her arm and met Rachel's gaze. "If Timothy agrees, I'll air express them tomorrow."

Rachel flashed her radiant smile. "My colleagues at the university are throwing a farewell party for me on Tuesday. I want you and Becki to come. Will you?"

"Becki would never forgive me if we didn't. She loves grownup parties. And—she has a going away present for you."

Dr. Rutledge watched her patient leave the clinic for the last time. Head high. Back straight. Her body much too thin. But Rachel left without regrets.

Dr. Rutledge had only one. She had failed Rachel McCully medically. But in her journal, she wrote: "I am not God. I am simply Rachel's friend, Rebecca's mother, and all of my training, all of my skills have not stopped the progression of Rachel's illness. She is in God's hands. Or perhaps that is where she has been all along. Her strength, her faith is somehow rekindling my own."

Four days later Dr. Rutledge canceled two of her afternoon appointments and pulled into the faculty parking lot at the university, and, hand-in-hand with her daughter went up the steps and into McClaren Hall.

Rachel McCully's dark lustrous eyes came alive when she lectured, danced when she laughed with friends, and sometimes teared when she quoted the Lake Poets. They were tearing now as the university president and the faculty from the English and history departments filed into her office.

"Bon voyage, Rachel," they chorused.

Nelson Rodgers walked in, balancing a cake with flickering candles. He looked smug as he placed the cake on her desk.

"What's this about, Nelson? It's not my birthday."

"That's what we want to know. We're not accustomed to a bon voyage party in the middle of the year."

Misty Owens's double chin quivered. "Quitting in the middle of the year doesn't make sense, not without an explanation. And not when so many students are clamoring to take your classes."

Rachel had to carry off her farewell with dignity, had to hide her fears from those who had known her for so long. She didn't want their pitying glances as the cancer took over. She laughed lightly. "Misty, I'm long past due for a sabbatical."

Nelson licked a bite of icing. "We should be celebrating your twelve years on our faculty, not sending you abroad."

Thirteen, she mused, *if you counted the two years part-time while I completed my doctoral studies and post graduate courses abroad on a Fulbright Scholarship.*

He went on: "Rachel, you're at the pinnacle of success. We know you've had some trouble with your health this year, but why leave now? We're here for you."

They were, she knew. But she was going forward with her plans for a year abroad. By then, she'd be in remission . . . or dead. "I really am going to England next week," she managed.

Watching their smiles fade was like seeing the sun slip beyond the horizon. Brilliant one moment. Thick dark clouds the next. She took in their expressions—these colleagues who admired her. A few envied her unequivocal success, her way of juggling schedules, but none of them wanted her to leave.

President Stokes caught her eye. "You'll be back before the year's over. Wait and see. We'll leave your room just as it is."

"But you are always scrambling for more space."

"This room has always been reserved for a McCully."

In the pause that followed, Nelson nosed around her bookcase and pulled out her high school annual. He flipped through the pages. "Listen to this. Your classmates thought you witty and wise. Fiercely competitive. Close to kindness, distant of heart. Rachel, does that ever describe you. It should say, next in line for department head—if I retired, that is."

Rachel swiveled her chair as he thrust the annual into her hands. Her full mouth and dark eyes were visible even in the black-and-white. Fiercely competitive? Yes. But on her last appointment with Eileen Rutledge, she had not even approached kindness of heart as they argued about her cancer treatment. Now as her colleagues broke ranks in the crowded office, she saw Eileen standing in the doorway, Rebecca by her side.

"I brought you a present, Rachel."

She smiled at the child. "That was very thoughtful of you, Becki."

Rebecca ran over and leaned against her.

"May I open your present?"

Becki nodded, then helped her tear the pink tissue, revealing a lampshade with tassels along its ridge and rabbits in blue and lavender. Rachel hugged Becki. "I'll cherish this forever," she said.

President Stokes extended his hand to Eileen. "It's Dr. Rutledge now, isn't it? How nice of you and your daughter to join us."

"Someday I hope to send Rebecca here for her university studies."

"Dr. McCully will be back by then," he said with a catch in his voice. "It is a tradition here to have a McCully on staff."

As Eileen glanced across the crowded room, her eyes locked with Rachel's. "Rebecca and I hate to see her go. Rachel's grandfather was the president when I was a student. Her father with the history department—her mother here at McClaren."

"We're proud of Rachel living up to the family tradition."

Tradition? Rachel thought. *It was my sister who wanted to follow in our parents' footsteps, not me.*

Steve Swanson, her friend from the history department, focused his camera and snapped a picture as Rebecca and Rachel puffed their cheeks and blew out the candles. "I think you have one space left on your wall for this snap." He pointed to the spot near the photo of Sinclair and Big Ben. "I'll hang it up before you get back."

Rachel took a quick bite of cake and swallowed her answer. She didn't want to party or pretend. She wanted to go back in time and erase the last nine months of illness.

31

Steve was scrutinizing her life from the pictures on the wall. *Look closely enough,* she thought, *and you will know what shaped my life—family loyalty, the mountains, the works of great writers.* But the photos on the wall said nothing about her unfulfilled dreams.

"Rachel, are you listening?" Misty Owens asked. "I envy you. Dr. Rutledge has been boasting about how you awaken your own love of literature in your classrooms. And what you have done for Becki."

Rachel started to say it was her sister's love of literature that had influenced her, but how could she explain the ambiguity of where her sister's dreams left off and her own began. Rachel carried yesterday's pain with her—those growing-up memories that even now veiled her in an elusive, diaphanous mist.

Misty murmured her disapproval again. "Dr. Rutledge, can't you persuade Rachel to stay at home? Why all this nonsense about going abroad for a year?"

"It's something Dr. McCully has always wanted to do."

"Whatever for?"

Because of Sinclair Wakefield, Rachel thought. *Because for me, England is Sinclair.*

How strange it seemed to her, that after all these years, Sinclair remained fresh and alive in her thoughts. The dappled images of him always at the back of her mind. Even now, like a quick whisper from the past, her skin prickled at the remembered touch of his hand on hers, his lips sweet and minty lingering on her own.

She wanted time to find Sinclair Wakefield again and tell him why she had failed to meet him on that rainy summer morning under the shadow of Big Ben. She owed him the truth and for her own conscience needed to tell him that she had loved him even though she had sent him away. If he knew the truth, perhaps she could bear the death sentence hanging over her.

In London, a month later, Sinclair Wakefield walked into the solicitor's office marked *Blackstone and Rentley.* He eased into the armed chair across from his old friend and stretched out his lanky legs. He had not felt so relaxed in a long time.

"So what's the good news you phoned me about, Bailey?"

"Your investments are holding steady in spite of a global market on a tailspin. With a few minor changes your losses will be minimal. We might even be able to increase your earnings."

"That's better than some of my friends are doing."

"You were always a cautious investor, a man with a strategy." He fingered his cuff link. "I have other good news. I took the liberty of leasing your cottage in the Lake District."

"Leased it?"

"It's part of your portfolio—"

"I was thinking about selling it."

"You're better off holding on to the property."

"Especially since you've already rented it."

"She's an American. She came to me on personal business. As we parted, she asked where she could find a rental in the North Country. She particularly asked me about Stradbury Square."

Sinclair reached up and straightened his tie, then clasped his hands again. "No one even knows that village is on the map."

"It isn't. That's why she surprised me. Once I told her about your place, that was it. She took it—sight unseen."

Wakefield felt a queasy sensation in his stomach. It passed quickly. "An American? What did she look like?"

Bailey leaned back in his chair. "Very attractive. But then, you always did have an eye for a beautiful woman."

"I wouldn't know what she looked like."

"I'm sorry—that was in poor taste considering Mary and your boy."

"It's been two years."

"Right, old boy. Hard to believe. I tell you, I miss that little fellow. Blake used to come here and climb up in old Bailey's lap and look for sweets in my pocket."

"He was always asking when he could go back to see Bailey."

"I can't even begin to imagine your pain. I wish I could have done more after your wife and son were killed. Of course, I'm still handling the lawsuit against the railroad company."

"Your idea, not mine. It won't bring my family back. But this American, what can you tell me about her?"

Bailey flipped his pen, end over end. "She's a university professor on sabbatical. An English professor, I think."

Sinclair's palms went sweaty, his mouth dry. "You said she specifically asked about Stradbury Square?"

"Yes. The minute I told her about Wakefield Cottage, she leased it for a year. No questions asked. Money up front. She had funds transferred from the States." He scratched his head and checked his notes. "She won't be living there full-time until the end of April or early May. Said she had appointments to keep here in London."

"I'm glad you leased the property. It's best to have it occupied. Does the place need any repairs before she moves in?"

An amused smile caught the corner of Bailey's mouth. "The fence could do with a fresh coat of paint. And the fireplace should be checked. I'll call a friend in Grasmere. What about you, Sinclair?"

"I'm staying on in the house in Oxford. I feel closer to Mary and the boy there."

Bailey shifted uneasily. "And you're back to lecturing?"

"Two days a week on C. S. Lewis. And I started another degree. Art this time."

"Art?"

Sinclair stood, stretched. "I was always interested in the arts. It has filled the hours since—"

"Sinclair, you haven't asked me the name of your renter."

Rachel! Rachel with those magnificent dark eyes. "I think I already know who it is. . . . We were supposed to meet under Big Ben once. Rachel McCully, right?"

Bailey's brows arched in surprise. Wakefield felt himself relaxing again, smiling. "She was long before Mary. I don't think she even knows I married and had a son."

Bailey whistled. "Should I tell her we've talked?"

"If she wanted to find me, she would. Whatever her reason for moving to Stradbury Square, I won't question it." He checked his watch. "I'm having dinner at the club. Would you care to join me?"

Bailey plucked his beard. "Sounds good. Are you staying a fortnight in London this time?"

"Just overnight. I'm driving back to Oxford in the morning."

Bailey put his calls on hold. He opened his desk drawer and took a pamphlet from it. "Miss McCully left this behind, quite accidentally, I think. It's a report on an anticancer drug being used here in London. Makes me think she's ill."

Wakefield frowned as he read it. "If Miss McCully needs anything, make certain she gets it." He cleared his throat. "If she is ill, as you suggest, she may need a housekeeper. The woman who worked for Mother might be available."

"Audrey? I'll look into it."

Outside, as they strode in silent companionship toward the club, the deep chimes of the Clock Tower rang out. As the resonant bell tolled, Sinclair Wakefield glanced up at Big Ben. The light at the top of the Tower was lit, the House of Commons still in session. The gleaming splendor of The Houses of Parliament reflected in the River Thames, but the peace and calm that had engulfed him when he entered his solicitor's office had vanished. Just when he had reached that point in life when he was ready to pick up the missing pieces—just when he was beginning to come to terms with the loss of his beloved wife and son—he was forced to remember Rachel.

As the bell stopped tolling, Bailey asked, "So . . . what happened to your appointment with Miss McCully?"

"She never showed up."

"Maybe she was delayed in traffic."

"I waited for more than an hour. Three hours to be exact."

"You should have waited longer. She's a beautiful woman."

They had reached the club. Sinclair held the door open for Bailey and with another glance up at Big Ben, said, "A man's pride gets in the way. But God more than made up for my disappointment when he brought Mary and my son into my life . . . even if our time together was far too short."

Three

A spectacular spring morning lay before Rachel with the splendor of the purple-tipped hills and the serenity of a shimmering lake, the lake a striking hyacinth blue this morning. For years she had loved the north country and the breathtaking Cumberlands from the words of the Lake Poets. Now she was drinking in the same beauty that Wordsworth and Coleridge had known. The meadowlands reflected myriad shades in emerald, russet, and gold from the surrounding hills, and that lavender patch high on the hillside above the lake must surely be heather in bloom, Rachel thought.

She longed to run along the footpath lined with brambles and wild Kiftsgate roses and foxgloves. To wander among the dancing daffodils. To catch an arced rainbow or a wispy cloud from the sky. She would give anything for the strength to climb the craggy heights, or even to walk along the zigzagging path on the lower hills. She dared not venture even a mile. But one day, when she licked this illness, she would run and climb again and nothing would stop her.

This was the unspoiled English countryside Sinclair Wakefield had shared with her. Her senses quickened at the remembrance of his unexpected closeness. His woolly vest had prickled her cheek as he held her. The tantalizing scent of his aftershave lingered long after he leaned down to kiss her.

Three weeks after they had started dating, he had stood in her office in McClaren Hall, waving two round trip plane tickets in his hand. "We don't celebrate your Thanksgiving at home," he had announced. "But we're going on holiday to England. Forget your turkey and dressing. I want you to meet my family."

They had taken their Thanksgiving break and padded it on both ends with added days. Still giddy with jet lag, they had driven north from London to his mother's house in Stradbury Square and the tiny village that had been his boyhood home. But Rachel's most lasting memory was standing on the lakeshore on that crisp, frosty morning in November, her arm linked with Sinclair Wakefield's. An early autumn had turned the hillside amber, the meadows in shadowed hues, the trees to patches of yellow. The lake barely rippled. Utter stillness.

In the shadow of the hills rising high above the switchback road, the windswept cliffs hung precariously over the lake. Standing there, Rachel and Sinclair had fallen victim to the allure of the Lakes and to each other. In that enchanting hour, she harbored the secret wish to come back to England with Sinclair when his year of teaching ended.

Sighing winds snatched away those dreams, buffeting her with the old fear of carrying the threat of cystic fibrosis into a marriage. Still she liked remembering that one moment in time when he had taken her back to his roots. Her no-nonsense, dignified professor totally different in a hooded jacket and casual corduroys, his shy smile showing his boyish side. He had been anxious for her to love his country. All she could think about then was loving him and knowing she could not destroy that love with defective genes.

This morning, standing once again on a tree-fringed lake, she wondered whether she had imagined Sinclair's love or only desired it. She snuggled into her thick sweater and checked the security of the scarf covering her soft, downy fuzz of hair.

The top branches of the trees reflected in the water. The high crags reflected there too, rising in gentle slopes and stretching to rocky peaks. The lake mirrored more than hills and trees. It mirrored her soul, past and present, filling her with joy at just being alive. She felt keenly aware of yesterday—Sinclair a part of it—and keenly aware of today, where time was precious. The reflection of past and present cried out for her to catch a glimpse of eternity while still occupying a space on earth. The God of the cattle on a thousand hills did not count years as she did. God did not cling to the cycle of twenty-four-hour days as she had done.

During those first months of illness, her fists knuckled in anger at him for robbing her of health and time. At first she had it out with God, long nights of pacing in the empty bedroom, back and forth to the toilet bowl retching from the effects of chemo. Crying. Cajoling. Begging to not be faced with her sister's agonizing journey.

Now she felt an odd acceptance of what she could not change. Still she was left with a thousand questions and with so many unfinished dreams. What had she accomplished in life? What lingering impact had she made on her students? Had any of them been changed by the imprint of her life on theirs?

At times—like yesterday—she still had it out with God, but in a more amicable way she had reminded him of those things she would still like to do. Browse the museums of Italy again. Sail a sloop off Hawaii with the wind in her face. Peek in on some of her students—especially Jude Alexander—to see whether they had measured up to her expectations. And simpler things like running or eating without feeling nauseous. Or skiing in Switzerland again or facing the challenge of climbing Mt. McKinley. And that cry of her heart for just one more glimpse of Sinclair! She realized that these thoughts didn't have spiritual ribbons attached to them, and yet wasn't wanting the wind in your face and the sea on your skin and being free on a mountain slope part of knowing the creation? Knowing the Creator?

Rachel watched a song thrush take flight and followed its upward path toward the sun-bathed summit. The thrush had left its nest and flown. Wasn't that what she had done? Set a course of her own by spreading her wings and breaking with medical tradition? She had made the right choice. For what it was worth—and it might be costly—she was back in control, deciding on her own course of treatment. She did not encourage it for others, but it was the path for her—the choice to have quality of life, however brief.

These months of being too ill to climb would end, one way or the other. Like the thrush, she would take flight on an earthly journey, or perhaps on an eternal one. Until now, she had almost lost sight of looking ahead—of looking up—of being all she could be for a day, a week, a month, a year.

As Rachel ambled along the west end of the lake, she was aware of hikers on the hillside, marring her solitude. They had been there all along, blocked from her senses, but now she envied their freedom to scale the fells to the top, and to come back down in the same steady gait with heavy rucksacks on their backs. She focused on a lone climber, a wiry man with a thick sweater tied around his waist, binoculars in his hand.

He paused, lifted the binoculars and focused them on her. Then his pace increased, slipping and sliding past several hikers sitting on the rocks in front of him. He stopped a second time, eyeing her through the binoculars.

She thought it strange, but she was flattered nonetheless. In spite of the hiking boots, the man ran those last few yards toward her. Cupping his mouth, he hollered, "You look lonely as a cloud, Doc."

She frowned, pointing questioningly to herself.

"Yes, you," he laughed. "You look lonely as a cloud."

She heard the familiar ring to his voice. It had to be Morrie Chadbourne, one of those transplanted Americans who loved this country. He was pithy to the point of bluntness but so un-British. He skidded to a stop in front of her and whipped off his sunshades. "Hi, Prof."

"Morrie."

He grinned. "You remember me."

Why wouldn't she? After spending so many months with Eileen who had once loved him, who probably still loved him. She expected him to say, *What are you doing here?* Instead he dropped his rucksack to the ground and grasped both her hands. "I should have known you would end up at the Lakes."

"You don't seem surprised that I'm here."

"I called the university recently, trying to reach you."

"Me?"

"Yes, I wanted a quote or two from you for my next project."

Seeing him again, she thought him perhaps thirty-five, his dark hair silver-streaked at the temples and unruly as it had often been. Of the hundreds of students who had passed through Rachel's life, Morris Chadbourne proved one of the most promising and most successful. His latest scholarly work, a comparative study of Coleridge and Wordsworth, had been well-received in the literary world at Oxford and at the universities of London. She was certain it hadn't made him wealthy, but surely it had put him high in the literary ranks.

"Morris Chadbourne, you've done quite well for yourself."

"I don't exactly own the bank, Dr. McCully. But I lecture now, and that puts food on the table. And you?"

"I'm on sabbatical."

"Are you here on a study program? That's what professors do with sabbaticals, isn't it?"

"Not this one."

"Do you think the university would give me so much as a clue? Nothing. Even talked to President Stokes, and all he could promise was he'd let you know I was trying to reach you. Did he?"

"Possibly. My mail is piling up in London."

"At least he admitted that you were in England. Look, let's go somewhere and sit down. Treat's on me."

"I need to be getting back to Stradbury Square."

"So that's where you're hiding out. Any street address?"

41

"The Wakefield Cottage."

"You're not getting out of my sight until we sit down for a visit. You look exhausted."

"You're the one who was hiking."

He frowned, studying her. "You should be. You need some color in those cheeks of yours." He swung his rucksack over one shoulder and took her arm. "Hungry?"

"Not really."

"But you like quaint atmosphere. I know just the place."

He led her into a country inn with stone-flagged floors and gas lighting. He waved at the owner. "I brought my old university professor with me, Hanley. Be good to her."

"Chadbourne, the wife's making you a mint cake." He winked at Rachel. "From what I see, Chadbourne, she's not old."

"Just a matter of speaking. Will you add some open-faced sandwiches and cream tea? We'll take the table by the fireplace."

"Any word from Lord Somerset, Chadbourne?"

"He and his wife are still planning that world cruise."

As they settled by the small round table, Rachel glanced around, liking the warmth of the fire and the pub's atmosphere. A cast-iron range with claw feet sat crookedly in one corner. A gas lantern swung from the ceiling above each table.

"You were right; this is a quaint place," Rachel acknowledged.

"I like it. A man can relax here. There are some tea shops where the proprietors don't appreciate dusty boots and sweaty hikers. It spoils their Victorian image, but Hanley welcomes climbers."

"I see that. Who is Lord Somerset?"

"One of the rich locals, if not the richest."

"He'd have to be for a world cruise."

"He's an art collector."

"You always had an interest in art—in stolen art, if I remember correctly."

His eyes shadowed. "I still do."

She rested her chin on her folded hands. "I never knew why."

"Someday I'll tell you." He cracked his knuckles. "Are you feeling all right, Dr. McCully?"

"I'm fine."

She hoped the fire in the stone hearth would bring a rosy glow back to her cheeks. Her mirror had not lied this morning—her complexion was still pasty, the luster in her eyes not like the old days. She hoped that Morrie would not take notice, and if he did, that he would not comment again. But Morrie was always quick to express his concern when something worried him. How could she hide her illness when it was so evident now?

When Hanley delivered the sandwiches and cream tea, he asked, "So, Professor, are you staying with Chadbourne at Lord Somerset's?"

In spite of the pallor, she felt her cheeks burn. "Of course not. Morris and I just ran into each other moments ago. I don't even know Lord Somerset."

Hanley's sea-green eyes pierced hers, amused, doubtful. "Have you not heard of Lord Somerset? He's the connoisseur of fine arts in the North Country."

"Quite knowledgeable," Morrie mumbled.

Hanley stood his ground. "Are you liking the Lakes?"

"Yes, it's been such a perfect day—and then running into Morrie here, that was special."

"He has never brought a fairer lady to my pub."

Again her cheeks burned. "My first visit here was in the fall some years ago. It was nice then too but much colder."

Hanley stroked his fleshy jaw. "Been here twenty years. April and May are good. We have more sunny periods, like today." He surveyed her, more amused questions in his glance. "You come to Hanley's Pub anytime. I'll be bringing my wife's cake shortly."

Morrie studied her as Hanley lumbered away. "Dr. McCully, I am sorry. Hanley's a bit of a romantic."

She rubbed her cheeks. "More embarrassing. Overbearing."

"You're not here on a study program, are you? You're ill."

"I'm better. But let's talk about you, Morrie. I've read several critical reviews on your study of Coleridge and Wordsworth. They were favorable. So what next?"

"A smaller study on the work of C. S. Lewis, and during my free time I'm researching lost art."

"World War II again?"

"Particularly a collection stolen in France. I'm on my own on that project, but I'm taking lectures at Oxford on Lewis."

Her cheeks flushed for the third time. "Have you studied under Sinclair Wakefield? He is well versed on Lewis."

"He just lectures two days a week. I'm petitioning for his seminars in the fall. How do you know him, Dr. McCully?"

"He was on faculty with us some years ago."

He held her gaze with a piercing glance. "Did you know Wakefield's wife and son were killed in a rail accident in France two years ago? Thankfully there were no other children— just the one boy, four or five when he died. But, of course, you would know that. You're staying in his cottage."

"I didn't know." *Why hadn't the solicitor mentioned it? Why had Audrey kept silent?* Pulling her sweater around her, she heard the tremor in her own voice. "I arranged for the cottage through a solicitor in London."

"You okay, Prof?"

"I'm all right." She straightened the tilt of her head scarf and wondered if the fuzz of hair showed.

He waved for the waitress. "Could you toss on another log? My guest is shivering with cold."

"You didn't have to do that, Morrie."

"The stone walls make it chilly." He took another sandwich and stowed it away in four bites. "I think I upset you. From the look on your face, you and Wakefield were more than colleagues."

"Good friends once." She touched the cuff of her sweater and checked the time. "I really should go."

"Not yet. Tell me about yourself."

Reluctantly, she settled back into her chair. "I finished my twelfth year of teaching a year ago. And then—well, we'll talk about that another time. What I really want to know is whether you still hear from Eileen Rutledge."

"We don't keep in touch. Do you?"

"She's been my doctor for the last several months."

He wiped his mouth. A flicker of understanding crossed his face. "Your doctor? Eileen is an oncologist."

"And a good one."

He reached across the table and squeezed Rachel's hand. "So that's why you're on sabbatical?"

"I told you, Morrie, I'm fine. I took a year off to take stock of my life as a teacher, wondering whether I left any lasting impression on the students who passed through my classes. You think about things like that when you've been ill."

"You were a good teacher. You know that, don't you?"

"I thought so."

"Don't get bogged down with that hay, wood, and stubble stuff you used to talk about when you graded our research papers."

She pushed her plate aside, the cake half eaten. "You touch their lives for a semester or two and they're gone. What I want to know now is whether they've succeeded."

"I turned out all right, didn't I?"

"But have all of your choices made you happy?"

"You mean Eileen?" he asked bitterly.

"I thought you two had something going between you."

"Just a college crush."

It was more than that, she thought. *There's a child. Do you know about Becki?* "I thought the two of you would marry."

"That affair with Eileen ended a long time ago. What happened to us after we left campus was not your problem. Your job was to teach the classics and you did a bang-up job."

She flashed a radiant smile. "I really must go, Morrie."

45

"I can't offer you a ride back to Stradbury Square, unless you want to ride on my handlebars."

"I have my own rental. But I'm surprised at you. You always had an old jalopy on campus."

"Part of my student image. I can't afford the luxury of a car here. I have a bike out behind the pub that gets me back and forth, and I depend on the underground or a taxi in the city."

They stood. "Doc, Stradbury Square is too far away. I have an extra room. Great spot to live. Spectacular scenery. A badminton court for when you're feeling better. Some private paths if you want to be alone. And, like Hanley suggested, an art collection that you won't believe."

"Then you're doing better in your writing than I thought."

"I make ends meet. But the art collection belongs to Lord and Lady Somerset."

His gaze shifted toward Hanley at the counter, who was nonchalantly wiping glasses. He lowered his voice, "I'd like to show you the Somersets' art treasures. The truth is, I'd give anything—do anything—to claim one of those masterpieces as my own."

Stolen art. For a second the look in his eyes troubled her.

"Doc, if you were close by, I could walk with you each day—help you gain some strength back. Maybe put some color back in your face." He looked boyish, eager. "If you won't share the house, there are guest cottages on the property. I'll arrange for you to stay in one of them. It's less isolated than Stradbury Square."

"I'm quite happy at the Wakefield Cottage."

He broke off a bite of the cake left on her plate and popped it into his mouth. "Will you come back soon?"

"We'll see."

"You'll have to do better than that. I want your word."

"All right. I will drive in someday. How's that?"

He caught her hand and smiled. "I'll count on it."

Morrie saw Rachel to her car and watched her pull out of the drive with a flick of her hand in farewell and that quick, warm smile. Old memories stirred with his first impressions of her when he was a collegian: striking, young, witty, desirable. And his own impudent belief that he could charm her, date her—he the young student from Kentucky besotted with his professor.

Now he wasn't certain whether it was his head or heart pounding—hammering, crushing his temples with its intensity. Years ago, back at the university, they seemed to move on the same wavelength. He could match her brilliance, and he knew it. But she had the confidence, the air of success, and he craved them both. She represented the position and popularity that he wanted.

In those early months on campus, he lingered after class or arrived early to engage her in conversation. He recalled sitting on the campus lawn a time or two, discussing the classics. All of that before Eileen Rutledge walked into his life.

Gripped by a fresh onslaught of loneliness, Morrie spun around, walked back into Hanley's Pub, and sat at the counter.

Hanley eyed him quizzically. "What will it be?"

"Another coffee. Black. And if Miss McCully comes back here again, no remarks. We are friends. Nothing more."

Hanley slapped an empty cup on the counter and filled it to the brim. "Just your old professor?"

Morrie gulped and felt the scalding drink going straight down. "Yes, that's it."

"She is much more a lady—more attractive than your other friends." He refilled Morrie's cup. "But you seem troubled at seeing her again."

"I didn't think it would matter, but I was wrong."

Hanley polished another wine goblet with his towel. "Another guest left a message for you."

Morrie glanced around, the coffee spilling on the counter as he turned back. "Who?"

"Didier Bosman, the museum curator from London. He was sitting in the far corner watching you and the lady, taking pictures, I think. He said to tell you he would call you later."

Hanley slapped the towel across one shoulder and leaned across the counter. "Stay out of trouble, boy, especially if that woman is going to become important to you."

Morrie fell heir to a lot of Hanley's counsel. His own marriage was a battle zone, but he liked to match up others who came through his door. It added spark to his dull, routine days.

"The professor is ill, Hanley. That's my only concern."

But some of those old enamored longings taunted him. What was it about Rachel McCully that always lingered in the back of his mind? That she believed in him? Expected the best from him? Or perhaps it was her solitary way. For all of her love of the mountains, her personable way in the classroom, she was an enigma, a woman who felt comfortable alone, a woman who never quit climbing or dreaming. There was always another mountain to conquer. Now she was grounded and this God that Dr. McCully believed in had tossed her the challenge of her lifetime.

And he was about to throw her safety to the wind. The museum curator's plan had sounded so simple. Fill the Somerset Estates with guests—just a few would be ample. Disconnect the intricate alarm system. Unlock the side gate. And go to the caretaker's cottage and sleep. Sleep! All for a painting—not for money, but for the possession of an Asher Weinberger work of art.

Morrie would awaken the next morning the same struggling scholar. And hate himself. But the Weinberger would finally be his. No, it had always been his right, his heirloom. No more legal hassles. Surely Dr. McCully would understand that.

Hanley took Morrie's empty cup and wiped the counter dry. "Looks like she is more than a professor to you, Chadbourne."

Had he been in love with her? Was he smitten again? No, he had been in love with Eileen Rutledge. Infatuated with Dr. McCully. Or was it that desperate need to prove himself to his professor once again?

Hanley whipped the towel from his shoulder and swiped the counter once more. "What is wrong, Chadbourne? A woman walks in here with you, and you fall apart."

"I must get back to the Somerset Estates."

"If you are responsible for them, you should. And take my advice, son. No woman is worth this kind of fretting."

"Hanley," his wife bellowed from the kitchen.

As Hanley shambled off, Morrie slid off the stool and with half a chuckle left the pub. But he couldn't shake off Hanley's question. *What is wrong, Chadbourne?*

He was about to betray Rachel McCully—the one woman who thought him clever, scholarly. She was proud of him. Respected him. No matter what advice Hanley could dish out, or what the museum curator demanded, one thing Morrie knew for certain: He did not want Dr. Rachel McCully to be disappointed in him.

$\mathcal{F}$our

Every day for eight weeks, except for those visits to the London clinic, Rachel awakened to a hermit thrush singing and to the happy patter of the housekeeper in the kitchen. She pushed herself to a sitting position, stretching her long legs beneath the cool sheets, and listened to the flutelike tones of the bird. Since coming to Wakefield Cottage, she shared the shyness of her feathered friend—its love of the woodland, its need for the privacy of her garden, its joy at awakening each morning. The bell-like music matched the song that quickened her own heart. Each time the sun burst over Stradbury Square, she felt pillowed by an eternal God, triumphant that she had beaten the odds by adding another day to her life, clearly defying the gloomy predictions of a year ago.

She ducked her head lower for a better view from her bedroom window. Stradbury Square was a peaceful village off the beaten trail where a few dozen or more thatched, white-washed cottages and old stone houses nestled against the wooded gardens. Roads snaked around the countryside. A tranquil lake mirrored the hillsides and the church spire. Neighbors leaned over the picket gates to exchange gossip and homemade buns and jellies with Rachel in the same way that they had undoubtedly done in years gone by with Sinclair's mother.

Some of the neighbors remembered Rachel's visit almost ten years ago. They welcomed her back, and the housekeeper who had fretted over Sinclair as a boy had moved in once again to watch over Rachel. Audrey must be all of seventy, of sturdy stock, and stronger than Rachel. They never mentioned Sinclair, but pictures of him hung on the cottage walls, and the boyhood mementos that his mother had treasured lay on the bookshelves in the drawing room. On Fridays, faithful as the clock ticking in the corner of the room, Audrey dusted them with obvious pleasure.

Slowly, Rachel forsook the comfort of the old-fashioned bed, slipped into a new pair of slacks and a long-sleeve denim top, and grabbed her work gloves. As she stepped through the conservatory into the garden, she breathed in the sweet fragrance of the rambler roses and flowering shrubs—much easier on her queasy stomach than the sizzling sausage in the kitchen. She knew the pleasing aroma of the garden changed with the seasons—sometimes honeysuckle scented the air, sometimes the pungent spicy odor of the trailing arbutus or an intoxicating whiff of sweet peas tickled one's senses.

The sun filtered through the broad-leaf evergreens and cut its path across the tapestry of flowers. She ambled over the pebbled path, cupping a pink camellia to her left, and stopping to trim a dead branch off her hollyhocks with her secateurs. Wakefield Cottage had become her sanctuary, her safe hideaway.

But it was not the haunts of poets that had drawn her to England. She had come here with a kaleidoscope of memories and fading portraits of Sinclair Wakefield. Treasured keepsakes. Vaporous shadows. Especially during her illness, she saw his face in the face of strangers. And now living in the cottage of his boyhood, she heard his voice in her dreams. Knowing that Sinclair had married and was now widowed, she resolved not to impose upon his grief. She had come to terms with the possibility of never seeing him again. Someday she would confide in Audrey, and if she lost this battle with cancer, Sinclair would one day know what really happened when he waited for her beneath Big Ben.

"Madam, you forgot your breakfast."

Would Rachel ever grow used to her housekeeper's greeting? She smiled. "Good morning, Audrey."

"Perfect morning," Audrey clipped. In truth, she was a soft-hearted woman who took pleasure in seeing to Rachel's needs. She wiped her red hands against the apron tied tightly around her ample middle. "You have a guest, Miss Rachel. Not too pleasant a man, I might add. Demanded admittance immediately."

"At this early hour?"

"Said he came for breakfast." She snorted, disgruntled again. "Said he knew you rose early. Such impudence."

That could only be Morrie Chadbourne. He was shamelessly bold—not a staid, polite British gentleman that Audrey would welcome. She pictured the two of them clashing at the door—Morrie demanding entry; Audrey reluctant to thrust company on Rachel before breakfast.

"What shall I tell him, Madam?"

"Is it Morrie Chadbourne?"

"He didn't give his name. Said you'd know right off."

Then it was Morrie—coming into town from Grasmere. He was lean as a rail, but his appetite would be ravishing. "Show him in, please. And, if you don't mind—"

"Will be no bother," she said in her simple country voice. "I'll crack another egg or two. Throw in more sausage."

"He can have my sausage and fried tomatoes." Rachel had no stomach for large meals, her poor appetite an offense to Audrey. "And I think we'll just breakfast out here."

Audrey cast a glance at the rising sun. "As you wish, Madam. But stay in the shade. No need to risk a sunburn."

She took Audrey's warning seriously. A hot sun could sap her energy or play havoc with the medicine that she was forced to take. "I will be careful. And, Audrey, Morrie likes plenty of toast and marmalade."

"Looks like he's never been fed before, but he won't go away from here hungry." She turned on her heels. "I'll see to that and have that breakfast for you both in a swift jiffy."

Rachel pocketed the shears, dropped her garden gloves on the workbench, and brushed the soil from her hands before tucking her short strands of hair beneath her scarf. As she heard Morrie's determined steps scrunching over the pebbled walkway, she squared her shoulders, standing tall as she had always done when she faced her students at the university.

A beguiling smile filled Morris Chadbourne's angular face as he came toward her, his dark-rimmed glasses making him look studious. "Hi, Doc McCully. Just getting in to see you was like the old days. I thought I was petitioning for a spot in your classroom."

She held out her hands. "Morrie, what a lovely surprise."

"You didn't keep your appointment—it's been three weeks since you promised to come see me."

"I have no excuse."

But she did. The trips to Timothy Whitesaul's clinic took time. Morrie's nose crinkled at the heady fragrance in her garden. "Are you really sorry?"

"Yes, now that I'm thinking about it . . . Morris, what tore you away from the purple hills of Grasmere?"

"You." He wrapped his strong hands around hers and bent to kiss her cheek. "You didn't call on me like you promised."

"I thought you were just being polite."

"When I make a date with a lady, I expect her to keep it."

She teased. "I trust you didn't pedal all the way here."

"No, a friend offered to drive me here in his truck."

"A long, bumpy ride for a checkup."

"We did get an early start," he admitted.

"I still think you should buy a car."

He grinned down at her. "I never got the hang of driving on the wrong side of the road. Besides, one can almost do the thirty miles of the Lake District without wheels."

"You must be hungry."

"Famished. Haven't eaten since five this morning."

She slipped her arm in his as much to steady her gait as to show her affection for him. "We'll have breakfast out here," she said as they took their seats at the wrought-iron table.

He crossed his gangly legs, a wiry, raw-boned man like Wordsworth—his eyes wide and intense as he surveyed her garden. A red-breasted stonechat fed at the bird feeder, while a honeybee buzzed the delicate petals of the morning glories.

"I want you to go back to my place with me so we can go hiking again. There are several places I still want to show you."

Surely he understood. She had little strength for hiking. "I don't hike much anymore, Morrie."

"When I was a student you were unbeatable on the mountain trails. The first to suggest a tennis match or a camping trip."

"Yes, I was all of that."

"So what happened? You said you were feeling better."

"I promised President Stokes I'd rest on my sabbatical. Hiking," she repeated. "I think not."

"Come on, Prof. It would be just what the doctor ordered."

"For now, I'm content just tending my garden."

He glanced back at the garden gloves and spade lying on her workbench. "Let someone else do the digging and planting."

"That's what I've been telling her," Audrey snapped as she put their breakfast tray on the table. "Just last week, I persuaded her to hire another gardener, a local man. But look at her—still out here exhausting herself with gardening."

Rachel smiled as Audrey turned back to the kitchen. "Don't believe her. I mostly just sit out here in my sun hat and tell the gardener what to do. I want my flower beds to be perfectly laid out for the people who live in this cottage next."

"I don't think the place is for sale."

"It will be someday."

She wondered, as she poured his tea, how much he knew about leukemia. How little she really knew about him. How much she imagined and admired. But there was the other side of Morrie that worried her. His anger at the mention of Eileen. The way his face clouded when he talked about the

54

stolen masterpieces from World War II. The thing that troubled her most was Morrie perhaps not knowing that his daughter, Becki, existed.

A bemused smile formed around his mouth. Rachel did not think him handsome but kindly. He had so much to give, a charm and warmth all his own. She would gladly claim him as a lifelong friend, so attuned were they in their love for the outdoors, great literature, and England.

Yet they were vastly different—she fashion conscious even in her illness and still buying her clothes from exclusive women's shops. He a scholarly man, a literary genius, and yet casual always, indifferent to the latest fads. Even today he was dressed in khaki slacks, newer than his frayed maroon shirt.

Morrie attacked his breakfast with a passion, but he was too busy a man to be dropping in for a carefree visit. "What brought you in from Grasmere?" she asked softly.

"I wanted a decent breakfast. I'm a rotten cook, you know." He popped another bite of sausage into his mouth. "And when you didn't keep your promise to come see me, I worried about you."

Rachel set her demitasse cup down, her tapered fingers still wrapped around it as her gaze locked with Morrie's. "You must not worry about me, Morris."

"Then tell me the truth. How are you . . . really?"

"Sometimes my white count goes off the charts. But I'm responding to the new treatment here in England and may go into remission."

"Not a cure?"

"One can always hope for a five-year cure. Or ten years."

"No guarantee?"

"My doctor thinks there is real promise with the new revolutionary drugs he is using for leukemia. He makes no promise of a cure, but what he offers me most is hope."

How much easier to swallow one giant-sized pill a day, she thought, *than to face that dreaded chemo.* Eventually, if she responded to the treatment, she would remain on a maintenance

55

dose. Already, in just a few weeks, her headaches were less frequent, her old energy creeping back.

Morrie leaned back, a piece of toast covered with marmalade balanced in one hand. "Come back to Grasmere with me. Then I'll take you into London for a second medical opinion."

"I have a physician in London."

"Come back with me. I'd be there to check in on you daily."

"Audrey does that."

"Rachel, you need a change."

"Before this disease takes me?"

"I didn't say that."

"Don't even think it. I'm going to beat this thing. I'll fight it all the way to the grave if I have to. That's better than surrendering. Giving up. Quitting."

"You were never a quitter."

"And I won't quit now. I'm not quite thirty-eight."

"Then you have three years on me. That's all." Frowning, he said, "In class you used to talk about eternity being in the hearts of men. I guess that goes for women too?"

He had nailed her with what had once been her unswerving belief in meeting God's appointments without quibbling. But her thoughts remained earthbound, wandering slowly back to Sinclair. "Morris, I had unfinished business when I moved here—a friend I wanted to find again. Seeing him, I think, is not possible, so I can never patch up those last unsettled moments between us. If I could, then maybe I would give up battling this leukemia."

"You're not a quitter! This friend of yours, do I know him?"

She held back for a moment, then said, "You travel in the same circles. Lecture on the same circuits. He was a teaching colleague of mine back at the university."

Above the rim of his glasses, his brows knit together. "Wakefield! Why didn't you marry him, Rachel? A husband could comfort you now."

"I have Audrey for a companion."

56

He nodded. "You're friends, but I daresay, not confidants. Could I help you find him?"

She reached across the table and patted his hand. "It's too late, Morris. I should have taken care of this a long time ago."

The sun rose higher, rapidly reaching toward their shady corner. "Perhaps I can help in another way. The last time we met, you said you wanted to see some of your students again."

"Such a silly dream. I guess I just want to know whether I accomplished all I intended to in their lives."

"Wasn't a dozen years in the classroom enough?"

"Not if I failed to leave an imprint on their lives. I intended to. I prayed that I would."

"Have no regrets. You were a magnificent teacher."

"But I have no permanence, no one to carry on my name at the university. A McCully on campus has been a tradition for three generations."

"Your students are your legacy."

"A nebulous legacy," she said sadly. "I sat on the platform year after year and watched them march by in caps and gowns. They grabbed their diplomas and were out of my life."

"You found me again. Aren't you satisfied with the results?"

"Morrie, I am proud of you. Do you remember that lecture on Coleridge when we discussed living well? Persevering."

He broke the stem of a flower from the bush. "Vaguely."

She knew by the changing shadows in his eyes that he remembered it well. Why wouldn't he? It was the day he met Eileen Rutledge. "We talked about Coleridge's qualities of greatness—about him not living up to his full potential."

"I'm not measuring up?" he scoffed. "The other day you bragged about my accomplishments."

"But something's troubling you. I think that's why you came here this morning."

"Come on, Doc. Just because I had a little run-in with your housekeeper when I barged in for breakfast?"

"When you came down the mountain the other day, you were full of charm and concern—the Morrie I remembered."

57

"And now?"

"You tell me. Back in the university, I told my students if they were ever in trouble, to call me. Collect, if they had to."

"I tried. But President Stokes wouldn't give me your forwarding address. I found you in spite of him. But I'm not your responsibility. So just to cheer you up, let's invite some other students back into your life for a big bash. A reunion of sorts. We'd be helping each other."

"You're serious." She saw by the intensity in his eyes that he was. "Oh, they'd be bored going back to the classroom. They may not remember me kindly. I didn't grade easily. And I know that I failed one—Jude Alexander—in more ways than one."

"I survived," he grinned impishly, "by transferring to Columbia's School of Journalism. It looked better on my resumé. You know, my views were too political, too liberal. I meshed better with the free spirits at Columbia."

"Was that your only reason for transferring?"

He stabbed at the last bite of sausage. "You want me to say Eileen Rutledge drove me away, don't you?"

"Only if it's true. I always thought the two of you were meant to be. I wanted you to work out your difficulties."

He snatched a dry piece of toast and smothered it with marmalade. "Working out a relationship is a tough call."

She waited until he met her gaze again. "I wish she knew about your success in the literary world. . . . Was it Eileen's family that kept the two of you from marrying?"

"Didn't she tell you? We married and divorced two months later. Maybe she wanted to forget our little spring fling during my junior year. Eileen was in her second year at med school by then."

Rachel felt a crushing headache coming on as she thought of the brief exchange across the desk in Eileen's office.

"Eileen, the child looks like—"

"Yes, doesn't she?"

"Morris, why didn't you give your marriage a little longer?"

58

"Eileen's family didn't think I was good enough for her. I was just a poor, barefoot Kentucky boy who read Wordsworth down by the river." His words crackled. "How could I support her? I hadn't published my first article when I told Eileen I wanted to do literary research full-time. Her father threw away the welcome mat even before he met me."

"And Eileen's mother—was she a social snob too?"

He looked chagrined. "No, Mrs. Rutledge was a good sort. She wanted her daughter to follow her heart."

"Why didn't you give Eileen a chance to do that?"

Morrie pushed his chair away from the table and squinted at the sun. "And why are you so stubborn about this class reunion?"

"The cottage isn't big enough. We'd have to rent a castle."

He gained time by sipping more tea. "There's nothing wrong with a castle, but I may come up with something better. You just get your invitation list written out—before we run out of time."

"If we have a reunion," she said softly, "I would put Dr. Rutledge's name on my list. And if she comes, she would want to see you."

He rose from the table. "She'd never come."

Thinking of Becki, Rachel smiled. "I rather think you are in for some surprises, Morris. Must you rush off?"

"My driver should be back by now. Maybe we can check out some castles on our way home."

"You are serious?"

"Where you are concerned, yes. Every good teacher deserves recognition." He pressed her shoulder, smiling. "No, don't get up. I can see myself out. Come for tea on Monday, and I'll show you the Somerset Estates."

"I have an appointment with my physician on Monday."

One brow arced as he looked at her, the eyes gentle as he was. "Do you want me to go into London with you?"

"That won't be necessary."

"But I have appointments in London myself. Wakefield and I are lecturing to a women's guild on Monday. If you're free in time, come and hear us."

She shook her head. "Not this time. But we could travel back from London together early Tuesday morning."

"No can do. I have another interview with an art dealer to discuss a painting I've had my eye on for a long time. The price he is demanding is still negotiable."

She reflected on Morrie's lifestyle, the job he held. Morrie had the quality of greatness but not the bank account to go with fame and fortune. "Morrie, neither one of us can afford to purchase a masterpiece."

His words sharpened. "Whatever it costs me—whatever I have to do—I want that Weinberger painting."

If she charted his breakfast mood swings on a graph, they would peak and dip, both ends shooting off the chart. This was not the Morrie she remembered sitting in the top row in her classroom, quietly debating, sometimes arguing the genius of literary giants. She remembered Morrie as a studious intellectual peering out on life through thick-rimmed glasses, pleasant to his classmates, yet preoccupied with rising above his boyhood limitations. He had been part of the basketball team but never a team player. Even then, he had been a solitary man, bedeviled with his obsession for art.

"Morrie, are you in trouble?" she asked.

The flecks of gray in his eyes darkened. "It's nothing I can't handle. Now, what about going into London together?"

"Protecting me again? Why are you being so good to me?"

He leaned down and brushed his lips gently across her cheek. "Because you are a remarkable woman, Rachel McCully."

$\mathcal{F}ive$

As he reached the swinging gate, Morrie Chadbourne's smile fragmented. He jammed his hands into his pockets and stumbled along to the truck with his eyes downcast.

"You took long enough," the driver said as Morrie hauled himself up into the passenger seat. "Did it go as planned?"

Morrie slouched lower and glared at the bearded driver beside him, a man younger than himself. "Not quite the way you expected, Chip. We didn't discuss having the reunion at the Somerset Estates. I can't do that to her. She trusts me."

"You'll get over it, Chadbourne. You're the one who wants that Weinberger painting. That means you figure out a way to deliver our share of the Somerset collection to us."

"I never meant to turn any of the collection over to you. It was all a joke on my part."

"Bosman isn't laughing."

Didier Bosman, the son of a European art dealer, was the museum curator he'd interviewed twice. Even his name threw Morrie into a tailspin. His image was easily recalled: medium height, rotund, thinning hair, respectably dressed, a nondescript face that would never be picked from the crowd. But the monetary value of each painting put a gleam in his eyes. After the interview, Bosman had tracked Morrie to Hanley's Pub, and was surely the sweat-togged figure prowling around the estates last evening.

Chip went on in his mocking tone. "A joke, was it? So you never wanted the Weinberger painting?"

Wanted it? Morrie could taste the desire. He knew the bitterness of trying to trace the ownership back to his great-grandmother in Paris. He had combed through sales records and art catalogs. Unless Morrie admitted who he really was, Weinberger's paintings would remain on museum walls and in private collections without restitution. And the others—those he could not trace—lost like the paper trail. How could he explain to anyone—even to Rachel McCully—why his interest in the works of Vermeer, Degas, and Monet was small in comparison? He had admiration for other artists, but he could live the rest of his life without a Rembrandt or a Goya or Matisse, if only he could lay claim to just one Weinberger painting.

"You tried the paper trail, Chadbourne. It didn't work."

His search had led him to the French-Swiss art connection, to the National Archives and Records in Washington, to the still-classified documents in France, and to the declassified documents in Germany. He could prove that the Chadbourne Collection had been well known in the city of Paris in the late 1930s—that it had hung on the walls of his great-grandmother's villa. But he could not prove he was the only heir.

"Cooperate with us. We can put that painting in your hands."

He hated the arrogance of the man. Chip was a bit of an actor. The acquired British accent was more midwestern American, as fraudulent as the man himself. Sometimes for the delight of it, he turned on an Irish brogue, claiming Ireland as his homeland. Morrie pegged him as more than a driver. Bosman gave the orders, but could he mastermind an art heist like this one?

"It won't work, Chip. Security is unbelievable. The gates electrified. The floor plan confusing. The alarm system—"

"Disable the system. We need two hours at most. Whatever you need, Bosman will get it. An electrician. A wire cutter. An explosives expert. The Millennium Dome heist failed. Bosman won't tolerate failure again." He swerved to avoid a rock in the road.

Morrie gritted his teeth. "I can't go through with it."

Chip shifted gears and took the hill at high speed. "It might cost you the professor if you back out on us now."

"Professor McCully is dying anyway."

The younger man's jaw clamped. "Dying? That's the end station for all of us. I didn't think she was that old."

"She isn't. She's sick. And whatever time she has left, I'm going to protect her. I'm going to see that she enjoys it."

"You're going soft for this woman?"

Once that might have been true—the university student infatuated with his professor. But not now. Morrie braced his foot on the floorboard as they took the narrow curves. He glanced back and could still see the Wakefield Cottage in the distance. He had been a fool to go there. Now Bosman knew where she lived.

"I'd say you can't protect her, short of marrying her. Maybe the wife can't testify against the husband. Either way, you wouldn't want anything to happen to her."

In cold fury, Morrie wanted to grab the wheel and take them both out on the next curve. "Leave Dr. McCully out of this."

The truck jerked forward. "Don't mess with us, Chadbourne. We need that Somerset house occupied in the next three weeks. And a better floor plan mapped out with the exact location for each painting—five from the drawing room, seven from the main gallery. Four from the library. The rest from the smoking room. See that you tag them and move the two Desmond oriental vases into the drawing room. Bosman has decided to take those as well. He already has a buyer."

He chortled. "Don't look so worried, Chadbourne. Somerset is heavily insured. He'll cut his losses with few questions asked."

"You underestimate him."

"No, my friend. You underestimate him. He wants no scandal."

He tossed a sheet of paper on Morrie's lap. "We want these two women invited to the reunion."

"Amanda Pennyman. Jude Alexander," Morrie read aloud. "How did you get these?"

"A museum contact back at the university. A simple matter."

"Forget Jude Alexander. She and Dr. McCully did not part on good terms."

"Then I'll take care of that one. You just make certain that Pennyman gets there. She has a live-in boyfriend. Kevin Nolan. Make certain he comes with her. That's an order. Just follow it."

"It's an irrational scheme. Just steal the paintings while the place is vacated—while the servants sleep and the Somersets cruise. There's no need for a reunion—"

"Scotland Yard is taking particular concern for private collectors on holiday. They would not expect a robbery with a house full of guests. For us, it will be a quick midnight entry. A quick exit. Nothing will happen to your guests."

"And innocent guests will be blamed for the art theft?"

"Right on. Knowing women guests, they will paw every vase and bronzed artifact within reach and leave their fingerprints."

Morrie choked on the lump in his throat. "Forget the Weinberger painting. I want no part of this."

"We know differently! Bosman doesn't question your motives, but I can't figure you out. The Weinberger must be worth two million. The rest of the collection much higher. Why were you willing to settle for just the Weinberger, Chadbourne?"

So they hadn't figured out Morrie's relationship to the Weinbergers. A distant relationship it was true, but his great-grandmother had married into the Chadbourne family in Paris. How long had she kept her Jewish heritage secret? Had it been her interest in the gifted Asher Weinberger that gave her away? Somewhere in the early '30s, Morrie's great-grandmother had

64

added Asher's work to her vast collection. But the art plundering in Europe tore the paintings from Sophie Chadbourne's walls—and stole her soul. His soul. *Where, Morrie reasoned, was Rachel McCully's God when that happened? Was her God dead in the '30s? In the '40s?*

"You're a strange man, Chadbourne. Brilliant. Persuasive. Greedy. Your greed will cost you—or cost the women in your life. But you puzzle me—I thought you believed in our cause."

"Bosman told me he was researching the provenance issue—tracking the ownership of World War II paintings for the heirs. That's why I interviewed him. That was why I got involved."

"That was a nice little twist for Bosman. The caretaker for one of the largest collections in the north walked right into his office to interview him."

"I thought Bosman was legitimate until he boasted about his connection with the Millennium Dome jewel heist."

"We won't have another failure like that one, and we wouldn't give Somerset's paintings another thought if we didn't know their value. The Somersets are rich. We believe they are also heavily insured."

They were well informed. Morrie had been researching an article on the foiled robbery at the Millennium Dome when he met Bosman. As the truck rolled along, he ran it through his mind again. A dozen men arrested by Scotland Yard and Didier Bosman not among them. Bosman boasted a link to the robbery, but Morrie could not be certain he was not just a copycat thief, foolishly planning on bulldozers and smoke bombs and a boat waiting on the lake to whisk them away—and a number of followers like Chip willing to take the risk for the money involved.

"A robbery in the Lake District?" Morrie had joked. "I assume I can quote you in the article."

"Do that," Bosman said, "and you'll regret it."

Morrie repeated the same thought to Chip. "All that planning for $500 million worth of diamonds. It didn't work. It won't work at the Somerset Estates either."

"Bosman didn't spend all those years as a museum curator studying the value of paintings for nothing. Twenty paintings, that's all he wants. Nineteen for us. One for you."

Twenty paintings out of three hundred. Morrie did not question the number. Bosman had done his homework. He had targeted the most valuable pictures in the collection. Those with the highest market value. Those most heavily insured. And four with questionable ownership and the least likely to be detected.

Considerate thieves? *No one loses that way,* he thought.

"Bosman has to be crazy. You can't put a boat on the Lakes for an escape route. And there's no way you can drive off with a truckload of stolen paintings without being caught before you reach Manchester or London."

"They'll be secure within an hour. When it's safe, we'll move them elsewhere, perhaps north to Scotland."

Thirty to sixty minutes distance? Grasmere? Some other city. Some warehouse that Morrie was unaware of?

Chip's cockiness increased. "The Somerset Estates is just another practice run. A little drive in the country. The British Museum is next. There we won't settle for just twenty paintings."

He slammed on his brakes a block from the pub, jolting Morrie against the dashboard. "Out," he said, his sardonic smile as cutting as his tone. "I think you can walk from here."

As Morrie's feet hit the ground, Chip gave his final shotgun orders. "We'll be in touch. Bosman wants to place men and women in the area—and in the Somerset Estates. So we need the place occupied. Replace the security guards you have. And you'll need a butler for that reunion of yours, one of Bosman's choice."

Before Morrie could slam the door, Chip accelerated and made dust of the road as he drove away. There was no way for

Morrie to redeem himself or to slip out of the net that surrounded him.

Back at Wakefield Cottage, Rachel lingered in the garden watching a bee light on the crusty egg on her plate. Why would Morrie even consider a school reunion, small as it would be? She questioned his motives.

He had betrayed Eileen.

Was she any safer under his spell?

At last she stood and carried the tray of dishes into the house. She found Audrey standing by the east window, her expression one of puzzlement. "So Mr. Chadbourne is gone? He is trouble, that one."

"Audrey, you don't know him."

Audrey turned, fire in her eyes. "I daresay, you don't know him either. In our village, you park in front of the cottage when you come visiting. Not down the road, out of sight."

"His friend had errands to run."

"In Stradbury Square?" She shook her head. "His friend was parked down there the whole time. That's their truck in the distance." Her tone softened. "Come, see for yourself and give me that tray. Cleaning up is my job."

Audrey took the tray but remained rooted by the window. "There is no place in the world like Stradbury Square. That's why we don't want strangers coming about, ruining it for us."

Rachel gazed out on the landscape, a harmony of nature on ancient hillsides. Stradbury Square was a world to itself with its cobbled streets and secluded gardens and its narrow gravel roads snaking around the tapestry of color. In the distance the truck rambled over the winding road and disappeared from sight.

"You're certain that Morrie's friend simply waited for him?"

"Like he didn't want to be seen or remembered."

For want of words, Rachel said, "I've been meaning to ask you, Audrey. I don't recall this window from my first visit here."

"Mr. Sinclair had it put in when his mother took sick. He had to cut into the wall. Brought in contractors from London. Mrs. Wakefield had such happiness sitting here, once she couldn't walk about the village or work in her conservatory—but promise me, Miss McCully, that you won't be seeing that young man again."

"He wants me to have a reunion with some of my students."

The cups on the tray rattled. "A reunion here?"

Rachel laughed. "Not here. I suggested a castle."

"Don't take on anything extra right now. You need your rest. Get your strength back and then worry about parties and guests."

"Audrey—you know, I might not get better."

"All the more reason to save your strength. You have job enough just trying to get well. But if you are going to keep seeing that young man, then it's up to me to find out who the driver was. Once I offer a plate of scones to my neighbors, tongues will loosen. It's a country style telegraph. We'll pass word along from cottage to cottage that we want to know about that truck and its driver." She looked determined. "If I pass enough scones along, we will have a description of that driver. It's my job to look after you. That's what the solicitor told me when he called to see if we needed any more repairs on the cottage."

"When I rented this place, he told me you went with the cottage. What a thoughtful man, looking after me like that!"

Audrey's throaty chuckle erupted. "Bailey Rentley just keeps the portfolio. It's the owner who pays for the repairs."

The owner. Sinclair. "How is Sinclair, Audrey?"

A fractional arc lifted the thick brow. "Still grieving for his wife and boy. But no one can tell that but me who knows him so well." Her shoulders heaved with a massive sigh. "I ought to tell him about your friend."

"Don't trouble Sinclair. He doesn't even know I'm here."

"I say he is fraught with learning, not stupid. If that solicitor Bailey knows you are living here, then Mr. Sinclair knows.

There's not much that happens here in Stradbury Square that passes by Sinclair Wakefield."

"If he knows—is that why he doesn't come around anymore?"

The tired eyes sought Rachel's. "Mr. Wakefield always hoped you'd come back to Stradbury Square to live."

"I did."

"He didn't mean for you to come alone." Her expression grew stern. "That day Mr. Sinclair went into London to meet you, why did you not keep your appointment?"

Payback time. What goes around, comes around. Audrey could be her mother standing there, her gaze razor sharp. "I *was* there, Audrey. I just didn't let Sinclair see me."

A puzzled frown spread the wrinkles on the older woman's face. The momentary anger eased. "He changed after that—never mentioned you again. Then he met Mary. She was good for him. And that boy—I wondered why they didn't have more children. Mr. Sinclair used to talk about a big family. But Mary almost died when Blake was born. And Blake—God bless that little fellow—he was always frail, happy but frail—funny the way things come about."

She lifted her apron and dabbed her eyes. "He used to come and bring the wife and boy when his mother was still alive. Nice little boy. Loved to play with his father's toys." She gave a quick wave of her hands toward the bookshelves. "Little Blake would put them back in the same place when it was time to leave and come out to my kitchen and thank me for the cookies and tea. He never drank the tea, mind you. He was such a nice little boy. Shameful to be gone like that."

She turned and left the room, moving laboriously toward the kitchen, one hip higher than the other. "Seems to me that there's too much of yesterday's garbage and heartache still cluttering this place," she mumbled. "We ought to get it cleaned up, and I just might be the one to do something about it."

"Audrey—I never meant to hurt Sinclair."

She glanced back, her red-rimmed eyes watery. "I wish Mr. Wakefield knew that."

⁓

Morrie's eyes focused on the gravel as he went to the back of the pub and unchained his bike. He considered going inside and pouring out his problems to Hanley, but he couldn't risk Hanley calling in Scotland Yard. Morrie had spent a lifetime working out his own problems, ignoring the need for God. Now it seemed impossible to call on a higher power to get him out of the mess he had walked into. With a helpless wave to Hanley in the doorway, he began the long ride back to the Somerset Estates.

He let himself in through the gate and entered the house through the back. He didn't turn on the lights until he reached the switch in the drawing room. As the room flooded with light, he moved to the stone fireplace, braced his hands against it, and stared up at the Weinberger painting that could ruin his life.

Morrie rarely grieved for his great-grandmother's violent death in Auschwitz. If he could lay claim to this one masterpiece, he rationalized, would he not be paying tribute to his great-grandmother and redeem a part of his own lost nature?

He only meant to right a wrong thrust on his Jewish family sixty years ago. Now in a twist of events, he needed Rachel McCully, a gentile, as his safety valve in the days ahead. If things went sour, Rachel would not suffer long. She was seriously ill, dying, wasn't she? No court in the land would lay the blame for an art heist on an innocent English professor on sabbatical.

That day when he had placed a call to the university to reach her, it wasn't the daffodils and rainbows in the sky that he needed. He wanted her wisdom about the straight and narrow, her personal integrity, her rock-hard way of facing life. Now, if he had it figured out right, he was on a fairly wide road to destruction. Perspiration dampened his brow. He never intended to be a thief. Still didn't. He just wanted to claim the painting that belonged in his family. How many museums had told him there were no heirs making claims against the Weinberger? A dead paper trail. They'd stolen more than an art collection from his great-grandmother in Paris. They had stolen her identity. His identity.

McCully could be his only hope. She had asked him about that lecture on Coleridge. His brain scrambled to remember that particular day at McClaren Hall. McCully was in her second year at the university, a distracting figure in front of any classroom. Long-legged, graceful. All of a hundred and twenty-five pounds. He remembered the quick swing of the hips as she turned from the chalkboard and faced the class with a brilliant smile.

"That's it," she had said. "My goals for the semester."

He had expected scribbling on the Lake Poets, not five pert sayings in chalk. For the life of him, he remembered only one. *Living well is costly. Living without integrity, futile.*

Not some sonnet or verse from the Lake Poets but her own rules to live by. It didn't take a genius to realize, young and attractive as she was, she intended to guide their minds beyond the classics to facing life beyond the campus. In her unassuming way, she had thrown God in as part of the package of learning.

"What if Coleridge had lived well?" she had asked that day. "At least better than he did. What if he had lived up to his full potential? To God's potential? What held him back?"

Someone had wisecracked, "Being the tenth son of a poor clergyman didn't help." Laughter. Agreement.

Bill Wong, the class joker, took up the mockery. "No wonder he had an albatross around his neck."

A more silky voice, a dreamer from the front row, said, "I think Coleridge was handsome, brilliant, talented, charming. Who else could have given us *Christabel* and *Kubla Khan?*"

Morrie cursed under his breath. *Five points for you.*

71

The same student added, "Being a charity pupil in school may have bothered him. Or maybe his impulsiveness stood in his way."

"Impulsiveness can be a good thing," Professor McCully had said. "And Samuel Coleridge did attend Cambridge."

"But he quit the university and joined the army," Morrie scoffed. "And his family and friends bought his discharge."

"So he bought his way out of trouble? Was that a good move for a man who possessed the qualities of greatness?" she asked. "He was gifted as a poet, as a literary critic, as a philosopher, but he left only a fraction of what he could have accomplished. What destroyed his creativity in the last years of his life?"

"Opium," someone suggested.

"Yes, he fell victim to that. Even his friend Wordsworth couldn't force that creative mind to go on producing when it was already dulled by drugs. What dulls your minds?" she asked.

Morrie, hearing the sadness in McCully's voice, realized that she was thinking beyond Coleridge to the students in front of her. She had made her point that day—you give your best, you don't buy your way out of trouble. The thought of his own creativity being destroyed worried him. Coleridge moved in acceptable circles with *The Rime of the Ancient Mariner* to his credit. What did Morrie have? One or two literary works that had placed him on the fringe of the literary world. Opium wouldn't destroy him, but he had allowed his smoldering resentment over the stolen art of World War II to lead him into wrong choices.

Morrie recalled, when the bell rang in McClaren Hall that day, students converged on the door, but he took his time gathering up his books. McCully had waited by the chalkboard as he came down the steps from the top row. He felt like he was entering the arena. Going for the death. "Prof," he said, "I can't worry about Coleridge digging himself out of trouble. I have problems of my own living down my childhood as a barefoot boy in Kentucky. No siblings—

but rotten poverty. No opium—but reason enough to slip into oblivion."

"Forget about living down your boyhood. Live up to your potential. Don't waste any part of your life or your talents. You are a gifted young man, Morris Chadbourne. Very philosophical. A good debater. So find someone or something to live for."

At that moment, he thought McCully might be the one to live for. He had walked her to her office in McClaren Hall, rehashing the life and works of Samuel Coleridge.

When they entered her office, a young woman smiled at the professor and then turned to Morrie, the smile still on her lips. Attractive. Wholesome. As their eyes locked, her cheeks flushed.

"Mr. Chadbourne, this is Eileen Rutledge, one of my former students. One," she said with a twinkle, "living up to her potential. Someone who doesn't buy her way out of trouble."

Morrie recalled his toes curling inside his loafers, the way his bare toes had curled into the haystack back on the farm in Kentucky. He excelled in the classroom, did well on the basketball court, but he was reduced to awkwardness as Eileen Rutledge extended her slender hand to him. He shifted his books to his other arm and allowed his sweaty hand to tighten around hers.

So much of Morrie was wrapped up in that one brief moment—so much wrapped up in his life from those two women. The professor who influenced his thinking and the young woman who walked into his life and grabbed his heart.

Now he stood, head bowed beneath the Weinberger painting, and leaned against the mantel. "What have I done?"

Six

Sinclair Wakefield managed a quick handclasp with the young American as they made their way from the lecture hall at the University of London.

A strong grip, he thought. Not like he had expected.

Morris Chadbourne had such a casual way about him. He was a lanky man with that annoying American wit and a charming smile for the women. He didn't seem to have a care in the world. His features were firm, his handgrip solid, and whether Sinclair wanted to admit it or not, Chadbourne had a scholarly mind.

As they left the building the rain came down in torrents. Chadbourne pocketed his tie, raised the collar of his thin jacket, and shrugged good-naturedly. Sinclair belted his Burberry and balanced his briefcase as he shoved his bumbershoot open.

"Sir, how about supper together?" Morrie said. "We could wait out the storm that way. There's no need to drown running for the subway."

"Sorry, old chap, I have an evening appointment."

He almost said, "Join us," but cut the invitation off at the impulse. His solicitor did not welcome uninvited guests. Besides, if Bailey Rentley's emergency call dealt with Sinclair's portfolio, he didn't want Chadbourne privy to his financial losses.

"Let's do supper the next time, sir?"

Sinclair didn't relish the idea at all. "Yes. Will do."

As he put his foot to the stairs, Chadbourne's casual farewell stopped him. "By the way, Don Wakefield, I ran into an old friend of yours near Grasmere a few weeks back."

Rachel! He disliked the jab in his midline. He turned, bent back his head and the umbrella. Rain washed his face. "Did you?"

"Rachel could do with a visit from an old friend, sir."

He was surprised at his own spark of jealousy. How well did this young man know Rachel McCully? Young? Why did he think of the American as young? There could not be more than six or seven years between them. But they were a world apart.

He ran down another three steps. "She's ill," Chadbourne called after him. "You know that, don't you, Wakefield?"

He disliked the American's constant use of contractions. Even more, he hated his confirmation of Rachel's illness. He paused when he reached the sidewalk and looked back up at the American. "Seriously ill?"

"I'd call leukemia touch and go . . . I'm not suggesting you stir up the old flames. You may not be capable of that."

Wakefield's anger flared. *How much did he know? How much had Rachel told him?*

"I'm sorry about your wife and son—but I think Rachel McCully could do with your encouragement."

Sinclair left Chadbourne, but impressions of the man and his message went with him. Was Morris Chadbourne spending time with Rachel in the Lake Districts? Was Chadbourne taunting him with her illness? Warning him? Mocking him? Or simply concerned?

She could do with a visit from an old friend.

Mary and the boy. *Dear God, what am I thinking? Rachel belongs to my past. I have no claims on her. Mary and the boy belong to—Mary and my son belong to my past.*

The rainy slime on the sidewalks of London splashed on Sinclair's trousers as he raced for the underground. He ran down another flight of steps to the tube, trying to decide

75

whether he liked Chadbourne or disliked him. Even as he scrambled for a seat on the subway, he kept thinking about Chadbourne's casual invitation to dine together—the sardonic smile on his lips as he announced that Rachel could do with a visit from an old friend. Sinclair wanted to go to Rachel. To take her hand. To tell her he was sorry. But he could not bear the thought of someone else dying. The pain would be too intense, the loss of Mary and his son still too raw.

He must return Audrey's phone calls, the ones he had ignored. He would ring her and ask how Rachel McCully was doing. But what if Rachel answered the phone? Pride stonewalled him as the toll of Big Ben resounded in his head.

Wakefield caged his pride by focusing on the afternoon lectures. He had given his usual speech on C. S. Lewis, adding from personal experience his understanding of grief and its impact on the human soul. Chadbourne, on the other hand, came up with new approaches to presenting the works of Wordsworth and Coleridge, skillfully weaving in his passion for art. Take this afternoon for instance. He spoke on the greatest art forms—the men and women who paint with words, those who paint on canvas, and those who give us music.

"They're all master craftsmen," Chadbourne had insisted.

Morris Chadbourne refused to separate the literary giants from the great musicians. He insisted on linking artist and author into the same mold. Invariably, his illustrations took his audience back to the looting of art during the Nazi regime. He stirred the listeners into a frenzy at the unfairness of heirs unable to claim what was rightfully theirs. Chadbourne's approach irritated Sinclair, boggled his mind.

Why? Sinclair wondered, did they continue to be booked on the same platform? And why not? He knew as the train rattled on toward his station that it was not the man or his subject that needled him. He braced his head against the muggy windowpane and felt the jolting to his neck as the train pulled into the next station. How could he seek out the woman he once loved? If Rachel McCully wanted to see him, she knew how to contact him. It was her move, not his. One who had been jilted did not rush in for a second rejection.

He reached the club twenty-five minutes later, feeling drenched from the rain and out of sorts with the world. He shook the rain from his umbrella and brushed his shoulders dry before pushing his way into the club.

The girl at the cloak check welcomed him. "Mr. Wakefield, what a miserable evening. The maitre d' said to tell you that Mr. Rentley will be late." She nodded up toward the private rooms on the balcony. "But Lord Somerset is already here."

"Lord Somerset? I wasn't expecting anyone but my solicitor."

"The table's set for four. There's the maitre d' now."

Leon approached with a bow. "We've set you up in a private room with a fireplace," he said, smiling. "That should help dry you out. Come, let me show you, Mr. Wakefield."

In the room, a lace curtain shielded the observation window. The window afforded a full view of the dining area, but those on the main floor would be unable to identify the guests inside.

Lord Somerset rose as he entered. "Sinclair, good of you to come. It's been far too long." His narrow green eyes remained unblinking beneath the gray-streaked brows. He said pointedly, "I haven't seen you since the funeral two years ago."

"My fault, James. Your wife sent me several invitations for dinner. I was not ready to socialize with others."

"Agnes understood. But I have no excuse for not meeting you at the club or driving into Oxford to see how you were doing."

"You were there for me, if I called. But I am surprised to see you this evening. I was told you were on a world cruise."

"My wife is. That's where I am supposed to be. If things go well this evening, I will join her at the next port."

"Problems?"

"Scotland Yard literally pulled me off the ship as I was about to board. That is what we are here to discuss."

"Scotland Yard? Am I part of the solution?"

"We hope so. Your solicitor should be along shortly. He told me to go ahead and order the evening's special for four."

"Lamb roasted in garlic, I trust."

They sipped coffee as they waited—one of those habits that Sinclair had developed in America, the year he met Rachel. He put the cup down and studied the man across from him. Lord Somerset's hair and sideburns were silver-gray, his lips thick, but easily given to a smile. He had a ruddy face, and at seventy-four was developing a double chin and sagging neck folds. Usually guests were expected to wear ties at the club, but Lord Somerset had come this evening in a maroon turtle-neck shirt and his tweed sport jacket, both giving him a more youthful appearance.

An amused smile crinkled his face. "Well, here comes Rentley now in his usual flurry—and with Inspector Farland in tow."

"Jon Farland? He specializes in art fraud."

"Right-o. The detective superintendent actually. He heads up the art fraud division. He usually gets his thief, as the saying goes, but someday, a thief is going to outfox that old boy." He stood, his grin broadening. "Good of you to join us, gentlemen."

The inspector gave a hearty laugh as he sat down. "It's the other way around, Lord Somerset. It is good of you to set your plans aside so willingly."

"I do have a personal interest in my art collection. I would hate to go on a world cruise and come home to an empty house."

"We don't think the house would be empty. Just some of the valuable paintings gone."

They were seated companionably when the dinner was served. Lord Somerset took a few bites and leaned back in his chair, his arms folded. "Well, Inspector, are we on a foxhunt, or just a false alarm?"

"We would not have troubled you, sir, if we were not concerned. I suggested that you meet us at the Yard, but Bailey thought it better to meet casually here at the club."

"A wise choice. That way I can slip out of town and out of sight as soon as we finish dinner. I understand from Bailey here that is what you expect me to do."

He lit his pipe, drew on it. "But I am more inclined to skip this meal and race back to my estate to protect my possessions."

"Do that and the thieves get away."

"They may get away anyway. You're asking a lot of me, Inspector. I will spend the whole cruise thinking of my place being ransacked."

"We won't let that happen. We will stay in touch with you." The inspector rubbed his chin. "We would like to keep the illusion that you are at sea. You understand, of course?"

Somerset gave a mocking bow. "Why don't you explain?"

"You no doubt read about that attempted diamond heist on the Millennium Dome some time ago?"

"Inspector, I am an Agatha Christie fan myself. The rest of my reading interests are limited to the financial page in newspapers and investment reports. But my wife was tied up in knots over the attempted diamond robbery. She insisted that we increase our insurance on our art collection immediately. That's why we left a caretaker in charge and increased our security before we left on what we expected to be a celebration of our fiftieth wedding anniversary."

"My apologies, sir."

Bailey Rentley flicked crumbs from his beard. With his mouth partially full, he asked, "How well do you know this caretaker?"

"My wife heard him lecture several months ago." He tapped the bowl of his pipe against the saucer and pointed the stem at Sinclair. "You share the same speaking lecture with Morris Chadbourne. My wife considers him quite gifted."

Sinclair nodded. "And quite charming with the women."

79

"Charming enough for my wife to convince me to give him a job as caretaker. I didn't mind. He seemed an amiable chap and quite committed to his research projects. A few brief inquiries and I knew he was not making a decent living with his books."

"James," Sinclair said, "you were always one to encourage ambitious young men to reach their goals. You encouraged me."

"Why not? Someone gave me a footing in the banking industry when I was young."

The inspector chuckled. "But you grew rich dabbling in the art world, an entrepreneur with his name on many charity bequests."

"Yes," he said, chest puffed. "I pulled myself up from the ground level and reached the top without the halls of higher learning as Sinclair has done. I earned respect and the right to friends in high places, including the monarchy. Yes, my wife and I were in full agreement to give Chadbourne a place to live . . . and the time needed to do his research."

The inspector turned to Sinclair. "Wakefield, you and Chadbourne were together at the University of London this afternoon. What can you tell us about him?"

"Outside of the lectures, nothing. We have no other contacts. But I agree with Lord Somerset. Chadbourne is ambitious. Brilliant. Committed to what he is doing."

"Committed enough for a robbery?" Farland asked.

Wakefield surprised himself by defending Chadbourne. "He is committed to art, not to stealing. We both have a great respect for artists. Past and present. "

Bailey Rentley washed down his last bite of lamb with scalding tea. "Lord Somerset suggested we contact you when he found out the renter at Wakefield Cottage is a friend of Mr. Chadbourne's."

"There is no need to involve Rachel McCully. Mr. Chadbourne is a former student of hers. That's all."

But could her former student be in this kind of trouble? "Inspector, I think you have the wrong man."

"I agree," Somerset said. "We don't know too much about our caretaker, but we like what we know. So, Inspector Farland, how did this come about?"

"Let's back up to another robbery. When Scotland Yard was tipped off regarding the attempted jewelry heist at the Millennium Dome, we had time to replace the real diamonds with crystal fakes."

Lord Somerset chuckled. "A bit more difficult for me to replace the paintings on my walls with fakes."

"We understand that, but to the Yard's credit, we had more than a hundred men in that diamond operation. At least a dozen people were arrested. As far as we know, we arrested everyone involved."

"I have no 200-carat, Millennium Star diamond at risk, and you can hardly hide a hundred officers on my property."

"I daresay your Rembrandts and Monets and Italian vases and bronze statues are of untold value, Lord Somerset. Since the attempt at the Millennium Dome, there have been several copycat art thefts, many of them within a seven-month window. They use the same M.O.—the same modus operandi as they call it. Bulldozers, smoke bombs, and masks and robbing museums or art shops near the river."

"Which means," Lord Somerset said, "that someone involved in that London robbery may have gone unnoticed."

"Or some clever gang has had ample time to plan another major heist. We have a man under surveillance, a rugby player by the name of Sean Larkins. Larkins has been in close proximity to two or three of these minor robberies, and he has a questionable record. MI5 Registry has a personal file on him here in London, and the CIA has a dossier in Langley, Virginia. Reason enough to watch Larkins' activities."

"Why not arrest him?"

"Lord Somerset, we cannot arrest him for being in the vicinity, nor can we arrest him for being seen in the company of Morris Chadbourne. But they hike together around Grasmere. They eat at the same pub. They were even seen together at the Norbert Museum in Bloomsbury recently, although that meeting may have been accidental. Larkins has let it be known that he has an interest in Lord Somerset's art collection—and Chadbourne is vocal in his lectures about wanting to own a Weinberger painting."

Somerset outstared the inspector. "My dear man, if you plan to rob someone, you don't go around announcing it."

"For me, the copycat robberies are announcement enough."

Somerset's green eyes were mocking. "I once told a museum curator that he invested too much time and money on security guards at night. I told him some clever thief will come along someday while the museum is full of Sunday visitors and walk off with a million-dollar painting."

"Impossible," the inspector snapped.

"I'm a mystery buff. Agatha Christie would come up with something like that."

"Agatha Christie is dead."

Somerset rubbed his hands together. "Think about it, Inspector. Get into the mind of the thief. Someone dressed in security garb politely removes a painting and disappears into the subterrain storage vaults. A delivery truck is waiting to whisk the thief and the painting away."

"In broad daylight—in a room full of people? Impossible."

"No, quite possible, Inspector. Surprise is the key. Scotland Yard should be looking for the unexpected. Some foolhardy plan that will work because no one expects it to. I daresay, if the thief thought himself under surveillance, he would set another plan in motion."

"Only a madman would plan a robbery so openly, sir."

"A genius, Inspector, not a madman."

"I deal in facts, Lord Somerset. We are making a detailed check on the London museums, but it is time consuming. Actually, there was an attempted robbery at the Norbert Museum some months ago. Foiled fortunately."

"Didier Bosman!" With care, Lord Somerset pocketed his pipe.

The inspector checked his notes. "Yes, Bosman is listed as the curator."

"I know for a fact that he prefers being called the Museum Director. Semantics, of course. He's an insider in the art world, his advice much sought after. But he sees every painting for its monetary value. I was on the board at the Norbert Museum, but I resigned a year ago."

"A personal problem?" the inspector asked.

"Bosman and I got on well at first. I believed him capable of putting the museum on a profit basis once again. He did within months. He even negotiated the purchase of two expensive paintings that my wife wanted. She loves spending my money, but she dreads going to the auctions herself. Her heart, you know."

He retrieved his pipe again and dipped it into his tobacco pouch. "Later, I withdrew my funding and had Bosman's background searched. It seems he was accused of fraudulent art dealings at his last posting in Paris—before he came to London."

"I'll contact Paris on that one," Farland promised. "As it stands, Miss McCully, Chadbourne, and Sean Larkins have all visited the Norbert Museum."

"It's open to the public, Inspector. All three are interested in art."

"So is my fraud division at Scotland Yard. Have you seen Mr. Bosman since stopping your funding at the museum?"

Somerset drew on his unlit pipe. "Once at the club. He told me I would ruin him if art buyers found out I was no longer supporting the museum. I simply walked out on him."

The inspector nodded. "That gives us one more reason why your collection could be the actual target."

Sinclair's coffee had gone cold. His appetite vanished. "James, you and the curator may be at odds, but do you really believe he would enlist Chadbourne's help to steal one or more of your paintings?"

Once again, Somerset leaned back and folded his arms across his chest. "It is the inspector who anticipates a robbery. I am a wealthy man, Sinclair, or so my wife tells me, but I have no intention of allowing my collection to be stolen, if that is what the inspector is suggesting."

The inspector obviously resented the put-down. "Morris Chadbourne is well-positioned to oversee that theft."

A flicker of amusement crossed Somerset's face. "In my absence, of course. This is a waste of time. The man is a scholar, a researcher. He dwells on the literary giants of the past and climbs the fells for exercise. He doesn't have time to mastermind a robbery while I'm away."

"That's why he must continue to think that you and your wife are at sea. Thankfully your wife can receive cables in your name until you are back on board."

"So I informed her. But she will never forgive me if I am delayed long in getting back to her. This was our fiftieth-anniversary celebration, gentlemen, preferably spent together."

Sinclair pressed his eyes with his thumb and forefinger, escaping Lord Somerset's steady, questioning gaze. Finally, he said, "I don't understand what you expect me to do. We haven't been in touch for two years, James." His tone took on a new edge. "And suddenly we are meeting together in a private room at the club calmly discussing the threat to your art collection."

"You heard the inspector. He promises me that nothing will go awry. I am personally holding him responsible for my Degas and Rembrandt and all of the other pictures that my wife treasures." Somerset's annoyance and sarcasm were evident in his voice. He was not as relaxed and unconcerned as he appeared. His anger was controlled, defensive, and Sinclair realized, he was depending on their friendship to fill the gap in his own absence.

Bailey leaned forward. "I told these gentlemen that you are studying art history and are acquainted with the major artists."

Sinclair's shoulder convulsed. "You know, I had to have something to do when I lost my wife and son."

Lord Somerset gripped Sinclair's arm. "Steady, man."

Even the inspector was silenced for a moment. "We are sorry about that, sir. But my department anticipates the possibility of a major art theft. Mr. Chadbourne could be involved. I have someone in every lecture hall where he speaks. I have an officer taking the same classes that he takes at Oxford. Unfortunately, my man is not scholarly. He's much more gifted for police work."

Sinclair looked at his watch. He had to call Audrey tonight and find out what relationship existed between Rachel and Chadbourne. Rachel would have every reason to be charmed by him. But at all costs, Sinclair had to protect her. Even his thoughts seemed plucked from the air.

The inspector cleared his throat. "We have no problem with Miss McCully. But how well do you know her, Sinclair?"

"We taught together in America. She is ill now; I believe she has leukemia. Why are you following her every move?"

"We know about her illness. We know her schedule, Wakefield. She mostly stays close to the cottage, except for her trips to see the medical director at the Whitesaul Clinic in Bloomsbury. She drives herself into London." He consulted his notepad. "Stays at the same economic hotel near the clinic. Takes her meals there and only ventures out for medical visits and brief trips to the British Museum and, less frequently, to the Norbert Museum."

The inspector drummed his pen on the notepad. "I believe your mother was a patient at the Whitesaul Clinic, Sinclair."

"Yes, she died under Timothy Whitesaul's care."

"Unfortunately, Miss McCully does know Mr. Chadbourne."

"I told you, she was his university professor."

"When we spoke to her housekeeper about that relationship, she said that she wouldn't tolerate anyone coming into

Stradbury Square and ruining it for the villagers. Or harming Miss McCully. Does she have reason to worry like that?"

"As far as I know the relationship between Miss McCully and Mr. Chadbourne is one of mutual respect."

"As you indicated, Miss McCully is ill. We know about her medical appointments with Dr. Whitesaul as soon as she does. We are very thorough, Sinclair."

Grudgingly, he admitted, "Mr. Chadbourne mentioned her illness this afternoon. I was unaware of it before."

"Chadbourne is apparently planning a reunion for Miss McCully—this according to the housekeeper. With Lord Somerset away on a cruise, Chadbourne would be free to invite the guests to the Somerset Estates."

Somerset's arms tightened against his chest. "Pure speculation. And you are expecting me to sit back and allow a possible theft of my art collection to go on? What kind of a fool do you count me to be?"

The inspector went from stroking his chin to rubbing the back of his neck. "What we want is a place on your property to set up a Scotland Yard surveillance team."

The gray-streaked brows arched. "You really do expect trouble. But a place on my property is easily solved, Inspector. I have guest houses. One is occupied by a cleric friend of mine. The Reverend Charles Rainford-Simms is a wise old chap."

"Then have him move out until after the reunion."

"No, but your men can move in. It will be crowded, but Charles will cooperate; a little excitement might offset his boring routine. A garden supply truck arrives at the estates every Monday."

"Good. Then I will send my men and equipment in that way . . . while Chadbourne is away lecturing. Sinclair can fill us in on that schedule. I'd like to add some of my own men to your security staff as well."

For a moment it looked like Somerset would refuse. Then he said, "I'll send word to Chadbourne that I have arranged for added security in my absence. He won't question that. He considers me an eccentric anyway."

He pushed back from the table. "We always have need for extra gardeners or kitchen staff. Just give me the word, Inspector, and I'll contact Charles to expect company, and I'll let Chadbourne know I've added on more gardeners and security staff for the summer. How many do you suggest?"

"Three or four on twelve-hour shifts. Eight total."

"And what do you want from Rachel McCully?" Sinclair asked.

"We want her to go ahead with the reunion. Since you were on faculty together some years ago, we want you on the guest list. And if her former student has made the wrong choices, we want you to help bring him up short."

"To turn him in?"

"You would do that for me, wouldn't you, Sinclair?" Lord Somerset asked. "It is hard enough for me to stay in the background—to even contemplate going back to the cruise ship. But if you would promise to be on hand."

"I can do that."

He would help a friend. But at all costs he would protect Rachel McCully first.

Seven

Sinclair shifted gears, stirring dust on the country road as he raced toward his boyhood home. In the distance, Stradbury Square looked as though it had been gouged from the imperial hillsides. Rugged drystone walls snaked across the countryside, dividing the fields into patches of Kendall green and golden wild flowers. Along the river's edge lay the old wool mill and the red sandstone ruins of the ancient Bruntwood Castle, places where he had played as a boy. Why had he stayed away so long and missed the richness of this familiar landscape?

He kept his focus on the fifteenth-century church spire that rose above the rooftops in Stradbury Square. The church lay dormant—its doors opened only when an itinerant bishop passed this way. The larger village just before Stradbury Square shared the visiting vicar, but Green Hills boasted its own English pub, a hotel that accommodated twenty guests, and the only grammar school for miles. Sinclair and Mary had considered sending Blake to the grammar school when he was old enough; he was too shy, too frail, to be sent away to a boarding school.

Ironic, he thought. *We never had to make that decision.*

The village grammar school had never been an option for Sinclair. He had grown up a social step above his playmates, financially positioned to be sent off to Weatherby School or Heatherdown Preparatory in Ascot. But as a boy, his infraction of the rules went against him when he was reported over and over for reading under his covers long after lights out. They took his flashlights away. He bought others. Embarrassed by his son's literary leanings, the older Wakefield insisted that his son attend Gordonstoun in Scotland to prepare for a military career. Sinclair refused. Instead, he embraced the traditions of Eton, proudly wearing its broad white collars and black-tail coats. But Sinclair, for all of his love of books, excelled in polo and cricket and horsemanship as well.

Just beyond the church, he spotted his mother's whitewashed house gleaming in the sun. He pulled off the road and stepped from the car. On his last visit Mary and Blake had been with him. He choked on the memory of his son's voice echoing over the wooded hills. His beloved son crouching down by a bush, and crying out in childish delight, "Oh, Daddy, there's a rabbit in there. I know there's a rabbit in there."

What right did he have to shut out those moments of joy with Mary and Blake? Yes, they were gone, but death could not take away those good memories. He pocketed the car keys and moved toward the walkway. Until now, he had been hidden by the bushes and hedges, but he could still see someone working in the conservatory. Rachel?

He stopped again, steadying himself and allowing his eyes to run the length of the side of the house. The kitchen curtain parted. Sinclair saw the aged face of Audrey peering out. He put his finger to his lips. The curtain swept back in place.

Sinclair held his breath as the door to the conservatory opened. Rachel whipped the straw hat from her head and placed it on the hook inside the door. Then she stepped from the conservatory and turned toward the house with a bouquet of flowers in her hands. Her lovely hair was cut short, not at all as he remembered it. She wore light-colored slacks and a long-sleeved blouse with the sleeves rolled up.

You've lost weight, he thought. But there was a hint of that same sprint to her steps as she walked toward the front door.

89

The pounding of his heart thundered in his ears. *Take it easy,* he told himself. *Rachel is part of your past. Part of your pain.* She was ill, but he would not allow himself to become involved emotionally. He braced himself against overt sympathy. He was here to help an old friend. End of commitment.

It was her voice, that lilting voice well-remembered as she called out, "I'm coming, Audrey."

He began to walk again, striding briskly to overtake her.

<hr/>

As Rachel turned the doorknob, her attention was drawn to the man coming up the long walkway toward her. She shielded her eyes from the glare. His confident stride stirred her memory. She pushed the front door open, her eyes still focused on the stranger, an unsettling discomfort rising in her. He rounded the last hedge on the winding walkway, his steps as steady as ever, his handsome face more than familiar. Her breath caught when she recognized him—her heart thumping against her ribs the same way it had so many years ago when she first saw him at the garden luncheon on campus.

Recognizing him, she let the flowers she was carrying topple to the ground. Her hands fled to her short cropped hair. Humiliation swept over her. Embarrassment. Resentment that he had come unannounced. "Sinclair!" she cried. "Sinclair Wakefield!"

"The same." He took another three steps and stopped. "I was afraid you might be out."

She touched her short bobbed hair again. "I don't go out looking this way."

"You look fine."

"Until three months ago I was bald for a long time." She was afraid she would cry. She tugged at a tuft of hair. "Now I have this thick, wavy fuzz coming in. At least it no longer comes out in clumps."

"I like you with short hair. You look youthful and carefree."

"And I like just being alive."

90

He seemed at a loss for what to do with his hands. He slipped one hand in his tweed jacket. "You have had a rough time, but Audrey tells me you are getting better."

"That's what I tell her. I don't want her to worry."

His facial muscles twitched. "Is the treatment not working?"

"My white count is down, my doctor supremely cautious. He won't call it remission, not yet. But he's hopeful. So am I, Sinclair."

He seemed relieved and went the rest of the way to the steps. She looked down into that face she had once adored and whispered a quick prayer for strength. For the right words. She was walking a tightrope, but she was plucky, tenacious. She had to make it. If only he would smile.

"I should have come sooner, Dr. McCully."

"I didn't expect you to come." *I wanted you to come.* She laughed nervously. "Have you forgotten my name?"

"No, Rachel, I have not forgotten anything about you. I was afraid to come. I have no excuse. I've known you were here for several weeks. I didn't know about the leukemia until yesterday."

It was out in the open, and she felt overwhelming relief. No excuses. No lies. No shams. The illness called by its name. "I'm doing fine, Sinclair. Cancer sapped my energy, but even that is coming back. Come in, please."

He climbed the last three steps, his eyes holding hers. As he stood facing her, she reached up and straightened his tie.

"I meant to do that in the car," he said. "But then I thought you would have forgotten what a devil of a time I have knotting it."

"I haven't forgotten."

He took her hands and pressed them against his chest.

She gave him her most captivating smile. "You'd better come inside. Audrey will want to see you."

Rachel watched him survey the room with pleasure, the expression on his face turning to joy. The drawing room still held its Victorian distinction, essentially the same way his mother had kept it. Her oak writing desk stood in the corner. Family portraits hung on the walls. The carvings and memorabilia from his boyhood, and the books he had treasured, still filled the shelves. Except for the throw pillows that she had bought in London and an extra bookcase for the books she had brought with her, little had changed.

"You remind me of Wordsworth," she said. "Pensive. Contemplative."

He stroked his chin, the grin spreading wider over his face. "That bad, what say?"

Rachel thought back to that first time she saw him. She had not intended to go to the university luncheon that day, but she stood as they were introduced. She wondered now if her hand was as clammy as it had been back then as their hands clasped. That strong face, his features as chiseled as they had been ten years ago. The clipped accent, welcomed now. His eyes seemed sadder, yet his gaze held hers as he looked down at her.

He glanced away quickly and scanned the room again, his gaze settling briefly on the mantel, as though he were searching for a missing item. She took his hand—if for no other reason than to remove the serious expression that was creeping back; she led him down the narrow hall to the kitchen. "Audrey, I have a surprise."

Audrey's cheeks turned as red as her work-worn hands. She wiped them dry on her apron and went into Sinclair's open arms. "Oh, Mr. Sinclair, you did come. I saw you from the window."

"And I saw the curtain fall back in place."

She laughed nervously. "But I didn't warn Rachel that you were here."

He wandered around the room and stopped in front of the water pump. Climbing ivy had wrapped around it. "Rachel, you could have had this old pump removed."

"I like its antiquity."

"Was the ivy your idea?"

"It gives the pump style."

He continued his inspection—lifting the lid from a cooking pot and peering into the oven. "Shepherd's pie, Audrey!"

"Made it just for you. And scones too."

He glanced at Rachel. "I don't want to impose."

"You're not imposing, Sinclair. This is your home."

"Right now it's yours."

Audrey glared at them both. "Out of here, both of you. Go back and visit in the drawing room. I need space here. And you two need to remember that you are friends, not strangers."

"Come on, Rachel. I learned long ago that it's best to do what Audrey says. Do you have guests often?"

"Not often enough," Audrey told him. "And the last one was one of her former students—that Mr. Chadbourne."

Sinclair could tell that Morris Chadbourne had left a sour taste in Audrey's mouth. He followed Rachel back to the cozy comfort of the living room. For a moment they were silent, awkward in each other's company. She was still beautiful in spite of her illness, her smile unchanged. He remembered that warm smile the day he met her at the school luncheon. The two moments merged. She tugged his hand, inviting him to sit with her as they had done on the wide stone bench after the luncheon so long ago.

As he sat across from her, he said, "You have kept the cottage much like Mother left it."

"I changed the bedroom. I had a brand-new wardrobe and bedside stand brought in from London—I needed a spot for a very special lamp. And Bailey Rentley gave me permission to have the room painted. I like it bright and cheerful when I wake up."

"You could have changed the whole place. I had no idea you had moved to England until Bailey told me. Why didn't you contact me, Rachel? I would have come at once."

"I wanted to call you, Sinclair—but I thought it inappropriate."

"Because of Mary? She died two years ago."

"I'm so sorry."

"So am I. She was a wonderful woman."

"Sinclair, you asked about my illness. I have told you as much as I can. Now I want to talk about you and Mary and your son. It was a tragic way to lose them."

"Coming back here awakened all the memories. We used to come here to visit Mother. When she was gone, we came because Blake loved the old place."

"You haven't been back since you lost them?"

"Not after the funeral. I wasn't able to face it. Now I wonder why I didn't come. We were here the weekend before they were killed." He glanced back at the mantel, looking for the picture of Mary and the boy. "I had a picture of my wife and child; Mother kept it there on the mantel . . . I guess you packed it away when you moved in."

"I didn't know there was one."

They looked up as Audrey appeared with cups of tea. "I took it to my room, Mr. Sinclair. So Miss Rachel here wouldn't be troubled. I'll go get it."

"No. Leave it where it is. You were fond of them."

When Audrey left the room again, he talked about Blake running over the rolling hills and loving being where his daddy had grown up. "He was a sickly child, but when we brought him out here, he ran and played as though he didn't have to struggle for every breath."

For two years he had relived that rail crash in France, chiding himself brutally for not being with his family. After that, he had rejected the comfort of friends and buried himself in the study of art, in the writings of C. S. Lewis, and in teaching his classes back at Oxford. He admitted now that he had shut away the longing to return to Wakefield Cottage, living instead in Oxford in the house that he had shared with Mary and Blake.

As the hour elapsed, some of the grief poured from him. Some of the pain of death began to ease. He was home! The woman who had cared for him since he was a toddler was in the kitchen preparing him a simple meal, one of his favorites. And Rachel sat across from him—pale, thinner, burdened with her own illness, but those lustrous dark eyes were fixed on him. Listening.

"I find great comfort in the evening vespers at Oxford—sitting in an ancient cathedral, hearing God's voice in the music and in the things that are said. I didn't want human comfort."

"Nor did I when I was first told that I had cancer. That was like a death knell. Like dying, in a way."

"I'm sorry, Rachel."

"I'm not sorry that you came. We both needed this visit."

It was too late to tell her his real purpose in coming. Chadbourne and his problems could wait. From the kitchen the aroma of the shepherd's pie reached them. He felt as though a balm had been poured into his soul as Rachel listened to him. He told her about meeting Mary, about marrying her three months later. "She was a wonderful woman—a governess to the children of friends of mine."

"I went past your home in Oxford twice. But I never had the courage to knock. What would I have said? 'Oh, Mrs. Wakefield, I'm an old friend of your husband's. Could I speak to him.'"

He laughed, a deep, unbridled laugh. "Mary knew about you. I wanted nothing between us. I told her you were my first love. Don't get me wrong. I adored my wife. She was special. If you had knocked on the door, Mary would have welcomed you."

"Once I found out what happened, I knew that I could never look you up." She paused, her brows knit. "Sinclair, you said that Blake was not a strong youngster. What did you mean?"

"He was perfect until he was two. He had colds and earaches, but we thought them normal. Then just before his second birthday, he was in the hospital with pneumonia. At least we thought it was pneumonia. It turned out to be cystic fibrosis."

Rachel paled. "Cystic fibrosis?"

"It was my fault. I knew it was in my genetic history. But I ignored it. I wanted children—"

"Three. You always said three."

"Yes, but when I found out what I had passed on to my son, I knew there could never be another child."

"You are a carrier?" she whispered.

"I must have been the one. It had bypassed my generation. I was so certain it would not affect my children. But Mary and I were willing to take the risk. She knew how much I wanted a child."

Rachel clasped her hands, the color totally drained from her face.

"Are you all right, Rachel? I didn't mean to upset you."

"I think I need to get some air."

"Of course." He stood and extended his hand to her. "Would a walk in the garden do? Blake used to love it out there."

Rachel's hand was cold in his as they stepped into the yard. The scent of lavender and rosemary and honeysuckle seemed to revive her. Scalloped hedges formed the boundary line. His mother had often mingled her flower beds with peas and carrots and cabbage heads. But all he recognized were the begonias and roses.

Rachel brushed a slug from the drywall, then Sinclair steadied her as she bent to yank a weed from the ground. She seemed as at home in the yard as his mother had been.

She pointed to the south slope, brilliant with sprawling geraniums. "The spring snowdrops are almost gone."

"They'll come back," he said.

"Will they?"

They ducked beneath Audrey's clothesline. "Rachel, you are not overdoing?"

"How can I? The gardeners do all the work. Audrey wants us to develop the garden the way it used to be."

"Don't do that, Rachel. This is your garden. Grow it the way you want it to be."

"But I thought it would please you—"

She was like a child wanting to please him, wanting to show him everything at once. The color was coming back to her cheeks now. "Sometimes the yard is thick with butterflies." She turned suddenly. "Why didn't you come sooner, Sinclair? You knew I was here."

"I knew you had rented the cottage in Stradbury Square. But I thought, if you wanted to find me, you would. And then Morrie Chadbourne confronted me about not seeing you."

"Morrie. He forced you to come?"

"He gave me the excuse for coming. I'm glad I did."

"He's a friend to me."

That tinge of jealousy hit again. "It sounds like you would defend Morrie Chadbourne to the death."

"If I have to, I will."

He had come here to warn Rachel against any reunion planned by Morrie Chadbourne. It was too late to warn her now.

An hour later the shepherd's pie had been eaten, the praises for Audrey sung, and now he must leave. He had not warned her about the threat to the Somerset art collection. He had not even mentioned that Scotland Yard would come at a moment's notice from him. Without knowing it, she was Scotland Yard's best bet to protect the Somerset collection.

"Sinclair, start visiting your friends again; won't you?"

"I'll give it a go . . . and you will tell me what comes of this plan for a reunion that you were talking about?"

"If you really want to know."

"I should be invited. My year at the university counts for something, you know."

At the door he looked down at her, "Rachel, there's one thing we haven't talked about today."

"One thing?"

"Why didn't you meet me that day under Big Ben?"

Tears welled in her eyes. "I was there."

"But I waited three hours."

"I know. But I just couldn't face you and tell you it wouldn't work out between us."

He wanted to draw her to him. "I loved you—you know that."

She nodded. "It's because I loved you back then that I couldn't face you."

"But why? Why, Rachel?"

"My reason no longer matters." She reached up and touched his cheek, her hand cool against his face. "It was far kinder to you for me to go away."

$\mathcal{E}$*ight*

Rachel left Grasmere and drove the winding country roads for an hour, trying to follow Morrie's directions. His distance was as a crow flies, his left and right turns remembered from a man's perspective for a trip that required no map for him. She had tired from driving, her strength spent in the long ride from Wakefield Cottage. She decided on a U-turn on the narrow road and driving back to Grasmere for better directions from one of the local pubs—or giving up and going back to Stradbury Square.

Suddenly, in the distance, one mansion dominated the rolling hillsides—not to the right as Morrie had suggested but to her left. For a moment, she considered the Somerset Estates an isolated monstrosity, out-of-place in this countryside. It loomed ethereal with luminous gray clouds hanging low around it, like a scene from Daphne du Maurier's books, or a place where Agatha Christie would gladly send Miss Marple or Hercule Poirot to unravel a crime. There would be servants, of course, especially a butler, but had Morrie mentioned anyone other than himself? Inside, the mansion would be a picture of wealth and beauty, incorporating style from more than one century. Today's weather fit the pattern for du Maurier, capturing the mansion in a gossamer mist. The thought of escaping into just such reading pleasure refreshed Rachel, taking her for a kilometer or two back to the delightful readings of her childhood.

The Somerset Estates dwarfed the neighboring villages, but as Rachel approached, the monstrosity became a magnificent work of art that possessed a character of its own with its stained-glass windows and a leaf pattern in the stone facing on the front of the house. Turrets protruded from the corners of the building. The entire property covered a block square with a wrought-iron fence on flagstone posts surrounding it. Grandiose. Lavish. But oddly placed on this country lane.

Many of the English country houses had been turned over to the National Trust in the economic fallout after World War II; others had fallen victims to an auction block. Lord Somerset had built his property in recent years, isolating it in the country—with the nearest neighbor a mile or more away. Rachel could see extensive gardens and outbuildings in the back. One of them had to be the caretaker's cottage. But cottage would hardly describe the place where Morrie lived. She parked in the circular drive on the side of the house and pushed the intercom button to the caretaker's cottage.

Morrie's voice boomed out: "Somerset Estates."

"Morris, it's Rachel McCully."

"Doc, I'll be right there."

Through the iron bars she saw him jogging toward her in a white T-shirt and tennis shorts, a towel around his neck.

He unlocked the gate and took her arm. "You didn't show up for my lecture in London."

"I stayed at the clinic for more tests."

His grip tightened. "Are you all right?"

"Dr. Whitesaul just wanted to make certain there were no side effects from the medicine. You know—liver, pancreas."

"And?"

"He'll call when the lab results come back."

"I have a confession to make. After the lecture, I told Wakefield about your leukemia."

"I know. He came to see me yesterday; but he has his own problems . . . I'm not one of them."

"I think he's beginning to see the end of his own tunnel. I told him you could do with an old friend in your life."

She threw back her head and laughed. "Is that how you see me, Morrie? As old?"

He gripped her shoulders. "No, I see you as beautiful. Desirable. I wished to God I could make you well."

She touched his lip. "Be careful how you express yourself, Morrie. God is my friend—and I don't want his name abused."

"I'm sorry."

She smiled. "I hope you get in Wakefield's classes in the fall. I think you'll learn a lot about C. S. Lewis's God."

"That's not my purpose."

"But it is my prayer. Now what about that tour you promised me?"

"First I want you to see the caretaker's cabin."

When they reached the brick walkway, she looked back. The mansion rose three stories; the bedrooms all had balconies, and a sunroom faced south waiting for the morning sun to hit it. Ahead lay the gazebo and picnic table and the cricket and badminton courts on the other side of an arched bridge. Landscaped flower beds lay on both sides of the walk.

Rachel sensed Morrie's nearness as he led her toward the guest houses in the back, and startled, gave herself more space. An older man waved from the steps of the smaller guest cottage.

"Good morning, Morris."

"Good morning, Charles." To Rachel he said, "That's Reverend Rainford-Simms."

"I noticed the clerical collar. Is he the vicar?"

"He was. The archbishop banished him to the North Country. Some squabble over defending an IRA terrorist in the Cotswolds."

"No wonder he was banned from the pulpit."

He squeezed her hand. "Charles is a nice sort. He cares about prodigals. Every man needs someone like that standing with him. But it means no parish. No funds to speak of. About all he does is putter and mutter in the flower beds."

"So he lives here permanently?"

"For now. The poor man's too old to work. Luckily, Lord Somerset set him up in the cottage." He grinned. "He's a peaceful sort. Takes life in his stride. We have great times running the gamut from politics to judgment."

When they entered Morrie's well-furnished cottage, Rachel took the soft chair and smiled at the untidy array of papers on his desk. He pulled another chair over close to her. "Are you still on for the reunion?" he asked.

She watched him, waiting for some sign of betrayal, then said lightly, "Of course, aren't you?"

"The castle is out."

She felt relieved. "Morrie, the idea was all I needed."

"I didn't say the reunion was out. I know just the perfect location. Great view of the rolling hills. Isolated from the crowds. Excellent accommodations. But more on that later."

His grin turned sheepish. "I started the guest list. I asked the alumni office to run a checklist and narrow it down to your classes on the Lake Poets. Then I asked for email addresses on any former students living abroad."

"Just like that they cooperated? Why all the rush, Morrie?"

"You're disappointed," he said.

"You did everything on your own."

He tensed. "I had to—believe me. I did have some help from your colleague Misty Owens. We wanted to conserve your strength."

He reached over and sifted through the mess on his desk, finally retrieving an email. "She really got things rolling."

"You've done all of this in just two or three days."

"Cyberspace," he said. "We're limiting the number of people to the first twenty—you being ill and all."

She ran her finger over the names. "Amanda Pennyman."

"She's living in London."

"I had no idea she was so close. Lenora Silverman."

"She's the lead singer in an opera in Rome."

"I know. I follow her career. And Sara and Lydia Arnold."

"Your friend Misty Owens suggested them. They'd have to fly in from the States. Nothing's confirmed."

"Sinclair Wakefield wants to be invited."

Morrie scowled. "Why him?"

"I told you. He spent a year at the university as a visiting professor." She looked up. "I don't see Eileen Rutledge's name."

His face hardened. "It would never work out," he warned. "I still come from the wrong side of the tracks."

Did he really see himself that way, this successful young man of hers?

"Stop it, Morrie. Once, Eileen was your joy."

"I told you, that ended when I met her grandfather."

It was Rachel's turn to lift a quizzical brow. "Since when does a grandfather control what happens to a marriage?"

"He was the patriarch of the Rutledge family. Eileen took me home to meet him, and from the minute I crossed the threshold of that mansion of his, we were at odds."

"You told me that, but I think you've left a lot unsaid."

For a moment he was silent. Then with a lift of his hands, he said, "You won't let it go until I tell you; Eileen and I were waiting for her grandfather in the library, working up the courage to tell him we were married. I disliked the man before I met him. He had such a control over Eileen. It was important to her to please him. After all, he funded her schooling. I resented the opulence, the power play in that house. I stomped over that oriental rug and that's when I recognized the oil painting over his fireplace. I went ballistic."

"Over a painting?"

"That painting didn't belong there. It came from the Chadbourne Collection in Germany a long time ago. When I saw that picture hanging on his wall, I was convinced it was part of the art looted decades ago by Hitler or Goering."

He looked away, his jaw chiseled in ice. "When her grandfather came into the room—a proud, stately old codger—I asked him outright where the painting came from, and before

103

I knew it I was accusing him of harboring one of the lost works of art."

"Is there no way he could have come by it honestly?"

"How? Weinberger's paintings were confiscated during World War II. Eileen's grandfather was stationed in Germany at the end of the war—in command of one of those art recovery units."

"It doesn't account for the painting coming under his roof."

"Doesn't it? I told him that Weinberger painting belonged to my family. Instead of welcoming me into the Rutledge family, he ordered me from his house. Then he did the unthinkable. He had my background checked. Found out that I—"

Morrie nearly choked on the words. "Found out that I did have Jewish blood coursing through my veins."

Rachel studied him. "Morrie, is it true? Does it matter?"

"I was so far removed—four generations. A great-grandmother from a wealthy Jewish family, but it mattered to Eileen's grandfather. He forbid her to have anything more to do with me."

"And she agreed?"

"We were already married. I didn't give her a chance to explain it to him. I broke it off." He shook his head. "It was a week later before I saw her again. Eileen was doing her residency but traded shifts with a friend. She was absolutely beautiful that night. Glowing. I don't remember ever seeing her that way before. She told me she had something wonderful to tell me."

He swallowed. "And I put my finger to her lip and said, 'Not now, Eileen. I've come to say good-bye.' She told me it didn't matter what my heritage was. That she loved me."

"But it matters to your grandfather," I told her. "And I know how much your family means to you. You can have a divorce. They'll never know."

Becki! He doesn't know about his daughter.

He clenched his fists. "In the end, her grandfather had the wedding annulled—by some sleight of hand or a large-sized check, no doubt. In his sight we were never married.

"Eileen told me she wouldn't let me go over some dumb painting, and I caught her by the shoulders and said, 'That dumb painting is worth a few million. I've spent a lifetime trying to track down some of my family's possessions through the Swiss banks, through the art retrieval efforts. And to walk into your grandfather's house and find a part of my past hanging on his wall—it was too much.'"

"Morrie, did you ever see Eileen again?"

He turned, a sardonic smile on his lips. "Does it matter?"

"It does if you loved her . . . and sent her away."

"It's been over eight years—almost nine—since I heard from her. It's good that you kept in touch, Rachel."

"Eileen's the one who told me about my cancer."

He threaded his fingers through his unruly locks. "What a mess I've made of friends. I tried unsuccessfully to prove the painting belonged to my family and lost Eileen because Jewish blood flowed through my veins. And now I'm living in a house with one of Weinberger's last works of art on the wall."

"Here at the Somerset Estates? Then let me see the work of the artist who destroyed your lives."

"It's in the main house. That's where we will hold the reunion, now that the Somersets have boarded their cruise ship."

She smiled, trying to ease the anger that stood between them. "Which means your first obstacle is out of the way?"

"Everything is fine about using the place. Trust me."

"That's my weak point. I'm not certain what your motives really are." She patted his arm. "Morrie, whatever is going on in your mind, please rethink it."

He led her to the house. It was more magnificent than she had imagined. Murals and paintings filled the walls. A copper statue stood in the smoking room. Two porcelain vases sat on the sideboard in the dining room. She fingered them

105

both. When Rachel and Morrie reached the drawing room, he went straight to the painting hanging above the fireplace.

She tried to see it from Morrie's eyes—tried to picture the empty canvas as Asher Weinberger picked up his brush. He had been born after the impressionist artists in France. But like them, he lived in France and had obviously been influenced by painters like Claude Monet and Renoir. Weinberger's painting caught some of the shimmering effects of light used by the Impressionists, but he had chosen a swollen river, not a garden or rural scene.

"When did he paint this one, Morrie?"

"In 1939 as the threat of the Third Reich moved in. You can feel the uncertainty in his painting—see it in the darkness of the river and in the face of the man entering the water."

"Symbolic?"

"I think so. His earlier paintings were happier ones. The last ones symbolic of his deep need to find a way of escape from what was happening as Hitler rose to power. In this painting, he didn't capture the movement, the quality of the Impressionists that he tried to imitate. That impulsive brush stroke is missing."

"Still there's a special quality to this work."

"Lord Somerset recognized Weinberger's genius and paid a great sum to own it. I've spent years trying to prove my right to Weinberger's paintings. I want to turn my research into a book."

"That will take years."

"I have time."

Rachel smiled at his confidence. A year ago she had felt the same way. Now she was buying every minute, savoring each new day. But it was the wrong time to lecture Morrie. His expression was pained as he stood beneath the Weinberger masterpiece.

"This reunion—this whole plan of yours—it's about the Weinberger painting, isn't it?" she asked.

He kept his back to her. "You don't understand. The Somersets have no right to this painting."

"And you do? Sometimes I'm not sure when you're joking, Morrie. Haven't the Weinberger paintings cost you enough unhappiness already?"

"Sometimes it's too late to turn back."

He didn't sound like Morrie Chadbourne, the student who had sat on the high tier in her classroom at McClaren Hall. He sounded like someone she didn't know, and the niggling doubts that Audrey had expressed became her own. But she had spent a lifetime defending the weak links in the chain. Her own sister. Students who struggled to get a "C." Mountain climbers who couldn't go the distance. And now Morrie. A gifted scholar, yes. But an angry man inside, and somehow the painting hanging above them was a clue to his bitterness.

"If you needed my help, would you admit it, Morrie?"

"I think not. I respect you too much to disappoint you."

"Then if you don't trust me, find someone else to help you."

"I could do that. But, Rachel, I need your friendship."

"You have it, Morrie."

"I want to protect you."

"Protect me from what?"

"You and I need each other."

"It can never be any more than a friendship."

"The old distance between professor and student?" He ruffled his dark hair and, with a sly smile on his lips, said, "Marry me, Prof."

She smiled. "So you can be a young widower?"

He leaned forward and placed his hand on hers. "I want to take care of you. You don't have to take this journey alone."

"I'm not," she reminded him.

"What do you mean?"

"God is with me."

"Charles could marry us."

"You're jesting, of course?"

"No, I'm serious. What about this weekend?"

"Not this weekend, Morrie. Nor next weekend. I'm not in love with you, and I would have so little time to offer."

"I'd like you to spend that time with me."

She felt pity for him, for herself. "You realize, don't you, that beneath this scarf of mine, my hair is just growing in."

"Big deal."

She threw back her head, and the sun coming in the window shimmered against her long silken neck. He took a firmer grip of her hand. "Please marry me, Prof."

She met his gaze. "I think you are stark raving mad. But it's a wonderfully kind madness." She pulled her hand free. "I'm fine with the way things are. I'm happy at Stradbury Square."

"I'd do my best to make you happy."

"Oh, Morrie. I don't know whether to laugh or cry. You were always so impulsive."

"You know I've always respected you."

"Marriage takes more than that," she said gently. "Now, I really must go."

She knew she was ill as she drove home, the flush of her cheeks more likely fever than distress over her visit with Morrie. It was almost dusk when she reached the cottage.

Audrey looked alarmed when she saw her. "You go on to bed, Miss Rachel. I'll bring you tea. I will call Sinclair—"

"Please don't. You were right about Morrie Chadbourne. He is a troubled man. I don't know how to help him."

"Would anyone?"

She thought of Eileen. Eileen and Morrie should face each other once again. "Give me a minute alone, Audrey. Please."

Rachel went to her rolltop desk, each step an effort. She sat down and took out a piece of pink stationery and wrote her first invitation: "My dear Eileen, Would you consider taking Becki out of school early? I am having a celebration in a magnificent mansion here in the Lake District. You and Becki must come as my guests. I want to keep my promise to Becki and take her to Hill Top Farm, but more, I need your help, Eileen, and all I can promise is a special surprise for you."

She sealed the envelope and was grateful to find Audrey standing there as she turned toward her bedroom. "Give me your arm, Audrey. I feel rather weak this evening." She was shivering as Audrey helped her into bed. "I must go into London in the morning," she managed.

"To post a letter?"

"That, yes. But I need to see the doctor."

"You have overdone today," Audrey scolded. "Driving in to see that Mr. Chadbourne."

"You tried to warn me . . . and I wasn't listening. Would you believe, he asked me to marry him?"

Audrey's hands fluttered to her chest. "No."

"That's what I told him."

"Rest now. Tomorrow I'll drive into London with you."

"Do you drive the motorway?"

A grin crinkled Audrey's tired face. "It's been a while, but it must be like riding a bike again. Once I get my foot to the pedal, we'll do all right."

It was three A.M. in London when Audrey finally reached Sinclair Wakefield. He sat on the edge of the bed in his room at the club, the phone gripped in his hand, his sleep-dazed mind trying to sort Audrey's jumbled words.

"It's Miss Rachel . . . in bed . . . fever."

Sinclair felt his heartbeat in his throat. "Slow down, Audrey. I am still half asleep. What's wrong?"

"Rachel is burning with fever."

"Try sponging her."

"I've *been* sponging her—I can't get her to stop thrashing or being sick to her stomach."

"Is she having difficulty breathing?"

"When the fever goes up, she breathes fast."

He was alert now. "Pain. Is she having pain, Audrey?"

"Some, I think."

"I'll see what I can do. Give me her doctor's number."

He scribbled the information on the paper by his bedside as he burrowed his bare feet into the rug. *Why was he getting involved? Why? Because she still mattered to him.* "Stay with Rachel, Audrey," he said, his voice raspy. "Do not leave her side."

"I won't, sir. I am here right now, holding her hand."

I should be. He went through the operator and declared an emergency. Minutes later, he heard a calm, reassuring voice: "Whitesaul Clinic. Timothy Whitesaul speaking."

"Timothy, Sinclair Wakefield here."

"Wakefield! You just caught me on my way out the door."

"Rather late to be leaving your office."

"I had some patients I wanted to check on. And some charts to tidy up. I'm off for the weekend. Wakefield, I haven't seen you since your mother was a patient of mine. How are you?"

"I'm concerned about my friend, Rachel McCully."

"You're acquainted? She's due in my clinic this week."

"She's sick, Timothy."

"Most of my patients are. What seems to be the problem?"

"Weakness. Vomiting."

"It goes with the disease."

"The housekeeper says she's burning up with a fever."

"She may have an infection. That's one of the risks."

"I know. She knows the risks. And I know what the results can be sometimes. We lost Mother that way. I don't want what happened to my mother to happen to Rachel."

"Your mother had age against her and a weak heart. McCully is a young woman."

"Timothy, I'm well aware that you take patients who are risks, young or old. White counts soaring. Failure to respond to the usual anti-cancer drugs. You're a risk taker."

"So is McCully. That's why I agreed to take her on in one of my clinical trials."

110

"Please, put my mind to rest. Drive up to the Cumberlands to see her?"

"At three in the morning? You know I don't make house calls. If she's not having trouble breathing, bring her down to London right away."

"I'm in London myself—overnighting at the club."

Another calculated pause. "Then it would waste precious time for you to drive up there and back. Find someone to drive her here. We may have to hospitalize her, and I want her under my care." His voice was tight. "Not everyone approves of my using experimental drugs, but it's Rachel McCully's only chance." He seemed to be thumping on the phone. "I don't understand. In these first few weeks, she responded well."

"Until now—can't you break the rules and go to her? The only person available to drive her is a housekeeper who's in her seventies. What if Rachel refuses to come with her?"

"That's foolishness. Is Miss McCully depressed?"

"I have never seen her happier. She's surrounded by—"

"She's out in public?"

The hour left them both irritable. They were baiting each other, each defensive of Rachel for his own reason.

"Our agreement was for her to stay isolated there in Stradbury Square, Sinclair. To live quietly."

"Doctor, she voted for quality of life."

"We're selective in choosing our patients."

"She's grateful."

The doctor's control slipped. "Noncompliant is not acceptable."

"Neither is dying."

Finally, Whitesaul relented. "The best I can do is cancel my plans for the weekend. I'll wait here at the clinic. If she gets in trouble en route, they should go to the nearest hospital."

Wakefield slammed the receiver down. He couldn't drive up to the Lake District to pick Rachel up. They'd lose too much time. He had to depend on Audrey. He forced calm

111

into his voice as he called her. "Find someone to help you drive Rachel into London," he said. "Dr. Whitesaul is waiting for her."

"Oh, dear. That means driving on the motorway. I don't think I can do it. I'll take her to someone here."

He heard panic in her voice. "Audrey—" His words dangled, lost in memories.

"I am still here, Mr. Sinclair."

"Audrey, I don't want to lose her. I just found her again."

There was a quick sob on the other end—Audrey having one of her romantic gasps. "All right. We'll come, but tell me how to get there."

He gave directions and could only pray that she had written them down. "How is Rachel now?"

"She doesn't look good, Mr. Sinclair. She did fall asleep moments ago though. . . . But driving all that distance on the motorway. What if something happens to her?"

"It won't. I will meet you at the clinic."

Nine

Rachel awakened in a different bed, in a strange room, in an unfamiliar setting, her arm attached to an intravenous feeding. Groggy, she searched her surroundings. Audrey was sitting by her bedside, patting her hand. Sinclair was standing at the foot of her bed.

His presence became a reality when she heard his deep voice. "Welcome back, Rachel. We have been worried about you."

"Where have I been?"

"Asleep for two days."

"You can't be serious."

"From what I know of Wakefield here," Timothy Whitesaul announced from the doorway, "this man of yours rarely jokes."

Man of mine. She focused on Timothy, looking professional in his white lab coat with a stethoscope around his neck. "I don't remember coming into London, Doctor."

Audrey sighed with relief. "Oh, wonderful. Then you don't remember my neurotic driving on those hairpin curves?"

"You drove me here, Audrey?"

"That I did. I sponged you all night long like I used to do for Mr. Wakefield when he was a little boy. But when your temperature went higher, I called him, even though you told me not to. I was so afraid for you."

"I was in London—at my club. I told Audrey to bring you right in. I thought she would ask a neighbor to do the driving."

"It wasn't like the bicycle," Audrey said nervously. "I kept closing my eyes to block out the headlights."

Through the grogginess, Rachel recalled with sudden clarity the blaring of horns. "Didn't I offer to take the wheel?"

"That's when I pretended I didn't hear you."

Whitesaul strolled across the room. "You arrived at my clinic without a dent in your car, but you gave us a fright with your high fever," he said as he reached for his stethoscope. "Fortunately, it turned out to be flu—a setback for you, but you'll be out of here in another three days."

He put the stethoscope to her chest. "Deep breath. Again."

"I'm still alive."

"That's how I prefer my patients."

"What about the shadow on my lung?"

"According to the X-ray, it's still there. But it hasn't grown."

"Doctor, Miss Rachel is not strong enough for any surgery."

He gave Audrey a gentle smile. "But Dr. McCully knows that we will have to remove it once she is strong enough."

"When will that be? . . . never mind." Rachel's voice faded. "Did I really sleep for two days?"

He tapped the IV bag. "With a little help from me. So what have you been doing—one of those exhausting spring cleanings?"

"I drove into Grasmere one day—and forgot my medicine."

He scowled. "You remember the agreement when you came on my clinical trial."

"Yes. But it was just one day."

"Fortunately for you, Dr. Rutledge made me promise that you would not be thrown out of the program."

"I'm grateful."

"One missed dosage should not exhaust you like this, Dr. McCully. Don't forget, I agreed to you living in Stradbury Square for its isolation. I thought it would do you good."

114

"It's been perfect."

"Then what happened?"

Sinclair stirred at the foot of the bed. "She tends to overdo. Now she is planning a reunion with some of her students."

Whitesaul sat on the edge of Rachel's bed. "Eileen Rutledge called me this morning. I keep her abreast of your treatment. She received your overnight letter—and your invitation."

"Is she coming?"

"This weekend." A sparkle lit in his eyes. "I look forward to seeing her."

"Oh, so do I."

Whitesaul arced one eyebrow. "Ever since I met Eileen, I've tried to persuade her to spend a year at my clinic."

"She has a daughter."

"I know. I was in residency at the medical center when Rebecca was born. Eileen doesn't go anywhere without her daughter." He pocketed his stethoscope. "I think the child could be happy in England, and Eileen would be so helpful here in the clinic."

"Is she considering it?"

"I like to think that she is. There is a postgraduate medical school in London. I want Eileen to attend there and prepare to work for me in cancer research and clinical trials."

"She likes what she's doing."

"We work with patients. She wouldn't lose out on that. She could make such a contribution to cancer research. She's good."

"She'd have to have a reason for making such a change."

He smiled ruefully. "She could marry me. Rebecca could do with a father."

He doesn't know about Morrie, she thought, and felt an over-whelming sadness. In wanting to bring Morrie and Eileen together, she was exposing all of them to even deeper pain.

Whitesaul tapped Audrey on the shoulder. "Time for you to get some rest. I'll send you back to the hotel in a cab." He turned to Sinclair. "We'll leave you two alone."

Alone with Sinclair, all the old feelings came back. Rachel had to contain them, not add to his pain. Her pain. Grappling for words, she asked, "Sinclair, when did they send for you? Was it Audrey's doing? She shouldn't have bothered you."

"Whitesaul let me know the minute he admitted you."

She blushed under his steady gaze. "You didn't have to come."

"I wanted to come. Isn't that what old friends are for?"

He took the chair that Audrey had vacated, and the familiar scent of his cologne flooded her with memories of what might have been. She tried desperately to hold them at bay, to cage them. He was here as her friend. Nothing more.

They fought silence for awhile. She smiled wistfully, without speaking, admiring the man that he was. His strength, his strong muscular frame was one of the things she most liked about him. He had such a keen mind, but it was his masculinity that struck her now. His strength comforted her. And then she laughed as he reached up to straighten his tie.

"What's funny, Rachel?"

"That tie of yours. And I feel uncomfortable when you don't say anything."

"Since my wife's death, I have come to appreciate the discipline of silence. That's why I spend so much time at the vespers at Oxford. I find them comforting and peaceful."

She placed her hand over his. "You miss her."

"I loved her."

His hand felt warm under hers. *You loved me once,* she thought. *And I walked away from that love.* "Sinclair, I was afraid of the silence when I learned about my cancer. I felt so alone, like you must have felt when you lost Mary and your son."

"But I have come to terms knowing that they did not die alone. God doesn't run out on tragedy. For different reasons, we were both frightened by our losses, Rachel."

"You lost the two people dearest to you." She waited a moment before speaking again. "I lost my dignity and my hair. And I lost control of my life—I hated that."

"I think we were both afraid that God had forgotten us."

"I'm learning," she said, "that he is always there."

"That is what brought me through the loss of my wife and son. Now you're faced with not knowing what's going to happen."

"With this cancer? I keep telling Morrie that I intend to lick this illness."

"For him?"

Sinclair's voice had tightened. She searched his face for double meaning. "You don't like him, do you?"

"The truth is, I don't trust the man. And I trust him less because of his involvement with you."

"We're just friends."

He placed his other hand on top of hers and rubbed her wrist with his thumb. "That's what you tell me."

She closed her eyes, not wanting him to see the mist forming there. *I need you,* she thought. *That's why I came back to England. But right now I need you for a different reason.*

Sinclair took one of those moments of silence to watch her. Even in illness, those dark eyes were brilliant, not with fever but with her love of life. A year ago her long hair would have fallen softly over the pillows. Now there was just a short cropping of silky dark curls covering her scalp. Her face was finely shaped, her features gentle.

Was he trapped with sympathy for her because she was ill? Or was that the old stirring inside of him, a love that had been shattered when she failed to meet him under Big Ben?

Take it easy, he told himself. He had stayed at her bedside for the last forty-eight hours, sitting in the silence of this room listening to her breathing, watching the IV fluid drip into her body. He had agonized at the thought of her never getting well again. Even when Whitesaul entered the room and placed his hand firmly on Sinclair's shoulder, he was afraid to ask. Finally, the doctor had taken him out of the room for a cup of coffee and a lecture.

117

"I don't know what your plans are, Wakefield, but I can tell you that I believe Dr. McCully will go into a remission."

"Then she will get well?"

"She will get better. We're trying an experimental drug; you know that. She'll probably be on the medicine the rest of her life. But I can't tell you how long she will live."

"You just promised me a remission."

"I can't promise you how long it will last. She has that other problem—possibly a benign tumor on her lung. Again no guarantees." He wrapped his stethoscope around his fingers. *"I have watched you watching her. Does she know how you feel?"*

"I don't even know how I feel myself."

He unraveled the stethoscope a second time. *"Don't make a commitment you can't live up to, Sinclair. Your mother was my patient and we lost her—and I know about your wife and son—the loss of someone else would not be easy."*

"But you believe in a remission."

"But I don't believe in a broken heart."

Then you don't know about Big Ben, Sinclair had thought. But he had shaken hands with the doctor, and considered the grip strong and therapeutic. He didn't know his own heart and mind as he went back to Rachel's bedside. Some wounds were still too raw.

Rachel interrupted his thoughts. "Will you really come to the reunion at the Somerset Estates?"

"Yes, but why are you so persistent about this reunion?"

"I'm going through with it to protect Morrie Chadbourne from doing something that could ruin his life." Tears fell gently down her cheeks. "There's a magnificent painting at Lord Somerset's that Morrie wants at all costs."

"Valuable? Nothing in Somerset's collection is inexpensive."

"Sinclair, Morrie is one of my most successful students, but he could never afford to purchase a Weinberger masterpiece. If he goes ahead with the reunion at the Somerset Estates, I will be there for him, perhaps to reason with him and to keep him from doing something rash. As a personal friend of Lord

Somerset, perhaps you will be there to protect the paintings on his wall."

No, I will be there for you.

Rachel was skirting the truth, repressing her fears, alluding to robbery. "I have never been very good at parties, Rachel."

"You are good at helping people who are lost."

For a second he wanted to tell her about Lord Somerset and Scotland Yard. The betrayal of confidence bothered him. He found his voice and said, "Mr. Chadbourne and I are acquainted at the professional level only. I find him an arrogant man. In his lectures, he frequently talks about the art theft and looting in World War II. This is a controversial topic in art circles. He knows that, but he won't back off."

"He's Jewish, Sinclair."

"Jewish? That's not a problem for me."

"It is the reason for his interest. One of the art collections stolen during Hitler's era belonged to his family."

"How would you know that?"

"Morrie told me." She hastened to defend him. "The Asher Weinberger paintings belonged to his great-grandmother."

"Is Chadbourne the heir then?"

"He hasn't been able to prove his ownership. He traced one of the Weinberger paintings to the walls of a retired banker back in the States. Now Morrie is convinced that your friend Lord Somerset has another of the Weinberger paintings in his possession. He said he's going to prove ownership at any cost."

"There are legal channels."

"Morrie claims he has tried them all. There are gaps in the ownership records over the last sixty years. Now he says those paintings will never be his, short of stealing them."

"A lot of art was lost and destroyed in Germany. Some of it was squirreled away and ended up in the hands of the wrong people. But I am here to tell you that Lord Somerset has been a legitimate collector for years."

"Morrie can't let it go. I wish Lord Somerset kept his collection in a vault—then I wouldn't be so worried."

Sinclair laughed. "He is not that kind of man, Rachel. He leaves the paintings on the wall for his guests to enjoy."

"I wish Lord Somerset knew about Morrie's plans for a party. I know the reunion is ridiculous. I don't know whether Morrie can pull it off. People just can't pack up and fly to England. And I don't have a legitimate reason to invite them."

"What better reason than a visit with you, Rachel?"

"That's what Morrie told me. But is that enough?"

If he was to help her, he had to ease her concern. For her health's sake, they had to approach this reunion with a light heart. Wasn't that what Rachel wanted? What she needed? In that year in America she had taught him the freedom of laughter. She loved life, laughed often.

He tapped his fingers, grinning unexpectedly, and saw her pleasure as his smile widened. "Rachel, we could turn this party of yours into a literary reunion, a learning experience. We could take your guests on side trips to Shakespeare's birthplace and Anne Hathaway's cottage in the village of Shottery."

"And stop and have lunch in Stratford–upon–Avon? But I would still be betraying Morrie."

"I think Mr. Chadbourne really wants to do something special for you. That is not fake. He's genuine there."

"It did start out with my wanting to know whether I had left an imprint on the lives of my students. Whether my life had counted. That's when Morrie came up with this plan."

He nodded solemnly. *That may be when Morrie found that you fit into his plans.* "I know you are worried about Morrie. But in fairness to the others who are coming, we will turn this reunion into something special. Can you do it, Rachel?"

She warmed to his plan. Her thoughts chased his. "We could walk in the Lake District where Wordsworth lived . . . at least you could walk with them."

"I will find you a white marble bench to rest on."

She looked away, but the sparkle had come back into her expression. "A bench like the one under the magnolia tree?"

"Would you like that?"

"I'd like it better if you would sit there with me."

"I might be too busy taking your guests to the site where Coleridge penned *The Rime of the Ancient Mariner*. Or herding them on a boat so they can sail on Lake Windermere. We'll work it out."

He met those lustrous eyes of hers, wondering whether she was still thinking about the bench under the magnolia tree. Or was she envisioning the vast lake as Wordsworth must have seen it—shimmering, glimmering, sparkling with sails?

Her excitement seemed unstoppable, her imagination running freely. "Oh, Sinclair, what a marvelous classroom. My students would love walking momentarily in the shoes of the Lake Poets and literary giants. Nothing will go wrong. Nothing. Maybe I'm just imagining Morrie ruining his reputation. Illness does that to you. We'll just keep him busy."

Had he been too lighthearted? She was overly confident now—foolishly confident—that nothing would go wrong, that nothing could threaten a reunion like that if she kept Morrie busy.

"Can I bill you as the visiting professor from Oxford?"

He saluted her. "I'd be honored."

"You won't forget the Dove Cottage in Grasmere? Everyone could pen their names in the guest book there." She sighed happily. "Morrie has a favorite pub—he knows the owner well. Perhaps we could all have lunch there."

The game they were playing strengthened her. "For those who dislike poetry and museums, Morrie can arrange to take a group for a strenuous hike in the fells of Lakeland," he suggested.

"In the steps of John Peel," she laughed without mirth. "Oh, how I wish I could climb again. But you must be careful. I don't want any of my students falling from some pinnacle."

"You are more concerned about the young man who may fall from grace."

It was obvious that Chadbourne's entanglement with this family painting worried Rachel. But Morrie's redemptive journey concerned Sinclair more than Lord Somerset's art collection. He strangled a sigh. Scotland Yard and Lord Somerset would never see it that way.

"For those with the child still in them, I can take them to the farm where Beatrix Potter wrote about Peter Rabbit and Mrs. Tittlemouse. You could go too, Sinclair. I promised Becki Rutledge I would take her there."

"You have color back in your cheeks just talking about it. I think things will work out for you, Rachel."

He leaned over and kissed her on the cheek. "Rest now."

"You too."

He met Timothy Whitesaul in the hall. "So you are leaving?"

"I will be back this evening. Can I use your phone?"

"For a toll call?"

"Scotland Yard."

If Whitesaul was shocked, he didn't show it. His broad hand spread toward his office. "I trust my patient is not in trouble."

"Only medically, doctor."

Sinclair walked into Whitesaul's office alone and across the room to the desk. He picked up the receiver and dialed. He was massaging his temples when a clear, efficient voice on the other end jarred him as she repeated, "May I help you?"

"Inspector Farland, please—yes, he's expecting my call."

Ten

Eileen Rutledge turned her travel-weary body toward the plane window. A pitch-dark sky loomed outside, black as night, like a web tightening around her and leaving her lost in its emptiness and space. She disliked flying and liked it less on this long journey abroad. But it was not the apprehension of hijackers or terrorists that kept her awake. It was Rachel's invitation to England that crowded her thoughts.

She tried to read between the lines of Rachel's invitation and came up with uncertainty. Rachel could be worse, dying; maybe she wanted to say good-bye. Rachel was better; she wanted to share her good news in person. Rachel was counting her days but wanted to keep her promise to Becki. She scolded her thoughts and sent them winging.

Back at the clinic, she had faced a mad rush for an early holiday, hurriedly transferring her patients to the care of her colleagues and writing detailed notes that revealed her own personal interest in each case. Within hours of leaving for the airport, she had spent two hours with a critically ill patient. Holiday scheduling rarely fit into a patient's life span. In Eileen's profession, someone was always losing the battle.

As midnight stretched into the wee hours of the morning, all she could see beyond the plane window was utter darkness and tiny blinking lights like glittering diamonds on the wings of the plane. All she could hear was the rumbling in the belly of the jet, and the annoying snores of passengers around her. She didn't risk slipping away to the lavatory for fear that Rebecca would awaken and be frightened in her strange surroundings.

Rebecca slept in the first-class seat beside her, looking angelic rather than an impish, soon-to-be third grader. Eileen stroked the child's long red-brown curls, the lump in her throat rising with a spontaneous burst of love. What a treasured, undemanding time this trip would be for the two of them.

Eileen's hand moved from the child's hair to the soft cheek and lingered there. Her life was too busy, robbed of moments like this. Eileen loved being a physician, but motherhood never agreed with her scheduling. Too often Rebecca was left with the live-in housekeeper, often picked up by her from the private school she attended, and all too often bedded down by this woman called Amy. Not by a woman called *Mommy*.

She smiled over the lost argument on what they should bring for Rachel. Rebecca had insisted that *The Secret Garden* and *The Tale of Peter Rabbit* would make Rachel happy.

"Oh, honey," Eileen had protested in the midst of jamming suitcases, "those are little children's books."

"Oh, no, Mommy. Rachel told me these are her favorites."

There was no dissuading her. Twice in flight when they slipped from her lap, Eileen tried to rescue them. Both times Rebecca stirred and closed her hands more tightly around them. The bond was there between Rachel and Rebecca, and for this reason alone, Eileen was taking the trip to England.

Both times as the books slipped from her possession, Rebecca cried out, "Are we almost there, Mommy?"

"We've a long way to go."

"Will we never get there?"

Rebecca was sizing up time, untroubled about her mode of transportation. For Eileen, with each flight, she considered the potential of not reaching her destination, but she shoved these fears aside, knowing that there would always be unfinished tasks and dreams at the end of her journey. But God had not brought her safely this far without a purpose.

She longed to visit England, but England stirred uncertainties from her past. Morrie lived there. Rachel, with her spontaneous love of life, was happy at the Wakefield Cottage. And Timothy Whitesaul, the Brit who had taken part of his residency at the medical center where she trained, lived and worked in London. They had remained friends through correspondence and phone calls, but there was a sense of embarrassment at seeing him again—this doctor who had been there in the birthing room, offering her his support and friendship the night Rebecca was born.

As the night wore on, the plane turned crisp and cool inside. The couple across from her kitted down with more blankets. The attendant turned her way and smiled.

"Pillows? Blankets?" she asked.

Eileen took two blankets. One to place gently over Rebecca's legs, the other to throw across her own lap. Rebecca had nestled against the airline pillow once again and drifted into a deep, even breathing. Eileen saw Morrie in the sleeping child and thought of Morrie's head on the pillow beside her during their honeymoon, looking rumpled and boyish as he slept, a relaxed, contented twist to his mouth.

Rebecca had Morrie's facial features—the firm dimpled chin, the high cheekbones. She also had his impulsive nature and insecurities. Were these Eileen's fault?

Why not admit it? She had brought her child into the Rutledge family with its high social snobbery, and under the care of the family patriarch, a dominating great-grandfather. The old man was ancient now and grumpy, tottering around the Rutledge mansion, still controlling the disbursement of his stocks and bonds. He spent his time reading the financial pages of three newspapers and watching the ticker tape slithering across the bottom of his TV screen, but he couldn't always remember where he put his car keys or false teeth. Little pleased him, not even the valuable paintings on his walls, nor Eileen's success as an oncologist—a dream he had shared with her. A dream he had funded.

Eileen had once been his pride and joy, Rebecca second fiddle—rejected because she was Morrie's child. With time, their roles would reverse because Rebecca adored her great-grandfather, grump and all. She had insecurities like Morrie—but what could Eileen expect for a child with an unforgiving great-grandfather, a missing father, and a working mother? Her child was surprisingly independent in spite of everything, and a good student.

Since Rachel McCully had gone away, Rebecca asked for little from her mother, save for chocolate-covered raisins and that promised trip to Hill Top Farm. When the invitation from Rachel came, Eileen grabbed the opportunity for three weeks where she could spend every breathing minute of it with her daughter, a desperate move to make up some of the missed times when she had been needed by her patients.

Maybe Timothy Whitesaul was right. Working at the Whitesaul clinic might offer her more time with Rebecca. With every report he sent on Rachel, he extended to Eileen his invitation to leave the security of her job in the States for the challenge of cancer research. At times the thought appealed to her, but perhaps sometime in the future when a drastic move like that would not uproot Rebecca from her private school and sheltered life. She laughed to herself—maybe that would be twelve years from now.

The flight attendant walked the aisle again, coming back for her periodic check on her first-class passengers. She dropped a hot towel into Eileen's hand. Eileen pressed it against her face and felt refreshed as she held it against her sleep-deprived eyes. As she washed her hands and inspected them, she was glad at the prospect of twenty-one days abroad, a chance for her betadine-scrubbed skin to be smooth again.

The attendant stood at her side, whispering, "We're going to serve breakfast soon for those who want it."

"It's so early."

"I know. But we want the trays cleared before we land."

She checked her wristwatch. "Breakfast at three-thirty in the morning? I think not. I promised my daughter we could eat at the hotel."

Eileen closed her eyes for what seemed only a moment, but when she opened them again the ribbons of sunrise glowed on the silver wings of the jumbo jet. The sky blushed in shades of begonias, from a pale pink to waves of coral and salmon. The plane drifted along on a bed of billowy white clouds that separated now and then for a glimpse of the glistening channel below.

She considered waking Rebecca, but the child was such a grump in the morning. Again, so like Morrie. So like her great-grandfather. Eileen let her sleep and rested her own head against the soft cushion to welcome the sunrise. The distant horizon still appeared faint, like a morning mist, but nature kept tossing its deceptive images at her. As the plane descended, she saw the island called England, surrounded by water. Now patched pieces of land beneath them appeared as lava-colored ridges, wave after wave of rolling lowlands peaking like distant mountains.

"Mommy."

She touched the soft cheek again. "Good morning, sleepyhead."

Rebecca stirred and stretched as she pushed her cramped body into a sitting position. "Where's my coat, Mommy?"

"In the closet." *Crushed and wrinkled no doubt, along with her own raincoat.*

Rebecca rubbed some of the sleep from her eyes. "Are we almost there?"

"Almost."

"Will Rachel be there?"

"I don't know, but someone will meet us, I'm sure."

But forty-five minutes later when they cleared customs and entered the crowded lobby, Eileen was startled to see Timothy Whitesaul waiting for them.

He stood, smiling down at her. He was a strapping man, over six feet tall and well-muscled. His face was as handsome as ever, and his hazel eyes still held that certain glow.

She offered her hand. "It's been a long time, Timothy."

"Much too long. I came early so I wouldn't miss your plane. A man can get lost in the crowd at Heathrow."

"Kind of like Kennedy back home."

"More like O'Hare International. That's the real nightmare."

He seemed reluctant to let her hand go. She was even more surprised when he pulled her to him and hugged her, but not half as startled as Rebecca. The child scowled up at him. "Who are you?"

"A friend of your mother's. And aren't you the young lady? All grown up now."

The scowl deepened. "I'm eight years old."

"I haven't seen you since you were eight pounds, one ounce."

"This is Timothy Whitesaul, sweetheart. He was at the hospital when you were born. He's the one who sends all the presents." Eileen patted her daughter's head, then turned her attention to Timothy once again. "Where's Rachel McCully?"

"Waiting for you at the Wakefield Cottage in Stradbury Square. I'll be driving you up there tomorrow."

"That's thoughtful of you, but, I plan to rent a car . . . I want to spend time with Rebecca and drive up there with her."

His smile caved. "Will you have any time for me this trip?"

"We'll see. I'm certain something can be arranged. I didn't sleep much on the plane. I really need to get to the hotel."

He hurried them along to the baggage claim and when the cart was loaded, he grinned wickedly and whipped Rebecca on top. He was strong as an ox, his hands broad, his smile broader. "You can direct traffic from there, Rebecca. Clear the path so we can get to the car. Your mother is worn-out."

"And I'm hungry."

128

To avoid Timothy inviting them to breakfast, Eileen said, "Sweetheart, I'll order our meal in the room. Tomorrow when we're rested, we'll drive up to Rachel's place."

Balancing on top of the luggage cart seemed to please Rebecca. "Clear the way. Clear the way," she announced, and surprisingly the path cleared for them.

Eileen put one hand on the handle, her fingers touching Whitesaul's. "I'll be more pleasant after I've rested," she said.

"I know. We'll be in touch. Can I call you? Would it bother your daughter?"

"Yes, to both questions. I assume you have Rachel's number?"

"And she has mine. She's planning some university reunion. She shouldn't be putting herself under such stress."

"There's no changing her if she's made up her mind."

"Clear the way. Clear the way. Look, Mommy, everybody is moving for us!" Rebecca observed.

"Yes, I see that." To Timothy she said, "How is Rachel?"

"The bout with flu set her back, but not for long. I think she is making progress . . . the shadow on her lung is another question."

"Then she's not in a crisis? This isn't an emergency visit?"

"No. She really wants to see you."

"What if the leukemia goes into an acute stage?"

He glanced at her as he maneuvered the luggage cart. "Eileen, you know the answer to that. A bone marrow transplant would be the only option then."

Her voice sounded professional, belying the ache inside. "She has no siblings, no immediate living relatives at all. That narrows her chance for a bone marrow match."

"Then let's not buy trouble ahead of time."

They were out of the terminal and moving toward his parked car. "Rachel insisted on the Ritz Hotel for you."

She stared up at him. "That's out of the question. Rachel can't afford that."

"Don't snub an opportunity like that. The French-styled rooms are grand. Rachel has already made arrangements. You can't rob her of that pleasure. And, Eileen, don't force Rebecca to have breakfast in the room. I won't stay."

She felt her neck turn scarlet. "I'm sorry."

"I'm not. You were always honest with me. I wouldn't want you to miss tea in the Palm Court. Rebecca will love the scones and jams."

He was silent a moment. "I don't suppose you've given any serious thought to moving abroad? To working with me in cancer research?"

"Every time I have a rough day—or lose a patient, I think about it."

"Then I'll pray for more rough days."

"You'd better pray for my daughter. Rebecca may not like England."

"How can she help but like it? Rachel McCully is here and I am too. And I want you both to come back and live here. I'd take good care of you," he promised.

Eleven

North, in the Lake District, Rachel sat in the drawing room at the Wakefield Cottage, her ringed hands clasped as she looked at the two men sitting across from her.

Sinclair nodded to his companion. "Rachel, this is Jon Farland. His chief interest is art fraud."

And you've betrayed me, she thought. *Bringing him here without asking me.* "I don't understand."

"Someone broke into the cottage during your trip to London."

"During my medical confinement, you mean. But, Sinclair, nothing was stolen. We haven't noticed anything missing."

She thought of Morrie and flew to his defense. Without naming him, she said, "If you are into art fraud, I don't know how you can help us. As Sinclair knows, there are only four paintings here at the cottage, none of them of interest to an art thief. It had to be a stranger passing through the village."

Sinclair countered in his deep voice, "Rachel, you know strangers don't come here. We're not even on the map."

"I found my way."

"No, I brought you here the first time, Rachel." When Farland's thick brows arched, Sinclair said, "You were my guest, Rachel. Mother's guest. Not a stranger. Why don't you tell Jon what you found when you got back? Let him sort it out for us."

Reluctantly she said, "We were gone several days, Mr. Farland. When we came back, the front gate was open."

"Is that unusual?"

"That would be unusual. I just thought in our haste to leave Audrey might have left it that way."

Although he looked calm, Sinclair sounded provoked. "Audrey said you didn't leave by way of the gate."

Of course, that made sense. The car was parked in the back. They would have gone through the garden. But she couldn't decide whether Sinclair was annoyed with her or with Audrey. Or was it his precious property that he wanted protected? She felt victimized by an intruder in the house, and Sinclair was incensed at the idea of a stranger passing through Stradbury Square.

Didn't he understand? She was sick, and Audrey was frantic when they left the cottage. The gate in the garden had been open too and some of the flowers crushed and in need of replanting. She wanted to tell him she would pay for the repairs, to just leave her alone. She hadn't sent for him anyway, and she certainly hadn't asked his friend Jon to come. She was about to speak her mind, but the look in his somber eyes was concern, not anger.

"I was sick when we left, Mr. Farland. I didn't take notice of anything." Her voice held a tremor. "I feel so violated, knowing that someone came in while we were gone."

Sinclair leaned forward and placed his hand on hers. "Stradbury Square has always been safe, Rachel. I don't think it will happen again. The neighbors will be watching closely, making certain you are safe. They've given me their word."

"Whatever happened, Audrey refuses to go to Lord Somerset's for the reunion. She insists she must stay here to protect the place. I can't let her stay here alone."

A prankish smile spread over Farland's square face. "She could handle it. I surprised her when I walked into her kitchen, and she had a heavy pot in her hand in a flash. She would have hit me with that thing if I hadn't told her who I was."

"And who are you?"

"A friend of Sinclair's."

Sinclair was less humorless. "I'll talk to Audrey. You will need her at Lord Somerset's. I want her there to watch over you."

"And you. She still thinks of you as a little boy."

He grinned sheepishly. "Much to my dismay."

"Go step by step," Farland said. "What was the first thing you noticed when you came back to the cottage?"

"The open gate. Then the trampled flowers in my garden. A flowerpot was knocked from the top of the dry wall—and broken."

"Yes, we think the intruder scaled the wall there, then forced the gate open when he—they—left."

"That's what I decided. The minute we came home, I went out to the garden for some fresh flowers. That's when I noticed—"

Farland scratched his temple. "Animals might have trampled the flowers." He didn't seem convinced as he jotted notes in his little black book.

"Then why the human footprints?" she asked. "A rubber sole crushed one of my pink camellias. I know that for certain. And I think somebody in a great hurry broke off my hollyhocks just brushing past them." She sighed. "I take great care in my garden, Mr. Farland. It's been my refuge during my illness."

From the quick exchanged glances with Sinclair, she knew he was aware of just how sick she had been. Had Sinclair used her leukemia to persuade Farland's personal interest in the problem?

"While I was in the garden cutting some roses, I heard Audrey scream. I found her in my bedroom, indignant at the shattered glass all over my rug. She kept saying, 'Mr. Sinclair will speak his piece, once he sees that broken window.'"

Farland's eyes sparkled, but he kept his voice businesslike. "The day after you left for London, your neighbor saw two strangers driving away in a red truck."

133

Her stomach tightened. She knew it was not the flu this time. Two men. Morrie and a man with a beard had driven into Stradbury Square in a red truck. She felt heartsick. Maybe Morrie was concerned about her. Maybe he had—

She met Sinclair's searching gaze and glanced away. "One of your former students came here in a truck, didn't he, Rachel?"

"Please don't quiz me like that, Sinclair. Whoever broke into the house didn't even take the money lying on my dresser."

Farland stroked his chin. "Perhaps they were just surveying the place for a future robbery."

"Really, old man," Sinclair snapped. "I want to encourage Rachel, not frighten her. I don't want to lose a good renter."

Is that all I am—a good renter?

Farland pulled them back to the break-in. "I checked your bedroom, Miss McCully. I'm quite certain that's how they entered the cottage. Once they came over the garden wall, they forced the window open and accidentally shattered the glass."

"So why did they leave a brick in the middle of the floor for a calling card?"

"Rachel, I will have the window repaired. Just try to remember. Are you certain that nothing is missing?"

"Don't press her, Wakefield. If she can recall anything important, she'll call us. Won't you, Miss McCully?"

She turned angrily on Farland. "I don't know who you are. You want me to tell you the truth, so be honest with me."

He brushed his flat top with his broad hand. "I'm *Inspector Jon Farland.* I'm with the art fraud division at Scotland Yard."

Scotland Yard? He had come with prying questions and a quick friendly smile. His pale eyes looked sleep deprived, his jacket less than pressed, and he smelled of stale cigarettes. She had noted his big, well-padded hands when he sat down, and thought him a repair man ready to suggest a paint job on the cottage. As they talked about art, she had imagined him an art dealer, or an intellectual acquaintance of Sinclair's from

Oxford. But an inspector from Scotland Yard—here to cover a break-in? Surely something more urgent brought him to Stradbury Square.

Aggravated, she said, "Mr. Farland, I brought no real valuables to England with me—just my jeweled watch and my mother's diamond ring. I was wearing them. The rest of my jewelry was untouched. There is nothing here of value to a thief."

"*You* may be the one of value to them. Perhaps someone you met in London. Or at the clinic. Someone from your past who thinks you can endanger them."

"That's foolishness. A former student and Sinclair are the only ones from my past who know I'm staying here. Tell me, Inspector, have there been other break-ins in Stradbury Square or the neighboring villages?"

He shrugged. "London is my jurisdiction. But Sinclair and I are friends. I've posted my men in the village. When you are at Lord Somerset's, they will keep an eye on your place." He laid a mobile phone on the end table. "That's coded in to my direct line. Call anytime. Someone will always be at that number."

"Is all this necessary?" she asked.

He stood. "Sinclair thinks so."

"You must be a good friend to go out of your way for a village off the beaten path."

"The truth is, we are concerned about you, Miss McCully. You are a guest in our country."

"One of thousands, Inspector."

"But the only one of importance to Sinclair Wakefield."

She blushed and fell silent. Inspector Farland patted her hand awkwardly. "Miss McCully, you just go and enjoy that reunion at Lord Somerset's."

Sinclair asked, "Have you heard from Somerset?"

"Not since he rejoined his cruise ship. Let me see, I believe their next port-of-call is New Zealand."

"Will you be in touch then?"

"Not unless there is something to report. No use worrying him. And you, Miss McCully, have nothing to worry about either."

"Did Sinclair tell you? I have guests coming tomorrow."

Again a whimsical smile covered the inspector's face. "I know. They are staying at the Ritz this evening. You should have seen my men scrambling for that duty."

Apprehension ripped through her. "You're worried about their security, even there at the Ritz?"

"Yes, because they will be guests in this cottage. They are driving up here with Timothy Whitesaul. Right, Sinclair?"

"That's the plan."

Farland hesitated on the front steps as Audrey came hurrying to them. "Phone call for you, Mr. Sinclair."

"For me? No one knows I am here, except the inspector."

"It sounds like Dr. Whitesaul," she whispered. "He said Rachel's guests are driving up from London by themselves. He wants to know whether that will be a problem for you."

Farland frowned. "Let me talk to him."

⌒⌒

Early that morning, Morrie Chadbourne climbed to the top of Old Man of Coniston, a rocky projection still snow-capped at the top, and isolated enough to give him time alone. The Coniston, old as the surrounding hills, was rumored to shelter goblins, fairies, and ghosts. He had ghosts of his own: a failed marriage; his planned betrayal of Lord Somerset; and his Jewish heritage. Charles Rainford-Simms had told him to be proud of his heritage. Morrie had a legal right to an Asher Weinberger painting, but legality was as close as he would get.

When he reached the memorial to the airmen killed in a navigational exercise in the fall of '44, he slumped to the ground and took some trail food and a slice of goat's cheese from his backpack. He quenched his thirst with bottled water. He'd been here before and pitied the young British airman and seven Canadians who died when their Halifax bomber crashed into the mountain.

Morrie took a bite of the cheese. He wondered whether any of the victims' families had ever climbed to this spot, to sit as he was doing to mourn for them. Below him, the village of Coniston rose above the water's edge. He figured that some of the old-timers still remembered the smoke rising when the plane crashed. He imagined some of them making the journey to the crash site to leave flowers on the unmarked graves of somebody's son. Somebody's husband.

At the foot of Old Coniston the day had begun warm and sunny, the air hinting to midsummer. High in the fells, the late spring seemed more like midwinter with its crisp chill. Trouble had dogged Morrie to the craggy top. He found isolation climbing alone, but he envied the airmen who had found oblivion. What had gone wrong with his own life? He was a successful scholar, yet he still blamed others for his miserable boyhood and Eileen's rejection. He still felt anger at Asher Weinberger for dying young and Lord Somerset for being so stinking rich. Morrie was good at climbing—better at running out when the going got rough.

The brooding rocks were as barren as his own pleasure. Far to his north lay the simmering firths of Scotland, a land scented with heather. To the south lay the bustling city of London. He was trapped between the two, caught in the shadow of the mountains. Toward dusk, Morrie came down the last few yards of the fells, half running. The good hike and climb on Old Coniston had cleared his mind and made him feel good inside. But the sight of the man standing there waiting for him churled his stomach.

Didier Bosman showed his anger in the way he stood guard over Morrie's bicycle—feet spread, legs rigid, shoulders squared, clenched hands jammed in his pockets.

"Bosman, what are you doing here?" Morrie asked, unchaining his bike from the tree.

"I waited for you at Hanley's Pub. When you didn't arrive, I came here to meet you. I'm staying at *The Old England Hotel* on Lake Windermere. We could eat there. Prince

Philip and Prince Charles found it a charming enough place to visit."

"I'm not dressed for that."

"Should we drive back to Hanley's Pub and have supper?"

He didn't want Hanley to see him in company with this man. "Whatever you have to say, Bosman, say it to me here."

Didier Bosman was sixty-ish with thinning silver-gray hair that left him with a high forehead. His face was full without flabby skin. Wide, black-rimmed glasses magnified the shrewd green eyes. Behind the sharp gaze lay the brilliant mind of an insider from the art world.

"We had everything worked out, Morris, but Chip tells me you were joking about helping us. You know I am not a joking man."

That art theft at Lord Somerset's had been Bosman's plan. Now with Rachel McCully's safety in question, Morrie was in too deep to pull himself free. For a second, he wanted to lure Bosman to the top of Old Coniston and leave him there with a smashed skull. Do that and he would never be at peace—and never discover who was really behind this intricate plan to steal another man's treasures. Bosman took credit, but was he discreet and clever enough to work out the details on the theft of the century?

Sweaty from hiking, Morrie felt shabby compared to Didier in his tailored clothes. Bosman probably had a dozen suits in shades of tan, with muted ties as blanched as his face. "Bosman, let it go. Just enjoy the paintings at your museum. There's no risk that way."

"No one notices me there. Even when I try to give the guests historical facts on the artists and their work, people don't listen to me. They make senseless comments and go back to their brochures for answers. I won't be ignored any longer."

"Change jobs then."

"Once we market the Somerset collection, I plan to retire."

"You're already a successful man," Morrie reminded the older man. "Curator at two major museums on the continent. You rescued the Norbert Museum from bankruptcy and put Norbert back in the tourist guides as a must-see museum on fine arts."

Gloomily, he said, "But it takes all my earnings to keep my ex-wives in high-rise apartments. What I need is money they cannot touch. Gold that they know nothing about."

"It won't work. The escape route is impossible."

"We go down. You go down. And my ex-wives are cut off without a sixpence. I like the thought of them moving to more economical accommodations. My two divorces have been most costly."

"Why steal the Somerset collection? The museum vaults are full of priceless paintings. You can market them."

"Too risky. Some of them date back to the Hitler era. I don't want Jewish families discovering them on the market and having the theft traced back to me because of some Jew."

Morrie raged at the prejudice. As he picked up the bicycle chain, his fingers trembled. "I won't help you, Bosman."

Bosman whipped a hand recorder from his pocket and thrust it in Morrie's face. He clicked the on-button. Morrie heard himself saying, "I have been the caretaker for nine months now. I know the Somerset Estates inside and out."

"Well enough to plan a robbery?"

He had laughed in Bosman's face, then, pressed for an answer, said, "Robbing the place would be a snap for a smart thief."

Morrie remembered Bosman snapping back, "I am that smart thief. I have been locked away in musty museums far too long. So what would you do if you planned to rob the Somerset Estates?"

For humor's sake, Morrie had flipped to a clean sheet of paper and sketched a map of the Somerset property. He pointed to the side gate. "This would be your safest entry."

Bosman's eyes had narrowed behind those rimmed glasses. "What would it cost for you to help me, Chadbourne?"

Without thinking, he bantered, "Promise to put the Asher Weinberger painting permanently in my hands."

Bosman roared with delight. "You'd hang the Weinberger in the caretaker's cottage—right under the nose of Lord Somerset?"

The tape kept running with Bosman's rambling thoughts and every one of Morrie's suggestions for a successful robbery. "Mr. Chadbourne, I don't intend to remain poor and unknown any longer. Sometimes I want to tear the pictures from the museum walls. But that has been my life for twenty years. People who love art come to gawk and admire. They have that right. But Somerset owns far more paintings than one man should; don't you agree?"

To humor him, Morrie had said, "Of course."

Bosman clicked the recorder's off-button. "We will go through with the plans, and for the safety of your guests, you will turn off the alarm system for us." Didier held up the recorder. "Do you have any doubts about helping us, Chadbourne?"

Morrie's own words condemned him. The salty taste in his mouth was more like fish oil.

"Most of your guests are of little interest to us. But this American, Rachel McCully, you seem to have an interest in her. I want those paintings, Chadbourne, at any cost. We know your schedule. Your every move. You won't be free to protect Miss McCully every minute; you do understand what I'm saying?"

Morrie understood. As he cycled back to the Somerset Estates, he sought for a way to fight back. But how could he leave for London early in the morning with his every move being observed?

He didn't know much about the wide and narrow roads, but pedaling through the countryside, he knew he was on the wide one with a deep chasm on either side. Somerset was worth millions. Billions, if his wife kept bidding for paintings. Bosman wanted only twenty select paintings. The most insured? The least known for marketing? No, he had targeted a Rembrandt, a Monet, and a van Gogh. Morrie could take off, run out. He was good at that. Eileen had warned him often enough that his introspection and bursts of anger and impulsiveness would ruin him one day.

Morrie didn't know for certain who his enemies were, but he could trust Charles Rainford-Simms. Charles dealt with prodigal sons. He found Charles at the back of the property, kneeling in front of a flower bed—his clerical collar smudged, his sleeves rolled up, his hands a mixture of soil and fertilizer. His lined face broke into a grin. "I missed our Sunday tea, young man."

Pushing to his feet, his knees cracked. Even with stooped shoulders, Rainford-Simms towered above Morrie, a kindly man with thick, snow-white hair, and translucent blue eyes that twinkled behind his glasses. His gaze neither probed nor threatened.

"I spent the day up on Old Coniston, Charles."

"Thinking? Praying?"

"Arguing with myself mostly. You should have gone with me."

"Ask me next time. I'd enjoy a good chat with you up there."

"You'd have me cornered, all right. . . . By the way, Charles, could you get me off this property without my absence being noted?"

The bushy brows meshed. "The garden supply truck comes again the day after tomorrow. I've asked for extra supplies so I can have the gardens looking superb when your guests arrive."

"But, we have gardeners."

"They have assignments. These flower beds are my joy."

"You're certain the truck can't come sooner?"

Charles smiled. "The rest of the staff would notice."

"That will have to be soon enough. Do you think the driver could bring an extra jumpsuit, large enough for me to wear?"

He sized him up, eyes amused. "I'll call and ask him."

"No questions asked?" Morrie was eager now.

"You have argued with yourself all day. I will not add to your burden. I'll tell the driver to count on a passenger when he leaves the grounds. How far do you need to go, Morris?"

"I want to catch the rail into London that morning."

Charles wiped his hands and slipped an arm around Morrie's shoulders. "I think we'd better have that cup of tea now."

Twelve

Jude Alexander left her desk at the American embassy in London and walked out the front entry, between what she called the Samson pillars. For a second she stood a stone's throw from a row of cement planters and directly beneath the bronzed eagle with the American flag fluttering above it. She had an indescribable, unexpected moment of homesickness. But she couldn't go home, not to the parsonage where her parents lived.

She had followed part of her dream into foreign service, but the glamour she had expected escaped her. Life was, after all, pretty routine. Jude was little more than a member of a secretarial pool, and if her clearance rating could be tagged, it would be at the lowest level. She hadn't seen one confidential report cross her desk in the twelve months she had been here. She had wanted so much more. Her last evaluation came as a warning. Failure to improve on the job meant closed doors to any other embassy assignments.

She was doing better, trying harder, and running faster away from her father's God. She glanced around, eyes wide with expectation. The stranger on the phone had told her he was Sean Larkins. He spoke with a charming voice and an Irish accent, but he said he was American born, running free as she was doing. If he expected her to recognize his name, she didn't. Adjusting her hair, Jude recalled the rest of their conversation.

"I think we went to the same university. Class of '98 for me. I've just seen the list for the Rachel McCully reunion. We're invited to the same party."

Party. Reunion. McCully. She didn't have a clue, but she recognized the name McCully and froze.

"Miss Alexander, are you still there?"

"I'm listening."

"It's a university reunion in the Lake District. We'll be honoring our old prof. Kind of nice, what say?"

She could barely say anything. She didn't want to honor McCully and never wanted to see that woman again. "I didn't do well in McCully's classes, Mr. Larkins. I don't think she'd like to see me put in an appearance."

"I hardly squeaked by myself. But she was a nice lady. Be good to see her again. You'll love the Somerset Estates where we're staying. I'm a soccer and rugby man myself, but they have a badminton court on the grounds. I'll challenge you to a game."

If he expected her to be a pro at badminton, she wasn't. "I don't have any holiday time coming."

"Then take a sick leave. Say, could we get together this evening? Talk, maybe have dinner? If we're going to drive up to the reunion together, we'd better get acquainted."

"I—I haven't been invited."

"That doesn't make sense. Maybe Morrie Chadbourne used the wrong email address—he's the one throwing the party. Well, never mind. I'll bring you a copy of my invitation. You're definitely on the list. That's how I got your name."

"I really have to go." *I'm being watched. On probation. You sound intriguing but I can't lose my job over you.*

"I'll wait for you. What time do you get off?"

"In thirty minutes. But you don't know where I work."

"Don't I? The operator said, 'American embassy' when she answered."

Jude laughed. "You are crazy."

144

"Crazy about finally meeting you. Do you have a favorite restaurant?"

"Surprise me."

"My kind of gal. I'm in Hyde Park right now, using my cell phone. I can reach Grosvenor Square by the time you walk out the door. I'll be waiting for you near one of those cement pillars."

She liked the laughter in his voice. "How will I know you?"

"If they don't arrest me for loitering, I'll be the tall, good-looking one with a polka-dot handkerchief in my pocket."

"I have blond hair."

"I know. You wear it pulled back from your face, but one lock of it falls over your right brow. You like dangling earrings and bright lipstick. And I already know you have big brown eyes."

She shoved her apprehension aside. "Be seeing you."

She saw him now doing exactly what he said he would be doing: waiting near the cement pillars. He was definitely tall and good looking, his deep-set eyes shadowed, his pale lower jaw looking as though he had recently sacrificed a beard. She walked toward him, taking note of his polka-dot handkerchief as he rose to meet her.

He took her hand and smiled, a captivating smile. "I didn't think you would be this beautiful, Miss Alexander."

In the tiny bedroom in their London apartment, Kevin Nolan booted up Amanda's computer. She wanted him to bring her emails when they met for lunch. With Mandy's workload in advertising, even a short lunch was a coveted time together. He decided to propose again today and knew what the answer would be. She ran scared when it came to marriage, to any commitment.

Amanda's only email was a fancy graphic design announcing a reunion in the Lake Districts with her old English professor. With Mandy's tendency toward sentimental journeys,

145

he considered deleting the invitation. But he ran the risk of making her mad and putting a locked bedroom door between them. Kevin didn't like life this way. He wanted marriage—he wanted to spend the rest of his life with Amanda Pennyman as husband and wife. But he didn't want to go to some crazy reunion with Amanda's professor.

Going off to the North Country for even an overnight lacked the excitement of going to the steeple races. Now that was excitement—the horses running neck and neck. Where was this reunion being held? He scanned it a second time: *The Somerset Estates*. Kevin felt such a revulsion that he cupped his mouth. Not at Lord Somerset's! James Somerset?

He'd had a run-in with the man, and once was enough. Somerset was a retired president, still holding office at the bank. Kevin was the boyish-looking auditor saying politely, "We have a problem here, sir. The books have been tampered with."

Somerset had faced him with his arms folded across his chest, his massive frame making Kevin shrink under his glare. "Look again, Mr. Nolan. I'm certain *you* have made the mistake."

They met a second time, but that time Kevin had the upper hand. "The bank has sixty days, sir, to correct this error."

Sixty days, or else, he had implied.

Kevin crushed the email in his hand and raced out the door. Amanda didn't like him running late. Not even for a lunch. He loved her. It was as simple as that. He had been a bachelor when he met her. She had told him right off: no drinking; no smoking. She had been less emphatic with his love of horses, but another few months at the support group and even that urge to put a little money on the race would be chiseled away. He needed to save every shilling for the day he married his little Asian princess—the beautiful girl with cinnamon skin and honest eyes who used her gentle humor and a dozen beautiful hats to make herself feel comfortable anywhere. She was one-fourth Chinese, just enough to make her long hair a silky brown and to give a slight slant to her dark eyes. His princess.

Amanda wanted the elegance of Georgian housing, but he feared they were stuck in this apartment for the next thirty years. Cramped as it was, it was busting their wallets. But it lay in the heart of London in close proximity to the museums and art galleries that Amanda loved; he felt drawn to Trafalgar Square with its political rallies and public meetings.

Public meetings sparked another unwanted memory of his last encounter with Lord Somerset: the betting line at the racetrack. He had stood in line behind a tall, overbearing man arguing with the bookie. The man turned, their eyes locking, freezing. Kevin had given him a quick nod. "Good afternoon, Lord Somerset."

Under his breath he had said, *See you here the next time.*

On his way to meet Amanda, he stopped at the department store to buy a bouquet of flowers. Balancing the flowers and Amanda's invitation in his hand, Kevin stepped out of Harrods and started down the sidewalk seconds before the bomb exploded in the art shop down the street. As he pitched forward, he remembered that Amanda Pennyman was waiting for him on the next corner at the lunch cafe.

He lay sprawled on the street, the crumpled invitation to Dr. McCully's reunion skittering from his limp fingers, caught by a frolicsome spring breeze.

As he drifted in and out of consciousness, a policeman knelt beside him. "Lie still, son. The ambulance is coming. I think this is yours," he said, tucking McCully's invitation into his pocket.

When he woke in a sterile hospital room, Amanda was at his bedside. He tried to tell her about the shards of splintered glass blowing against him. He felt the sting on his face, looked at his bandaged hand, felt his swollen lips.

Amanda's soft voice reassured him. "You're going to be all right, Kevin. There was a bombing in an art shop near Harrods. The clerk there was killed. Thankfully—" Her voice broke, trailed.

"Oh, honey, I missed our luncheon date."

"It doesn't matter." She rested her fingers on his bandaged hand. "I love you, Kevin."

"Then marry me."

"Someday."

"No, as soon as I get out of here. When are they going to release me?"

"Not until tomorrow. By the way, I found this in your pocket."

"The invitation came via email; I was taking it to you. Who is she anyway?"

"The English professor who was kind to me the day Lee died."

Lee, the dead fiancé—the reason Amanda feared another commitment.

"Will you go with me, Kevin?"

"I don't care to go, but if you want to go to this reunion by yourself, okay."

"No, we both go. Or we both stay home. Dr. McCully prayed for me the day Lee died—"

"Wait! This isn't going to be a religious retreat, is it?"

"No, Kevin. Just a reunion. I really want to go, but Dr. McCully would be disappointed to know we're living together."

He took her fingers and kissed them with swollen lips. "Then marry me, Mandy."

She avoided his eyes. "We'll probably talk about great literature at the reunion."

"Sounds boring."

"She's anything but boring. Will you go with me, Kevin?"

He felt trapped. "Give me one good reason why I should?"

"Because you'll like her. She's very classy. And very compassionate. I remember the day I sat in her office and told her about Lee. She came around and put her arms around me and held me until I stopped sobbing . . . I always had the feeling she knew what it was like to lose someone."

A moody silence hung between them. "Kev, when I heard about the accident near Harrods, I couldn't get to you fast enough."

He turned his bruised face on the pillow and touched her cheek with his bandaged hand. "And all I could think about was you coming. But this reunion—I'm not sure, Mandy. Spending several days with strangers."

In the dressing room in Rome, Lenora Silverman turned on her agent. She blessed him in English, a peppery blasting of words that accompanied a quick stomp of her foot. Realizing what she was doing, she switched to a fiery Italian. She could as easily have scolded him in German or French.

"No, you listen to me, Tomas." She waved her invitation to Rachel McCully's reunion in the air. "I want to go to that gathering in England. I could leave after the Sunday performance. Please book me on the midnight flight. On any flight."

He threw up his hands. "Your fans expect you to sing in *Madame Butterfly*. You have the lead part. You are Cho-Cho-San."

Cho-Cho-San, the lovely geisha girl. The opera in its beauty and tragedy was one of her favorites. She loved the part of the young Japanese girl married to the American navy lieutenant. No matter how many times she had heard it, she teared when he promised to come back "when the robins nest again."

"I have a stand-in. She is very good. She longs for the opportunity to prove herself. Please let her take my place."

He nodded reluctantly. "Perhaps she will make a better Cho-Cho-San."

Offstage, Lenora felt unattractive—stocky and too short. But when she filled her lungs and sang, her chest rising with the volume, she felt beautiful. She escaped into the parts she sang, regardless of the language, and for months now, had been Cho-Cho-San in *Madame Butterfly*.

"I would only miss five performances."

149

His hands shot in the air again. "Five too many."

She closed her eyes and tried to think back to her classes at the university. She barely remembered the other students, but she remembered her English professor, Rachel McCully, saying, "Lenora, you don't want to teach. You want to sing."

"But I am afraid to tell my parents. I'm afraid I'll fail."

"You won't know unless you try. Change your major."

"But I won't be able to take any more of your classes."

"The world won't disintegrate if you stop your English classes. But if you don't change your major to music you will never sing professionally. You were born to sing. You have the gift of languages. The gift of music."

Lenora had sung in all the great works, feeling the power of drama and music in grand opera. She had sung at all of the great opera houses—minor parts and lead soprano—in Paris, Rome, Vienna, Budapest, and at the Royal Opera House in London.

She looked at Tomas and stomped her foot again. "I must go, Tomas. I wouldn't even be here if it weren't for the influence of Rachel McCully on my life. She taught me more than English literature. She taught me to believe in myself. To follow my dreams."

Two hours across the Canadian border sat the sprawling Tallard farm, visible from the motorway. It spread over rolling hills with a whitewashed farmhouse and barn and Guernsey cattle grazing lazily in the morning sun. Seven years before Janet Tallard had made the decision to throw her education to the winds and marry the Canadian widower with three young sons.

The three boys needed a mother. No, they needed mothering, and that burly man, her gentle giant in jeans and boots, needed a wife. Someone to share his heart and hearth and faith. She never looked back. Her ready-made family delighted her, and three young boys who had barely known their own mother found in Janet someone who could fill that empty void: Paul, Mickey, and Jared. Four, seven, and nine back then. Eleven, fourteen, and an awkward sixteen now. She loved them the day she married Tad, loved them even more when she discovered that she could not bear a child of her own.

It had not been seven years of smooth sailing. They argued over the boys sometimes. Argued about the sermons they heard on Sunday mornings. Argued about the long hours it took to make a go of the farm with so few hired hands. Farming was new to her. Pitching hay deplorable. Rising at dawn exhausting. The needs of three small boys bewildering. The kitchen had been a safer haven, but even there she was a novice. Tad had come to her rescue. He didn't buy cookbooks but taught her the recipes he loved.

"Give a man his meat and potatoes seven days a week," he told her, "and he will rise up and call you blessed."

It took some doing on her part to convince the boys, and finally their father, that they couldn't eat and run. Dinnertime would be family time, and the vegetables and fruit were not to be left on their plates as garbage.

Janet had pitched in, side by side with Tad, because she was determined to prove her love and the wisdom of marrying an older man—she twenty and he thirty-five on the day of their wedding. She had no regrets even now as she made her way to the postal box hugging the motorway. Her ponytail flapped against the small of her back as she crossed the tractor-mowed lawn in her boots and jeans, the jeans too tight now, Jared had told her. But the boys needed new school clothes, and new shoes for church and Sunday school, and the mission project for starving children was more urgent than a new pair of work pants.

She yanked open the lid to the metal mailbox and pulled out the ads and bills and junk mail. And the good mail—a card from an old college friend and a letter from home. And a thick envelope marked Airline Ticket Enclosed.

151

She tore the envelope open; the ticket bore her name. The departure flight was days away. Destination: London, England.

What kind of a lottery was this? What kind of a joke? It had to be Tad, always planning special surprises. Her whole life she had wanted to travel to England, but it was one of the dreams she had set aside to become Mrs. Tad Tallard.

The ticket looked legitimate. She had to tell Tad. Racing across the property toward the barn was almost an impossibility in heavy boots. Her feet felt weighted to the ground. Her heart raced. She burst into the barn. "Look at this," she cried.

Four pairs of eyes looked up from their work. Tad and the boys. Tad and his three look-alikes.

"I just got the mail," she announced.

The boys exchanged glances, smiling. Tad put the feed bucket on the barn floor and wiped his big hands on the sides of his overhauls. "Anything for me?" he asked.

"Bills. And the cattle magazine. There's an article on a new kind of feed. And more on the cattle disease in England."

"And?" he pressed.

"An airline ticket for me. It's from you, isn't it? Oh, Tad, I love you. I love you."

"You never gave me cause to doubt it."

"But why a holiday just for me?"

He pointed back to the boys and waved them closer. "Their idea. You had an invitation to a reunion in England. It came by email. Jared here thought we should surprise you."

"We even put in some of our spending money," Paul said.

Tears brushed her eyes. "Are you trying to get rid of me?"

"Naw," Mickey admitted. "We'll be stuck with Dad's cooking."

Jared poked him. "Dad can handle it. We just wanted to thank you for being our mother."

Janet Tallard. Twenty-seven. The mother of three. The proudest mom in Canada. "I wanted to be your mother. . . .

152

This ticket says I leave this week. Tad, why aren't you going with me?"

"Somebody has to tend the farm. You won't be gone that long, but I miss you already."

"Where am I going exactly?"

"To the Lake Districts for a class reunion with your old English professor."

"Rachel McCully?"

Days before she left the university in her sophomore year, she had convinced herself that marriage to a dairy farmer didn't need a university degree, but her counselor—an energetic English prof named McCully—had disagreed. But once Janet's decision was final, she had come to the wedding and sat on the bride's side.

"What is she doing in England? Oh, I remember. She always traveled abroad in her summers."

"She's living there now," Tad said quietly. "She's ill, Janet. I don't know how seriously."

She looked down at the ticket, faced him again. "Ill? Not Dr. McCully. You remember her, Tad. She came to our wedding. She has boundless energy."

"The truth is I don't remember her. Only that you talk about her. At our wedding I had three kids to keep in tow. And a beautiful bride coming down the aisle to me."

"Dr. McCully took the boys off your hands at the reception."

"Yeah, I remember her," Jared said. "She grabbed me two pieces of wedding cake just to keep me quiet."

"Dad doesn't dig the computer world, so I e-mailed an answer back to the man throwing the party." Mickey was an exact replica of his father: sandy hair, big grin, burly. Muscled and tenderhearted. "The man who is throwing the party told me your friend has leukemia. We want you to go, Mom."

"Leukemia! Oh, not Dr. McCully."

Tad cleared his throat. "The first twenty invitations accepted were on their way. We just got in under the wire." Awkwardly, he said, "You'll need some dresses for the trip."

Janet looked at this beloved family of hers. Knew that Paul needed shoes. He couldn't go on wearing hand-me-downs. And she was secretly pinching pennies from her grocery money so the boys could go to summer camp. "I don't need any dresses, Tad. I'll make do; but I could use a new pair of shoes."

"That and a new hairdo. The boys made an appointment for you. They want you to have your nails done too."

She looked down at her work-worn hands.

"They have those fancy, make-believe nails. They glue them on, I think," Mickey informed her. "At least I think that's what the lady at the beauty parlor told us."

Tad couldn't take his eyes off her; he was looking at her the same way he had on their wedding day. "I love you, Janet. It will be the first time we've been apart, but I want you to go. And if your professor is ill, maybe you can help her."

He opened his arms, and she went into them. He smelled of the barn and the farm, but it was like a sweet fragrance to her.

⌒

In the Los Angeles *Race for the Cure,* Lydia Arnold, a high school teacher, stood waiting for her sister to finish the race. The pack of runners streamed toward her. She still could not pick Sara from the sea of faces, but she knew Sara was there, running her heart out for another social cause. Why had she chosen to run the marathon against breast cancer? Lydia could not be certain. But she was grateful. Until two years ago, a mastectomy had always been someone else's battle.

Exhausted runners were crossing the line now, and there was Sara, young, vibrant, determined, her strong legs stretching toward the finish line. Her tank top was wet with sweat, her hair damp from running. She crossed the line and stopped on the edge of the crowd to catch her breath. She bent over, hands to her knees trying to fill her lungs with air.

You did it for me, Lydia thought, *but you don't know that.*
It was another five minutes before she could reach twenty-two-year-old Sara. "Great job, sis. I'm proud of you."

"You sound like an old mother hen, but I didn't win."

"Was that the goal? I thought you ran in the race against cancer. . . . I have my car. Can I drive you home? We could go out for breakfast first."

"Dressed like this? Lydia, don't be such an idiot. Drop me off at my apartment. What I need is a hot shower and a long nap."

And to be as far away from me as you can get.

"What about dinner this evening?"

"I have other plans."

As they made their way toward the parked car, Lydia asked, "Sara, do you remember Rachel McCully?"

"Of course. She turned the dull poets of yesteryear into music. I loved her classes."

It was one of the few things they had in common.

"What made you think of her, Lydia?"

"They're throwing a party for her in England. The invitation came by email. It's for both of us. It looks like marvelous scenery in the Lake Districts."

"And a crowded tour bus and rotten accommodations."

Like the only trip we ever took together. "No, we'd be staying in an old mansion. Will you go, if I pay the way?"

She whipped the sweatband from her forehead and wrung it out. "A free trip to England? First class or nothing."

"First class then. I called my travel agent. She's working on a booking. I'll tell her to make it first class."

"You'd blow a whole wad on me?"

I'd do anything to win your favor. Your love. Your respect. "The money is yours when I die. Might as well spend it now."

"Why cross the ocean to see a teacher?"

"You know why. McCully was special to me. I was in her first creative writing class. Older than the teacher. But I learned so much from her . . . and I always wanted to go to England."

155

"Then go. You don't need me tagging along. We don't always get on, you know. We're sisters all right, but we had a crazy set of parents. They doted on you, and I came along nineteen years later. Unexpected, you know."

"Don't be cruel, Sara. Mom and Dad are good to you."

"I know. But they're more like my grandparents. Right now, I don't seem to have much in common with them, and you and I are practically strangers."

"Not my choice." Lydia bit her tongue, thinking, *They are* your *grandparents. Someday I will have to tell you the truth, and then I will lose you forever.*

She had never told anyone the truth about Sara until that year in the creative writing class. She had written about a child, a lost child. About an empty womb, a dead heart. And Professor McCully had written across her paper, "Lydia, you shouldn't bear your pain alone. My office door is always open."

It was wide open the day she went to her. McCully glided across the room and told her secretary, "Hold my calls." Then she closed the door and said, "Lydia, where is that lost child?"

They emptied a box of tissues that day, the two of them. The next semester when Lydia ran out of funds and was leaving the university, she went to Rachel McCully to tell her good-bye. "I have no funds or scholarship to go on with my studies."

"You have to finish. You have the child to think about."

"I think about her all the time."

That night, Rachel McCully took her out to dinner and handed her a thousand dollars. "This should keep the registrar happy until we can find you some scholarship funding. I've already started the ball rolling."

She had shoved the money back across the table. "Oh, you can't do that, Dr. McCully."

"Oh, but I can. Call it a loan if you feel better about it. If you can't pay it back, we'll just consider it an investment."

She paid it back three years later during her first year of teaching. As she started the car she said, "Sara, read the small

156

print at the bottom of the invitation. It looks like Rachel McCully has cancer."

"Cancer? Then she didn't send her own invitation, Lydia. She'd never tell us something like that. She took on our problems, but she'd never share her own."

"I know. That's why I want to go. She gave me a lifetime of memories. That invitation just asks me to give her back a few days. Will you go with me, Sara?"

"I'll sleep on it."

But Lydia knew she would go. She had just run a marathon in the race against cancer. Yes, Sara for all of her outward indifference, had a tender heart. She would turn this holiday into a continued race, this time in the fight against leukemia.

In New Zealand, the sleek, white cruise ship bobbed gently in the bay as a stretcher was carried down the gangplank. Few passengers noticed. Those who did showed little interest.

"Just another elderly passenger," an American deckhand said to the steward standing beside him. "Those old ones wait too long to travel like this. A rich diet does them in. Sets the old heart pumping."

The steward saw it differently. The Somersets had tipped generously, especially the woman. He had been making up their bed for them, when she clutched her chest and said, "I need the ship's doctor."

He tried to help her. Things like this happened on board. Heart attacks. Broken ankles. Even deaths. He tried to ease Mrs. Somerset into a chair, thinking, "Where is Lord Somerset when he is needed?"

At the slot machines, he was certain.

"You'll be all right, Mrs. Somerset," he promised. But he knew from her ashen face that it was serious. He watched now, feeling a personal sadness for her. He turned away from the rail unable to watch the proud man following the stretcher down the ramp. *Worthless man. Wealthy man,* he thought.

157

Ah! If he the Italian steward from Milan could lay his hands on even a fraction of that man's investments. He was too busy to know how sick his wife really was.

⌒

An hour later, Lord Somerset ran alongside the stretcher as it was taken toward the medical evac plane standing on the tarmac. He smiled down at his wife, her small hand in his.

As he ran, he leaned down and whispered, "We did it. You really fooled them. Thank you, my dear, for getting me off that cruise ship. I need to be getting back to the mansion."

"Trouble?" she whispered.

"Nothing for you to worry about, my dear."

She was silent again, her eyes closed. Slowly she opened them. It was then that he realized how chalky and clammy her skin was. Her eyes were listless, her hand limp in his.

"I'm not pretending, James," she managed, as they settled her inside the plane. "I really did have another heart attack." She struggled for each breath. "A mild one, the doctor said."

"But you told me—he told me—"

"He told you what I instructed him to say. James, you always told me that a man would tell you anything for a price. But that's your world, not mine. I'm so ashamed, James—"

"It's all right. We can go on another cruise as soon as you're better."

"You will have to go without me. I'll never be well enough to risk it again."

"Nonsense, Agnes. We've spent fifty years together. We're not going to quit now."

"You told me that's a long time for spending your money."

I can't make it fast enough. . . . You'll put me in the poorhouse. . . . Not another painting, Agnes? No, I'm spending evenings at the club just to get away from you.

Didn't she realize he was joking? That he couldn't live without her? That she was his strength, the only woman he had ever wanted to come home to? He lifted her hand to his lips and kissed it.

Her eyes closed, the long lashes glistening with tears. Lord Somerset hated himself for forcing her to take this trip. What had he done to her?

"James."

"I'm here."

She tried to cup his cheek. Her hand dropped to her side. "I'll be all right, James. I want to rest now."

He wanted to say "Happy Anniversary, darling," but the words strangled in his throat.

Thirteen

Morrie Chadbourne stood beneath the squeaking gilded sign with the face of Mona Lisa engraved on it. "Coventry Art Theft Registry," it read. He didn't know whether he had the strength to walk up the long narrow steps to the second floor. Walk them and he might be throwing his career to the winds. He hesitated. How could he face the people upstairs? Should he barge in and announce the biggest heist in Lake District history? Who would believe him? His motives were mixed. Steal the Weinberger painting first. No; his stomach turned sour at the thought.

The eyes of the Mona Lisa made him squirm. He did what he always did. He ran off, ran toward the River Thames to the hub of London and the melting pot of people who would swallow him into oblivion. His legs cramped on the second block. Before him, the broad sweep of the Thames rippled and glistened. He couldn't miss the Houses of Parliament and Big Ben across the river. The Union Jack fluttered from the Victoria Tower. Beyond them lay St. James Park and Buckingham Palace. There would be police constables, mounted and walking, and somewhere in the maze of London, Scotland Yard. He'd given the Yard little thought until now and repressed it. Better to risk his confession to a stranger at the Coventry Registry.

He turned back, retraced his steps, and scowled up at the squeaking sign as he went up the stairs to the second floor. A framed copy of the Mona Lisa hung in the Coventry office. It was balanced on a ledge above the company motto: ART INVESTIGATORS: RECOVERING MISSING MASTERPIECES.

Art gawkers had stared up at da Vinci's masterpiece for decades, trying to figure out what the lady herself was thinking. He was struck by her hands, her eyes, her low-cut dress. But he was mostly annoyed by the gaze she fixed on him as though she had deliberately turned his way. If the investigators at the registry were anything like Mona Lisa, they could put a thief in his corner and have a confession with that same scrutinizing gaze.

Right now, with Mona Lisa's eyes on him, the only loss Morrie wanted to report was a man who had lost his way. That kind of problem was best dealt with in the company of Charles Rainford-Simms or at St. Paul's Cathedral or Westminster Abbey, places where he sometimes felt more dead than alive, places where he was constantly drawn back again.

The irony of it struck him. The art registry investigated and tracked down the loss and theft of some of the most valuable art treasures in the world, yet they obviously worked under a tight budget of their own. Everything looked practical, efficient: no plush chairs; no rich carpeting; no gilded frames with Claude Monet or Pierre Renoir paintings.

Why wouldn't an art theft registry have at least copies of Rembrandt's *Portrait of an Old Man* or Seurat's *Seascape*? There were no still life, no Henry the VIII glaring down at him, no troubled mental distortions by Picasso to break the plainness of the paneled walls. No angels or religious paintings at all to remind him of his Jewishness and to cause him to wonder.

Not even a secretary to man the front desk.

What had he walked into, an office full of modern-day sleuths? One wall was covered with an orderly display of black-and-white photos of famous paintings. The one nearest him was a lost Matisse drawing. Another section was marked: Missing art 1939–1945 with names like Goya, Cezanne, Van Eyck, Vermeer. Under another picture, it said: from the David-Weills Collection. The whole display was made up of art lost, stolen, stashed away in the vaults of some museum or possibly even stowed away at Lord Somerset's. And this registry seemed bent on finding them.

Several rooms shot off from the main lobby, the larger office to his right with the door ajar and the sound of angry voices coming from it. He could see two men: one blustery; the other a more easygoing chap with his smile more tolerant than the man behind the desk. The director of the registry and a client, no doubt.

Morrie's wait seemed eternal, but in truth he had been there less than ten minutes, long enough to hear some of the exchange from the director's office and the man with heavy jowls shouting, "No, I will not release Jillian for that assignment in Brazil."

"She's the best investigator we have."

"That's your usual claim. She is the most attractive, so I am not sending her to South America with you."

"We're friends. I have the bravo. She has the brains."

"Sorry, Joel; Jillian asked for the desk job until she gets restless being hunkered down in London or quits glowing like a schoolgirl when her bridegroom walks in. Whichever comes first."

"They've been married two years."

"They don't know it. Those foolish kids act like honeymooners."

"That job in Brazil deals with a Van Stryker painting. It needs a woman's touch."

"Choose another woman."

As they continued to ignore him, Morrie's thoughts drifted, but he spun around at the sound of light footsteps and caught sight of a flesh-and-blood Mona Lisa walking briskly his way. What Morrie saw on a quick head-to-toe glance was elegant legs and lively eyes, tawny hair lying smoothly over narrow shoulders, and a beguiling blush of innocence when she smiled at him. He was about to trust his life and career—to say nothing of his heart—to this attractive young woman in a trim navy suit.

"Hello, I'm Jillian Reynolds. May I help you?"

"I wasn't expecting you."

She laughed. "Nor I you."

Her voice matched his first impression of lighthearted.

"I'm sorry. Our secretary must be out for a moment."

"A long moment," he told her.

Now that she was closer, her eyes were perceptive and definitely blue, brilliant like sapphires. It was easier to keep eye contact with her than the Mona Lisa.

"I saw your sign outside."

"Most people come looking for it. This is an art theft registry. You've either lost a great painting and come to report it, or—"

He didn't let her finish. "I want to stop a robbery."

"That's a switch. But how would you know about that?"

"I'm Morris Chadbourne, and I'm involved."

"You should talk to Scotland Yard."

"No, I won't do that. You record lost works of art, don't you? I want to register twenty paintings before they are stolen."

"Are you certain they are of value?"

He noted the large diamond on her hand. "Yes, Mrs. Reynolds, there's a Rembrandt and Monet and Weinberger among them."

"Not one of them worth less than two mil. Mr. Chadbourne, I think you'd better talk to Brooks Rankin. He's in charge here." She glanced toward the director's office.

"They've been raking you over the coals," he said.

"I'm fair game. Most of the Coventry investigators are men. I broke that tradition. But it looks like Brooks and Joel will be another hour ironing out their differences."

"I can't wait that long. I'm already changing my mind—"

"Then you'd better come into my office."

He followed her and sank into the chair across the desk from her. For the next twenty-five minutes he told her about the planned robbery. How they were going to pull it off. How deeply involved he was. She jotted notes but said noth-

163

ing. So far he had not mentioned Didier Bosman or Chip by name. He did so now with a hollow sound to his voice.

"Not Didier Bosman from the Norbert Museum? I know him."

Now for the first time she seemed to doubt him. He hastened to explain the school reunion for Rachel McCully. The mess he was in. The Asher Weinberger painting that involved him. "Weinberger is my particular interest."

"My particular interest is all of World War II," she said. "That's my specialty now. I spend my time tracing the paper trail, particularly the loss of art under Hitler. Even Picasso hid some of his work during that time. We're still trying to find it. There are so many gaps in the ownership. And now so many dispossessed owners. So many frustrated heirs."

"I'm only interested in that one painting," he said.

She pulled a thick notebook from her shelf. "According to our records several of Weinberger's paintings were destroyed."

"Because he was a Jew."

She smiled as though she knew. Understood. "Perhaps. But we don't have a record of any of his work surviving the war. And we have no living heirs listed here, unless—"

"I've seen two of his paintings, Mrs. Reynolds."

"Genuine? Then they may be the only two not destroyed."

"Are you no longer searching for them, Mrs. Reynolds?"

"I never stop looking."

He liked this girl.

"Morrie—may I call you that? I recognize your name now. My husband writes music and art reviews. He did an article on one of your lectures on Wordsworth and Coleridge. In the article, Chandler wrote about your interest in artists like Weinberger, men who were lost along with their art. You're quite a scholar."

"All I am now is a thief, ma'am."

"You're just thinking about being one. I want to help you. You want to stop the theft without hurting your guests. In recent art thefts, people have been injured. One man killed. Can you really pull off this reunion without someone being hurt?"

He nodded.

"Morrie, you have told me everything about this robbery but the exact location. Am I to guess that?"

"Are you familiar with the Somerset collection?"

The delft blue eyes glowed. "Lord Somerset from the Lake District—that eccentric old gentleman? He's worth millions."

"Several. His property alone makes him a wealthy man."

"Coventry asked permission to view his collection. Somerset refuses every time. He tells us that he won't have Coventry coming into his place and ripping the paintings from his wall."

"That implies some illegal ownership beyond the Weinberger."

"I don't think so. He's just very possessive of his collection. He would never deliberately acquire a stolen painting or a vase—or whatever—not knowingly. He's quite a man of integrity, or so we've been informed."

"Do you know him?"

"I met him at an auction and a second time at the British Museum when he was browsing for his own pleasure. The only time he spared me ten minutes of his time was at a banquet in London."

"Lord Somerset and his wife are away on a world cruise. I can get you in to see the collection in his absence."

"You can! What's the exchange rate?"

"Your promise to come to the reunion that I'm holding there. Can you pretend to be one of Dr. McCully's former students?"

"Hardly. I did most of my university studies in Europe and took my degree in Rome."

"What about this scenario? You started a course under Dr. McCully and left for Rome three weeks later."

She seemed amused. "A possibility, but if I'm going to help you, I need to know the whole truth. Are you trying to stop a jewel heist like London's Millennium Dome robbery?"

"No, the theft of fifteen or twenty paintings from the Somerset collection."

"He must own three hundred paintings or more. Why such a few paintings?"

"For quick disposal."

"Why is this so important to you, Morrie?"

"I'm the caretaker at the Somerset Estates. Lord Somerset trusts me."

Again she nodded toward the director's office. "I will have to talk to Brooks and Joel Gramdino. They may not want to get involved without notifying Scotland Yard."

"Please don't."

"If they decide to help you, how will I let you know?"

He pulled a copy of the invitation to the reunion from his pocket. "This is your personal invitation to Dr. McCully's reunion. The second sheet is a list of the guests. Just show up."

"Brooks may turn these papers over to Scotland Yard."

"I will have to trust you. But if you and your husband show up for the party, I'll know you are going to help me. You'll be helping yourself as well. It will be a close-up view of Lord Somerset's entire collection."

"That excites me. But what happens when Dr. McCully and I meet? You can't recognize someone who never sat in your class."

"I'll tell her what's happening—not about the art heist, but about you. I'll tell her I need your help—that I owe you one for an old favor. Rachel won't like it, but if anyone can pull it off, she will."

"Can you pull it off, Mr. Chadbourne? If we stop the robbery, you will be involved. Most likely arrested. I won't pad the Coventry reports. There will be consequences."

"I know. Maybe I will feel more at peace when it is over."

Thirty minutes later, she looked up to see Chandler standing in the doorway and wondered how long he had been there. He gave her that special smile that he reserved only for her. She still thought him a handsome man—this husband of hers—with his dark red-brown hair and Grecian features with a finely chiseled mouth. Those smoky-blue eyes would absolutely dance when she told him about the positive pregnancy test. But do that now and he would never agree to the Lake District reunion. She was torn with telling, but would two more weeks make that much difference?

"I wondered when you would notice me, Jillian."

"I was just thinking about you. You wrote an article on the man I interviewed this afternoon—Morris Chadbourne. Come see, Chan. I've been putting my notes on the computer."

Chandler was a music critic but had expanded his reviews to include all arts. At times, he served as a consultant with Central Intelligence, assignments that she dreaded. He grinned. "You're using that code of yours that drives your boss crazy."

"As long as it doesn't drive you crazy. . . . Honey, we've been invited to a university reunion in the Lake District. Here, take a look. Our names are already on the list—which says that Mr. Chadbourne was really sure of himself."

He scanned the invitation. "An American university? You went to school in Rome. So who is this Dr. McCully? It says she was your teacher. You've never mentioned this woman before."

"I'll be amazed if Professor McCully remembers me."

"No one who meets you ever forgets you, Jillian Reynolds."

"That's where the lie comes in. I'm to tell the professor I took one of her classes for three weeks before moving to Rome."

He frowned at the guest list. "Looks like I'll go with you."

"Why the sudden interest? I imagined this would bore you."

"But Langley might want me there with Sean Larkins on the guest list. I doubt he ever attended an American university."

"Neither did I. Does that make me of CIA interest too?"

"I'll vouch for you. Larkins is a rugby player. On his last visit to America, he was asked to pack up and leave quietly."

"Did he do something wrong?"

"It's the company he keeps. He's always a stone's throw away from trouble. Kevin Nolan here presents a different problem. You may remember the name—he was in the vicinity of that bombing near Harrods where a London art clerk was killed. Nolan was injured. Now he's going to a reunion where a valuable art collection is on display? It may not be significant. . . . But wherever Sean Larkins is, trouble could be just behind him."

"So we have our separate agendas at the reunion?"

"Yes, and I won't let you out of my sight. But why the lie, Jillian? This pretense of knowing McCully—it's not like you."

"It may prevent an art theft."

The third phone call came to Hanley's Pub early in the afternoon. Hanley's wife was out of earshot when he put his lips close to the mouthpiece. "Hanley's Pub."

"Is Morris Chadbourne there yet?"

He recognized the caller. Who wouldn't after three calls? The man was from the North Country, but was this a toll call? The static on the line was more long distance. But he'd play the man's game. "Not yet."

"You will let Bosman know the minute he walks in?"

Hanley didn't need any more trouble. He was already worried about the use of the sheds behind his property. If his wife discovered what he was up to, his life would be more miserable than ever. "Of course, soon as he walks in," he said.

But he liked Chadbourne and wouldn't betray him, not unless the price for his services was right. He needed a break. He'd like his expenses paid to the French Riviera, especially if his wife agreed to man the pub while he was gone.

He yanked the towel from his shoulder and wiped the countertop. The bike hadn't been chained behind the pub all day.

Wherever Morrie Chadbourne had gone, he hadn't started out on his cycle. It wasn't often that a man as smart as Chadbourne had time for the likes of Hanley. But Hanley knew fishing and the Lake Districts and how to listen when a man was down. They were good friends, but he felt sorry for Morrie. He seemed unhappy, ever since that old professor of his showed up at the pub.

Morrie had told him once that it didn't take Oxford to make a man intelligent. He would be surprised at how cunning Hanley had become. It wasn't every day that old Hanley could outsmart the art critics of the world.

At the Wakefield Cottage that evening Rachel and her guests were in the drawing room, enjoying cups of cocoa when Audrey appeared. "Miss Rachel, that Mr. Chadbourne is on the line."

Eileen's color drained. "Not Morris? Rachel, you tricked me into coming here?"

"No, Eileen. I invited you because I wanted you to come."

"Does Morris know I'm here?"

"He will soon enough."

"Mommy, who is Morris?"

"An old friend, honey. Rachel, he'll be—he'll be furious."

Audrey fidgeted in the doorway. "Miss Rachel, you know Mr. Chadbourne doesn't like waiting."

With a faint smile for Eileen, she picked up the extension. "Morris, this is Rachel. Where have you been?"

"In London. I just spent six miserable hours in a bus on the motorway. Are you all right, Rachel?"

"I'm fine."

"Good. The party is a go. The details are finalized."

"I can't believe anyone will come."

"I had to turn people away. But I'll keep the final list a surprise. I have friends coming, a man and a woman, and I need you to pretend that the woman spent time in one of your classes."

She felt an upsweep of rage. "You turned away some of my former students for strangers? Why the deception, Morris?"

"Please, Rachel, just help me."

She watched Eileen whisper something to Becki, and then she was on her feet rushing from the room. "Yes. Yes, I am listening, Morris. And who is this student that I am to remember?"

"Jillian Reynolds. Jillian Ingram in your classroom."

He spent the next few minutes describing her. "Really attractive. Quite a number. Oh, yes. The specifics. About your height, Rachel. Brownish hair. Blue eyes. Really blue."

His description annoyed Rachel. *Your ex-wife is here, as lovely as ever, and you're thinking about someone you just met.*

"The rest of the guest list will be a surprise."

I can count on that, she thought. Strangers, perhaps.

"Morrie, I will need two bedrooms with a connecting door."

"For you and Wakefield?" he teased.

If he had been standing in front of her, she would have slapped him. "You can house Sinclair Wakefield wherever you want. My rooms are for personal friends. And I want comfortable housing for Audrey."

"She's the housekeeper, Rachel."

"And you were a barefoot boy in Kentucky. Find Audrey a room as nice as the one you have chosen for yourself."

"I'll be staying out in the caretaker's cottage."

"Very well furbished. Put Audrey as close to me as possible. I may need her if I have a sleepless night."

He did not ask the names of her guests, and thankfully not their ages. A guest of eight would not please him.

"Everything is set for next week. Wakefield and I have mapped out some tours. He'll take our guests to Oxford and Stratford-upon-Avon. You can grab a free day and rest up."

There he was switching back and forth between conniving and kindness. "I'll enjoy a rest day."

"Rachel, you and your guests should arrive just before dinner. That way everyone else will be settled in, and you won't have any extra work."

"That's asking too much for you."

"You're the guest of honor, remember. It's going to be a special party. Trust me, Rachel."

She glanced at Becki, who was sitting in a chair much too big for her. She looked frail and diminished, a Beatrix Potter book still in her hand. "Morrie, we will see you around five on Sunday."

She hung up and leaned down to kiss the top of the child's head. "Where's your mother, Becki?"

"She went outside—she's crying."

"Wait here. I'll just be a minute."

"You'll be in trouble. Mommy wants to be left alone."

"I'll risk it."

She found Eileen in the garden, staring up at the stars. "I'm so sorry. I should have told you, Eileen."

"I should have guessed. I knew I would have to face him someday. I won't spoil your party, Rachel. It means too much to you."

"You won't mind? In spite of seeing Morrie again?"

Eileen wiped away her tears. "I never told him about Becki. . . . He never liked children."

"Once he sees her—" *No, she was not certain what would happen.* "He loves you. I'm certain of that, Eileen."

"He loves himself more."

She tried again. "He needs our help, Eileen."

"Yours, perhaps. He always liked you." As Rachel watched, the moon caught Eileen's lovely face in shadows. She folded her arms across her chest, warding off whatever blows lay ahead.

But before she could apologize again, Eileen said, "Poor Morris. He has always needed somebody's help. Perhaps that is why I fell in love with him. He needed me back then."

171

Fourteen

Sinclair ran the back of his fingers over the bristly growth on his chin. He had shaved poorly this morning, shaved and showered in haste because his alarm clock had failed to ring. He'd raced through the whole day, played center forward in a rough soccer game between faculty and undergraduates in midafternoon, and was back in time for his last lecture with a deep gash on his finger and his muscles aching from soccer abuse.

Yet the whole day put together had been one of unexpected pleasantries: young scholars prepared for a definite exchange on thought and purpose. A light lunch at a favorite corner cafe. A personal triumph—as though he had arranged it—when the rain of the dismal gray morning gave way to a cool afternoon. And that sense of renewed physical strength participating in a hard fought soccer game, with the faculty winning.

From the window of his office, he looked out on the town and hills that he had come to love. Oxford, situated between two rivers, had been home for Sinclair since his undergraduate days. Even this glimpse reminded him of his life here. The morning rush to lectures. The town and gown rivalry. History and tradition. Medieval towers and cloisters. Ancient spires and narrow streets crowded with students on bicycles—he had been one of those students once—and the leisurely movement of boats on the rivers. Given the opportunity he could still enter the annual rowboat competition on the Thames and come in first place. Then came the end of the day with its reluctant stride home to an empty house.

He was not quite forty-two, yet he had spent years here. Four years of studying the classics, his honors high enough to stay on and research for his doctorate in literature. After years of browsing through the libraries—Bodleian was one of his favorites—he still delighted in stretching his mind. His boyhood choice to pursue an intellectual career proved even now to be the right one for him. He would have made a poor soldier or captain of a ship; he found challenge in stirring minds, not winning battles.

Life had not been all cranial pursuits. He excelled in sports and still did. He'd earned the title of *blue* in rowing and rugby competition with Cambridge and could still fit into his dark blue blazer that represented those matches. Much to his credit on the social level, he had friends among the townspeople.

He heard the distant sound of the chapel bells calling the listeners to evensong. Until this moment, busyness had marked his day, allowing him to send any thoughts of Rachel and Mary scudding to the background. Should he skip vespers to go home to his seventeenth-century house with its frontage flush with the sidewalk? He still slept on the third floor, waiting for total exhaustion before wending his way nightly to the room he had shared with Mary.

The vesper bells kept ringing. Was it always to be the ring of bells that tore at his soul? Big Ben in London, reminding him of Rachel's rejection. The pealing of church bells in Stradbury Square on the morning he said farewell to his wife and son. The vesper bells at Oxford—calling him to evening prayers, offering him hope. As the tolling continued, he set his books aside and in the long flowing robe of an Oxford don, strode toward the cathedral, his aching muscles stretching the distance with him.

Inside, daylight still filtered through the thirteenth-century stained-glass windows. He sat alone toward the back of the sanctuary, willing that no one would come near him.

Daring God to be the only one. The boys' choir came first, somber and singing a cappella; they looked like well-scrubbed cherubs and sang like angels. At least the way Sinclair imagined angels could sing. It was a long procession of children and adults in white robes with red bows, with hymnbooks held reverently in their hands.

After the first reading in the Psalms, Sinclair took his pen and notepad from his pocket and balanced it on his knee. As the sanctuary filled with the choir's anthem, he wrote, "My beloved Mary, life is so empty here without you. No flesh and blood for me to see, to touch. Just memories. And I find myself still blaming God for robbing me of my happiness. But, Mary, I find myself blaming you for taking our son away."

He crossed the last line out, feeling guilty for having written it. The pen twirled in his fingers, rubbing painfully against the miserable gash from the soccer game.

"Oh, Mary, do you remember how you loved the soccer games and went to cheer me, with Blake on your lap? I miss that."

Mary as honest as the promises of God, a little nobody, as she called herself, finding him when he most needed her. She berated herself that she had not gone to university. Sinclair insisted that their marriage was built on love, not on higher learning or scholastic prerequisites. In her plainness, she was beautiful to him. In her simple easygoing way, she filled his life with boundless happiness. Laughter had died for a little while after Rachel, but Mary brought it back into his life.

He put pen and paper together again. "Without you here, I have difficulty seeing the beauty in a sunrise. I have only recently been back to Stradbury Square, twice since losing you and Blake, but I remember how much you loved the sunrise there. On Easter I rose early from a sleepless night and went out on the rolling hills behind Oxford. I watched the sun rise, and for the first time since I lost you, I really found you again.

"In a way I let you go that morning. Now I am struggling again, wanting you back, needing you to protect me from

174

falling in love again. For six years, you were the sunrise in my life, the flesh and blood that became one with me, the union that gave us Blake. You would tell me to go on with living. But, my beloved Mary, it is Rachel who has come back into my life, not you.

"She is here in England. But she is ill, and I cannot separate first love from sympathy. Every time I want to reach out and take her hand, I think of you and my longing for you. I cannot separate my longing for you—my longing for her. But you are dead. She is here. She is as beautiful as ever. But time is against her. Dear Mary, I cannot bear the thought of losing someone else. Sitting here in the evening vespers, I admit to myself that I have loved you both."

Mary had come to him in the most unexpected moment, at a time when he had decided to remain a bachelor. She was walking ahead of him on the rolling hills behind Oxford. Flowers in bloom. The sky a peacock blue. The beginnings of an evening wind whipping against his face. Suddenly a hardball careened into his chest, winding him, angering him. A young woman and three children charged toward him and stopped dead in front of him.

Clenching the ball in his fist, he said with what dignity he could muster, "Madam, you should teach your children how to pitch a ball properly."

"They're not mine," she said, looking at him unabashed.

He held the ball up, his fingers still gripping it. "Not yours? Then perhaps one of those sheep tossed it my way."

She eyed the condemned sheep grazing nearby, an amused smile on her face. "The ball is ours. The children are not mine. I'm their governess. If you are so concerned about pitching the ball properly, then you teach them."

His jaw locked.

"Mary, why is he wearing that funny robe?" This from the smaller of the three, all of five years old, Sinclair concluded.

"He's from the university, a teacher like your daddy."

175

"You're our teacher, and you don't wear funny clothes."

The child was right. Mary was attractively dressed: Flannel slacks. Cool blouse. A brilliant scarf at her neck. Long lashes shielded pale blue eyes. Her makeup was modest, her face ordinary. But when she smiled, he said, "Don't go. I apologize for my robe, but I came straight from my lecture. A good walk clears my mind after a long day."

Walking delays going back to an empty room. "When one cooks like I do, Mary, there is little to rush home to."

"Mary will cook for you," the older boy informed him, the boy named Darrel.

For the first time, her composure slipped. To tease her more, Sinclair said, "I look forward to testing your cooking."

"May we have the ball back?" she asked. "It truly is ours."

"But I need it to teach the boys how to pitch."

They walked back to the campus together, the three urchins running ahead of them, his flowing robe over his arm. In front of the house where the children belonged, she said good-bye.

"May I see you again, Mary?" he asked.

"Not without knowing your name."

They married three months later. "Someone had to rescue you from the children," he said.

But it was Mary who had rescued him, filled his life, completed it.

⚋⚋⚋

Another anthem filled the cathedral. He took his pen and wrote again. One word: "Rachel." And the scribbled notation: "My beloved Mary, I feel that Rachel is coming between us."

He capped and recapped the pen. Silence engulfed him. The sanctuary had emptied. He was the only one left in the pew.

"Don Wakefield! Remember me?" a young man asked. "I'm Darrel Moreland. Mary was my governess."

"The boy who slammed that hardball into my chest?"

"Afraid so. I'm at the university now as an undergraduate."

"Has it been that long ago that I met you?"

176

"Yes, sir. . . . And I was at the funeral—"

"Yes, I remember. We named our son after your younger brother."

"That was a point of contention between us for a long time."

Sinclair chuckled dryly. "I warned Mary that it might not sit well with you, you being the oldest son. And then, of course, we never had another child."

A grin cut across the young man's face and lingered there. "It's a good thing, sir. I never liked the name Darrel."

"That's what I told Mary about my name when she wanted to name our son after me."

He felt suddenly peaceful inside, uplifted. His colleagues at the college never broached the subject of Mary and Blake. Yet here was this undergraduate talking about them as though they had just this minute stepped from the chapel. It was good to discover that someone else remembered his wife and son had lived.

He clapped Darrel on the back as they walked down the aisle toward the chapel door. "Darrel, if you need help—have problems, or any questions on your tutoring, in fact if you just want to talk or pitch a hardball, come see me."

"I was afraid to impose on your grief, sir."

"No, Darrel. If you had not tossed that ball, I would never have met Mary."

They were actually laughing as they stepped into the cool of the evening. He could not recall a word from the evensong, not even a phrase from the anthems sung, but he remembered Mary and Blake with great pleasure and a new sense of freedom. They parted outside the cathedral, and Sinclair made his way to his empty house, his thoughts on tomorrow's commitment and deception.

Tomorrow he would drive to the Somerset Estates and walk and live in the company of Rachel McCully for the next several days.

He wanted to go. He dreaded going.

The following afternoon, Eileen helped Rachel pack the car for their trip to the Somerset Estates. Rachel seemed distracted as she turned the keys over to the young constable from London.

It was the same policeman who had followed Eileen to the Lake District. "Doctor's orders," Timothy Whitesaul had said.

So far, no one had explained the cause for alarm, but Eileen remained on guard. Now, with a police guard left at the cottage, something was seriously wrong. Rachel had said that Morrie was in trouble. From the caution taken at the Wakefield Cottage, Eileen dreaded what lay ahead.

She buckled Becki into the backseat. "Mommy, I can do that myself. I'm not a little child."

"I know. I'm sorry, sweetheart."

Eileen offered to drive, but Rachel took the wheel. She was backing out when the constable stopped her. "You forgot this." He thrust the cellular phone through the window. "Sorry, Miss McCully. Farland's orders."

"Yes, I know. It's coded direct to his desk in London."

"Don't worry, Miss McCully. Everything will work out. The inspector has men stationed at the Somerset Estates."

She put her finger to her lips.

"I'm sorry. My error. I forgot the child was with you."

"I'm not a child, and Mommy says I have big ears. So there."

He grinned. "We'll take good care of the cottage, Miss McCully. And you have a good trip, Miss Becki."

Grumbling from the backseat, Audrey said, "Keep the kitchen clean. I'm not coming back to a bunch of dirty dishes."

He saluted her and grinned again. "We'll leave the place spotless. Now you go on. We're sending an escort behind you."

Sitting in the backseat beside Audrey, Becki giggled. "If you don't want him to leave the dirty dishes, Audrey, why did you let him take care of the house?"

Rachel turned and exchanged glances with Audrey. "We—we just don't like to leave the house empty."

178

The age lines on Audrey's forehead deepened further. "You just don't want the flowers in your garden crushed again," she said. "Nor the gate left ajar. None of it my doing."

"Audrey, that's enough."

Eileen checked the passenger's side mirror as they drove away. Nothing was said until they reached the main turnoff and the car behind them followed at a polite distance.

"We do have company, Rachel."

"I know. Get used to it."

"I feel like we're going to a policeman's ball."

Rachel sighed. "That might be more fun. Stop fretting, Eileen. I don't know any more than you do. Sinclair guarantees our protection. Morrie swears that we're going to have fun."

"Am I risking my daughter's safety? If so, find me a phone. I'll call Timothy Whitesaul to come and take us back to London."

"No, Mommy, Rachel promised to take me to Hill Top Farm."

Rachel caught Becki's eye in the mirror. "I plan to keep that promise on Wednesday, Becki. We'll have a grand time."

As they drove on in silence, Eileen took note of Rachel's soft hands relaxed on the steering wheel. There had been a big change in Rachel in these weeks in England. She did look better; even her skin had taken on a more rosy glow. Her profile was as strong as ever, her eyes bright again. She was still much too thin but glamorous enough in her choice of clothes and makeup; it was unlikely her guests would guess how sick she had been.

"Do I pass inspection, Doctor?" Rachel asked.

"Yes. You look great."

"As long as I don't look older. Before the party ends, I'll be thirty-eight."

They had been driving for an hour when a smile spread across Rachel's face. She pointed to the pretentious gate, swung wide for their arrival. "There it is. Our home for the next several days."

"Wow!" Becki exclaimed. "Is it a castle?"

"Sort of."

"It's certainly impressive," Eileen agreed.

The Somerset Estates appeared like an ominous looking structure high on a rocky hill, with sloping emerald green hills that reached lazily toward the river behind it. It reminded Eileen of a castle on the Emerald Isle—one she had seen a long time ago. Before Morrie. Before Becki.

"Rachel, it's magnificent. And, Becki, you have to be careful. You mustn't touch a thing."

"Good. Then I won't have to wash my hands or help Audrey in the kitchen."

"You know what I mean, young lady."

"Eileen, she'll do just fine. I'm so nervous about seeing some of my former students that I'm more apt to be the one who breaks something."

"Then we'll both be in trouble, Rachel."

As Rachel parked in the front drive, Becki wrapped her arms around Rachel's neck. "I like your wig. You look just like you. And that's very pretty."

She patted the child's hand. "With Becki's vote of confidence, I think I'm ready."

"It's beautiful," Eileen observed.

"Me or the house?"

Eileen poked her playfully. "Both."

"Wait until you see the inside. Let's go in."

"Rachel, I feel a bit ill. Just nerves, I think."

"I guarantee—Morrie won't bite."

"Does he really live here?"

"Not in the main house, in the caretaker's cottage in the back. But don't feel sorry for him. It is well-furbished. He has three bedrooms and lots of work space."

"It's more than he ever had."

"Then be glad for him."

"Do you think he's happy here, Rachel?"

"Has Morrie ever been truly happy?"

"I don't think so."

She took the keys from the ignition. "Not even in those two months when you were married?"

Eileen frowned as she glanced back at Becki. But Becki was busily piling out of the car, talking excitedly with Audrey.

"Rachel—I'd almost forgotten those two months. They were the happiest of my whole life."

They went up the seven flagged steps, Becki walking between them and Audrey lagging behind. Before Rachel could ring the chimes, the double doors swung back. A balding, dignified man welcomed them into the domed, marble hallway. "I'm Mr. Freck. Do come in," he said.

Awestruck, Becki whispered, "Do people really live here?"

"Yes, miss." The butler smiled, patted her head, and then said to Rachel, "Mr. Chadbourne and the rest of your guests are waiting for you in the drawing room. Your luggage will be delivered to your rooms."

"Don't forget my books," Becki told him.

"They'll be in your room, miss."

"The rest of you go on," Audrey told Rachel. "I'll see to the kitchen."

With the same warm smile he had showered on Becki, the butler led them to the drawing room, into what was obviously one of the Somersets' favorite rooms. It spelled comfort and coziness, splendor and magnificence. The room went silent as they entered. Rachel scanned the group and was delighted with the familiar faces and the tapestry of memories they stirred.

She was tempted to say, "Put down your pen and papers, class," but all she could do was smile at them.

Before Rachel could find her voice, one couple rose and came toward her. They made a handsome couple crossing the room. He was tall and muscular with a dimpled grin, she vibrant like a fashion model in her Italian suit. Her radiant blue eyes met Rachel's. *Morrie's friend, no doubt,* Rachel thought.

"Dr. McCully, I hope you remember me."

How can I? We have never met.

She took a quick survey of this student who had never been her student—a lovely girl with a lively step and an enchanting smile. Long tawny hair swept across her shoulders. She held out her hands to Morrie's friend. "Jillian Ingram. Of all people."

There! She hoped she got it right.

"It's Jillian Reynolds now," the young man said, taking her hand. "I'm Chandler, Jill's tag-a-long husband."

Chandler Reynolds had a guileless smile, his gaze direct and friendly. Rachel liked him immediately—she didn't have to remember him from her classroom.

"My wife and I are grateful you invited us."

"The pleasure is mine, Chandler."

His eyes danced with merriment as he talked to her, but she knew those alert eyes would not miss a thing. He was sizing up her guests, acquainting himself with Somerset's art treasures.

"Were you in class with some of the others, Jillian?"

She blushed. "So far I haven't recognized anyone."

But Rachel did. Misty Owens, her colleague from the university, and Elsa, the last secretary that she had on campus. Bill Wong, who had gone on to be a chaplain in the army. Her eyes settled on the Arnold sisters. She ached, wondering if they had ever settled their differences.

"Oh, Lydia and Sara, what a joy to see you."

Feeling weak in all the excitement, she linked her arm with Eileen's and felt the tremor in Eileen's body. She didn't dare look at Morrie. Not yet. Instead she said, "Amanda Pennyman." It netted a quick wave from Amanda, and a supportive hug from the young man beside her. "Amanda, what are you doing these days?"

"Kevin and I are living in London. I'm in advertising."

That was the job Amanda's fiancé had wanted, the young man who was killed on a motorcycle. Lee. Lee something. She turned to Kevin. "Are you in advertising too?"

"I used to be into horse racing until I met Mandy," he said, as though a confession were expected of him. "Now I've settled down with a real job—"

"He's a bank auditor." Amanda sounded unsure of herself, nervous to have the attention of the room drawn to them.

Slowly Rachel looked from face to face. She caught her breath when she recognized Jude Alexander sitting alone, the girl's gaze burning with resentment as their eyes met.

She groped for another name or two. Remembered others, especially the girl with the golden voice. "Lenora, I thought you were doing the opera *Madame Butterfly* in Rome. Lead soprano."

"I am—thanks to you. My stand-in is filling in for me."

Janet Tallard stood by the piano, looking as calm and sure of herself as the day she went down the aisle to marry her beloved widower. Her face still glowed. "Hello, Dr. McCully."

"You came all the way from Canada, Janet—without Tad? Just for this reunion?"

"I left Tad home with the boys—tending the farm and milking the cows."

The room broke into laughter. From the corner of her eye Rachel saw Morrie stumble to his feet, glaring angrily at his past. Taking Eileen's arm and Becki's hand she crossed the room to meet him. "Morrie, dear. You remember Eileen—"

His looked ashen, gray like his temples. That he still cared about the woman standing in front of him, Rachel had no doubt.

He gave her a quick hug. "It's been a long time, Eileen."

"A few years. . . . This is—my daughter, Becki."

"I didn't know you married again."

"I didn't."

His expression twisted. "Neither did I, Eileen."

183

"Becki, this is Mr. Chadbourne," Eileen said. Becki offered her hand.

Rachel nudged him. "Aren't you going to say hello to Becki?"

Words seemed to lodge in his throat. He brushed back his unruly lock of hair. Timidly, Becki drew back her hand. He murmured, "She's a bit young for a university reunion."

⁓

Afterwards—after dinner and dessert—the guests settled back in the drawing room where Asher Weinberger's masterpiece was central to the room. It hung above the fireplace in solemn beauty, its darkness overshadowing the reunion. Seeing it, Rachel hesitated in the alcove and held her breath. This was the painting that could hang like an albatross around their necks—the painting that could ruin Morrie's life.

Morrie moved to the front of the room, dimmed the main lights, and pressed a panel beneath the stone mantel. It threw a cataclysmic effect over the painting, spotlighting the brush strokes of the gathering black clouds and the last ribbons of sunlight.

An eerie silence fell over the room, a silence broken by Becki. "That's kind of pretty, Mr. Chadbourne. Did you paint it?"

A quizzical frown spread over his face. "No, I didn't."

"My great-granddaddy has a painting like that."

Sinclair came to stand beside Rachel in the alcove where their voices were muted, and where his steadying hand comforted her. "It's amazing how light changes the face on that picture."

"It's frightening what Morrie is trying to do."

"Everything is going to work out."

"Not between Morris and Becki," she whispered.

"Everyone else finds her a charming child."

Morrie's voice demanded their attention. "Lord Somerset developed an intricate lighting system in order to mute or brighten or cast shadowy images on the artwork on his

184

walls. Somerset's art collection is one of the most valuable ones in England. There are paintings in every room—even in the rooms where you're staying. You can look, but don't touch. That goes for you too, Smidgen," he said, glancing down at Becki.

"I can't touch. I'm not that tall. And my name is Rebecca."

"That was my mother's name."

More of Rachel's happiness stole away. "Sinclair, the guests should retire, but someone should stay up and make sure—"

"Nothing will happen this evening. I'm certain of that."

"Do you have Inspector Farland's word on it?"

"Farland has it covered. You concentrate on your guests, Rachel. Especially Jude Alexander. I sat with her at dinner, and I don't think you are her favorite person."

"I told Morrie she would be unhappy if he invited her—that she could make the rest of us miserable."

"According to the invitation list, she was definitely invited: *Jude Alexander and guest.* But she came alone." He shrugged. "I challenged her to a game of badminton tomorrow. She was dead on the button with her answer. She told me she had no time for batting a feathered shuttlecock across the net with an older man."

Rachel smothered her chuckle against his shoulder. "At least I like older men," she teased.

Morrie stood beneath the Weinberger, his voice modulated as he said, "Weinberger's earlier works imitated the Impressionist painters. Bright and full of sunlight. But in 1939 his paintings began to show the darkness that was descending over Europe." He pointed toward another painting, his smile warm when he gazed at Amanda or Jude, shadowed and wounded when he looked at Eileen. "The smaller painting over there by Eileen is a work by Degas. The one by the piano a Claude Monet, and that one by you, Jude, is a Cezanne. But the Asher Weinberger overshadows them all simply by a flick of this switch."

He turned the dimmer, forcing the light changes to high-light the picture. "Note the shimmering effects of light in the far corner of the canvas as though the sun just set." But there was darkness and rage in the swollen river, fear in the face of the boatman as he tried to push away from the shore.

"Sinclair, what is Morrie trying to do?"

"Maybe he's sending a signal to one of the guests—letting that person know which paintings to target—which ones to steal."

She looked away to hide the hurt in her eyes. As she turned, Morrie glanced her way, and she saw rage and dark-ness in his expression—as though Asher Weinberger had painted Morrie's portrait and hung it on the wall.

Fifteen

Rachel slept with the curtains open, using daylight like an alarm clock. But greeting the first streak of dawn as it cracked the darkness was not to her liking even in this luxurious bedroom. What had awakened her? The wind? Someone prowling in the corridors outside her door? Light steps? Heavy ones? Bare feet?

Listening, she finally distinguished Becki's steps pattering to their adjoining bathroom, and Eileen saying, "No, Becki, we are not going to Hill Top Farm today. That's Wednesday. So come back to bed before you wake Rachel."

Rachel turned and twisted for another fifteen minutes before tossing the bedding aside and standing up. Sleepless nights often made her argue with herself about the outcome of her cancer treatment. Mostly, she was optimistic, determined to go on with living, to prove the doctors liars. The next moment she felt uncertain about the outcome. Unhappy about this reunion. This was not her gathering. It was Morrie's.

But this miserable battle with cancer was her own, and she had no intention of it spoiling the week for Morrie or anyone. She thrust thoughts of her sister's early death aside. This didn't happen twice in one family, did it? Whatever the label—cancer, cystic fibrosis—it seemed unfair.

I'm still young. Days shy of thirty-eight, she thought.

No, she had already lived twice as long as Larea—and lived it to the fullest for both of them. She went to her dresser, uncapped her medicine bottle, and tapped out one pill. *Timothy's miracle cure.*

This morning she cupped it in her hand. "Okay, wave of the future, Timothy Whitesaul believes in you. I'd like to believe in you too." She rolled the pill over before popping it into her mouth. "Are you living up to your rave reviews and blasting those cancer cells so I can get back to mountain climbing?"

Not letting her hopes wander beyond that, she pushed her fresh grief for Larea and the longings for Sinclair back into the darkness as she picked up the glass schooner and, like a chaser, sent the water and the pill down her throat.

At the first real glimmerings of day, Rachel dressed and made her way down the long cascade of steps on the spiral staircase, running her hand over the polished balustrade with its oak leaf motif and pressing her feet into the thick red carpet. The house lay quiet except for the murmur of voices coming from the kitchen and the whispering of wind coming through the open windows and stealing down the long marble corridor.

Even the silent hallway was an art gallery with murals of battlefields on both sides of the corridor. Standing guard beneath each mural was a life-sized ivory statue with the carved features of the monarchy and the world's political giants: Queen Victoria, King George IV, Churchill, Roosevelt, Lord Nelson.

She switched on the lights as she entered each room, switched them off as she left. The clock in the main gallery said five. It coincided with Rachel's jeweled watch. The gallery with its graceful domed ceiling was as magnificent as the cathedrals in London. Portraits of the Somersets hung on the end wall—Lord Somerset with an arrogant smile and his arms folded across his massive chest. *A vain man,* she decided, yet the eyes looking down at her twinkled in the morning light. His wife seemed more regal in her deep lavender gown, a diamond necklace at her breast, but Rachel saw unhappiness in her eyes.

You own all of this, and you have missed joy.

The rooms teemed with art treasures, the opulence the vanity of one man. The Somerset Estates had imperial grandeur but no heirs. The owners had a legacy of affluence and excess, but they had squandered so much of their wealth on themselves and yet had built their name with charitable giving. In a museum she would find the display awesome, but here it brought her sadness. The Wakefield Cottage was serene in comparison, the home she had grown up in on faculty row near campus ordinary and livable. Her own well-furnished condo had not been elaborate.

She made her way from the smoking room back to the drawing room, knowing that the Asher Weinberger drew her there. She looked up at it in the darkened room and longed for the picture to reveal its secrets, its control over Morrie.

"Good morning, Dr. McCully."

She whirled around. "Chandler Reynolds, you frightened me."

Jillian's husband stepped from the shadows in a navy jogging suit. "I thought I was alone too. Did you take the grand tour?"

"Yes. I had trouble sleeping."

Turning to the tapestry drapes, he opened them, allowing early daylight to steal into the room. Grinning at her, he said, "There, that puts the Weinberger back in the limelight."

"Morrie . . . Morrie is obsessed with that painting."

"Are you? That picture says volumes, Dr. McCully, but I don't think it has the answers you're looking for."

They took turns focusing their attention back on the painting. "I'm not certain I know the questions yet. But why are you up so early this morning?"

"I've been out for my morning run."

"I envy you. I used to be a mountain climber and could sleep anywhere. Campsites. In the cramped space in the back of my van. Today—in this luxurious setting with its oak bedposts and headboard, the tapestries over the windows, a bathroom bigger than my bedroom at the cottage—I woke up at four. Maybe the seventeenth-century bed kept me awake."

"Jill and I got an eighteenth-century mattress like my army cots."

"You were in the military?"

"Army intelligence—stationed with the American troops in Bosnia. I considered reenlisting and then I met Jillian in Vienna. But after talking with Chaplain Wong about this latest unrest in the Middle East, I would be willing to serve again."

"As a chaplain?"

"No, with intelligence. Or with the Army Rangers. My wife goes ballistic at the thought of my going army again. But I still have a mind for trouble."

"So do I."

"Then did you notice anything different about this room, Dr. McCully?"

She looked around, perplexed. The dirty cups and saucers from the night before had been cleared away. The cushions on the chairs fluffed. Dear Audrey's hands at work again. "No, I don't see anything unusual."

"Look again. Look over here on this wall—where Eileen Rutledge was standing last evening, where I'm standing now."

Her gaze shot to the empty space where the light from the window cast its morning rays across the cream walls. She stared in disbelief. "One of the paintings is gone, Chandler."

"That's right. The small Degas."

"Why would anyone take that painting?"

"It has a nice monetary tag. At least a million. I doubt that Lord Somerset's alarm system can detect his paintings walking, not if someone has free access at the gate. But we have time and that alarm system on our side. No one goes out those locked gates without permission or a code key in hand."

She felt a jumbled mistrust of Chandler. Last night she had thought him guileless, trustworthy. Betray that first impression and she shared his guilt of being the only ones in the drawing room before the other guests awakened. Or should she go with her instincts? He had been with Army intelligence. Was he intelligent enough to unravel this mess?

"Chandler, we must tell Morrie."

"Not yet."

"He's the caretaker. Either you go find him or I will."

"Let Chadbourne discover the loss. That gives us time to find out who else had a case of insomnia this morning."

"And it gives the thief time to get away."

"You, my dear lady, have nothing to worry about. You are no thief. And don't look at me that way." He held up his hands. "I'm wearing a jogging suit. No backpack. I didn't take the painting."

As she moved toward the door, he strolled across the room and blocked her way. "Don't sound the alarm. We'll be having breakfast in a very short while."

"Are we to pick the thief from the way he chews sausage?"

He held up a handkerchief. "Or if someone claims this."

Jude's! Her stomach tightened. With effort, she maintained her dignity but raged inside. "None of my former students would take that painting."

"That leaves Becki," he said, eyes twinkling. "But she told us she is too short to touch any of Somerset's treasures. So, dear lady, that leaves someone outside of your classroom. Someone like me. But I'm an art and music critic. Not a thief. I'm your friend. You have to trust someone."

"Everyone at the reunion claims me as a friend." *Except, perhaps, Jude Alexander,* Rachel thought.

Chandler's lips curled. He glanced past the empty spot on the wall to the dangling Claude Monet. "One of those *friends* of yours attempted to take that painting as well."

The Monet hung catawampus, tilted sideways, askew like Sinclair Wakefield's ties. A clammy chill started at the base of Rachel's spine. She rubbed her arms to ward off the goosebumps. "Please, straighten it, Chandler."

"And leave my fingerprints? I daresay the person ahead of us wore gloves. Last evening Chadbourne told us we could look at any of the paintings in this mansion but not to touch them."

He urged her to sit down on the French settee. "You must not get involved," he cautioned. "Whoever moved that Monet must go on trusting you. . . . Now, just think about the missing painting. It may trigger your memory. Something you saw or heard. Something or someone who awakened you."

Becki had awakened her. Perhaps the wind. But they were not connected. She tried to remember what the Degas painting looked like. She knew more about the artist.

Edgar Degas. She searched her mind and placed him in Paris, born into a wealthy Parisian family. Surely that meant an Impressionist painter. A man with a high brow and searching dark eyes. Beardless, if she remembered his self portrait correctly. "He was an Impressionist painter, wasn't he? Sunlit landscapes."

He smiled. "More neoclassical. He chose jockeys and ballet dancers and ordinary women for his subjects. Did you know Degas lived to a ripe old age, unusual for that time in history. I'd buy all of those years if I could spend them with Jillian . . ."

He was back on track when she said, "I'm sure you're aware that Degas was known for his sculptures of horses and ballet dancers. There's a horse sculpture in the smoking room—a marvelous craftsmanship."

"Then I'm sure we both have our fingerprints on it. Morris warned us against touching things, but he may have been tempting us to do just that. We expect to find his fingerprints in the mansion. But if something goes wrong at this reunion, suspicion will fall on any of us who left a print on a vase or sculpture."

He eased into a chair and stretched his long legs. "Degas had his own style; his color and compositions influenced the art world of his day. But he broke with the Impressionists in midlife and later became a recluse. I suspect that will ultimately happen to the Somersets. Since his wife's heart condition, they have become virtual recluses here in the Lake District."

"Recluses? They are on a world cruise right now."

"Oh! Well likely they'll touch ports where they can acquire another masterpiece to hang on these walls. And for what? No moving van will follow their hearse to the grave. The Somersets will check out empty-handed, like the rest of us."

Rachel stormed from the room with Chandler close behind her. In the dining room, she wrapped her arms around her chest as she stared out the glass doors toward the gardens and guest cottages.

"I'm sorry, Dr. McCully. That Degas may date back to World War II. My wife is interested in the art thefts of that era."

"You sound like Morrie. He believes the Weinberger painting was stolen from his great-grandmother back then."

"If he's an heir let him lay claim to it. But what if he's an ordinary thief planning to use all of us here at the reunion?"

She whirled on him. "Many of those collectors in World War II were Jewish like Morrie. He can't come up with the sales records and art catalogues demanded of him. The paper trail stopped there for Morrie."

"He'd lose anyway. Lord Somerset would never hang a painting on his wall if he thought it was stolen. It would be stowed away in the subterranean vaults."

The thought of a subbasement on the property came as a surprise. But why not a temperature-controlled room for his paintings? "Maybe that's where the Degas is now."

"As small as it is, the Degas could be anywhere. In one of the rooms upstairs. In the trunk of one of the vans parked outside. In a guest cottage—or in the toolsheds out back."

She shivered. "Or in your room, Chandler."

"Or yours." He smiled. "Don't get involved. Let Jillian and I handle it for you. . . . Mr. Chadbourne told us you were ill."

"Is nothing sacred with Morrie? Maybe he was afraid no one would come if he didn't play on their sympathies."

"He told my wife the Somersets don't need the Weinberger painting. I'd keep my eye on that if I were you, Dr. McCully."

"I don't understand you, Chandler. You're friends."

"Friends with Chadbourne? I just met him yesterday."

You are playing with my mind, trying to make me mistrust my guests. Playing the devil's advocate and asking me to trust you. And now I find you are not even Morrie's friend.

"My wife and Chadbourne have mutual interests. History, for one. And art." He seemed suddenly amused, this guileless man mocking her. His deep chuckle filled the room. "Jillian is not a thief, Dr. McCully, but if my wife finds a sculpture or painting she's been searching for, she simply picks it up or takes it off the wall and goes on with her business."

"What is her business?"

"She dabbles in magnificent paintings like the Weinberger and the missing Degas."

Rachel's attention was drawn toward a stranger making his way from the back of the property toward the main house. The man was wearing a raincoat on this warm sultry morning. "Who is that, Chandler? For a moment I thought it was Morrie."

The stranger passed the badminton courts and drew closer. Slightly taller and better looking than Morrie, he carried a metal briefcase, large enough to hide a million-dollar painting.

"That man was not with us last evening—and he is definitely not one of my former students."

Chandler said quietly, "His name is Sean Larkins."

"You know him?"

194

"I know of him. He's a popular rugby player from Ireland. He usually sports a beard. People who know him call him Chip. That man should never have been invited here. . . . If you'll excuse me, Dr. McCully, I think I'd better shower and change for breakfast. My wife was sleeping when I left the room."

The stranger slipped behind the side bushes to the front entry. Moments later the musical chimes at the front door sent the butler running. Rachel cut across his path. "I'll get it, Mr. Freck."

"But, madame."

"It is most likely one of my guests."

She opened the door and smiled up at the stranger. He was handsome in a sullen sort of way with height to his credit and a cleft chin to distinguish him. He flashed a winsome smile. "Well, the saints be praised—the professor herself. I would know you anywhere, Dr. McCully. Just as full of beauty as ever."

She considered matching his blarney. "And who might you be?"

"It's Sean. Surely you remember me? Sean Larkins." His hurt was as forced as his accent. "I'm a friend of Jude Alexander's."

Warning enough, she thought.

"She did tell you I was coming late?"

"Jude really hasn't said anything to me."

"Shy as ever, that girl."

Hardly the description for Jude. "I was the lad in the top row in your Chaucer class," he said.

"Were you now?"

This was not a face she remembered. His bone structure was well chiseled, chin firm and determined. He was most presentable in his gray suit and tie, his raincoat slung over his arm now. His deep-set eyes blazed as he waited for Rachel's appraisal to simmer. One thing she knew for certain. He had never been in her classroom.

"Mr. Larkins, I never taught Chaucer."

Undaunted, he said, "Really? Well, it was *one* of those challenging classes of yours. Luck runs with me. If you don't remember me, at least I'm not in trouble."

You are in more trouble for trying to deceive me.

"I'm looking for Mr. Chadbourne," he announced.

"So was I."

"But I'll settle for Jude. I'm here as her guest."

It's everybody's party, Rachel thought.

As she stood back, Sean stepped inside and gawked up at the magnificent gold pillars and domed ceiling. "I think I'm going to like this place. As lovely as the castles of Ireland."

"Well, Mr. Larkins," Rachel said graciously, "if you want to freshen up for breakfast, Mr. Freck will show you to a room with a balcony. I'm certain you'll enjoy your accommodations."

The butler frowned his disapproval. "Follow me, sir."

Rachel walked down the hall and found Morrie in the dining room. "It's turned into quite a gathering, Morrie," she commented.

"I'm glad you like it."

"I didn't say that. It may be my reunion, Morris, but many of the guests are strangers to me. The young man on his way upstairs is Sean Larkins, a friend of Jude's."

Morrie managed a quick glance from the doorway, a sudden rage filling his eyes. "Chip Larkins? Your friend Jude is keeping poor company. How long has she known him?"

It was the wrong time to tell him about the missing Degas. She didn't trust the Morrie looking at her now. She said cautiously, "Would it matter how long they've known each other?"

"He is someone I'd rather see outside the gates. I'm going to keep my eye on him, Rachel. Inviting him was a big mistake."

"I didn't send the invitations."

"Someone sent his."

She didn't argue but admitted, "I've made some mistakes with Jude Alexander. This is the first I've seen her since she failed one of my classes. She still despises me."

His mood mellowed. "If someone didn't pass, was it your fault, Dr. McCully?"

"I feel that I let her down. That one course kept her from graduating. Jude meant to go into foreign service."

"She did. She works at the American embassy. Your friend Jude is just lucky she isn't waiting tables in some restaurant. Hanley could do with an attractive waitress at his pub."

"At Hanley's? Jude would probably make more on tips than I did teaching at the university." She smothered a sigh. "Until last evening I wasn't certain what happened to her. She's a minister's daughter. Angry with everyone." *Angry like you are.* "What grieves me the most is she put God on the back burner."

"With me, Rachel, God isn't even on the back burner."

"Then I failed you too, Morris."

Sixteen

The guests left in separate cars for Windermere and Grasmere, leaving Rachel alone to fret over the missing Degas. She found no time to snatch a few moments alone with Sinclair before he was out the door with the others. Even as they moved toward each other after breakfast, Morrie had whisked him away to the drawing room. Sinclair cupped her chin in passing, "I'll see you this evening. Are you certain you want to stay home alone?"

"Certain," she had told him and wondered whether he heard the uncertainty in her voice. Maybe even the tremor.

When the massive front door closed behind her guests, Rachel went upstairs to her room to mull over her own stubbornness behind a locked door. She didn't have Audrey to confide in. With the beds already made up, the floors swept, the bathroom tiles scoured clean again, the shower stalls wiped dry, the staff would be resting.

She was already tense as a circus wire. How many more paintings would slip from the walls of the mansion in the next several days? With her old indomitable spirit, she had tackled a gathering that directly opposed Timothy Whitesaul's cautious approach to recovery. Timothy constantly urged her to avoid a crowd for the sake of her immune system, to get plenty of rest, good food, fresh air, and exercise. His parting words were always, "Keep the stress level at a minimum, Rachel; just relax."

Didn't he understand? With Rachel, it was grabbing at time, reaching out to help Morrie, reaching beyond that to help herself. Had her choices in the classroom prepared any of her students for life in the real world? Had she been prepared for it herself? The delight of seeing some of her former students took a nosedive. Could she face several more days when even the next few hours seemed daunting, crushing, insurmountable?

Rachel opened her purse, took the cell phone, and pressed the coded number to Inspector Farland's office in London. "Someone will always be at that number," he had promised.

A polite voice informed her, "Your party is unavailable at this time. Leave your name and number; he will return your call."

Before another painting disappeared? She snapped the off-button and tossed the phone back into her purse. Outside her room, she heard footsteps in the corridor. Whispers. Doors opening quietly, closing again. Her breath came in tight gasps as she unlocked her door and cracked it open. Someone had just disappeared into a room across from her. Kevin's room? Sean's. Chaplain Wong's. No, she had seen all three of them leave.

The door opened again. The butler slipped on to the next room and went stealthily inside. Rachel did not wait for him to reappear but went quickly downstairs. Even there, came the whispering sounds of someone in the drawing room. Determined, she stepped inside and startled Jillian and Chandler Reynolds.

Jillian had a camera in her hands. "Jillian, I saw you leave less than an hour ago! What are you doing?"

"Taking pictures."

"I can see that. But this is a private collection."

Jillian went on snapping the Weinberger from varied angles.

"Stop her, Chandler. We're here to protect Lord Somerset's collection, not photograph it. We have trouble enough."

"We have more trouble than you think." Chandler stood by the piano pointing to where the Monet had tilted only hours ago. Like a mockery to Morrie's Jewishness, a copy of van Ruisdael's *Jewish Cemetery* hung in its place. "I tried to tell you earlier, Dr. McCully. My wife is here on official business."

"What happened to the Monet painting, Chandler?"

"It's anyone's guess. Someone took it while we were all straggling in and out for breakfast. With two paintings missing, everybody at this reunion falls under the umbrella of suspicion. Jillian is starting in this room—getting as many pictures as possible. That way we will know when something else is missing."

Rachel clutched her jaw. "There are over three hundred paintings. It's impossible for Jillian to photograph them all."

"We have to start somewhere. And do so quickly. Dr. McCully, we're both here trying to help Morrie Chadbourne." Jillian's eyes went back to the Weinberger. "I need pictures to compare with the ones we have at the Coventry Art Theft Registry."

"Dr. McCully, my wife is an art fraud investigator."

Her camera clicked again. "This could be one of the masterpieces confiscated in 1939—and lost for all these years. If it is a genuine Weinberger, it is listed at the Registry."

Rachel calmed. "You know Inspector Jon Farland?"

"We've worked together in the past. They respect the work the Registry does. We have a comprehensive list of art missing from all over the world. We're constantly adding to our records. But I need proof that this is a genuine Asher Weinberger. Lord Somerset has refused all requests to view his collection."

"Surely Lord Somerset is a cautious investor. He will have legitimate documentation to prove his purchase."

"That only makes proof of rightful ownership harder. We thought all the Weinberger paintings were lost. Now Morrie may be right. Three or four of the originals may have survived the war."

"You seem so sure of yourself, Jillian."

She faced Rachel, the camera at her side. "It's my job. Name any of the great artists and their names are no doubt on our registry. Some painting missing. Some drawing. An unfinished canvas. An unclaimed Spanish tapestry. A charcoal sketch. Wood panels. Sculptures. Rare books."

"You make it sound like everything was stolen."

"Thousands of works were. So many of the paintings smuggled out of Germany are still unaccounted for. A pastel by Degas is still missing. Bruegel's *Enchanted Island*. A Rembrandt drawing. One of the Vermeer paintings from the Rothschilds' collection. Even a Gutenberg Bible—at least an excellent fake—is missing."

"Maybe they were destroyed by bombings."

"Dr. McCully, more were destroyed by violence and greed. Some were deliberately demolished because the artists or owners were Jewish. In the last days of the war, truckloads of stolen property were transferred to underground shelters and the salt mines of Austria. And heaven knows where else."

Jillian gave an elegant sweep of her hair back from her face and turned with the sparkle of a fashion model, her perceptive eyes lively as she looked at Rachel. Gently she said, "Dr. McCully, gaps in ownership—that's the problem today. A lot of marketing went on during the war—the sale of property that belonged to somebody else. Now, sixty years later, heirs are dying or dead. The newer generation has little interest in lost or stolen art."

"We'll have to tell Morrie what's going on when he gets back—"

"By the time he gets back the film will be on its way to the Registry. But Morrie really did ask for my help, Dr. McCully."

The cell phone in Rachel's purse rang. She took it out, pressed it to her ear. "Inspector, I'm glad you called back." She nodded as she listened. Relief spread over her. "Yes, they're here with me. Lunch? Yes, I could drive in there to meet you."

She smiled at Jillian and Chandler when the call ended. "That was Inspector Farland. He said for you to be careful; I'm sorry, I didn't realize—" She gave them an apologetic shrug. "I've been invited out. Charles will be the only one having lunch with you today. He's the older gentleman who works in the gardens for love of it. Poor man. He lost his parish when the Archbishop of Canterbury banned him to the North Country."

It was Chandler's turn to be surprised. "Not Charles Rainford-Simms? I stayed at his rectory in the Cotswolds. He is really a nice old man. He took a raw beating protecting an Irish prodigal." He looked at her. "You may not be able to trust any of us, Dr. McCully, but you can trust Charles Rainford-Simms."

When Rachel left, she found Charles kneeling by a flower bed near the side gate. He rose to meet her. His stooped shoulders had cut him down to six-two, but he still towered above her.

Soft ridges had been chiseled into his face through kindness. "Don't look so unhappy, my dear," he said.

"I'm just worried about Lord Somerset's art collection."

"Everyone seems to be. I wouldn't worry, my dear. Mr. Chadbourne doubled the staff before the reunion. Even the butler was a last-minute replacement."

"Mr. Freck is a replacement? That worries me. He was just up on the second floor going through the rooms."

He brushed his brow with the back of his hand, streaking his snow-white hair with soil. Thick bushy brows tented as he seared her with his brilliant blue eyes. "There you go adding another care to your narrow shoulders. Next thing you'll be telling me about the missing paintings. Morrie told me as he left this morning. I may even know who took them."

She stared at him. "And you're doing nothing about it?"

"I'm gardening. It's a wonderful vantage point."

He could be dotty, forgetful. His imagination was in overplay. The crook in her neck tightened as she looked up at him. "One of them was stolen before dawn. The other during breakfast."

"Two thieves," he said calmly. "Those paintings are still on the grounds, I'm certain of it. So are you running away needlessly, my dear?"

"I'm just going to lunch."

"With Morrie, I trust? He admires you, Miss McCully."

"No, with someone else. Morrie was one of my most gifted students. That's why I agreed to this reunion. But I worry about his obsession with art."

"Can you fault a man for his love of art?"

"If it forces him to steal."

"I see."

"Charles, can you stop him from whatever he's going to do?"

His blue eyes shone with merriment. "Morrie may be a prodigal son, but I don't like to interfere with the Lord's business unless he wants me there."

"Morrie doesn't even know that Becki is his child."

He considered that. "I thought so. She looks like him. But a man on a redemptive journey doesn't need interference from me, he needs someone running alongside of him. Guiding him a little."

"Like you did for that Irish terrorist in the Cotswolds?"

"So you know about young Conon O'Reilly?"

"Even hearing about it made Morrie angry with the Church of England for taking your parish away."

Amusement twinkled his eyes. "Tell Morrie I broke the rules of the church; that's why the parish was given to a younger man."

She kicked a pebble from the walkway. "You know Morrie doesn't believe in our God."

"Neither did the Irish lad. But, like that boy, perhaps Morrie believes in God more than we realize."

He let his hand rest comfortingly on her shoulder. "I think you need someone running alongside of you too. If you need me, Rachel, I'll either be at my cottage or at one of these flower beds." He took a crumpled handkerchief from his pocket and wiped her eyes. "You seem to be searching for answers yourself."

"That's how all this reunion came about. I have leukemia—"

"I know."

He sounded as though it were merely a headache, or the nuisance of a runny nose. Seeing it from that perspective, she smiled at him. "I had eternity in mind."

"So did God when he created you. I see from your guests that you have touched more lives than you will ever know. You are well-esteemed. Let that be enough. Whatever accolades are due you will be waiting for you when the time comes."

"I may not have long to wait."

He wiped the soil from his hands and chuckled merrily. "Take me, my dear. I'm more than halfway there. Or three-fourths. Or maybe I will simply go back to this flower bed and get that call Home. Time is important but not a cause for fretting."

"Chandler Reynolds said you were a wise old man."

Another chuckle erupted. "And did he put the emphasis on the old or on the wise?"

⌒

Sinclair Wakefield drove four of the guests into Grasmere for the day so they could explore Wordsworth country. Excusing himself for a business appointment, he pointed the four women in the direction of Dove Cottage and suggested that they have lunch at *The Swan*, an oak-beamed restaurant with an excellent view.

They synchronized their watches and agreed to meet late in the afternoon for the drive back to the Somerset Estates for a late dinner. He waited until they slipped into the crowd, then drove to Hanley's Pub to meet Inspector Farland. He considered the pub a poor meeting spot to discuss stolen art when the inspector's blustery voice could easily echo across the room.

Coming in from the bright sunshine, he allowed his eyes to adjust to the darkness. Inspector Farland sat in the far corner with his back to him. There would be no noisy greeting to draw everyone's attention to them. He crossed the room and took the seat across from him. "Good morning, Inspector."

"Jon will do."

Sinclair took the rebuke in stride and scanned the menu as the pub's owner lumbered over to their table. A man that size was a heart attack waiting to happen, his skin gray as he faced the inspector. Sinclair settled on trout; Farland took smoked ham.

When Hanley walked away, Sinclair asked, "Does he know who you are?"

"I think so, and I don't think Hanley takes to strangers."

"He took to me quickly enough."

"Right. He takes to the climbers and the locals. He's always crowded, but he seems ill at ease with me this morning."

"How would you know that with your back to him, Jon?"

"That mirror by the fireplace lets me watch him when he doesn't know it. So what's this about missing paintings?"

"Two of them. A Degas and a Monet."

He whistled. "And how is Chadbourne handling that?"

"He was expecting trouble, but not one painting at a time."

Hanley was back. When he lingered, the inspector frowned. "That's all. Thank you." His voice carried too loudly, trailing behind Hanley. "I don't feel comfortable with that man."

"You'd do better not letting him hear you," Sinclair cautioned.

Grudgingly he lowered his voice. "So Chadbourne admits that he's expecting more trouble. Do you think he's involved?"

"Inspector, I think today took him by surprise. But remember, we are acquainted at the professional level. Not close associates. He won't be confiding in me."

"Because of Dr. McCully? She's a beautiful woman."

He leaned forward. "Then don't cheapen her. I am there at the reunion to make certain that no harm comes to Rachel."

"Lord Somerset believes you are there on his behalf."

"Then I've already failed him with the missing paintings."

⌒

Hanley wiped the glasses on the counter for a third time, then took the wet towel and rubbed the countertop with vigor. His wife screamed for him from their back kitchen. He long ago tired of her whining. Now he hated the sound of her voice. But he had to admit, her cooking pleased their guests: Cumberland cheese and sausage. Trout from the streams or the cucumber sandwiches preferred by some guests. And her mint cake drew others who would prefer the more picturesque tea shops.

Yesterday his wife questioned him about the phone calls that kept coming to him ever since that reunion started over at the Somerset Estates. "I know who that caller is, Hanley."

Acidy fear ate at his gut. Did she really know the name of the caller? Had she listened on the extension?

She had put her hand on his and begged, "We should close the pub for a month and go away—we don't need the money, Hanley."

But he tasted the money, savored the prospect of more. He longed for the time when he would have wealth in his pocket, extra money that she knew nothing about. Money that would not be recorded in the expense record or taxed by the government. Money that would guarantee him the chance to leave her forever.

Go away? Go away with her? Did she think that they would be safe by going away? Didier Bosman was not a man to be crossed. Now Hanley had discovered that Chip was part of the reunion at Somerset Estates, so Bosman had a man on the inside and boasted there were others. "Someone to keep an eye on Morrie Chadbourne."

Hanley worked out the truth after recognizing that arrogant voice on the other end of the phone. A theft had been planned right under his nose. All along, he credited the planning to Didier Bosman and Morrie Chadbourne. Now he had pinpointed the mastermind behind the Somerset robbery. He celebrated his discovery with a burst of uncontrollable laughter, suppressed with a schooner of beer. There were those—like Scotland Yard—who might pay for his knowledge. But old Hanley knew how to keep still. When to keep still. The adrenaline pumped through his body every time the phone call came. But he valued living, treasured keeping his knowledge under wraps until just the right time.

The sun reflected through the goblets on the shelf. He rearranged them and still the light caused shimmering pictures in his mind. He could pack tonight. Take some of the earnings from the week and fly to the Riviera. Stay in some hotel on the beach. Watch the sunbathers. Maybe find the courage to take his own oversized body into the warm water. He could still float. Still let the warm Mediterranean flow between his toes. How cheaply he had been bought—and how wealthy he could become. He would wait. Take pictures of the paintings in the shed. And someday—

He slung the wet towel over his shoulder and leaned against the shelves. His body trembled so that the crystal behind him rattled. No one was buying his silence. He chose to be silent for his own safety. He would keep the pub open long after midnight on Saturday as he had been ordered to do. That was all. That meant nineteen paintings would be stored in the sheds behind the shop. For how long? Maybe he could forget to unlock the sheds. Then Bosman and the others might head for the motorway to Manchester or London—and never come back to Hanley's Pub.

His thoughts raced back to his younger, thinner days when he could swim. That was how he met his wife on the beaches of France. For the first time in many years he needed her again. Needed the woman she once was when they were both young, and she the strong one, certain that he could make a go of the pub. He glanced down at his rotund belly, the white apron snugly around it. His hands too chubby, his jaws too fleshy. A fat man too heavy for his stature. His wife had not fared much better. But they had made a go of their pub—twenty years of making a go at it. Clients liked them. The locals came often. Two generations of customers. They had a thriving business. Everybody liked old Hanley. Everybody tolerated his wife for her cooking.

Their favorite guest was the American, Morrie Chadbourne. Hanley kept his friendship with Chadbourne under wraps. He wanted to warn Morrie of the danger, but not at the cost of his own safety. He prayed that the man would not come again, that he'd never park his bike behind old Hanley's pub again.

Hanley stood with his feet planted on the cold, stone-flagged floor, pain radiating through the calves of his legs, the clogged vessels kicking up a fuss again. He glanced toward the table by the window. The two men had been there for hours. When he refilled their coffees, he heard snatches of their conversation. Wakefield the one man had been called. And Inspector Farland, the one smelling of cigarettes. Scotland Yard sitting in the far corner of his pub, and Hanley felt trapped.

Now he stiffened even more. Coming through the front door was the lovely Professor McCully, walking sprightly, smiling at him. The empty goblet in his hand crashed to the stone floor as the two men at the table by the window rose to meet her.

Seventeen

By the third evening, a spirit of pretense hovered over the guests. They agreed on a formal dinner with candlelight and pre-dinner music and no open discussion on the missing paintings. Most of them had spent leisurely side trips to Ambleside and Derwent Waters. Now, in spite of the tensions over the thefts, they appeared an amicable lot as they gathered to listen to the music.

Eileen arrived first in a slim-fitting turquoise evening dress, the color of Becki's eyes. When she saw her name tag beside Morrie's, she quickly rearranged the place settings.

"Oh, Eileen," Rachel protested.

"It's best this way."

As the guests took their seats, Chandler played his mother's Stradivarius, a faraway look in his smoky-blue eyes as he tucked the high-glossed violin under his chin. Skillfully he glided the bow across the strings, filling the room with waltz music and ending with the lively notes of "The Blue Danube" waltz.

Sinclair held out his hands. "Dance with me, Rachel."

She went happily into his arms. Soon others joined them. Even Jude and Sean seemed lost in the music, and in spite of his bandaged hand, Kevin was light on his feet and more than content with Amanda's head on his shoulder.

"Mommy, dance with Morrie," Becki urged.

"Yes, dance with me," Morrie said.

When the waltz ended, they silently took their seats again, their faces flushed, the paintings truly forgotten.

Amanda had come in her Georgette gown, her lap computer in her hand. Now she slipped the laptop beneath the table and smiled apologetically at Rachel. "As soon as dinner is over, I'm going to finish designing an advertisement page on hideaway estates in Britain. Once my boss learns I'm staying at the Somerset Estates, he'll like my idea. Kevin has given me some graphic arts ideas; I'd so love to see him work at my advertisement agency."

"I thought Kevin was content with the job as an auditor."

She blushed. "Rachel, if we worked together, he'd be too—"

Kevin shot Rachel a lopsided grin. "Too busy for betting at the horse races. I can't convince her I'm a reformed man."

"You don't mind my bringing the computer to the table?"

What I mind is how blind you are to Kevin's love, she thought. *How tempted you are to mold him into your dead fiancé. Oh, Amanda, you have to learn to trust Kevin. Or lose him.* She smiled at Kevin, liking his boyish appearance, his sincerity.

"It won't do any good to argue with Amanda, Professor. That laptop is my biggest competition." He sounded bitter, but there was a gentleness as he held the chair for Amanda. Once she was seated, he leaned down and kissed her on the cheek. Rachel liked Kevin Nolan, but in just these few days she was well aware that the Reynoldses were watching him closely. But why? What had he done?

Even Sean had appeared at the last minute in a borrowed tuxedo, looking handsome and guarded. His churlish expression made his eyes seem even more shadowed. He stood in that familiar stance, one hand in a pocket, the other resting on Jude's shoulder. Rachel tried to catch Jude's eye, to reassure her, but Jude and Sean had their own agenda.

Sinclair took his place at the end of the table, opposite from her, and she was grateful for his presence, his strength. The loss of his wife and child had left deep ridges by his eyes, and he had a tightness around his mouth that she did not remember, but he looked more handsome than ever, his white dress shirt a direct contrast to his coppery skin. He smiled across the flickering candles—a brightness to his hooded brown eyes. Strands of silver had crept into his dark hair, but they only made him more distinguished.

Sinclair lifted the ornate dinner bell and rang it. Rachel's thoughts leaped back to Big Ben tolling. "Reverend Rainford-Simms agreed to have the meal with us—and offer a dinner prayer."

Charles, a cleric without a parish, stood like a gentle giant with a slight stoop to his shoulders. "Methinks," he said, eyes twinkling, "that it would be better to sing an old Welsh song." Promptly he began to sing in a deep, resonant voice.

Lord of the hills and lakes, bring peace and calm.
For friends beside us, all around us,
Let us offer You our hymn of praise.

An age tremor struck his voice midway, but he went on singing, his fingers tented, pensive. His eyes remained wide open, full of merriment with secrets of his own.

Oh, Lord of the hills,
We ask for hearts that see You everywhere.
We give Thee thanks.
We give Thee praise.

Rachel decided that the Very Reverend Rainford-Simms had made up the words as he sang them. But who could question his honest face? His sagelike appearance. He had sized up his divided company and had directed their attention toward the Lord of the hills. Whether her guests saw the hills would be an individual matter. Whether they found peace at this reunion would depend on what they did with the Lord of the hills.

"Are you my other grandfather?" Becki asked as the song ended and the food was passed.

211

Charles caught her eye as grandfathers do and said, "Perhaps we could talk about it after dinner."

The adults smothered their laughter. One eight-year-old bobbed her head. Happiness welled up in Rachel. The conversation passed easily at first, but then Jude challenged them with the Weinberger painting in the sitting room. "Morrie here tells me that the Weinberger is a stolen masterpiece."

Morrie's eyes smoldered. "I said, 'What if it were stolen from the Jews during the war?'"

Rachel glanced at Eileen and saw that she had retreated into silence. She sat, eyes downcast. Charles Rainford-Simms's voice boomed across the room to her. "Didn't you tell me that your father owned one of the Weinberger paintings, Dr. Rutledge?"

She barely lifted her eyes to meet his. "My grandfather has a very large collection; Weinberger's work is just one of them."

"Great-granddaddy doesn't like the Jews," Becki announced, her mouth full of sliced lamb.

"Hush, Rebecca."

"But it's true, Mommy. He told me that himself. He went to war. He was a soldier. And when he came home he hated the Jews."

"But we don't," Eileen assured her daughter.

Morrie's gaze searched the face of the child, and then her mother's. "Tell me, Dr. Rutledge, why did he keep such an expensive painting when Weinberger is a Jewish artist?"

"I don't share my grandfather's prejudices, Morris. And neither does my daughter. In fact—when I was in med school I went with a young man who had Jewish blood. But my grandfather destroyed our relationship."

Rachel felt the icy chill passing between Morrie and Eileen. She wanted to slap Morrie's hand, wanted to wrap her arms around Eileen. But what had Eileen said? *A young man who had Jewish blood.* She didn't identify him as Morrie.

Chandler Reynolds leaned forward. "My wife has made a study of the lost art from World War II."

"Much of it looted and destroyed when the Nazis took over."

"You're right, Morrie," Jillian said. "But even now, a number of good organizations are still searching for those missing masterpieces."

"How well I know! But they're turning them over to the Louvre and other museums around the world when they find them."

"Never intentionally." Jillian stared Morrie down, forcing him to lower his eyes. "Imagine how difficult it is to trace the original owners. Proving ownership is like fitting a jigsaw together, piece by piece. It's a painstaking search. So many of the victims died. There are no records to prove ownership."

Calmly Sinclair said, "The Rothchilds and Rosenbergs and Weinbergers were only three of the collections stolen in France during the war. The looting went on all over Europe. But it was that five-hundred-million-dollar jewel heist in London's Millennium Dome that sparked my own interest in studying art history."

Jillian flashed him a warm smile. "Then you do know that paintings by Rembrandt, Monet, van Gogh, and Vermeer were ripped from the walls of art collectors and private collections by the Third Reich? The whereabouts of works like Cezanne's *Snow Scene* is still unknown. But we'll go on searching."

Once disgruntled, Morrie could not shake it. "We know that wartime partnerships existed between neutral countries. Nazi depositors used money and art stolen from innocent victims. Strangers gained financially with other people's possessions. And still do. We know all of that, yet today the heirs are rebuffed by officials who fail to return these assets to rightful owners."

He turned his anger and frustration on Eileen. "I still want to know how that Weinberger painting found its way into your grandfather's private collection."

"My grandfather came by that painting honestly."

"Did he?"

Charles propped his elbows on the table. "Young man, do you think any of us in this room approve of stolen art? Not even the heart of a thief—should one exist."

"I'm not a thief," Becki declared.

Expressions around the table masked. Feet shuffled. Hands reached for half empty water goblets. Sinclair kept his eyes on Rachel, his lips sealed.

Rainford-Simms remained himself. "I'm glad you're not a thief, Becky. But it is the people behind those paintings that matter to me. Great artists. Collectors. Individual families who loved the masterpieces. And the twisted thinking of those who looted them. It's what happened to them that matters."

He tapped his chest. "What matters is what's going on inside of us. We cannot hang those paintings back on the walls, not sixty years after they were looted."

Morrie challenged him. "Charles, don't you understand? Nazi gold was stolen from slaughtered Jews. Billions in money and property never restored."

Charles looked from Morrie to the faces around the table. "I understand. But stealing another painting will not right the injustices already done."

He glanced at Jillian. "It is the same with art, is it not, Mrs. Reynolds? Someone has already stolen the Degas from the walls of this mansion. We must be on our guard. But what do we know about Weinberger? I think that is the painting that most concerns Morris."

"He could have been a great artist," Jillian said.

"But he died in Auschwitz," Morrie snapped.

She stared him down. "Some of Weinberger's work was destroyed. But according to you, some of his paintings are still out there. He just didn't live long enough to be well-known."

"Jillian, if that painting in the sitting room is a genuine Weinberger, what then?" Jude asked.

"Then we'd better treasure it."

"I rather think it would be fun to steal it."

"Jude," Rachel said.

214

"Oh, come on, Professor. You never could take a joke."

"Stealing is not a joke."

Jillian's soft voice took control again. "At least we get a glimpse of the heart of Asher Weinberger. He could have been a great artist. Could have known world acclaim. He didn't live long, but he lived long enough to paint his heart on canvas."

Audrey appeared from the kitchen carrying a tray of steaming plum pudding. She shuffled around the table, placing a china bowl in front of each guest. Last of all she put a small portion in front of Rachel and smiled. With that smile, Rachel knew that this woman's rough hands had painted her heart for all of them in the meal she had prepared.

"Thank you, Audrey," she whispered.

At the last bite of plum pudding, the guests began to excuse themselves, one by one, leaving half empty crystal goblets and sticky china bowls. Candles flickered. The stereo played softly. When the last guest left the room, Sinclair walked the length of the table to sit beside her. "Are you all right, Rachel?"

"The arguments about art and Nazi gold unnerved me."

"Why don't you take Eileen and Becki and go back to Wakefield Cottage before something awful happens?"

"And leave Audrey and my other guests?"

"The missing Degas was merely a warning. It won't stop there. Send the guests into Grasmere. Cancel this reunion."

"And disappoint Morrie? You don't like him, do you?"

"I believe him capable of anything. He's not the same light-hearted man who lectures with me. Whatever is going on in his life is related to that painting that's worth two or three mil."

"I think it's worth more than that to him." As her cheeks flushed, she started to rise. He cupped her hand. "Don't go."

"I should help Audrey clear up this mess."

"I arranged for additional help in the kitchen. Audrey will supervise. She's quite capable, you know."

He lifted the bell and shook it. When Audrey appeared, he said, "I'm trying to keep Rachel from tiring herself."

"Try putting a lid on an active volcano. It's just in her to work." Audrey gave Rachel an affectionate pat on the shoulder. "You have a full-time job just entertaining your guests."

"We plan an easy day tomorrow. Sinclair is taking our guests to Oxford for the day. And I'm taking Becki to Hill Top Farm."

Audrey blew out the candles. "Mr. Sinclair, you need to walk off that dinner. You two should catch some fresh air before evening sets in."

Rachel started to stand. Sinclair put his hand over hers again. "Don't go, Rachel. Stay here with me," he urged.

"But we should spend time with our guests."

"*Our* guests have things pretty much in hand."

She glanced out the wide window. Jude and Sean had separated from the others and were standing against the iron fence. Sara and Lydia sat on the stone bench watching the badminton game. Janet Tallard looked at peace with her world, her head thrown back in laughter, as she talked with Lenora. *High society and a pretty farm girl together.*

She searched, but Morrie and Eileen were not together. Would they ever be? "Sinclair, I look at all those students, and Janet is the most content. The same happy girl who sat in my classroom. The same young woman that I tried to counsel against dropping out of school to marry. And do you know what she told me?"

"I won't know until you tell me."

"She said all she ever wanted to be was a wife and mother."

A shadow clouded his eyes. "Mary was content like that. She made my life complete."

In a way I never could have done. "I wish Eileen and Morrie would get back together again. Did you see them dancing?"

"I was too busy watching you, Rachel. You can't force a couple back together. Becki, as dear as she is to you, is not your responsibility."

216

"In a way she is. What Becki wants more than anything else in the world—"

"Is for you to get well."

"More than that. She wants a daddy like her friends have. Eileen never told Morrie about Becki." She turned to face Sinclair and confided, "They met at the university and were married briefly and divorced. Actually, Eileen's grandfather had the wedding annulled."

"Don't meddle, Rachel. The child would only be hurt."

"Morrie is angry because he thinks Eileen bore a child out of wedlock."

"Then he doesn't think very highly of her!"

"It's a long story."

"I have all night," he said as Audrey scooped up the last stack of dishes. "We can turn on the electric log in the fireplace."

"You do that, Mister Sinclair," Audrey suggested. "Take Rachel into the drawing room, and I'll bring you some hot tea. And don't worry about Becki. I'll go for her soon and give her a bath."

"Tell her I'll be in to read to her."

She glanced at Sinclair. "Not tonight, Miss Rachel. I'll do the reading. You two just enjoy each other."

Moments later, Sinclair's eyes darkened as he pushed himself to his feet and stared down at the fireplace. "Rachel, I haven't been totally honest with you. I expected trouble at the reunion. That's why I'm here, but Inspector Farland and I were both surprised at how quickly the Degas and Monet were stolen."

"Morrie didn't take those paintings! I'm certain of it."

"But someone may attempt to steal more paintings while we are here. That's why Inspector Farland is keeping an eye on us."

"Is half of Scotland Yard here?"

"Several officers are mingling with the staff. They will be ready for anything."

"Then nothing will go wrong. Does Morrie know?"

"No. And he is not to know. Are you aware that Jillian Reynolds works for the Coventry Art Theft Registry?"

"Yes."

"Then you know that the registry is committed to recovering stolen masterpieces, no matter where they've been taken."

"Yes, Jillian has been sizing up the Weinberger. But why would Morrie invite them here?"

"You invited me."

"I'm glad you came. I needed you here."

He cocked his head at a rakish angle. "If you hadn't invited me, I would have invited myself."

The firm jaw relaxed into a smile. The lights in the room caught his rugged good looks. And for the tenth time since he stood at the gatepost at Stradbury Square and came up the walkway back into her life, she regretted breaking her promise. If she beat this cancer—if she went on living—she would never think of Big Ben or hear it chime again without aching inside.

"What are you thinking about, Rachel?"

"About the day we were to meet at Big Ben."

He took a step toward her. "Are you ready to tell me what happened? I waited there for you. A long time."

"I know. I watched you."

He took her hands. "Tell me what happened."

Behind them they heard the labored footsteps of Audrey coming with her tea. Rachel pulled free and smiled wanly. "I think this is the wrong time."

"But soon?"

"Soon," she promised.

Eighteen

As the ferry took them across the lake to the village of Sawrey, Rebecca's excitement mounted. "Oh, Rachel, I wish Beatrix Potter would be there today. I wished she hadn't died so soon."

Rachel smiled. "Shall we pretend she's there?"

"Mommy and Morrie will think we're foolish."

"Then we shall be foolish."

"Why did Morrie have to come with us?"

"To be with your mommy, I think. Do you mind his coming?"

"He's not much fun. I don't like him."

"Because he calls you Smidgen?"

"I don't call him names." She ran ahead for a moment and came back and slipped her hand in Rachel's.

The springtime fragrance of lilacs filled the air. Castle Cottage stood across the street. A few Herdwick sheep grazed in the meadows. Spruce trees grew in the woods. Rushes lined the edge of Esthwaite Water. Rachel pulled Becki back from the water's edge, but she broke free and ran through the rolling countryside, her feet trampling the wildflowers.

She went back and clutched Rachel's hand again. They half ran, searching for the sand bank where Flopsy, Mopsy, Cottontail, and Peter had lived. They discovered a big fir tree, but only a squirrel scampered for cover. They looked for the farm where Jemima Puddleduck lived and found instead a nest of robins. Crossing the stone bridge hunting for Jemima's woods, they found only fields of radishes, lettuce, and parsley. They hunted for rabbits, toads and mice. Rebecca wanted to find Squirrel Nutkin sailing on a raft and saw only a nightingale in the orchard.

"I wish Ribby the cat was still alive. And Tom Kitten and Samuel Whiskers and Pigland Bland," Rebecca mused.

"But they are. Remember, we're pretending. If we find Ribby the cat, Duchess the dog will be right behind."

"Mommy said Miss Potter married when she was middle-aged. So don't worry, Rachel. You can still marry Sinclair Wakefield."

"I'd have to wait for him to ask me."

"Mommy thinks he already asked you."

A long time ago, she thought.

Finally they went past the stone wall at the bottom of the garden, through the wicket gate. Rachel held tightly to Rebecca's hand as they went up the sloping path to the cottage. Hill Top Farm overlooked the village, keeping watch on a sprawling acreage of land. It was just as Beatrix had lived it, just as Rachel remembered it from her last trip, just as Rebecca dreamed it would be. Ahead of them lay Miss Potter's two-story house with a weather vane on the chimney and ivy vines growing up one wall. Pots of geraniums sat on the windowsill. Rhododendrons grew in the yard. The garden was filled with some of her favorite colors: pink foxgloves, yellow snapdragons, blue larkspurs.

Inside were the carved oak furniture and the stairs leading to the small cozy rooms on the second floor where Beatrix Potter wrote with her quill pen. Rebecca whispered that the pantry in the large kitchen surely held nibbles for the squirrels in the neighborhood; Rachel whispered that she smelled veal pie baking.

Together they pictured Beatrix Potter—a plump woman in her long tweed skirt sitting at her desk with a quill pen in hand and writing her animal stories. They pictured her going down the long, narrow stairs and putting on her wide-brimmed straw hat before lumbering along in her clogs out to her Herdwick sheep.

"Mommy said she had rheumatic fever when she was twenty."

"I'd forgotten that, Becki."

"Her hair came out in clumps—like yours did."

"I haven't forgotten that. Did you know, she had lively blue eyes like yours, Becki?"

Morrie and Eileen lagged behind them, but Rachel could hear them talking and knew it was not going well.

Moodily, Morrie said, "I should have gone to Stratford-upon-Avon with the others instead of coming to a kids' farm."

"Why didn't you, Morrie?" Eileen asked him.

Rachel heard the wretchedness in his voice, the longing. "I wanted to be with you, Eileen. Like old times. I thought the two of us could go off and spend the day together. Rachel and the Smidgen don't need our company."

"I'm not leaving. . . . Morrie, did you know Beatrix Potter died during World War II—she died just before Christmas."

"Did she now? Do you think Rachel will live to Christmas?"

"Of course. She's getting better."

He tried again. "Rachel is good with your daughter. I guess it's easy. She's such a happy little girl."

"Her father was that way a long time ago."

His voice cracked, cleared. "I have been wanting to find the courage to ask you. Who was he?"

"Rebecca's father? Surely you have guessed by now?"

Rachel felt her heart pounding and wondered whether Becki was listening too, and knew that she was. She heard sadness in Eileen's voice, and even though her words softened, Rachel heard her say, "Morrie, you are Rebecca's father."

As they went back through the side gate at the Somerset Estates, Eileen tugged at Becki's hand and dragged her away without a word. Before they reached the main house, Becki glanced back and gave an uncertain wave intended for her father.

Morrie toed the ground, his eyes downcast.

"She's your daughter, Morrie. Are you just going to let her walk away?" Rachel asked.

His jaw tightened. "A child I've never seen before drops into my life and—" He ran his hands despairingly through his thick hair. "Don't you understand, Rachel? It's too late. I'm a scholar, not a father. I wouldn't know what to do with a child."

"Give yourself a chance to know her. Let her know you."

"I'd be a disappointment, Rachel. You can see how I disappointed Eileen. Like Eileen told me this afternoon, I'm more interested in the Weinberger painting than in an eight-year-old that I never knew existed."

"So you are punishing Eileen?"

"She should have let me know. I had a right—"

"Did you leave a forwarding address or simply vanish?"

"That's what her grandfather wanted. I didn't measure up. If she wanted me to know about the child, she could have reached me through the alumni office."

"The child has a name, Morrie. Rebecca Lynne."

"My mother's name."

"So it's the past then? Not today. A war sixty years ago, not your child? Oh, Morrie, be careful what choices you make."

"What happened sixty years ago affected my life."

Your reason. Your feelings, she thought. "What happened just now will affect your daughter for the rest of her life. She's eight, Morrie. Vulnerable. Don't hurt her."

He started to walk away, and called back, "I don't want to hurt Rebecca. But tell Eileen it would be best if she packed up now and took her away."

"I won't do that—unless I leave with them."

"It would be safer for you as well."

"You're being destroyed by what happened sixty years ago."

He cracked his knuckles. "I'm being destroyed by what might happen this week. There's a tie-in with that war and Eileen's family. Eileen's grandfather was in the military, involved in the postwar art restitution. It seemed strange that I found one of those missing paintings hanging on his wall. And now the one in Somerset's possession. You can tell how he values it by the place he has given it in his home. The value I place on it."

"You don't really believe Becki is your child! You are more willing to believe that a painting belongs to you than your own child."

"I know for a fact that my family accumulated an art collection before Hitler came to power. In the case of Asher Weinberger, he was a distant relative; my family purchased many of his paintings along with works by Degas and Claude Monet and Cezanne. All looted from my great-grandmother's estate in Paris. Those facts I believe in. But to say that I'm a father? I don't have much time, Rachel. I only have the time left before Somerset gets back to prove that painting belongs to me."

"Do you plan to steal it?"

He looked smitten. "I didn't take the Monet or Degas."

"Someone did."

"I don't make much as a lecturer, but if I could own the Weinberger, I could sell it and send the money to Eileen."

She stared at him. Something he had wanted to possess for years, and he would sell it for Rebecca? "You'd do that for Becki? Is supporting her more important than knowing your child? Oh, Morris, what has become of the caring student I once knew?"

"An art historian I read about said he was tracing a thread back through time. That's what I'm doing. And I think that's what you're doing too. Tracing your own life span. You want to help Rebecca because she belongs to one of your students."

"To two of them. Your thoughts are evocative, Morrie. But not quite accurate. I know where I've been. What I've done.

223

Right now I want to know where the threads knotted. Where the tapestry was marred. Whether I can unravel some of the past and change the tapestry of my life. Or the lives of my students."

"Isn't that what I want to do? Prove that thread of ownership. Get some of these masterpieces back in the right hands. Provide for my—for my daughter. I call it righting a wrong. You call yours the tapestry of life."

"You've lost me."

"What I'm saying is we're no different, Rachel." He stomped off, angry with himself. Angry with her. Angry with the world.

Jude and Amanda passed Morrie on the walkway. "Is something wrong, Dr. McCully?" Amanda asked. "Mr. Chadbourne looked upset."

"That's how she affects people," Jude said.

"We were just discussing the tapestry of life." She smiled at them both, then said quietly to Jude, "I'm glad you came to the reunion."

"And I'm wondering why I came. I'm not part of your legacy, you know."

Amanda turned on her. "Don't talk to Professor McCully like that, Jude."

Amanda fell in step with Rachel, allowing Jude to saunter on ahead of them, sulking. "Professor, I'm sorry about Jude."

"She's not your problem. Do I dare tell you that I'm glad that you and Kevin are here?"

"We know. You didn't have to tell us. I've been wanting to talk to you alone—about Kevin and me. Do you think we'll have time on the cruise on Lake Windermere?"

"We'll make time, Amanda."

Eileen sat down at the desk in their room as Becki kicked off her shoes and flung herself on the bed. "I'm sorry, Rebecca."

"It's no big deal."

"You've wanted to know your father for so long."

"No big deal." She rolled on her stomach. "Did you bring me here to meet him?"

"No."

"Did Rachel?"

"I'm afraid so."

"Then I hate them both."

"You don't mean that. Not after you and Rachel had such a lovely time at Hill Top Farm. The two of you are the best of friends."

"She can't be my best friend and Morrie Chadbourne's friend too." She grabbed a book and buried her face in it.

Eileen had brought her black logbook to England with her, the one with weights and dosage charts, the one where she kept the diary pages about Rachel. She reached for it now and wrote: *Rebecca met her father today. And I may have lost my child . . .*

The tears kept her from writing more. She brushed them away and turned back to the notes she had written since arriving in England.

Sunday—May 26: Our first day in England: Timothy Whitesaul met us at Heathrow. Surprised us, I should say. I had forgotten how ruggedly attractive he is. How kind. He welcomed Rebecca as he would his own child. But then I had forgotten how involved he was in my pregnancy, how caring, never asking me who my child's father was. Never knowing that I had been married. And he was there when she was born—more father to her than Morrie would ever have been.

Monday morning—May 27: I am waiting for the bellboy to carry our luggage down to the car. Rebecca has gone off with Timothy to see the sidewalks of London, whatever that means.

Timothy surprised us by arriving at the Ritz for breakfast. He insisted on treating us before we left for Wakefield Cottage. I asked about Rachel. He is optimistic. He couldn't take his eyes from me at the table. I blushed like a schoolgirl and Rebecca asked me why my face was red. I remember that same look when Timothy held Rebecca in the delivery room, those wide eyes of his filled with love. He asked me again if I had given any thought to moving to England and becoming part of the Whitesaul Clinic. How blind I have been. Corresponding with him all these years. Enjoying the unexpected phone calls from him. Calling back to thank him for Rebecca's birthday presents, and Christmas presents, and just special-day presents. His invitation goes beyond cancer research. Without couching his desire into words, he is asking me to become part of his life, part of Rebecca's life. I am flattered, but is this what I really want?

Monday noon—May 27: Driving on the left side of the road is a challenge, especially on the motorway. I soon had my heeled foot to the pedal, and kept abreast of the wildest of drivers. Thankfully, Rebecca was absorbed with the countryside, the crowded towns, but even more with the expectation of seeing her friend Rachel again. I did not tell her that the car behind us was there for our protection, that the young man behind the wheel belonged to Scotland Yard.

Late Monday—May 27: What joy to see Rachel so happy in Wakefield Cottage. She is at home here. She is still much too thin, her once gorgeous complexion still sallow. But those eyes and that smile will never change. Seeing her now, I am confident that Timothy is right. Rachel will lick this battle with cancer. Or am I being selfish, not wanting my child to lose her friend? Not wanting to lose her myself. I feel like a student again—looking up to her professor. Learning from her.

Tuesday—May 28: Rachel has betrayed me and I am angry. This reunion that she plans is with Morrie Chadbourne. "I meant to tell you," she said. Had she told me, Rebecca and I would never have flown to England. I wanted to call Timothy Whitesaul and beg him to drive up here and take Rebecca and me back to Heathrow. That was my plan until I saw Rachel and Rebecca talking about going to Hill Top Farm. I won't take this dream from my child.

Sunday—June 2: Today I saw Morrie Chadbourne for the first time in nine years. I have never stopped loving him. Could he possibly feel the same about me?

Tuesday—June 4: Rachel amazes me. She is everywhere at once, the gracious hostess. Yesterday she walked across the grounds with Janet Tallard, arm in arm and laughing—as though they had secrets of their own. Of all the guests, Janet is the most at peace, the most calming on Rachel after her argument with Jude Alexander at breakfast. Is Jude capable of stealing the paintings? Does she dislike Dr. McCully that much?

Tuesday afternoon—June 4: Amanda Pennyman seems to be avoiding any time alone with Rachel ever since the name Lee passed between them. I suspect that she and Kevin are not married. That Amanda's past has been awakened by being here again. But knowing Rachel, she will find time to spend with Amanda. At least that is her plan. Time alone with each of her former students to encourage them—to leave another imprint on their lives. Kevin enjoys talking to Rachel—he talks about horses and she about the gardens here on the property.

Wednesday at breakfast—June 5: I saw it again today. Rachel's eyes light up whenever Sinclair Wakefield walks into the room. He is an attractive man. And I remember that day back in the clinic when I asked her whether there had ever been anyone special in her life. When I asked her why she never married and had children, she turned away with tears in her eyes. Could Sinclair be the reason for those tears?

Wednesday evening—June 5: Hill Top Farm. Becki could not have been happier. She and Rachel pretended the whole trip. Seeing rabbits and squirrels and imagining Beatrix Potter still tending her sheep. It would have been perfect if Morrie had not gone with us—for today he discovered that Rebecca is his child. What should have brought him joy left him staring at Becki. "You mean the Smidgen is mine, Eileen?"

⁓

Eileen closed her logbook where she had made her Hill Top entry. She brushed the burning tears from her eyes, forced a smile on her face and steeled herself against the pain inside. The pain that Becki must surely be feeling.

"Rebecca," she said cheerfully, "let's—"

But Becki was gone.

Nineteen

Becki wanted the pain and hurt to go away. She didn't like Morrie Chadbourne. She didn't like him one bit. Her tummy felt like it did when she got sick. Her cheeks felt hot, like they did when she had a fever and her mother stayed home from the hospital to take care of her. She squirmed for several minutes before she rolled over on her stomach. Her eyes kept filling with tears as she propped herself on her elbows and balanced her book on the pillow.

Today had been the best day of her life. Today had been the worst day of her life. Hill Top Farm with Rachel—that was the best part. When they walked toward the meadows in the village of Sawrey, Rachel promised that she would get well.

Rachel loved animals as much as Becki did. That's what she liked about her. "I never had an animal," Becki had confided, leaning against the fence.

"Neither did I, Becki. My sister was ill all her life. She had trouble breathing, so we could never have animals in the house."

But they had a host of imaginary animals at Hill Top Farm. And live ones too. The sheep grazing. The cat scampering across their path. The squirrel in the hedge on the stony path up to Beatrix Potter's Cottage. Right now Becki would like to sit on the sandbank and maybe cry a little. Maybe cry a whole lot.

Becki wished now that Rachel had let her fall into the Esthwaite Water on their trip today. She'd be gone now, not hurting like this. She wanted to be Squirrel Nutkin sailing away on a raft so that no one would ever find her again. She risked another side glance at her mother, the moment stolen between pages from the book she was reading. *No big deal,* she had said.

But that had been a lie. It stung more than when she had skinned her ankle on the playground. It hurt more than those times when her classmates teased her about the daddy who was never there. It made her sadder than when Great-granddaddy shouted about the man who ran out on her mother.

"So where is your daddy?" the kids would ask her.

And that smarty pants Emily, saying, "I bet you never had a father. That's what my mother thinks."

"Oh, he's away. He'll be back someday."

She had come up with wonderful excuses, pretending as she had done all day today at Hill Top Farm. Excuses like, "My father is on a secret mission for the president." Or, "My father is an army general. He'll come home when the war is over."

No one thought to ask her, "What war?"

Great-granddaddy said there was always a war, people killing each other for no reason. He didn't like anybody outside his country either. And he always seemed unhappy about the blood that ran in her veins.

The lump in her throat was familiar. Usually it came when she was mad at her classmates, peeved at the sitter, or just plumb annoyed with her great-granddaddy. Her eyes ached from fighting back the tears. She wouldn't let her mom see her cry. Not over Morrie Chadbourne. When she was naughty or slow to obey, her mother told her, "You are just like your father. Good looking. Smart as a whip like he is. And stubborn and proud."

Rebecca thought about that. Morrie was tall. He knew a lot about art and books. He always won at badminton—she liked sitting out on the bench watching him. The other guests liked him, especially Jude and Rachel. And he really liked that dumb painting in the drawing room. He liked it better than he liked her. He called the painting a masterpiece; he called her Smidgen.

Just a week ago she had wanted to be like her father because the imaginary father was perfect. But not the real father. She liked Sinclair Wakefield so much better than Morrie. Sinclair was kind to her and told her about his son Blake. Sinclair still loved Blake, the way she wanted her daddy to love her. And Kevin Nolan talked to her about horses and called her by her proper name. "Stay in England long enough, Rebecca, and Amanda and I will teach you to ride one of our favorite stallions."

Of all the people in England, Becki liked Timothy Whitesaul the best because he always sent her presents. The next time the kids at school asked her about her father, she would tell them that he was a famous doctor who lived in England and was fighting cancer. She thought about Chaplain Wong and decided that his children were lucky because he missed them all the time; she liked it when he told her about Jesus loving children. Morrie Chadbourne didn't seem to know anything about loving anyone.

Now what she had longed for all of her life—finding her father—turned out to be the worst day of her life. She stole another glance at her mother, who was still leaning over her black logbook. Wet tissues lay on the desktop. Her mom reached for another tissue. Then she started writing again, a fountain pen clutched in her hand, the one she called her lucky pen because Timothy Whitesaul had sent it to her from England.

The Secret Garden caught Becki's attention again. She longed for a secret garden of her own with friends to hide away with. She was angry at Rachel for being Morrie's friend. Hill Top Farm had been such a wonderful day of pretending.

All of that turned into the worst day of her life when her mother's words thundered in her ears. *"Morrie, you are Rebecca's father."*

The man who called her Smidgen.

She had dreamed of meeting her daddy one day, always picturing him as someone strong and brave. Someone handsomer than any of the dads she knew. He would come back into her life and say, "I'm here . . . for always."

Sometimes she talked to her imaginary, perfect dad. And told him secrets. And made up stories about what they would say to each other. But Morrie Chadbourne didn't want to talk to her. He didn't want her to be his daughter.

Mommy seldom talked about her daddy and never in front of Great-grandpa. He called him the miserable scoundrel. That always made Mommy cry. Suddenly, Rebecca felt very angry at the miserable scoundrel. Without a word, she pushed herself to her feet and ran into the adjoining bathroom. She flushed the toilet, and turned on the faucet. Splashing her face with cold water, she felt hot tears merge with the water. She grabbed a towel—Rachel's towel she thought—and wiped her face dry. Dropping the towel on the sink, she peered into Rachel's room. Rachel was gone.

Quietly she went through the room, out Rachel's door, and down the long, curving stairway. The balustrade no longer looked like a marvelous slide. Nothing mattered except finding her father and telling him she hated him for making her mom cry. *A Smidgen, am I? I'm sure that's better than being a scoundrel.*

She wandered through the empty hallway into the kitchen. Audrey dropped the potato peeler and opened her arms wide. Becki flew into them.

"There, there, child." She wiped Becki's tears with her apron. "What's wrong?"

"I have to find Mr. Chadbourne."

"From the looks of you, I wouldn't want to be in his shoes. So why don't you tell old Audrey all about it?"

"I can't right now. Mommy always says we talk to the person who makes us mad first. Then we won't tattle to others."

"Wise, that mother of yours. Do you want some scones and milk first? Then you can get your thoughts together."

"If you please, I'll come back for the scones and milk. I have to see Mr. Chadbourne first."

Audrey glanced at the wall clock. "All right. Off you go then." She put two cookies in Becki's hand. "One for you and one for Morris." Her eyes twinkled. "A peace offering. He should be out in his cottage right now. Should I call him and check?"

"No, I want to surprise him."

With a quick hug, Audrey let her go. Once outside, Becki ran toward the back of the property, not even stopping to pick one of the flowers that she loved. She was racing past the first guest cottage when Charles called out to her. "Good morning, little one. Where are you going in such a hurry?"

I'm not a little one, she thought. *I'm not a smidgen.* "I'm Rebecca Lynne Rutledge and I'm looking for my father."

He tented his fingers to his lips. "I see. That is an important mission. But you won't find him at the cottage."

"Audrey said he was there."

He shook his head. "I know for a fact that he went out to the toolshed about thirty minutes ago. Would you like me to go with you? The shed is kind of a creepy old place."

She considered his offer, some of her bravado wearing thin. "No," she said politely. "I want to talk to him by myself."

The door to the shed creaked as she pushed it open. A stale, musty smell hit her nostrils. The room was much bigger than she expected, but it was dark inside, with one lightbulb dangling from the ceiling. Shovels and garden hoes hung on hooks on each side of the room.

"Morrie," she called.

No answer.

She walked in slowly. The door slammed behind her sending a cold breeze across her bare legs. It took a minute before she could force her feet to keep moving. She crossed to the end of the room and found a staircase leading down toward a cellar.

A heavier door blocked her entry. She tugged at it and finally opened it wide enough to slip in. Here the corridor was lit much brighter. She tried to call Morrie's name again, but managed only a squeak. The corridor branched off into several tunnels, a basement playground. It was cold here, and very dark. She listened and then walked toward the sound of a phone ringing.

Closed doors lay on one side of the tunnel. Seeing another light toward the middle of the hallway, she followed it, running her hand along the damp wall so she would not stumble. She felt terrified that she had come this far without Charles. She wanted to run back and find him when her father stepped into the hall and said, "What are you doing here?"

Morrie stared down at his daughter, feeling as cold and empty as the corridor in which he was standing. She looked small and vulnerable, yet her chin stuck out defiantly.

"What are you doing here, Smidgen?"

"Looking for you."

He pointed to the door he had come from. "Come in then. In here. We need to keep the door closed. This is a temperature-controlled room."

She shivered as she stepped inside. "You don't seem surprised to see me."

"Not really. Charles called and said you were on your way."

"I heard the phone ringing. That's how I found you. It's scary down here."

"That's why we don't invite people down. But now that you're here, look around. These are the chambers where Lord Somerset keeps his extra paintings and the ones not catalogued as yet."

He felt hopelessly unable to strike up a conversation with a child. What did he know about what children liked? He knew nothing about this child. Not her birthdate. Not her favorite colors or what grade she was in. Finally he mumbled, "Did you enjoy the trip to Hill Top Farm today?"

234

"Yes—until I found out you were my father."

"I was just as surprised as you were."

Her lip quivered. "Are you really my father?"

"That's what your mother says."

"She never tells a lie. . . . You made her cry."

"I didn't mean to. Go back to your room, and don't tell anyone you followed me here."

"Audrey knows. And Charles told me you came in here."

"Good. Announce it to the world. So what do you want?"

She was a plucky sort. "I want to know why you dislike me so. I always dreamed my daddy would be a nice man."

He choked at the thought of shattering her dreams. "I never dreamed about you. I never knew you existed until today."

"Don't you like my mommy?"

The kid could hold her own, the way he used to debate in school, winning verbal wars, throwing his knowledge about as a weapon. As a cry for acceptance. *Like* Eileen? Always.

"I loved your mother from the day I met her."

She frowned. "Great-granddaddy says you had a funny way of showing your love."

"So he's still alive?"

"Mommy says he's too mean to die."

"Do you believe that?"

She shrugged. "I like him. I think he's a nice old man, but not as nice as Charles."

"Maybe you and your great-granddad are two of a kind."

"No, Mommy says I'm like you—like my daddy. But I would never run away from Mommy. So why did you run away?"

He could think of a hundred reasons, but only the truth mattered to this child. "Your great-grandpa sent me away."

"He said you could never afford to take care of my mom."

"Well, she won't have to worry. She'll be a rich woman when he dies."

"No," she said matter-of-factly. "I'll be rich. He's leaving all his money to me." She seemed to be crooking her neck looking up at him. "I don't care if he does or not. Money hasn't made him happy. Besides, he might spend it all before he dies."

He raged. "He's leaving nothing to Eileen?"

"Just a dumb painting."

"The one in his living room?"

"You know about that?"

"It's a long story."

She was looking around the room again with those curious blue eyes of hers. She cocked her head to stare into the vault, then ran her wrist over the pile of soft cloth used to protect the paintings. A quizzical frown arced her brows as she looked at the metal container that stood like an oversized briefcase—leaning with the Degas painting against the table leg.

"I think that's one of the stolen paintings," she said. "So where is the other one?"

"I don't know, but I assure you, Smidgen, I didn't take it."

"I know. But I saw who did."

He lunged for her and grabbed her arms. "What are you talking about?"

Her fist tightened. "I saw the man who took the painting."

A man. So a man had stolen it. What kind of lies did this child tell? "Don't say anything like that."

"But I did see him with my own eyes. I woke up when it was still dark out. I went downstairs by myself."

"You expect me to believe that?"

"I'm used to visiting my great-granddad in a big old house. So I wasn't afraid to go downstairs alone. I was in the drawing room when I heard the man coming—so I hid behind the drapes."

He shook her, not violently, but born of the fear inside him for the safety of this child of his. "Don't tell anyone what you just told me. Don't tell your mother. Don't tell Rachel—"

"You're the first person I told. I saw the man, and I saw him go out the doors with that metal box in his hands." She pointed. "That metal box right there."

"Out through the French doors?"

"I don't know what kind of doors they are. He just pushed them open and went out."

"You're wrong. You have to be wrong."

Fear clouded her face. "I don't like you. You don't want to be my daddy. You don't even believe me when I tell you the truth."

With forced unkindness he said, "My life is too busy for a child's vivid imagination." He was being deliberately cruel, desperate to protect this child of his. "I want you to go back to the main house. I wouldn't mention this visit to your mother. It would just upset her to know you had been down in these tunnels." His voice cracked. His fist doubled against his weakness. "Eileen is always careful to protect you. She's a good mother. Now go before I send you packing."

She flung one of the crushed cookies at him and ran, her footsteps echoing in the hollow corridor. Morrie did not follow, but stood in the tunnel blindly watching her go. But it was all right. Charles would be waiting for her at the top of the stairs.

~

"That was quite a touching scene."

Morrie did a double take as Sean Larkins stepped from the inner vault, a teacup in his hands. Larkins eyed the Degas. "The child said she knows who took the painting. I am sorry to hear that, Morrie."

"She's just a child. She has a wild imagination. You should have seen her at Hill Top Farm today."

"You went with her?"

"I'm her father."

"You amaze me, Morrie. You have endless surprises up your sleeve."

You can't even begin to imagine what surprises I have for you and Bosman before this reunion ends. He would be glad to see Scotland Yard cuff them and lead them away.

"What are you doing down here, Chip?"

"Checking the place out, tagging a few more paintings Bosman may want to collect. If he doesn't want them, I do. By the way, Morris, I suggest that you stop calling me Chip at this reunion."

"It's the name I know you by."

"My name is Sean Larkins."

"I know that now—your name as Irish as your fake brogue."

"I am Irish, third generation back. It gave me an in with the rugby team."

"You made a good name for yourself on the team."

"That I did. I'm still negotiating a new contract so I can play professionally again."

"I would think a famous name would be good enough for you. Why get yourself messed up with Didier Bosman?"

"I'm like you, Morris. Greedy for both fame and fortune." He looked around at the uncatalogued paintings. "It seems to me that it would be a simple matter to remove one or more of these magnificent paintings from the vault and go undetected for some time. Long enough to market them. If Bosman is not interested, I am. What say we work on this together?"

"You're forgetting the elaborate alarm system we have here."

Larkins flashed a cocky grin. "How effective a robbery can be when it's far removed from a major city!"

"You're forgetting our staff is well-trained, efficient."

"Would you raise the battle cry with cooks and gardeners? Or did you bring a special detail from Scotland Yard for this unique gathering?"

"I should have thought of that."

His cocky grin remained. "Maybe someone did. But don't forget. Make certain that alarm system is off Saturday night."

"Saturday then?"

"That's right. The robbery is set for Saturday. By the way, is Kevin Nolan's room the first or second door on the left?"

"What do you want with Nolan?"

238

"It's payback time. We have a surprise for him. He lucked out at the bombing near Harrods. If he hadn't stopped and gone shopping for his girl, he would have been by the art shop when the bomb went off."

"You and Bosman were involved in that? Kevin was the intended victim? You are mad, Chip. An innocent clerk was killed that day."

"Plans are sometimes costly," he said.

"What about Jude Alexander? How did you rake her in?"

"You told me you wouldn't invite her. I had to work around that invitation myself. I make a dandy escort, don't you think?"

"Is the girl involved, Chip?"

"She pleases me. I find her most attractive and useful. She dislikes McCully enough to do anything we ask. All that points in her favor."

Larkins put the teacup on a shelf. "I am delighted to know your daughter, Morris. For the child's safety, I suggest that you keep her from announcing to others that she observed a robbery. I'll see you at dinner . . . and don't forget. Have the decks in the main house cleared by midnight Saturday. Bosman and the truck will be here around one."

He sauntered off and was whistling as he reached the stairs.

Morrie stared at the metal container with the Degas painting leaning against it. He wondered where the Monet had been hidden. Wondered who had taken it.

But Rebecca was more important than the paintings. Rebecca, his child! Yesterday he did not care what happened to her. Now, her safety was in his hands. With a despair he couldn't control, he kicked at the Degas painting and left an irreversible tear in the canvas, cutting its value from four million to two.

Twenty

Rachel stood stock-still, motionless by the French windows that overlooked the lovely gardens. The Somerset house lay quiet all around her, a strange stillness echoing in its vastness. The house seemed undisturbed—the morning mute, all noise suspended in the vaulted ceilings above her. Though she strained to hear, she heard not even the muffled sounds of the staff in the kitchen. Even the wind sent no whispers across the corridor. She wanted to hear the whimper of a voice. A murmur behind one of the closed doors upstairs. The rustle of the leaves in the gardens. The swish of a maple leaf tumbling to the ground.

She wanted last evening back with Sinclair whispering old promises as he blew a breath across the tip of her ear, stirring old memories. Old longings.

She thought back to those marvelous camping days in the woods back home, to her contentment before cancer, before chemo and her hair coming out in clumps, before her move to England. She had loved the quietness of an early morning in the woods. The awakening of birds. The canopy of the sky, with moss and fallen leaves for the carpet beneath her feet. She liked the memory of a rucksack on her back as she started up the mountain. The water cascading over the cliff. A tossed rock rippling the water. The smell of the pines and wildflowers. The feel of her boundless energy going higher. What had happened to all of that? Tomorrow she would be thirty-eight, not old in the sequence of time, but her body, struggling to regain its old strength, would not be able to scale the smallest fells. And never Scafell Pike as the rest of her guests would do on Saturday morning. Today, the guests were left to find their own excitement. She was left to spend the day alone. They had made it five days into the reunion with two paintings missing, one attempt to remove another one, and Morrie stirring a ruckus when he found the Desmond vases sitting on either side of the fireplace in the drawing room. But perhaps, the major threat was over. Perhaps the fears had been imaginary and Scotland Yard needlessly concerned.

Opening the French windows, she had a better view of Chaplain Wong. He was sitting alone with his back braced against one of the landscape boulders, a writing pad on his knee. She smiled to herself, remembering him as the class joker with a quick laugh and a love for poetry. He still had his quick wit, but poetry had taken second place to his two sons. Back on campus, would she have guessed him destined for the chaplaincy and fatherhood?

And where were the others this morning? Kevin and Amanda had gone off to browse through the Windermere Steamboat Museum on the banks of Lake Windermere. The women traveling on their own had taken a picnic down by the lake. Jude and Sean had escaped to the hills above the Somerset property, and even now could be seen off to her left in what could only be described as the beginnings of an argument. Eileen and Rebecca took off without her this morning and were walking in the gardens. But were they aware they were walking in the direction of Morrie's cottage?

Rachel turned from the window and went wearily up the great curving staircase. What she had meant for good had backfired. The differences between Eileen and Morrie kept escalating, trapping Rebecca between them. And she, Rachel McCully, had expected the miracle of reconciliation by bringing them together. Timothy Whitesaul's arrival this evening would light the fuse even more.

Rachel paused at the top of the steps. She had ventured little on the upper floors of the mansion, staying mostly to her own elegantly furnished bedroom at the top of the stairs. Now, she strolled toward the end of the hallway—past Lydia and Sara's room, beyond the room that Lenora and Janet were sharing.

At the end of the corridor, Rachel discovered double doors in an arched alcove near Jude's room. They led her into a smaller hall with a spiraling staircase at the far end where a skylight flooded the stairwell with sun. The sound of organ music reached her. She started up the stone-flagged steps and paused to listen again. Following the notes to a landing, she saw a sign that read *Somerset Chapel.*

From all she had heard, Lord Somerset was not a man given to religion. Whatever he did seemed only to magnify his wealth and position. Inside the chapel, she saw Sinclair sitting at the organ, his back to her. Not wanting to disturb him, she slipped into a pew and took in the magnificence of the carved, vaulted ceiling and the stained-glass windows. The chapel was a miniature cathedral patterned in the shape of a cross with the organ at one transept, the baptistery at the other, and a semicircular apse with a highly carved pulpit and a cross that was at least eight feet high. Somerset had spared no money in this chapel, but for what purpose? There was the damp, musty smell of a room seldom used and a faint coat of dust along the top of the highback cushioned pews.

She realized that this was the high spot on the mansion, the oblong-shaped building that she had viewed from the gardens. The turrets and towers on the corners of the building intrigued her, the spire on the roof puzzled her. Now she knew it rose above the chapel. Had Somerset built this sanctuary to please his wife? Or his own ego? Did Charles even know it existed, or had he been brought onto the property as Lord Somerset's personal priest?

Her mind raced. The guests had agreed to spend Sunday sharing the great writings of the poets of the Lake District.

In the early afternoon, they would gather on the stone benches and feast on the picnic prepared by Audrey and cheer the ongoing men's competition on the badminton court. With Rachel's discovery of the Somerset Chapel, they could really make it a proper Sunday. She would ask Sinclair to play the organ, Chandler to play his violin again, Lenora to sing. Perhaps "Ave Maria," since that was her favorite. And Charles, the man banished to the North Country, could stand behind a pulpit, and Chaplain Wong could offer the benediction.

The organ music stopped. Sinclair turned and discovered her sitting there. "Rachel, I thought I was alone."

"Don't stop playing on my account."

He grinned. "My playing leaves a lot to the imagination."

"I didn't know you played."

He came down the aisle and sat beside her. "Mary tried to teach me a song or two."

"Sinclair, I have a plan for Sunday."

"Do you now?"

And so she told him. He nodded in agreement. "But Chaplain Wong and Miss Silverman are leaving early Saturday morning before the Scafell hike. One of Inspector Farland's men is driving them into Heathrow."

"I'd forgotten in the excitement. That means Lenora is going back to being Cho-Cho-San in *Madame Butterfly*."

"And Wong is heading back to his post in the Gulf."

"You liked them, didn't you, Sinclair?"

"Especially Wong. He makes good company. But you need to know, Inspector Farland intends to have their luggage thoroughly inspected at Heathrow."

"That's awful."

"That's necessary. He wants their forwarding addresses."

"Try Rome and the army."

He smiled. "Don't be offended. I'd rather they be cleared that way, wouldn't you? Neither Farland nor I expect any problem for Wong or Miss Silverman. It's a safeguard really."

"Then why all the fuss?"

"There will be a reckoning day when Lord Somerset gets back and finds paintings worth millions missing. We're personal friends—I should have told you, but I was backed against a retaining wall. I wanted to be at the reunion with you. But I promised Somerset I would be here to watch over his art collection."

"A heart divided," she said. "What is Somerset like?"

"James? He's very wealthy, of course, protective of his art collection. Less protective of his wife, Agnes—although he provides for her liberally and would be lost without her."

She turned to a safer topic. "Why did you come up here?"

"I was looking for the missing paintings."

"Sinclair, you shouldn't wander off alone like that."

He laughed. "And what brought you up to the chapel?"

"Curiosity."

"Mine went wild too. I can't believe those paintings left the property. How could they, do you think?"

"What about the garden supply truck that came on the grounds the morning after we arrived? And Audrey tells me there have been two food deliveries."

He slapped his forehead with his broad hand. "The garden truck! That's how Inspector Farland brought in his men. Of course, two paintings could go out the same way."

"But it doesn't make sense. We've been gone for hours each day, plenty of time for someone to break in. Why not rob the mansion when it's empty? Why fill it up with so many guests?"

He scowled severely. "Because one of your guests may be involved. Or—and I've mulled this over in my sleep—one of the guests may be planted here deliberately, in an act of vengeance."

She shuddered. "That kind of thinking points back to—"

He touched her lips, a sadness suddenly touching his expression. "Whatever happens, a friend may be involved. Your friend or mine."

She allowed his comforting caress. "I wish we had canceled this reunion."

Gently he pulled away, cupped her chin, looked down into her face. "That's like wishing away our chance to know each other again. That's what is important to me right now. But as far as I'm concerned, you pulled it off, Rachel. Your guests seem happy. You're holding up—I hope Timothy thinks so when he sees you. I asked him to join us when we climb the fells on Saturday."

"Don't let anything happen to you, Sinclair."

"I won't. That's why I asked Timothy to join us. I think it wise to have a doctor along. He's an excellent climber as well."

"You are expecting trouble on the mountain?"

"Aren't you? I'm just sorry you can't take the climb with us. You love climbing. You won't mind being left here alone?"

"Audrey will be here with her pots and pans to defend me. And surely Eileen won't take Becki on a climb like that. Don't worry. It's the art collection that's in danger. Not me. I still think everything is going to be all right. Maybe Inspector Farland has wasted his time sending men here."

"Wasted?" he challenged. "Someone did take those paintings."

"But nothing horrible as I expected. No gang of thieves breaking in on us."

"Rachel, anyone who knows our schedule so far knows that we will be gone on Friday and Saturday. I think I should stay here when you take the Lake Windermere cruise tomorrow."

She clasped his hand. "No, I want you there with me."

He sighed, expelling the air from his lungs. "Are you up to talking about Morrie, as in where did he go this morning?"

She pushed her fears aside. "He went off on his bicycle quite early. The Reynoldses left right after that. I'm certain they weren't together. I don't think Morrie really wants to face Eileen and Becki again this morning. The child is really upset."

"Perhaps that was just an excuse."

"Now, you're trying to worry me again."

245

"Morrie and Sean Larkins are obviously at odds. And Sean and his girlfriend Jude are not the adoring couple that he wants us to believe. . . . What kind of a student was he, Rachel?"

"Sean? He was never my student."

"What? He told me he took your Chaucer class."

"And I told him I never taught Chaucer."

He squeezed her hand. "Sean is looking for an excuse to avoid the climb on Saturday, but I want him where I can keep my eye on him. You're not to be here alone with him on Saturday."

"Inspector Farland's orders?"

"No, mine."

The sun shining through the stained-glass windows formed its own shadowed reflection on Sinclair's handsome face. She wanted to talk about them, to forget everything else. "It has been a strange reunion," she said. "Will any good come out of it?"

"Haven't you discovered your answers yet? I've watched you these last few days, and I'm convinced that as a teacher you left a deep impression on your students."

"Sinclair, did you know I never intended to be a teacher?"

"You didn't?"

"Being a university professor was my sister's goal. Apart from Larea, I would have left the great books of literature on the shelf in my parents' study. But Larea was ill, and I would read to her for hours at a time. The Brontë sisters and Milton. George Eliot. Dickens. Thackery. We'd laugh about the styles and the way people talked in the Victorian period. We spent so much time reading together that I started loving literature."

His somber eyes grew serious. "What did you want to do?"

She squinted as she glanced up at the windows. "Honestly?"

"Honestly."

"I wanted to climb mountains. Swim rivers. Win Olympic medals. Be famous in the sports world. I didn't want to follow the McCully tradition at the university."

"In my year on campus with you, I envied your popularity with the students. To me, you were a born teacher. What changed your mind about the mountains and rivers and medals?"

"My sister's illness . . . her death."

Their eyes locked. "I could never get you to talk about her."

"When I do, the pain seems raw again."

"Rachel, no one knows we're up here in the chapel. We can stay here the rest of the day if we have to. There are no demands on our time. It seems a good place to talk about what happened. I've waited a long time for some answers."

"Big Ben?" she whispered.

"You told me it no longer mattered. It does to me, Rachel."

She managed to get her words beyond the lump in her throat. "You wanted children; I didn't. It is as simple as that."

"I don't believe that. You adore children. I've watched you with Rebecca. You would have made such a wonderful mother."

She shook her head. "I decided against children long before I met you. I could never bring myself to tell you why, not when being a father was so important to you. I planned to tell you the truth when we met under Big Ben. . . . Do you remember telling me that Blake had cystic fibrosis?"

She watched his expression change from firmness to bewilderment. From confusion to understanding. "Not meeting me under Big Ben—it has something to do with cystic fibrosis?"

"It ran in my family too."

"What? You should have told me."

"My sister died from complications from that miserable disease. I could have been a carrier—"

"We could have talked about it."

"You would have tried to convince me that it didn't matter. It did to me, Sinclair."

"Genetic defects should have mattered to me too," he said. "But I wanted a son so desperately that I risked being

247

a father. Blake suffered from that. After that, Mary and I decided against more children. Rachel . . . I want to know more about your sister."

She nodded and found her voice. "It was a terrible struggle growing up with a sick sibling. Even at the university, few people knew what was going on. Mother considered Larea's illness a private affair. Mother didn't intend for it to become a shameful matter for me, but I decided it was my fault. I felt guilty that I was well and Larea wasn't. So I started spending long hours reading to her. I knew she would never be well enough to follow her dream. We both tried to protect our parents—pretending that Larea would get well."

"You tucked all of that inside?"

"I was younger, but I was the strong one—off skiing and climbing and swimming. And she wanted to know all about it. We spent hours on her bed just talking. We were great friends."

"She certainly changed your life."

"I hated losing her, but my sister never lost hope. She believed she would one day be well enough to run and climb and teach. She was determined to carry on the family tradition and make it a third generation of McCully teachers on campus."

"Is that why you took up her dream?"

"Partly."

"Did you ever qualify for an Olympic team?"

"Yes, I did. I'd been away for a week at one of our training bases. When I got home from skiing, I burst into the house, anxious to share my time with Larea—she lived for those times. I can still remember crying out, 'Larea, I'm home.'"

He slipped his arm around the back of the chapel pew, barely touching her shoulders. She felt comforted by his nearness. "I kept shouting, and there was no answer. I started up the steps and saw my mother at the top of the stairs leaning over the banister. 'Your sister is dead, Rachel. And if you had been home two days ago, like you promised, you would have been here in time.'"

He stiffened. "What a cruel way to tell you."

"Mother was hurting. Devastated. I ran up the stairs and brushed past her into Larea's room—and it was empty."

"And right then you gave up your own plans?"

"Circumstances changed my plans. By the time the funeral was over, I had missed the ski camp and the chance for the team. Back then the games were every four years. By then I could have my university degree in English, and that's what I did. If it hadn't been for Larea's love of literature, I would never have found my way down the mountain slopes into the classroom."

"She really influenced your life, didn't she?"

Her words came slowly. "Larea could rarely attend church and never climbed mountains. She thrived on good books and music and taught me so much about life and God from the limitations of her own room. And sometimes from her hospital bed."

"I grew up alone, the only child. At least, as a growing lad, I didn't have to lose someone as close as your sister."

You lost Mary and Blake, she thought.

"I hope being a teacher pleased your parents."

"It pleased me. I found I was good at teaching. I figured I'd spend fifteen or twenty years in the classroom and then start traveling and seeing and doing some of the things I dreamed of doing. . . . Then, a year ago, I was diagnosed with leukemia."

"Tell me, did Larea's illness and death have something to do with not meeting me at Big Ben?"

Sitting in the quiet of the Somerset Chapel, Rachel pictured the Parliament buildings glimmering as they had done that day. She recalled Big Ben ringing out the hour from the Clock Tower. She had stood there, watching him, crying, and then caught a boat up the Thames past the Parliament buildings. Big Ben had cried out in resonant tones again. She could almost feel the spray of the Thames on her face as she had felt it that day.

No, a tear was stealing down her cheek.

"Sinclair, I was going to tell you I couldn't marry you."

"Were you going to tell me why?"

"No. It sounded so cold to say I wouldn't marry you because I didn't want to take defective genes into my marriage. I wouldn't bear you any children. Whenever you told me you wanted children, I would go home and cry myself to sleep."

She reached out and straightened his crooked tie as he said, "We missed so much time, didn't we? And yet, if you hadn't walked out of my life, I would never have known Mary. I've been very fortunate. I have loved two women . . . Rachel, I'm still in love with you."

"I'm a poor risk. This leukemia—I can't make any promises."

"I'm willing to take the risk."

"Sinclair, you haven't been listening to me. It's too late now. I'm a health risk. A remission will only buy me time."

His eyes turned brilliant as he slid closer to her. His arms tightened around her. "I've been listening to my heart. Rachel, I am still in love with you," he repeated. He went on happily, "This Somerset reunion won't last forever."

"Neither will I, Sinclair."

But suddenly she felt utter freedom. Time didn't matter. She went willingly into his arms, and lingered there comforted, content, free to love him again.

⌒

Hanley had come to the point that he was hearing the phone ringing even in his sleep. He was fully awake now and winced as it rang again. He took the receiver and gripped it in his hand on the third ring. "Hanley's Pub."

He heard the croak in his own voice and the cold indifferent answer on the other end. "Are they there?"

A lie would net him nothing. "Morrie and Chip arrived a few minutes ago. They're at the table with Bosman now."

Hanley didn't like Didier Bosman, a decolorized man with a devious plan that could ruin all of them. They would end up on the run, and all Hanley wanted was a trip to the Riviera. He had no hankering to hang a Rembrandt in his cramped lodgings. Hanley had less to lose than the rest of them. Take Bosman for instance. What was wrong with being the administrator at the Norbert Museum? If you listened to the man, his stewardship as keeper of famous works of art had failed him. Hanley figured his greed, his revenge would be his downfall.

But Chadbourne really worried Hanley. Morrie had dragged into the pub, pale and listless, looking like he hadn't slept in a month. He had stalked across the room to Bosman's table without even a nod to Hanley. But then, he didn't know Hanley was working with them.

"Freck is here too," he announced over the phone. "He said to tell you he took care of the painting."

"Which one? The Monet?"

"Should I ask?"

"No, just tell Bosman I want no mix-up on Saturday night."

Hanley digested the warning personally. How was he to slip away from his wife at the midnight hour? Better to leave the toolsheds unlocked and stay away from the property to save his own skin.

"Sir, Bosman was talking about using the delivery trucks on Monday, maybe driving north into Scotland."

There was an explosion on the other end. He held the phone away from his ear. "You tell Bosman the plans are made. No changes. No delivery trucks."

Hanley pressed the mouthpiece closer again. "My wife—"

"You deal with your wife. Nothing will go wrong."

Hanley's hand trembled as he cradled the phone. He set four goblets on the countertop and filled them. The man on the other end had instructed no liquor, but Hanley needed a chaser, and from the looks of the men at the table, they could do with a bracer themselves.

Especially Chadbourne.

As Hanley lifted the tray to carry it to them, a young couple came through the door and stopped by the counter.

"We're pushing our luck, Jillian, coming in here."

"Morrie came in moments ago. I saw him. You know he recommends this place for lunch, Chandler."

The tray in Hanley's hand shook. The girl eyed him with a smile. "I'm looking for a friend. He comes here frequently. . . . Oh, never mind. There he is over there. Is the tray for them?"

Hanley nodded.

"Chandler, you take it. Help this poor man."

She sashayed across the room. Hanley stayed on her heels and heard her say, "Morrie, we've been looking everywhere for you. We wanted to talk to you about the Weinberger painting."

"What about it?" Sean Larkins asked.

What about it? Hanley wondered.

Without a hint of a surprise, she smiled at Sean and brightened as she recognized Didier Bosman. "Mr. Bosman, remember me? I'm Jillian Reynolds from the Art Theft Registry in London."

Bosman half stood, smiled politely. He peered at her through his wide, black-rimmed glasses. His thin lips were tight as he answered, "We meet again. So you like eating at Hanley's too? I often drive up for a meal myself."

Hanley felt as though he had been punched in the pit of his stomach. No one ever drove six hours to Hanley's Pub. Bosman would hang them all if he said another word. But the girl kept talking. "I haven't been to the Norbert Museum since that attempted robbery."

"Thanks to you, we've had no more problems. Would you and your husband care to join us?"

Chandler placed a glass in front of each man and then sat down beside his wife and acknowledged the balding butler. "Mr. Freck, no wonder you didn't help serve breakfast this

252

morning. It must be your day off. The coffee lost its flavor without your expertise."

Hanley hovered behind Bosman's chair, waiting for recognition or dismissal. He had to get the message across to Bosman and hit on a feeble plan. "My wife was asking—can you all come back for a midnight supper Saturday?"

Bosman drummed his fingers on the goblet, his gaze sharp. "If you'd be so good as to tell me what's on the menu on Saturday."

Twenty paintings from Lord Somerset's collection, Hanley thought. "My wife's special."

"If we can't make it by twelve, what about one? Would that be convenient, Hanley?"

"I'll check. And you, Mr. Chadbourne?"

Morrie shoved back his chair. "I have other plans."

Twenty-one

Hills and dales surrounded Lake Windermere with the higher blue-green mountains rising in the north and the gentle rolling hills to the south filled with spring daffodils. An early morning mist had risen, leaving the lake an electrifying blue like Becki's eyes. The sun glistened across the tranquil waters turning the crest of the ripples into glittering diamonds.

The Daffodil, their sleek luxurious motor yacht, lay anchored at the end of a long wooden dock—25 tons of grace with a resident chef and an area for sunbathing. As they waited to board for an all-day cruise, Rachel turned to Jillian. "Jillian, you're not worried about seasickness, are you? I promise, the lake is so calm."

"It's another kind of sickness. I've been ill every morning since we arrived at the Somerset Estates."

"You don't mean? Oh, dear. Does Chandler know?"

"I didn't dare tell him before we came; but once I do, he'll be ecstatic. He wants to be a father."

"I think he will make a wonderful parent."

"That's what I think about you, watching you with Rebecca. You should have been a mother, Dr. McCully."

"Even if I had married, there would have been no children."

"You're so adamant!"

She moistened her lips. "My sister was ill with cystic fibrosis all her life. When she died, I vowed I would never have a child. Treatment is much better today. Patients live longer. But my parents knew their pregnancies would be high risk.

They took the chance—I wouldn't do that to a child of mine."

Jillian placed her hand gently on Rachel's arm. "It is strange," she mused, "this exact same group will never meet again. But we will always hold good memories, won't we?"

"Interesting ones, albeit tainted with stolen art."

"Morrie was afraid of something like that. That's why he came to the Art Theft Registry and asked for our help."

"He did?"

"Yes, he said he wanted to stop a robbery. It will take months to prove it, but initial checks at the registry indicate that Morrie is right about the Weinberger. We're petitioning the courts to take that painting. That means Lord Somerset may have to find a replacement picture for over his fireplace."

Her gaze went to the group again. "Tuesday we'll be going our separate ways. But, Dr. McCully, I have a feeling there's one person here that won't be slipping out of your life again."

Rachel felt her cheeks blaze. "I don't see him yet. Maybe he's off buying my birthday cake."

"I rather thought it would be difficult to surprise you. At least pretend. Sinclair is planning a birthday party for you at dinner. You mustn't disappoint him. The cake—that's when everything fell into place for me about the two of you." She laughed, her sapphire eyes glowing. "It's funny, Dr. McCully. I never noticed Don Wakefield during my three weeks in your classroom."

Rachel bantered back. "In a way, Jillian, I really wish you had been in my classroom."

"In a way, I feel like I have been. I hated using a lie to gain entry into the Somerset Estates. But in my line of work, we do use devious ways to track down missing masterpieces."

⁓

The Daffodil launched at nine, only moments after Sinclair and the cake were safely on board. They navigated around islands of trees in the center of the lake, glided past acres of gardens along the lakeshore, passed bustling market towns and villages perched on the banks of the lake, and to Becki's delight, glided past Hill Top Farm on the western shore.

Rachel strolled casually along the rail, talking to her guests—knowing that one of them could be an art thief. Any one of them could leave the Somerset Estates with a framed two mil in a suitcase or be led away by Inspector Farland at Heathrow and booked as a common criminal. That was the agreement with Lord Somerset should a robbery occur: No one would be taken into custody at the mansion. A scandal would be avoided at all costs.

As Rachel moved along the rail, she thought how pleasant it was being with these young adults. She would spend the day with them, marveling at the scenery, conversing with them as they sunbathed or swam, and eat beside them on the flying bridge. Only a few years—twelve at most—had passed since they had left her classroom, but Rachel clearly remembered their faces. Yet the details of how they acted or dressed on campus seemed vague, except for Amanda in her hats, Chaplain Wong in his baggy khakis, and Sara like a walking model. Wong was the class joker. Jude the rebel. Lydia the poor girl working her way through university. And Janet her gifted, happy-go-lucky poet.

How quickly Rachel had slipped back into her teacher's role, expounding on Wordsworth and Coleridge in the evenings, reminding them of how often she had prayed for them, and discovering that they had left an imprint on her own life. They had come into her life for brief periods, and now her only commitment to them was friendship. Even Becki would soon put away the Beatrix Potter books, their charming moments with rabbits and squirrels almost gone.

Since the robbery, she had dreamed about Scotland Yard mug shots. All of their faces were there, young as they had been on campus. She wanted them to be the carefree, frolicsome students that she remembered. Even the glare of the sun on their faces now—mature faces with the air of innocence gone—were important to her.

Sleep had been troublesome during her illness, but the stolen Monet and Degas had given her fitful nights of dreaming as she flitted through the mansion in a negligee and gown searching for missing paintings and discovering a sonnet or haiku or simple message hanging in their place: *Something of beauty is gone forever. The Tales of the Missing Monet. The Rhyme of the Lost Museum.* She tried to shake free of her worries. She wanted to take mental snapshots of her students and guests back to Wakefield Cottage. Suddenly she laughed at herself. She sounded ancient, not thirty-eight.

And still laughing, she heard Sara Arnold say, "Why not share your joke with me, Dr. McCully?"

She slipped her arm around Sara's slim shoulders. "And why don't you tell me what you have been doing since graduation?"

"Running marathons in the fight against cancer. I ran the last one for Lydia—maybe I'll do one for you someday."

Not thirty minutes later, while they were waiting for the lunch bell, Rachel found Lydia leaning against the rail watching a sailboat moving effortlessly across the water with its sails into the wind.

"It's so beautiful here, Rachel. It reminds me of John Keats: 'A thing of beauty is a joy forever.'"

"That was always one of your favorite lines, and mine. Did you recall that Keats died as a young man? He wrote of beauty, Lydia, but he also feared dying. Feared that he would cease to be. He was afraid of leaving no immortal work behind him. I have wrestled with thoughts like that since I knew about my leukemia."

"Are you afraid?" she whispered.

"Only of not being all I could be and of not being here next week, next year."

"I had cancer too."

"I know. Sara told me. She said she ran the Los Angeles marathon in the fight against cancer."

"Yes, I was proud of her."

257

"She said she ran it for you, Lydia."

"For me? She knows? She knows I had a mastectomy?"

"And she knows that you paid her tuition at the university. Your parents told her."

"Why? They agreed we would never tell her."

"They were afraid you might die with your cancer. They wanted Sara to know the truth. The whole truth, Lydia."

"How can I tell her who I am? We're constantly at odds."

"Why do the two of you keep on pretending? If you run out of time, Lydia, she may never know who she really is. Who you are. This reunion could be a time of healing for both of you."

⁓

The crew served their three-course lunch on the aft deck with a choice of smoked salmon smothered with mint and seasonal vegetables or chunks of Lakeland Lamb with an apricot-almond sauce for their main dish. Jude and Sara were still in their swimsuits, Jude with her skin turning pink; Sara with an even tan. They had just come back on board from water-skiing. Kevin, who had gone with them, was toweling himself down, his thick, blond hair clinging to his scalp. Amanda stood by his side, holding out his T-shirt and fretting that swimming had not been good for his facial wounds.

As the afternoon lake winds died down, dusk crept in slowly, eerily. The setting sun hovered on the horizon. The hills turned to purple-rimmed shadows. And then they feasted again, this time on smoked trout and new potatoes and curried chicken with ginger and garlic. Dressed to the nines, they ate in the dining room with its wide viewing windows. Sinclair sat on Rachel's right, Kevin on her left, wearing his bright yellow dress shirt. Morrie remained distant, moody, his eyes on Becki. Rachel tried to draw him back as the others jostled about campus life and teased her about her love of hiking.

Amanda smiled at Kevin. "You should have been at university with us. Dr. McCully always made learning fun."

He gave Amanda a boyish grin. "I like the sound of her mountain trips better than a class on poetry."

"Kevin, the minute my classes were over on Friday, I headed right for a campground or a mountain trail," Rachel said. "Eileen and Amanda went with me a couple of times. Several students did."

"But why take students with you?" Sean asked. "I would have thought you'd like to be alone."

"They were my life. The classroom went with us. We'd sit under giant redwoods and talk about great writers and thinkers and preachers. Sometimes we didn't get back for evening chapel."

"That's what some of the students liked about her, Sean," Sinclair told him. "Rachel was willing to take her faith beyond the pew and the school chapel."

She laughed. "Sinclair, you know some of the faculty opposed my unorthodox ways. Just ask Misty Owens here. But students opened up. The mountains and the rivers set them free to discuss their fears. Their hopes. A lot of sonnets came out of those trips. I still have copies of the poems Lydia wrote."

"Lydia wrote poetry?" Sara asked.

"Poems about you, Sara. You should ask her about them."

Sara stared at her sister. "What were they about, Lydia?"

Rachel waited, prayed. From deep inside, Lydia found her strength. Without wavering, she said, "About a lost child. An empty womb. A dead heart."

Sara gave an impatient shrug. "Oh, that sounds morbid, Lydia."

"No, I wrote them out of my love for you."

To break the silence that fell over them, Kevin turned to Rachel and said privately, "I didn't want to come to this reunion. I didn't think I'd be welcomed here after I had a run-in with Lord Somerset over a banking incident."

"But I am glad you came. You're very fond of Amanda."

"Yes; but I'm tired of my mother asking me if I've found the right girl yet. I've found her, but I don't dare let them meet. She'd be so busy lecturing us on immorality that I'd have a tough time convincing Mother that the one thing I want to do is to get married and spend the rest of my life with Amanda Pennyman."

"And your mother would disapprove of that?"

"Not about—"

Before he could finish his sentence, Timothy Whitesaul slipped into the chair that Sinclair had vacated. "Happy birthday, Rachel."

She patted his hand. "You made it possible with your miracle pills! It's been such a long journey. But I've always known that even in death, I would have a refuge."

"It will be a while before you take that refuge."

"Is that a promise, Timothy?"

"It's a known fact." His broad face creased with a smile. "Your white blood count is coming down. Way down. Normal, in fact. Sinclair convinced me to save the news for a birthday present. So . . . Happy birthday, Rachel."

"You mean—"

"Your leukemia is in remission. But we'll keep watching that shadow on your lung. Like I tell all my patients, now is the time to go skydiving or to take up the Argentine Tango."

She was too happy to cry. "I won't get that radical."

She glanced up as Sinclair placed the cake in front of her. Their eyes locked. "I love you," he mouthed. "Happy birthday, darling."

As Dr. Whitesaul munched his first bite of cake, he turned to Sara and Lydia Arnold. "Rachel tells me you are sisters."

Sara gave him a defiant toss of her head, but tears brimmed in her eyes. "We're trapped in the same blood line—actually we're trapped in Lydia's lies." Tears brimmed. "She doesn't have the courage to admit who I really am."

"No, you're wrong, Sara." All eyes turned on Lydia. She glanced at Rachel and then said, "We're not sisters. You are much more important to me, Sara . . . You are my daughter."

Sara stumbled to her feet and moved toward Lydia.

Dusk kept slipping away as the rising moon sent new streamers of light across the rippling lake. Rachel was still slicing the birthday cake when a sudden wind squall hit without warning. Rain clouds swept in. Dusk turned to a blackened sky, and rain pelted against the boat, rocking it unsteadily. The yacht tilted precariously starboard as plates full of birthday cake slid across the table and crashed to the floor.

On the deck, crew members ran toward the bow of the yacht. The captain barked his orders over the intercom. Kevin and Morrie were on their feet at once, running out of the dining room, Sean and Jude on their heels. Sinclair shoved back his chair and whispered to Rachel, "Wait in here."

Along the shoreline, Rachel could see the villagers hurrying to batten down their thatched roofs. Leaves blew like tumbleweeds. Tree limbs swayed, splintered, crashed. The sheep were skittish in the pasture, running blindly into the fences.

The storm whipped across the lake, turning the tranquil waters into rolling waves. Sailboats dipped with the waves, cutting the surface with their riggings. Rachel stood frozen by the window, watching the frantic move to lower the sails.

The Daffodil listed with the wind, tossed about without a rudder. As the captain fought the mechanical difficulties, he attempted to radio his position. Static filled the air waves. Another violent gust of wind swept over them. Another rolling wave stirred the lake waters. The next swell lifted the yacht and sent it crashing against a rowboat, capsizing it. The occupants sank beneath the waters, struggled to the surface.

Screams erupted, "Man overboard! Man overboard!"

Rachel saw Amanda leaning over the rail, crying pitifully. She made her way toward the deck. "Go back, Rachel," Sinclair cried. "Stay inside the cabin. I'll come back for you."

Rachel shook her head and slid across the deck until she reached them. "What did we hit, Sinclair?" she demanded.

"A rowboat. Two or three passengers. At least that many heads bobbing. I've never seen a squall like this one—now take Amanda and go back inside."

Rachel shivered in the drenching rain and stared down into the semidarkness as the crew dragged the injured on board. Rachel pulled Amanda against her. "What is it, Amanda?"

"Kevin is gone. I saw him go overboard."

Beyond the damaged rowboat, a long figure bobbed face-down in the water. Rachel recognized the yellow shirt, the blond hair. She pointed. "There ! That has to be Kevin!"

Sinclair stripped to his waist, kicked off his shoes, and dove off the front of the yacht. They watched him surface, gulp in more air, and plunge beneath the waters again. When he surfaced this time, he had locked his arm around the chest of a man and was towing him toward the yacht. Willing hands reached out to hoist Kevin Nolan and Sinclair back on board the rocking vessel.

But the cheer of the rescue caught in their throats.

Kevin lay on the deck—limp, pale, waterlogged.

Twenty-two

Rachel was up early to watch the mountain climbers gather in the lobby. The men were going in full force, but she was surprised to see Amanda Pennyman hurrying down the stairs in her hiking boots, sun goggles around her neck.

"Amanda, are you going on the climb too?" she asked her.

"I have to be there for Kevin. I don't want anything to happen to him again today."

"It won't. Sinclair said that yesterday's storm was unusual. Try to focus in on a twenty-four-hour day. That means no looking back—no rushing ahead."

"I can't forget what happened yesterday. I almost lost Kevin on Lake Windermere."

"I know. That was such a tragic accident."

"I don't think you understand. It was no accident, Dr. McCully. Last night, Kevin told me someone pushed him overboard."

"But, Amanda, everything happened during the storm."

"No, Dr. McCully. Someone deliberately pushed Kevin overboard. We're determined to find out who did it."

The reality hit her. She forced herself to remain calm. To tread lightly. Surely, Amanda was overreacting. Surely—no, she knew that Amanda had told the truth. She formed her words carefully, safely. "I think Kevin means a lot to you."

"He does."

"But you're not married yet?"

She flicked her hair back from her cheek. "You knew?"

"You're still talking about Lee. A bride doesn't talk about another man like that."

Her cheeks flushed. "I wanted Kevin to measure up to Lee."

"Kevin can't measure up to an imagined perfection. Lee was a wonderful young man, Amanda, with his whole future ahead of him. I remember how you grieved for him, but he was the kind of person who would have wanted you to go on with your life."

"How can I? I still blame myself for his death."

"Amanda, did you tell Lee to break the speed limit? Or cut corners too quickly on his motorcycle? You know he was careless behind the wheel. Lee was brilliant, but he took too many risks."

"We quarreled that morning."

"I thought so. We don't get to choose what our last words are with someone we love. Lee would have understood that."

"I think he took his anger out on the motorcycle."

Rachel had known Lee. Known them both. He was an easygoing young man, spirited down to his boots. A risk taker and an honor student. A young man who made friends easily and who had swept Amanda off her feet.

The diamond came three weeks later, just one more of Lee's impulsive decisions. But the motorcycle always came first. He kept it polished even at the cost of keeping his dates on time. But for Amanda, Lee could do no wrong.

In her eyes, he was just about perfect. And in many ways he was. But it was Kevin who mattered now. Amanda had to choose. Or she had to set Kevin free. She had to set both men free.

"Kevin is his own man, Amanda. He loves you, but he can never wear another man's shoes. What is it you like about Kevin?"

She seemed perplexed with the question, as though Rachel McCully of all people would see the qualities in him. "He's honest and kind. He tries to please. He's a hard worker—"

264

"He's boyish and funny, and very much in love with you. But he feels that Lee is like an albatross around his neck."

"I never meant for that to happen. But, Rachel, he gambles."

"So did Lee in his own way. I thought Kevin was going to a support group, getting help for his gambling."

"He is. Ever since we came to the Somersets', Kevin keeps telling me that Lord Somerset should be in a support group too."

"With Kevin getting help, you're running out of excuses. I watched you last evening when you thought he wasn't going to wake up."

"I thought he was dead. It was like losing Lee again."

"Amanda, let Lee go, before you force Kevin to walk out on you. He likes being an auditor. You know that, don't you?"

"I want him to do something more glamorous."

"Do you want a makeover or someone who loves you?" Her voice cracked, trailed. "I'm afraid of commitment. Of something happening to Kevin again."

"Nothing will happen. I promise you. Sinclair and Timothy will be there. And Morrie is an experienced guide in these fells. Go on. Everyone is ready to leave, and Morrie hates waiting for people. If you get tired, stop and rest."

"And if Kevin gets tired?"

"He probably will. It's a demanding climb and he's still traumatized from yesterday, and still wearing scars from that bombing near Harrods. That's a heavy plate for any young man. So if he gets tired, stop and rest and talk about your future together."

Her smile turned impish. "Dr. McCully, you said I should just think about twenty-four hours at a time."

"I'll make an exception—just this once."

Amanda gave her a quick hug and ran to catch the others. "Wait for me!" she cried.

When Rachel turned, she saw Becki standing by the window with her face pressed to the windowpane.

"Will my daddy be all right?"

She had called Morrie daddy. Was there still hope for Eileen and Morrie? Was there hope for the three of them? Becki turned from the window, waiting for her answer.

"Your daddy is a very good climber."

"Somebody tried to hurt Kevin yesterday."

"Oh, Becki, who told you that?"

"Timothy Whitesaul."

Rachel thought of the buffeting winds on the high hills. The brooding peaks. The slippery trails. The amateurs climbing with the group today. The weather could change at a moment's notice, change without warning as it had done on the lake yesterday. Another wind-driven rain on the craggy heights could be deadly.

"Everyone will be fine," she said, trying to convince herself.

Becki looked up and shared her secret. "Morrie told me he would sit with me at dinner tonight."

She felt rage. Morrie intended to have the climbers stop off at Hanley's Pub for a late supper. Had he heard Becki correctly? Had he lied deliberately? Rachel swallowed her anger and said gently, "If Morris gave you his word, then he'll certainly get down the mountain safely. Sinclair and Timothy went with him. Nothing will happen."

"Did Sinclair promise to have supper with you, Rachel?" Becki asked.

"Not tonight. He doesn't always remember his appointments, not if he's lost in one of his books. A long time ago, I persuaded him to go on a camping trip with the hiking club."

"Did he keep his promise?"

"He forgot. When I arrived at his apartment, I expected him to be out on the sidewalk with his camping gear, but he was sitting at his kitchen table, reading a book on art restoration. All he could say was, 'Oh, Rachel, I forgot.' But I didn't stay mad at him forever."

"You don't think Morrie will keep his promise, do you?"

"I don't know, Becki."

"Did Sinclair make you cry when he didn't keep his promise?"

"A little."

"Maybe I'll cry too."

Maybe, Rachel thought, *you'll cry a whole lot. Morrie will not be home for dinner.* "Come, why don't we walk in the garden?" she suggested.

⌇

Since moving to the Lake District, Morrie had spent many an hour scaling the craggy hills, seeking their grandeur and isolation at a trout stream or within sight of a herd of deer watering by a brook. After yesterday's near tragedy on Lake Windermere, a somber mood swept over the guests. But Morrie determined to keep his promise to the men game enough to tackle the strenuous climb on Scafell Pike. Reaching the summit was the only way for these men to enjoy the true beauty of Lakeland. That was the place for mountaineers and backpackers, for the rock climbers and the locals accustomed to reaching the heights. Today he must inspire these men to break away from the thick gray mist that hovered over the reunion, that shrouded the Somerset Estates in darkness.

He was resolute that nothing in the high steep fells of Lakeland would keep the men from climbing. He wanted them to reach the summit, even knowing that one of the guests might not want them all to reach there safely. The pinnacles bred rugged men. Perhaps the climb would unveil the uninvited guest as well, but as he joined the men at the appointed hour, he was shocked to see Jude Alexander standing there in her shabby hiking boots with a backpack slung over her shoulders, and Amanda, smartly dressed and ready for the hike.

Kevin looked less prepared. His face was still colorless from yesterday's mishap. He would keep his eye on Kevin. Until now he had considered Kevin a possible problem. Now he believed differently. Before that first wave hit their yacht, he had seen Kevin tumbling headfirst into the water.

Someone had helped him over the side.

"So the three of you are going with us?" he asked and headed for the cars without waiting for their answers.

They rode through rural countryside on the way to the peaks, over a grassy slope, past a remote river valley, and on to the wooded lowlands and high tarns. The easy part was over as they stepped out of the cars and checked their shoelaces and trail food.

"If you're going to turn back, do so now," Morrie warned them. "Once we start, we keep going."

At his signal, they adjusted their backpacks and began the single file ascent toward the sun. They climbed steadily, up toward England's highest peak, up toward the crags and cliffs.

Taking a trail break two hours later, they looked up and saw the jagged promontory, a rough, bouldery summit.

"Jude, a person could take quite a fall from there," Sean said.

"You frighten me with your crazy remarks," she said, replacing the cap on her water bottle.

The trail led the group across a footbridge, past a well-kept sheepfold, and up a zigzagging path toward steep fellsides. They took another break at the watercourse where a stream of silvery water tumbled between the gleaming walls of rock.

"Are you still with us?" Morrie asked Amanda.

Amanda shook her head. Her heels had blistered. The pounding of her heart hindered her climb. She looked at Kevin, and he nodded his agreement. "Morrie, Amanda and I are going to wait here until you get back. We've decided to call it a day. We'll wait on the boulders where we saw a herd of red deer watering at the tarn."

Sean eyed them contemptuously. "You're quitting already? We might come down a different trail."

"Then we'll make our own way back."

"No," Sinclair said. "If the others choose another route down, Whitesaul and I will come back this way for you."

Amanda looked exhausted, Kevin even more peaked. Sean shook his head. "What's wrong, Nolan? You can't swim. You can't climb."

"Let them alone," Morrie warned. "If they can't get to the top, that's no disgrace. Look how far they've come."

Sean shifted his rucksack and started climbing again as Kevin told her, "Amanda, I've lost my wallet."

"Where?"

"I don't know. It was in my rucksack."

"And Sean was walking behind you."

Morrie overheard them. "I'll keep my eyes open. We'll settle this back at the Somersets.'"

"But what would he want with my wallet?"

"I'm wondering the same thing."

Sinclair gave them a reassuring smile. "Do you have enough water? Trail food?"

"We're set. We're just sorry we can't push any further."

Sinclair nodded. "You've made a wise choice. Maybe even a safe one." He shaded his eyes to watch the others pushing ahead, then he shook hands with Kevin and followed Morrie up the path.

Progress was slow as they clambered up to the heights and stepped from boulder to boulder, but Jude was gutsy, sticking close behind Sean. It was rough work crossing the boulder fields. Sean Larkins was leading the climb now, taking over in his mocking way. Morrie fell behind him, scowling. The man had a volcanic nature, like his own. *They were two of a kind,* he admitted to himself, *time bombs walking through volcanic ridges.*

Their ascent path to Scafell Pike rose southwestward into the thickly wooded fells, and higher to the barrenness of Scafell Pike. By the last twenty feet, the weather turned. Tempers soared. Sighing winds whipped around the precipitous cliffs. Looking down a kilometer away was another tricky path crowded with hikers.

269

Looking back, they could see for miles, but a mountain mist was rapidly closing in on them. "The rest of you get started down," Morrie told them after they had rested and eaten. "I want to have a talk with Sean."

Wakefield and Whitesaul had gone only a short distance when they heard the cries of other climbers. They looked back and saw Morrie and Sean wrestling on the edge of the promontory. They ran back up the hill as Morrie's head cracked against the rock. Fists flew. The two toppled, rolled closer to the edge. Morrie was on top now, blood pouring from his temple. He jammed his hand angrily against Sean's jaw, backing him closer to the precipice.

It took both Wakefield and Whitesaul several minutes before they could tear the two men apart. They dragged them to their feet. "What's wrong with you fools?"

"Just a friendly argument, Sinclair." Morrie winced as Whitesaul examined the jagged cut on his temple.

Sinclair shoved Sean ahead of him. "That's a pretty angry scuffle over a friendly argument," he said.

Becki and Rachel were waiting for the climbers when they arrived back at the mansion. Morrie was the last one to come through the door. "Morrie," Becki cried.

He turned and frowned. "What are you doing up, Smidgen?"

"We were going to have supper together. You promised."

He put his hand to his wound, as though he were willing himself to remember. "I'm sorry. We'll have to make that another time. I am sorry. It was your mother's idea, not mine."

Timothy Whitesaul caught Rebecca on the run, picked her up, and carried her upstairs. Rachel watched them go and then turned angrily on Morrie. "What has happened to you, Morrie? Must you hurt that child at every turn?"

"I'm trying to protect her, Rachel. We have problems. The safest spot for that child is with her mother."

270

She retreated. "Morris, you should let Eileen look at that wound."

"I can take care of it." He tried to smile, but the swelling on his face stopped him. "Charles scheduled a chapel service for us tomorrow. So it's up to you to have our guests in bed before midnight," he urged.

"I can't ask them to retire at a certain time. They aren't children. They're on holiday with just a little more time together. The reunion is almost over."

"Thankfully," he said.

"It was your idea to hold the reunion here."

"And it's my job to protect Lord Somerset's property. I didn't think about that enough before the reunion. I've thought a great deal about it since I met my daughter." He fixed his weary eyes on her. "Just help me, Rachel. Make sure the guests retire early. It's important. I'll be staying in the main house this evening in Wong's old room, if you need me."

She shook her head. "The guests have formed some special friendships. Chandler and Kevin have a chess competition going that goes past midnight. The women like sitting up and chatting by the fireside, beneath your Weinberger painting, I might add."

Morrie winced. "It isn't mine yet. It may never be mine. But someone took the Monet and Degas paintings, and now a Rubens is missing. I can't risk something else coming off the walls."

He strolled off, but at the foot of the stairs, he turned back. "Rachel, I'm grateful for what you tried to do. But you do know, don't you, that it will never work out for Eileen and me."

She bit into her lower lip. "And Becki?"

"I could never be permanent in her life."

⌒

Charles found Rachel sitting alone in the garden. She was holding a cup of tea and sipping it.

"Good evening," he said. "I see the climbers are back."

271

"Yes, and they're an irritable lot. Morrie was injured. He didn't say how. And he broke his promise with his daughter so Timothy carried her upstairs."

"I don't like to tell you, but another painting was taken off the wall in the drawing room."

"That's what Morrie said. That narrows it down, doesn't it? Most of the men were gone all day climbing the Scafell Pike."

"But the painting was taken before dawn this morning."

"Then Morrie knew before he left for the climb? So someone is really laughing in our faces."

"No, someone is trying to distract us. To keep us from suspecting anything major."

"And I'm just worried about Morrie and the man he has become. He has a child, and it doesn't seem to matter to him."

Charles sat beside her. "I gather he just isn't very keen on God either. He doesn't like sermons, so I can't practice mine on him."

"I try to engage him in discussions on Michelangelo's Sistine Chapel and on the Italian Renaissance. Maybe through the paintings, he may discover the truth for himself."

"More things are wrought by prayer—"

She laughed lightly, grateful for Charles and his wise ways. "Than this old world ever dreams of. Alfred Lord Tennyson."

"So you see, my dear, I know the poets too."

"Charles, you have one of those hearts of gold."

He threw back his head, stretching the flabby skin of his neck, and roared with laughter. "Sometimes, dear child, I still see myself as a man with a heart of stone."

"You're much too kind for that. Maybe a polished stone with one side of the stone stamped 'to Ireland with love.' Or with Conon O'Reilly's name. I still marvel at all you did for him. Most people would shun an Irish terrorist."

"Did you know my daughter died in Ireland at the hands of terrorists?"

"Oh, Charles."

272

"So you see, my dear, God has a lot of polishing to do on this hard heart of mine. The rough edges are being hewn away. Hacked sometimes. I miss my parish, but I have the sky and earth for my sanctuary. And little ones like Rebecca as a friend."

"And the rest of us as part of your flock?"

His eyes met hers again, blue as the larkspurs. "One prodigal at a time. I am a fortunate man. And you are a fortunate woman."

"How so?"

"Chaplain Wong and I have had some good chats. You left a great impression on him."

"On Bill? Really? He was the class joker at the university. He took my classes just to meet graduation requirements."

"I dare say life is more serious for him now. Did you know that he credits you for choosing the chaplaincy?"

"Me? We never discussed his becoming an army chaplain."

"But you told him there was more to life than daffodils and sonnets."

"I had to, Charles. Bill was not all that keen on studying literature—except he liked writing poetry."

"Oh, he enjoyed your classes—at least in retrospect. But what he most remembers—so he tells me—is that day on the mountain trails when you prayed with him. He did a turnaround after that. Said you told him to choose a career that would put him in the thick of ministry."

"But we never discussed the army."

"But you told him to be a good soldier for Jesus Christ."

Her eyes misted. "When he leaves here he is going on re-assignment—hopefully, home to his wife and children."

Charles brushed the soil from his hands and touched her arm. "No, his posting is back to the Gulf."

"On the front lines? Surely not with the ground forces or the Army Rangers?"

"If there are covert operations still going on, he would want to be with them. He's parachuted in with them before.

I had that privilege in World War II. Jumping with British commandos as their chaplain. I understand Bill."

"Charles, he might get killed."

"He wants to be with the soldiers—in the thick of ministry." Charles knuckled a tear from her cheek. "He wants to leave a safe and goodly heritage for his children. He told me that if anything happens to him that I was to thank you for touching his life and leading him to Jesus."

"Nothing has happened to him yet, Charles."

"I know. But my memory gets shabby now and then, and I might forget my promise—should it ever be needed."

Over the lump in her throat, she said, "Thank you for telling me. Charles, I will miss you when this reunion is over. I hope you will come to Wakefield Cottage to see me."

"I'd like that."

"There's a centuries-old church there. Rarely used. A cleric visits once in a while, but not since I've been there. Why don't you—"

"The banished shepherd?" he interrupted.

"You could come. It doesn't have to be in an official capacity. The villagers would repay you in food and lodging."

"That's how I began my ministry. Perhaps I could end it in the same way. Have they had any wedding ceremonies there lately?"

"No, and no young couples planning one that I know of."

"I have a couple in mind."

"Amanda and Kevin!"

"That would be good," he said. "But I have someone even more special in mind. I think the laws and my licenser would still permit me to marry someone. They banished me to the North, but they didn't strip away my rights."

"You mean me." She flushed scarlet. "Charles, it's ever so beautiful when the sun comes up over Stradbury Square."

"I'd be up to meet it."

"You could have your own garden, or help me with mine."

"Once you're well, you'll be going home again."

274

"No, I want to stay there forever. But you probably won't want to leave the Somerset Estates or these lovely gardens."

A dark cloud crossed his face, veiled his kindly expression. "Perhaps when this is all over, the property will be vacated or turned over to the National Trust."

"Why would you say a thing like that? The Somersets have no plans to leave."

He smiled. "Mrs. Somerset is not well. She finds this forced isolation deplorable. But I have no right to put an added burden on you. You don't even know them."

She stood and looked around her. "Nor envy them. It's magnificent here but not cozy like my Wakefield Cottage."

He tucked her arm in his, and they walked down the bricked pathway toward the main house. "You have brought a measure of sunshine to this place. I wish Mrs. Somerset could have been part of it. She is such a lonely old woman. Old like I am."

Rachel walked a few more steps and stopped. She was worried and didn't know why. How could she explain the brooding premonition to Charles? She looked up at the magnificent mansion and felt nothing but dark, shadowed oppression. "Morrie wants me to have all of the guests in bed tonight before midnight. He's adamant about it," she said.

"So that is the hour? Take his advice. Do what he says."

"Then our lives are at risk?"

He squeezed her hand. "Only if you interfere. Our prodigal son is merely hours from disaster. But there are so many twists and turns for a man on a redemptive journey. We have to believe that, in the end, he will make the right choices."

Twenty-three

Midnight! Rachel listened for the sounds of silence, wanting them. Wanting everyone to be safely asleep. She heard instead the whisper of the wind, the roll of distant thunder, the rumble of a heavy truck on the country road so seldom heard at this hour. She strained to hear the hollow sounds of the mansion, the creaking of steps, the mumble of voices, and would have welcomed some outcry, some din or racket, the clatter of a dish to reassure her that she did not keep vigil alone.

At the scratching of a tree branch against her windowpane, she caught her breath and slipped through the darkness to her open window. Crickets sang. A possum rattled across the top of the balcony rail. Two shadowy figures stole across the back of the property. They stepped cautiously. Halted. Drew back into the chimerical darkness of the pine trees. She strained her eyes, waiting. Then movement again as they skirted the flower beds.

Clammy fear tugged at her. She hurried through the adjoining bathroom into Eileen's room. "Eileen. Eileen, I need your help."

Only Becki lay in a curled knot on the big bed. She went over and kissed the damp brow of the sleeping child. *Where? Where is your mommy?* she wondered.

She cracked the door. Across the corridor came an uneven snore. Down the hall the flush of a toilet, the running of water. And midway down the corridor she saw someone. Eileen. Her hand on the doorknob to Morrie's room. Impulsively, Rachel darted out, closing the gap between them.

"Eileen, that is not the way to win him back."

Eileen's grip on the doorknob slackened.

"Morrie is in trouble, Eileen. You can't help him that way."

"What way, Rachel? I know how it must look, but I want to have it out with him. I'm sick of the way he's treating Becki."

"Dear Eileen, you can't force him to love her."

"That's what you intended when you invited us to come."

Rachel felt stunned. "I know . . . and I was wrong. . . . I am so sorry."

"It hurts. He doesn't believe that Becki is his own child—"

"He knows. But he's not the Morrie we knew. Not the young man who came down the hills just weeks ago, running over to me there at the lake. Carefree. Jaunty. Laughing. He is so ill-tempered now—and worried and obsessed with that painting."

"He was always vulnerable, but he's become a puzzle to me."

"To both of us, Eileen. You were married to him. Can you trust him for one more thing?"

"As Becki's father? No."

"I mean, can you still trust his judgment? Can you trust him to stop whatever mischief is going on at this reunion? We need to talk to Morrie. Confront him for his own sake."

A grumpy, sleepy voice said, "I told you that man is trouble. Told you that from the beginning, Miss Rachel."

Startled, they turned and saw Audrey peeking out her bedroom door, her cotton nightie rumpled, her upper teeth missing. She covered her mouth and mumbled, "Miss Rachel, are you all right?"

"I'm fine. I just have to find Morrie."

Audrey glanced apologetically at Eileen. "He's been prowling around all night. Sneaking some old lady up the stairs. Older than me," she explained.

Puzzled, Rachel asked, "A stranger? Not one of our guests?"

"Came in thirty minutes ago. Mr. Chadbourne had me make up the master bedroom—said he could trust me to help him. Wasn't to my liking. But he has been nice to me these last few days. Making it a point to thank me for my meals and for being friends to Becki and to Miss Eileen here. Who wouldn't be nice—"

"The woman," Rachel said impatiently. "Tell me about her."

"Not much to tell. We had to help the poor soul up the stairs. She stopped almost every step to catch her breath. Course that helped me breathe too, what with not knowing what I was into with that Mr. Morrie. He's a charmer with all that flattery." She looked disgusted with herself. "I even get taken by it."

"Audrey, who is the woman?"

"She didn't give any name. About dug the skin off my hand, she held so tight. Just said she was glad to be home again. Sweet face. Tried to smile. Acted like the lady of the house—fancy enough clothes." She paused. "Touched the things on the dresser, like they were hers. Ran her hands over the bedpost. Fluffed her pillow like she'd done it before. I've done right by her. I've been looking in on her. She's still breathing."

Worry clouded Eileen's face even more. "Rachel, do you think it's Lord Somerset's wife?"

"Impossible. The cruise ship is halfway around the world."

"Makes no matter to me, Miss Rachel. After I helped her into bed, I asked Mr. Chadbourne about her. He just stomped off back downstairs."

Eileen stared at his closed door. "He's not in his room?"

"His room is empty. No one has slept in that bed," she huffed, forgetting to keep her nearly toothless mouth covered. "See for yourself, if you don't believe me."

Rachel touched Audrey's shoulder. "We believe you. I'm going downstairs and have a look around. Morrie can't be far."

"I'll go with you," Eileen offered.

Rachel suppressed a chuckle. "In that robe and slippers? Go back to the room and stay with Becki. And take Audrey with you."

"I am not going anywhere, not without my teeth."

"Then get them. Eileen, maybe you should look in on the woman. Make certain she's all right. After that, let her rest."

Rachel went down the grand staircase and followed the light into the smoking room. The drapes were drawn back from the wide French windows, and the vast backyard eerily lit with the night lanterns that surrounded the property.

Chandler and Kevin were bent over the chessboard in the far corner. At the sight of her, Chandler grinned. "Kevin is winning so we can stop if you want us to, Dr. McCully," he offered.

She crossed the room to them, feeling exhausted inside. "It looks like we're all suffering from insomnia this evening."

Chandler nodded. "Sinclair asked us to keep a watch here. He's out patrolling the property. Whitesaul is with him."

Rachel gave a sigh of relief. "Then it was Sinclair and Timothy I saw out in the garden." She glanced at their game board. "Please. Go on with your chess game."

"Actually we don't even remember whose turn it is. Do we, Chan? We're busy keeping an eye on Mr. Freck. The old butler's been busy dusting the paintings. Going from room to room."

"At this hour, Kevin?"

"It may be more than dusting, Rachel." Chandler pointed to the painting of Lord Nelson on the wall above them. He picked up a flashlight and beamed it on an iridescent marking on the gilded frame. For a second, it glowed.

"What a strange thing to do to an expensive frame."

"Not odd, if you are tagging it for easy identification."

She braced her hand on the table, her uneasiness growing. Kevin patted her hand. "Don't worry, Dr. McCully. The marking will wash off. So far we've found three paintings in this room marked that way. As soon as Freck decides to call it a day, we're going to check the other rooms."

"So it hasn't been just chess that keeps you up late?"

"No. Jillian asked us to help out this way. She had to go into the Art Theft Registry yesterday with more pictures."

"A long drive."

"The inspector arranged for a private plane. She'll be back later this morning." He grinned. "By the way, I insisted that she make an appointment with an obstetrician while she's in London. I want Jillian and our baby to have the best of care."

She felt the smile creep along her cheek. "You know then?"

The roar of a truck on the country road caught their attention. Rachel glanced at her watch: Twelve-fifty. She had forgotten the truck. Thought it long past the mansion. Had it parked on the lonely road and waited? Yes, it was definitely coming closer, turning on the corner by the side of the mansion.

Chandler glanced out the windows. "Company?"

"We'll know soon. It's driving our way without headlights. I have to find Morrie."

"You can stop looking, Rachel." Chandler pointed to his cell phone. "Charles called. Morrie went out the side gate just before you came downstairs."

"Then he's—" Hot tears burned her eyes. "Why didn't Sinclair or Charles stop him?"

"I don't know, but back home we would say the ball is set in motion. We have to let it keep spinning."

She nodded at the windows. "If you see anyone moving along the side of the house toward the drawing room, go upstairs as quickly as possible. We'll want someone up there with the women."

Kevin stumbled to his feet. "I'm going to Amanda now."

"Sit down," Chandler said calmly. "Do what Rachel says."

Rachel heard the engine die. The truck doors open. The side gate creak. From where she stood, she saw the outside lights dim, go out. An uncanny darkness settled around the house. The interior lights in the smoking room and hall flickered. Darkened. Flicked on again. Something was wrong.

She raced for the door. "No," Chandler warned. "Stay right where you are, Rachel."

She dashed ahead of him and came to a running stop in the great hallway. Four men in black ski suits and balaclava masks were positioned inside the hall. One man was coming out of the drawing room with a painting in each hand, a handgun tucked in his waistband. He froze at the sight of Rachel.

The black-clad man closest to the main door stood beneath the statue of Winston Churchill. He was of medium height; his mask stretched skin-tight over a high forehead. In his right hand, he brandished a .45 semi-automatic, the sight of it forcing Rachel to remain motionless.

The powerfully built figure by the French windows was silent, yet he seemed to be in charge. His gray-streaked brows showed through his mask. "Get her out of here—and get those paintings in the truck," he demanded.

Near Rachel, the tall and lean thief fastened his eyes on her. They were Morrie Chadbourne's eyes. A nausea worse than the kind she experienced on chemotherapy hit her. Her skin prickled. Her knees locked. She was about to utter his name when from the corner of her eye she saw a sudden movement. It was Jude, a pajama-clad Becki beside her. They started down the stairs together. They stopped, immobile at the sight of the strangers.

"What's happening, Rachel?" Jude asked.

"Jude, take Becki back to her room."

"But, Rachel, we want milk and cookies. Don't we, Jude?"

"Go back to your mommy, sweetheart."

Jude took another step down. One of the masked intruders glared up at her. He leaned the paintings he was holding against the wall and grabbed his Beretta. The dim lights in the hall reflected off the gun as he barked, "Go back to your room, Jude."

"Sean? Is that you, Sean?"

He shrank back. Jude took another step. "Sean, I know it's you. I know your voice."

She was running now, down the grand staircase, leaving Becki standing on the first landing, her small hand gripping the rail.

"Sweetheart, please go back to your mommy," Rachel cried.

Her voice was drowned out by Sean's: "Don't force me to hurt you, Jude." He aimed the Beretta, his finger tightening on the trigger.

"Sean, you were going to the pub with Morrie. What are you doing here?"

"Taking a little of a rich man's treasures."

The man in charge raged. "Shut up, you fool."

"Don't call me a fool. What I know could cost you a hundred years, if you had that many left." Sean tore off his mask. "Go back, Jude. I care about you. I don't want to hurt you."

"I can't let you do this, Sean."

"You can't stop me."

She was seven steps from the bottom when the gun exploded.

"Oh, no. No." Sean's voice broke with a strangled cry. "I didn't mean it, Jude. I'm sorry."

For a second, her eyes stared widely, questioningly at him. She balanced on the step. Swayed. Then toppled headfirst down the stairs, leaving a bloody trail on the thick carpet.

From another direction, three shots fired wildly. The statue of Winston Churchill toppled. A Desmond vase on a pedestal splintered. The hall mirror cracked. The glass in the French windows shattered. Becki screamed.

Becki stared at Jude's crumpled form, and cried, "Help me."

Morrie stood immobilized in the shadows. But at her second cry, *Help me, Daddy,* he stumbled toward her and caught her in his arms. He loosened her grip from the balustrade and threw them both on the floor. "It's okay, Smidgen. I'm here."

She rasped, "Why are you wearing funny clothes, Daddy?"

As Jude moaned, Rachel braved a halting step toward her. The man in charge boomed out, "Dr. McCully, not another step."

He was a tall man, barrel-chested, strands of gray hair showing beneath his cap.

"My friend is hurt, sir."

"And we don't want the same thing to happen to you." He pointed to the man by the door. "Bosman, deal with her if she crosses us. Sean, snap out of it."

Sean's voice agonized, "But my girl is hurt."

"Forget her. You and Freck get the rest of the tagged paintings from the other rooms."

Boldly, he crossed Rachel's path as she crept toward Jude. He jerked her unmercifully. Behind his mask, his eyes were cold and mocking. "You could ruin everything. Where is Kevin Nolan?" He pressed the nerves in her upper arm. "Where is he?"

She tried to break free. He squeezed harder, the pain excruciating. "He's playing chess."

Becki screamed again. A piercing wail. "Let Rachel alone!"

Morrie tucked his daughter's face in the crook of his arm. "Lie still, Smidgen. Everything will be okay."

She protested with a muffled cry, "He's hurting Rachel."

Freck and Sean reappeared, each carrying two paintings. Sean stared at Jude lying helplessly on the floor, then glared at Morrie. "I have the Weinberger for you."

"Put it back. I no longer have any need for that painting."

The powerful grip on Rachel's arm slackened. "Mr. Freck, that's the wrong picture. They both are."

For a second Freck looked confused. "They're tagged, sir."

As Jude moaned, the man turned his fury on Morrie. Without warning, he cracked the butt of his revolver across Morrie's cheekbone. Blood gushed out. "You betrayed us, Chadbourne. You marked the wrong paintings."

"I had to stop you somehow."

"Daddy, you're bleeding . . . I want my mommy."

From the stairwell, Eileen cried, "I'm coming, sweetheart."

"Another step," the man warned, "and you'll need a doctor."

Morrie caught her eye. "Go back, Eileen. These men intend to take what they want. Becki is okay."

"Morrie, I can't let Jude bleed to death. I'm a doctor."

"Don't come. She'll be okay."

"No, I'm coming down to our child—and to help my patient."

Something snapped inside the stranger. "This child is yours, Chadbourne?"

"Yes . . . she's my daughter."

He laughed ruefully. "Confound it. Then it's over. All over. I've lost." He moved with surprising speed toward the French doors. Before anyone could stop him, he crashed through the shattered glass. Fell. Rolled. Was on his feet again, running. Darkness swallowed him up as he raced toward the back of the property.

Sinclair waited outside the French doors with Inspector Farland's iron grip on his arm. "Inspector, I'm going in for Rachel. There's already been one round fired."

"We negotiate first. Panic them, and there will be more gunfire. More injuries. My men have the property surrounded. As soon as Morris Chadbourne gives the signal, we go in."

"You still think you can trust Chadbourne?" Sinclair asked.

"I have no choice. I am counting on that child making an honest man of him. We know he deliberately tagged the wrong paintings. His idea—"

As he spoke, the masked figure ran from the mansion and raced toward the back of the property. "Let him go, Wakefield. He won't get beyond the gate."

Sinclair shook himself free. "I'm not waiting, Inspector."

Farland smiled in the darkness. "I'll send one of my men with you."

Sinclair knew the truth before he reached the musty toolshed. The sense of betrayal overwhelmed him. The man's breach of faith. His corruption. How long had they known each other? Sickened, he kicked in the door to the shed. It sprang back. He went down the narrow steps and into the tunneled basement—into the vaulted room filled with art. The room was temperature-controlled, but Sinclair felt a naked emptiness inside, a glacier-chill to his bones. His old friend stood there facing him, a revolver in his hand. His face was ruddy, his thick lips parted, his silver-gray hair slicked back. The black turtleneck shirt caught him at the double chin. He was surrounded by what he had treasured all of his life. Masterpieces. Paintings in every size. Sculptures. Framed paintings. Unframed canvases. The Degas. His mask lay on the table, his pipe pouch beside it.

"Lord Somerset." Even saying the name pained Sinclair.

"I've been expecting you, Sinclair. It was not like you to be sleeping on the job. How long have you known?"

"Long enough, James, to keep hoping I was wrong. Thank goodness my wife, Mary, never lived to see this."

Somerset looked unperturbed. "I never meant for you to be involved. Actually your solicitor and the inspector forced me to seek your help. I liked the idea of a town and gown mentality with a distinguished academician like you. In my absence, you would defend my name and property to the last kilometer."

"What happened to you? You are a wealthy man. Why mastermind this insane robbery, James? Why target Kevin Nolan?"

Lord Somerset leaned against one of the musty crates. "Surely you guessed I'm in debt. Heavy gambling debts mostly. And I left errors on the bank books. I was safe until young Kevin Nolan did that last bank audit. Unfortunately, we gambled at the same racetracks. It didn't take him long to learn about my gambling losses. I had to destroy him before he ruined me. But it looks like I've botched this whole affair."

"Perhaps you never wanted to succeed."

He slapped the revolver against the palm of his hand. "That's good of you to suggest, Sinclair. Yes, a game maybe? I was

285

bored with retirement. Frustrated with being useless. I thought I could play my curtain call like Hercule Poirot."

"Put the gun down, James."

Somerset's mouth twisted into a sardonic grin. "You think me mad, my friend? You're young enough to be my son, but you represented success to me. You probably don't have an extra schilling to your name, but you had the academic life—the acceptance of everyone at Oxford; I coveted that." His arrogance melted into desolation. He put the gun down. "My poor wife! Agnes will be devastated by all of this. All she ever wanted to do was spend my money and grace the walls of our home with beauty. But do you know how difficult it is to live with a woman for fifty years, Sinclair?"

"Mary and I never had that opportunity."

Somerset turned as Inspector Farland entered the vault. "Ah! Inspector, we meet again, under less favorable conditions."

Farland plucked at his bristly jaw. "I've come to arrest you, old friend."

Somerset folded his arms across his hulking chest. "I daresay when we had dinner at the London club, I expected you to arrest me then."

"I never guessed how deeply involved you were until later. You must have thought us gullible fools that night."

"Yes, I almost changed my mind seeing you again, Sinclair. You had gone through so much with the loss of your wife and son, yet nothing changed your character. The financial mess that I faced only pointed out my own weaknesses. In the past, what was money? My wife and I had only ourselves to please."

"Lord Somerset, you could have sold your paintings—and pulled yourself out of debt."

"For how long, Inspector? Agnes would go on buying paintings. I would go on gambling. Sell them and my wife would rant and rave at me. But a robbery—she would be furious at the thieves, not at me." He gave the inspector a mocking smile. "She'd comfort me at our loss, and the insurance would bail me out. Young Nolan was my solution. Once the robbery happened—Nolan's past gambling addiction would mark him as a suspect."

For the first time, Sinclair saw Lord Somerset as elderly, confused, his features ridged with years. The more Sinclair heard his old friend try to explain himself, the more he pitied him.

"I had willing conspirators, Inspector. A museum curator and Mr. Larkins were unlikely thieves. Chadbourne walked into our hands. And that butler," Lord Somerset said with contempt. "A greedy little cur. And old Hanley over at the pub was pure putty; all he wanted was a trip to the Riviera—a chance to get away from his wife. Poor bloke. Prison won't have the same appeal."

His chest heaved involuntarily. "Agnes constantly bid on a Rembrandt or Rubens. But without wealth, how welcome would I be in the clubs in London? Or esteemed in Grasmere and the Lake District? How easily we'd be forgotten if we could no longer support our favorite charities. How often would I have an invitation to have tea with her Majesty and Prince Philip?"

"Was all of this worth it, Lord Somerset?"

He shook his hoary head. "I will have to face my wife's humiliation, Sinclair, and risk her turning against me. She stood at my side for fifty years—and now my wife will have nothing."

Grief for an old friend rocked Sinclair. "I could speak to my solicitor, James. He could contact the National Trust. It might salvage the property. Agnes deserves more, but that's the best I can offer."

The gray-streaked brows knit together. "When I learned of my wife's heart condition, I would have bought her the world to please her." He choked out the words. "All I had to do was bluff my way financially for a year or two, and then Agnes would be gone. It wouldn't matter what happened to me after that."

Behind them, Rachel and Morrie had crowded into the vault. She glanced at the powerful figure with his arms crossed. "Sit down," Somerset invited.

"Where would you suggest, sir?"

"The crates are quite comfortable. I'm Lord Somerset. You must be Dr. McCully, the one who kept Morris from being a thief."

"I thought you and your wife were on a world cruise."

"My wife took sick. We came home early."

As Sinclair slipped his arm around Rachel, Somerset glowered at Morrie. "Chadbourne, trusting you was one of my biggest mistakes. You betrayed me. You intended to stop this robbery."

"I have to live with myself, Lord Somerset. But most of your paintings are safe, except for the Rubens and the Monet and that Degas. I thought a mathematical genius like you would appreciate the final tally."

"Three out of three hundred. A fair score," he agreed. "But what about the injured girl, Morrie?"

"It's touch and go for her. Dr. Whitesaul is transferring Jude to the nearest medical facility. They'll airlift her to London." He rubbed his eyes. "The bullet penetrated her abdomen. It fragmented. Ricocheted off the bone."

"I'm sorry," he said wearily. "Perhaps Charles could—"

"Right now, Charles is with your wife."

Somerset's eyes misted. "I should be."

Inspector Farland moved closer and led Somerset toward the stairs. "I just had word that your wife wants to see you."

His face twisted. "May I go to her?"

The inspector nodded. "As soon as I can arrange to send some of my men with you. She's waiting in the master bedroom."

⌒

Pushing his way ahead of the inspector, Morrie strode from the basement without a backward glance. Outside, the men from Scotland Yard waited for him. A June rainstorm had darkened the sky. Black clouds hovered low over the mansion. The distant thunder and lightning inched closer.

"Daddy." The voice out of the darkness seared him.

He bent down and engulfed Becki in his arms, holding tightly to this flesh and blood that he had never cradled as an infant. "I'm sorry, Smidgen."

"Are they going to take you away, Morrie?"

"They have to."

"I won't let them. Mommy and I won't let them hurt you."

He felt her hot tears on his neck and saw Timothy White-saul standing in the downpour with his arm around Eileen. More pain, like burning fuel, licked at his skin. He knew he didn't deserve Eileen. Whitesaul did. Morrie had no one to blame but himself.

He hugged his child tighter. "Becki, listen to me. If they don't take me away, I'd only run away. I always go off alone."

"Don't you want to be with mommy and me?"

The emptiness was an ache deep inside him. An impossible longing. How long would it last? Today. Tomorrow. He'd run again.

A voice boomed across the night, "Let Chadbourne go."

Lord Somerset filled the door of the toolshed with his massive frame. His black sweat top was skin tight, his wrists cuffed. "The child's father was a pawn in my hands. Let him go."

The inspector massaged his scrubby jaw. "We have evidence to the contrary—and Chadbourne's own confession."

"The man is a fool, but, Inspector Farland, you would need me to file complaints against him. I won't do that. As my caretaker, he has done an impeccable job. . . . He rescued the very thing I would have destroyed. He kept the art collection at the estates. You have the others—Bosman, Larkins, Hanley, and Freck. Deal with them. . . . And, Inspector, you have me."

But they would not have him for long. In his persuasive way, he convinced everyone that he had a right to spend a few moments alone with his wife, his hands uncuffed. The men from Scotland Yard, Sinclair and Wakefield waited respectfully outside the door to the master bedroom. Five minutes. Ten. Twenty.

"Should we go in, Inspector?" one of the men asked.

Farland scowled at his watch. "Give him five more minutes.

The commotion and weeping in the room erupted seconds later. A frail voice cried out, "No, James. No, darling. Not that way."

The sound of a long wail. A crushing thud. Sounds they could hear even in the hallway. Sinclair shouldered the door open. Agnes Somerset lay weeping against her pillow, her finger pointing toward the open glass door that led to the balcony.

Sinclair knew before they crossed the room to peer over the balcony rail that Lord Somerset had taken matters into his hands one final time.

⁓

In the aftermath, Rachel considered it incongruent that in the midst of the turmoil inside the mansion and the death of Lord Somerset, Janet Tallard came down the blood-stained stairs with suitcases in her hands and that warm congenial smile on her face.

She stopped when she saw Rachel and Sinclair standing together. Her eyes grazed the room. Men from Scotland Yard moved efficiently through the chaos. Others bore the shrouded form of Lord Somerset through the garden toward the gate.

"What happened, Sinclair—not one of our—?"

"No one that you knew, Janet. It's been a nasty ruckus. An unprovoked robbery. Thankfully, we didn't disturb your sleep."

"I use earplugs," she said, embarrassed. "I can sleep through anything."

He smiled, his serious face handsome. "You just did."

At a signal from Sinclair, Kevin was at her side, taking her luggage into his own hands. "I'm driving you as far as the train station. Are you ready to go, Mrs. Tallard?"

Rachel hugged her. "Kevin will explain everything. Go. And try to remember the good times we had these last few days."

"I can hardly wait to share it all with Tad and the boys."

With another quick hug and with a puzzled frown on her face, she stepped gingerly through the shattered glass and debris and out through the main door of the mansion.

Rachel squeezed Sinclair's arm. "I envy Janet's happiness, Sinclair. She is heading home, back to her uncomplicated life with Tad on the dairy ranch in Canada—where Guernsey cows graze contentedly and three growing boys call her Mom."

Epilogue

Rachel awakened in time to watch the sunrise over Stradbury Square and to hear the first flutelike tones of the thrush greeting the morning. She padded barefoot to the window, dropped to her knees, and propped her elbows on the windowsill. The sun spread its path across her tapestry of flowers. A gentle breeze caught the pungent scent of lavender and honeysuckle.

Everything was as she had left it. The sky as blue as the crescent lake. The garden and the birch and aspen trees in full bloom. She let her gaze run along the dry stone walls to the hills dressed in imperial purple and dotted with yellow wild flowers. The neighbor's sheep grazed. Winding roads snaked around the countryside. She was eager to get her hands in the soil and to trim back her rambling roses. The smell of baking came from her kitchen. Sausage to please Sinclair. Scones to please her.

There were good memories from Somerset Estates. She would keep those. The painful images she would sort through in the months ahead. She had a long time. She had forever. She pitied the fragile hold that Lord Somerset's wife had on life. In time, Rachel would find it in her heart to be charitable toward James Somerset's memory, a man who needed forgiveness from all of them and went without it. The few guests from the reunion who had not flown home were staying on at the hotel a few miles from Stradbury Square. And dear Audrey, with her starched apron and swollen legs and as faithful as the ticking clock, was back in her kitchen, doing what she had done for decades, pleasing Mr. Sinclair.

Just beyond the neighbor's whitewashed cottage stood the ancient church with its fifteenth-century spire stabbing the sky; its empty pulpit would surely appeal to Charles. He was right! The first wedding would be her own. Rachel was certain of it.

As she thought of Sinclair, Becki burst into the room and latched her arms around Rachel's neck. "Oh, Rachel, don't let Mommy take me home today."

She pulled Becki down beside her. "You can come back someday."

"Promise?"

Was it a promise Rachel could keep? She said, "We'll see. And if you can't, Sinclair and I will come and visit you."

"It won't be the same that way."

It would never be exactly the same. "If we're to get to Heathrow in time, we'd better get dressed, Becki."

"Mommy said Morrie is taking us, so you can stay home."

There was a flicker of hope and then despair. "But, Becki, I thought Inspector Farland wanted Morris to stay in the area?"

"Inspector Farland made him promise that he'd come back."

She sounded so grown up, so matter-of-fact. Had the truth caught up with her that this daddy of hers would not be going home with them? Ever. She forced back her despair and said quite cheerily, "Up. I'll race you for the shower."

"Audrey said we can have breakfast in the garden."

"Oh, that will be grand, Becki. Now off with you."

"You said we were racing—"

"I changed my mind. You're my guest. So you go first."

At the door, Becki turned back. "We found Kevin's wallet."

"You did? I bet it was in his suitcase all the time."

"No, in your garden. Inspector Farland said it was planted there." She shrugged as Eileen came up behind her. "Mommy

293

said Jude and Sean wanted to hurt Kevin. Didn't you, Mommy?"

Eileen tousled Becki's hair. She met Rachel's inquiring glance. "Becki seems to know everything, Rachel. Did she tell you we found the Monet painting behind the hedge?"

"One of the stolen paintings? Here at Wakefield Cottage?"

"They intended to put the blame on you and Kevin."

She shuddered. "Jude's parents are coming. They'll stay as long as they have to—in order to take her home with them."

"It may be a while. Timothy said her wounds will heal, severe as they are. She can function on one kidney, but it will take longer for her to change inside. Although, Timothy said she's asking for you, Rachel. I think that's a good sign."

"I told her I would stand by her."

"You're a remarkable woman, Dr. McCully."

She touched her throat. "Someone else told me that once."

"Morrie?" Eileen shooed Becki off toward the shower. "Don't look at me that way, Rachel. It will never work out between us."

"But Becki said he's driving you to Heathrow."

"I owe her a chance with her father. Inspector Farland agreed. He said with Lord Somerset dead, they have little to hold Morrie on, except his conscience. He did stop the robbery." She shook her head. "Morrie had so much potential. But he resented my coming from a wealthy family. Unless Becki told him, he doesn't know that my grandfather intends to leave his wealth to Becki—his Weinberger painting to me."

"And what will you do with the Weinberger, Eileen?"

"I know what it's worth, but I'd like to give it to Morrie. It's rightfully his. That painting would be too painful for me to keep. I would always think of him. Do you understand?"

"Yes."

～

As Morrie unloaded the luggage at Heathrow, Eileen exclaimed, "Morrie, what are you doing with suitcases? You promised Inspector Farland that you would go right back after you saw your daughter off safely. You're not running away again?"

He did what he always did. He flashed a dimpled grin to cover his insecurities. Becki had his impulsive nature—and his eyes, blue and piercing. "I just need time alone, Eileen."

"You're breaking your word to the inspector."

"I broke my word to you too, a long time ago. I promised you 'until death do us part.'"

"What you broke was my heart."

They stood on opposite sides of the car now, their gaze meeting across the rooftop of the rental. "I love you, Eileen."

"I know."

"I never meant to hurt you."

"I know."

"Will you be all right?"

"Will you, Morrie?"

He nodded. "I'm catching a plane to Paris. Once we're inside the terminal, can you and Becki make it to your departure gate without me?"

We've made it for eight years! This was the same Morrie she had fallen in love with. The vulnerable Morrie who had needed her was running away again. "Of course, we'll be all right. We can go on from here."

"Will you tell that old codger that you saw me?"

"Why upset my grandfather?"

"That's right. He might cut you right out of the will for lining up with this old Jewish boy."

"Stop it, Morrie. Becki is going to be proud of her Jewish heritage."

"You're going to do that for me?"

"I'm doing it for Becki. And just for the record, my grandfather has tried to make it up to me ever since you went away. He didn't realize how much I cared about you until you were gone."

His eyes darkened behind the glasses. "He told you that?"

"He shows it in the way he showers Becki with his love. Don't worry, Morrie. Granddad is not leaving me any inheritance."

"Because of me?"

"He never says. But everything he has will go to Becki when she's of age . . . except the Weinberger painting. That will be mine."

He flinched. "Becki told me. So, it's payback time," he said. "You win after all, Eileen."

He picked up the heavier suitcases, and they started walking, side by side. Like it had once been. Like it would no longer be. Rebecca ran ahead of them toward the tiled concourse. Morrie watched her go and said sadly, "I feel like I've lost everything. When you board that airplane, I have nothing left."

"God will always be there for you, Morrie."

"God? I'd like to believe that. Charles kept urging me to consider eternal matters before it was too late."

"Is it too late, Morris?" Eileen whispered.

"I don't know. I hope not. That's one of the reasons I'm going away. To sort everything out. I posted a note to Inspector Farland, telling him I'd be back." He glanced at her, looked away again. "I can't believe God would love me. Forgive me. I've made such a mess of things."

"He wants you just as you are, Morrie."

"Without you?"

"Your choice."

Rebecca was peering around the crowd. "Mommy, hurry or we'll miss the plane."

"I'm coming, darling. . . . Morrie, aren't you at least going to say good-bye to her?"

"I don't know what to say."

"You'll think of something. You're always good with words."

He walked over awkwardly, set the luggage down, and knelt by his daughter. "I'll miss you, Smidgen. Maybe your mommy will bring you back someday, and we can spend some time together."

"Don't make her promises that you won't keep, Morrie."

He embraced Becki, almost crushing her. "I'm sorry, Smidgen. I wish it could have been different."

"No big deal," she said, catching her breath, but there were tears in both of their eyes.

He straightened, grabbed his own luggage. "I'll leave you here. I hate long good-byes. . . . Have a safe journey, Eileen. Write sometime. Send me pictures of Rebecca Lynne. Of yourself."

As they entered the terminal alone, Timothy Whitesaul was waiting for them. He stooped down and Becki flew into his arms. He held her tight. "Go ahead and cry, honey. I know it hurts."

Eileen wanted to burst into tears. Timothy was everything that Morrie could never be, a man with unexpected tenderness.

He looked up at Eileen and said, "Rachel called. She said Morrie was driving you in to Heathrow."

"He did."

"Will you be coming back to him?"

She shook her head. "It's over. Really over. He's running away, Timothy."

"I saw him racing in with his luggage. He ran past me. Never noticed me. Where is he going?"

"To Paris, I think."

"He's trying to find himself. Rachel McCully has deeply influenced him. And then—discovering Becki, I think he'll be back. He'll do what's right. Charles Rainford-Simms said he's on a redemptive journey so Morrie can't run far. You know him, Eileen. You loved him. There has to be some good in him."

And so much good in you, she thought. She compared the two men: Morrie charming and beguiling, Timothy practical. Morrie fought the world he lived in; Timothy lived to improve his world, quietly pursuing his cancer research with little praise from his colleagues. In a crowd, should he choose, Morrie—her first love—could be the center of attention; they often met in a crowd, their eyes catching across the auditorium. In that same crowd, Timothy would stand on the sidelines, or engage in a quiet conversation with one or two. She had met Timothy on an emergency room rotation—she the intern, he the resident-on-call. In the chaos, he remained calm.

In the chaos, they discovered each other.

Becki walked between them now, her hand securely in Timothy's. She was the center of their lives. It was as if she belonged there. As though she were really his.

"Will you come back to me someday, Eileen?" he asked. "My offer is still good."

She glanced up as he guided them through the crowd. "Do you mean that job at your research clinic?"

"No, the one by my side."

When they reached the departure gate, he said, "I want you to marry me. I want to make a home for you and Becki here in England." He touched her cheek gently, the feel of his broad hand comforting. "I have always loved you. And I think you know that for me—in a very real way—Becki has always been mine."

She managed to surmount the lump in her throat and said, "I know. You're so good to us."

"Will you come back, Eileen?"

"Will you give me time to sort out my feelings?"

He smiled, their eyes locking above Becki. "You can have all the time in the world as long as you come back into my world."

⌒

Kevin Nolan and Amanda Pennyman watched Rachel and Sinclair walk out through the garden gate at Wakefield Cottage and down the country lane. "I envy them," Kevin said.

"They are happy, aren't they? It seems so funny seeing Dr. McCully radiantly happy like that. I just never thought about her that way."

"What way is that?"

"You know, silly goose. Romantic and all."

"She's a wonderful person, Amanda. I liked her from the start. Thanks for inviting me to the reunion."

"I almost got you killed."

"I don't think that was in your plans," he teased.

"How do you feel, Kevin? Really?"

"With all that's happened?" He patted the wallet in his pocket. "Like a sacrificial goat."

"Kevin."

"Hmmm?"

"You haven't asked me to marry you lately."

"I did two weeks ago. And the week before that. And in April when I was afraid Mother was coming to visit us."

"But not lately. Lately, you haven't wanted to make an honest woman of me."

He looked at her. Everything had changed except his deep longing to marry Amanda. He looked away, fixing his eyes on Dr. McCully and Don Wakefield. They were not much older than Kevin himself. He watched them walk leisurely over the stone-flagged path, side by side at first, then hand in hand. He envied the joy they had found in discovering each other again.

Amanda nudged him. "Kevin, ask me to marry you again."

He turned, met her anxious gaze, and gave her a crooked smile. He tried to quiet the drumbeat of his heart. "I won't take the risk of you turning me down again."

"Maybe I won't this time. . . . What if I propose to you?"

Don't mock me, he thought. "Things have changed, Amanda."

"Forever?"

"It has the forever quality to it."

"I don't want to lose you. I want us to stay together."

He felt pained. "Not without a permanent commitment."

299

"When that bomb exploded near Harrods—when I heard it on BBC—I was so afraid, Kevin. I knew you were in the area, waiting for me. I was certain something had happened to you."

"Something did." How could he tell her?

"I was afraid you were dead."

"Like Lee?"

"No, like you. I thought I had lost *you*." A tear tracked down her cheek. "I love you, you big galoot."

"So you've told me for three years. You still wouldn't marry me."

Her gaze strayed down the path. "Dr. McCully told me that true love only comes along once in a lifetime."

"What about Lee?"

"He was my first love." She brushed at her tears. "I was strong-willed back in college, always living on the edge. I don't think Lee and I would ever have married."

"You were engaged."

"I know. But I've grown up in the last ten days. I know what I want now. Rachel told me not to let you get away because God brought us together."

"It's not that easy, Amanda. It's that religious jargon, isn't it?" he challenged.

"It's more than jargon, Kevin."

"I know." His brow arced. "You don't have to explain. I knew all of that as a boy. Threw it over as a teenager. Blocked it out when you moved in with me. In these last few days, I knew that I couldn't go on without God in my life. That's why I went off fishing with Sinclair yesterday. I knew he had something I didn't have. We talked about it."

"You certainly didn't catch any fish."

"But I caught hold of eternity for time. That was better than trout. I haven't felt this peaceful and clean in a long time, Amanda."

"God forgave you even after we broke his laws."

"He's in the business of forgiving, Amanda."

"That's what Dr. McCully told me when you fell overboard in Lake Windermere. Everybody thought it was an accident—that you had been goofing off, standing on the rail. I knew differently. I told Dr. McCully that someone pushed you in."

"It happened so fast, but I think it was Sean. I hit my head on the way down so I couldn't be certain with my senses dulled."

"Dr. McCully and I had a long talk after you were hurt. That's when I told her we weren't married."

"There was never anyone else for me. I look at the professor and Wakefield and marvel at how little time they may have left to spend together. But no complaints. They're content. Happy."

"They're in love, Kev."

"They wasted all those years. I won't go on wasting mine."

"Then you won't marry me, Kevin?"

He grinned finally. "You haven't asked me yet."

~

As they turned back toward the garden at Wakefield Cottage, Rachel smiled when she caught sight of Kevin and Amanda.

"Sinclair, do you think we have given them enough time?"

"From the way he's kissing her, I rather think so. If they don't watch out they will break off your hollyhocks."

"They were damaged when the house was invaded, remember?"

"Inspector Farland put a tag on that one, as he calls it. Sean's fingerprints match up. I think they had Plan A and Plan B. If they couldn't defame Kevin at the reunion, then they planned to leave his wallet and the Monet painting here at the cottage."

"Poor Somerset. Trying to destroy the man who audited his books. And poor Morrie. Involved with him just for a painting."

"At least Amanda is one of your success stories, Rachel. And Kevin—he's a poor fisherman, but a jolly good man. Now let's walk back toward the lake and give them more time together," he said with a rakish grin.

She slipped her arm in his. "That suits me fine. I like being alone with you. Sinclair, Eileen called from Heathrow. Morrie is not coming back. He boarded a plane to Paris."

"He'll come back. He'll do it for Rebecca. Thanks to the challenges in your classroom, he is an intelligent young man. Now, dear Rachel, let's talk about us."

She knew he was about to propose. She was created for this moment in time. Not to fill her sister's role as a university professor—although she had filled the role well. Not to go down in history as an Olympic gold medalist, nor just to leave an imprint on other lives, but to find her soulmate, her companion, her lover, her fulfillment in God's choice for her. All else had come to this moment when she could let someone else love her for herself.

"You fought a good fight in your battle with cancer, Rachel. I think you've been laying up treasures in heaven— some that will surely bear the names of your students, but now it's time to think about us. I want to marry you, Rachel."

"I'm on bonus time. There's no guarantee on my remission."

"There's no guarantee on anyone's tomorrow. Let's just enjoy every moment we have. Will you marry me, Rachel?"

"Can I give you my answer tomorrow?" she teased.

"I won't wait until tomorrow. I want my answer today."

She tilted her head and met his gaze. "And Audrey would be furious if I didn't say yes."

"Then say yes."

"Yes—but people will think you foolhardy marrying me."

"I've been accused of being self-sufficient. Independent."

"I rather liked that about you."

They made their way back along the country lane, over the pebbled path that led into the garden. "Rachel, I promise you, tomorrow—for all of our tomorrows—we'll spend as much time as we can at Wakefield Cottage. You're happy here, aren't you?"

"Radiantly happy, Sinclair."

"I'll go into Oxford three days a week for my classes."

"But you will come home to me again. There will be many days to watch the sunrise over Stradbury Square. We did that when we first came here together, ever so long ago."

"You remembered?"

"You told me it was the only place we could be alone."

He said thoughtfully, "Mary would be pleased about us."

"That's an odd thing to say."

"No, Mary knew about you. Sometimes she said that a corner of my heart and a nugget of my memory would always be yours. She was right, you know. I adored Mary, loved her. She made my life complete, but part of me always remembered you. Can you understand that, Rachel?"

She felt vibrant and alive like the day they met. "I think so. And all those years, you were always in my mind. A kaleidoscope of portraits and shadowy images. The sound of your deep rich voice whispering in my ear, shouting in my dreams. Somehow you were always there even when you weren't." Her voice lowered. "But you know there can never be any children. Timothy Whitesaul doesn't want me to risk it, not after my cancer and my family history of cystic fibrosis."

"But there *can* be children."

She leaned her head against him. "It would be too risky."

His fingers tightened around hers. "Charles told me about a little girl from his last parish at St. Michael's. Tesa was sent away to live with distant relatives, but it didn't work out. She's unhappy there. He wants to find a permanent home for her."

"A little girl of our own?"

"She's younger than Becki. Shy and bright-eyed and small for her age. I already plan to add another wing to the cottage—a couple of small bedrooms and a small bath. Tesa would have a room of her own."

"Won't it be too much for Audrey?"

303

"She can be Tesa's nanny. We'll hire help in the kitchen."

"Audrey won't like that."

"But she will love Tesa."

"Oh, Sinclair. A little girl of our own? I will adore her. When can we go and get her?"

"Slow down, love. We could arrange for Charles and Audrey to go for her while we are on our honeymoon. But we can stop and see her on our way, so she will be comfortable with us—and so we will have someone special to come home to."

"I love you, Sinclair Wakefield."

He smiled, his eyes teasing. "How gratifying."

Even as they stopped on the cobbled path, she knew as he took her in his arms, his lips on hers would be sweet and tender. She went gladly into his embrace, and time no longer mattered.